HIS FATED ONE

A CAIRO'S ROGUE SERIES

ANNA RING

Cover Design by Anna Ring
Formatted by Phoenix Book Promo

To my readers and followers who have been with me from the start.
This one's for you!

GLOSSARY

(NOT IN ALPHABETICAL ORDER)

Rogues: Feral, packless wolves. Shunned or exiled out from packs.

Moon Goddess: The Goddess who created werewolves. Werewolves pray to the Goddess instead of God like humans do. The Goddess is who grants wolves soul mates.

Mates: A term that werewolves use to call their soul mates.

WG: Werewolf Government

Serenity: Alek's gift. One touch can put anyone to sleep instantly.

Last Sight: Zia's gift. Can send anyone to the moon to see their dead loved ones. Together both can draw extra strength from the moon but only when together.

The Moon: The werewolf version of Heaven.

The Forsaken Place: The werewolf version of Hell.

Their Wolves: Each werewolf-human has a wolf they shift into. The wolf mainly controls the wolf form with suggestions from the human inside. The wolf can portray their feelings to the human side when in human form. They can also momentarily take over the human form in extreme cases of anger or fear.

Scents: The personalised smell that every person has. A werewolf can find their mate by the particular smell of their scent. It will feel like their scent has been turned up to the max and will smell like the best things in the world to that person.

Mind Link: Werewolves can mindlink family members, and people in their pack. If they are rogues, they cannot mindlink with other rogues, wolves or other members from different packs. Mindlinking will appear as:

CHARACTER: *[...]* in the book.

Masking: An ability all werewolves have to shield their scent. When masking their scent they appear as Humans.

Alpha: The leader of the pack.

Beta: The alphas second in command.

Luna: The female leader of the pack and mated to the alpha.

Seer: Seer wolves cannot shift into a wolf. They instead receive visions from the Goddess. They can be good visions or bad, or warnings of danger coming. Every pack has a Seer. Their appearance is also different from regular werewolves/humans. Their skin is a variety of ash grey. Their hair is white with silver streaks that represent the moon and when they receive visions their eyes go pure white like their irises disappear. When they don't have visions, their eyes are violet.

Mark: A bite mark mates give each other at the base of their necks/shoulder to show other wolves they are mated and to complete the bond. Once healed they appear as scarred teeth marks.

Quick Note: When full "..." sentences appear all *italicised*, that means characters are speaking another language.

Prologue

Dear Diary,

Today the rat that has been stealing my food while I slept, has died.

Courtesy of me, of course.

Every morning I wake up I'd find little bits or just whole chunks missing out of my food. It's already sparce as it is, but I don't need a dirty furry thief taking what I desperately need. But alas, I finally caught him. Pretended I was asleep and when I heard the proud squeaks I struck. Now I'm stuck with his little decaying body. I didn't think this through, and I don't want to risk my chances and try toss him out the steeled barred window in my dungeon cell that's too high for my little body to reach. I don't want to toss him up and risk him hitting the bars and breaking apart of his flight back down.

Then again, I could leave him near the cell door for the other rats to see that I mean business. This food is off limits!

Mmm, I think that's a good idea.

Brb, gonna go prop him up for the others to see.

Okay I'm back, where was I?

Oh yes, my cell. Would you like me to describe it to you?

May as well or else I'll go insane. Currently I'm feeling okay. Usually, I'm wracked with panic attacks and PTSD episodes and new ones being made. But right now, I'm feeling good. Doing my daily diary entries so I don't go insane.

I'm not allowed visitors, so I don't need to clean up.

The wall I'm currently leaning on is cobblestone, the wall to my left is cobblestone, the wall to my right is cobblestone. The wall in front of me is cobbles-

Jokes got you!

The not wall in front of me is all bars. Steel of course so any wolf that dare even touch the bars will be burned. But it's so dark down here I can't see out beyond the bars into the corridor. The only light that's coming through is from that small, barred window I mentioned earlier. It's not as clean as you would think either. That window doesn't stop the snow from blowing in, sheeting the ground which then gets wet and muddy. There's nowhere in this little room that I can move my thin ass mattress, so it doesn't get filthy and soiled. I can't remember the last time I've ever had a great night's sleep without waking with pain and covered in dirt from a dirty mattress.

My captor is an asshole, an evil sadistic asshole that was born without a heart or soul.

He threw me in here and gave me not one blanket to ride out the typical Siberian winter. I can only shift into my wolf for a little while longer but soon I'll grow too weak to shift. It becomes harder with every turn. My face, it's taking longer to heal. My right eye is still swollen shut from the last beating my captor gave me when I refused to acknowledge him as my mate and my ribs are broken for sure. I can't say how many but all I know is that it hurts to breathe.

Sighs

Oh, who am I kidding?

I'm never getting out of this fucking cell.

So many people are dead because of me, and my pack is better off without me. If it wasn't for me the Rogue War would have never happened. Pack members wouldn't have been injured, lost their soul mates, wouldn't have lost their lives because of me.

I wipe a stray tear away with my bruised fingers from the one eye that isn't swollen shut. It hurts so much to touch which only makes the crying worse. I try to use the tears to wipe the dried blood from my swollen cheek. My supernatural healing hasn't been the best since I was thrown in here. It's almost like my wolf has abandoned me too. She lets me shift sometimes but every day she fights the shift more and more. I can't lose her too. I can't or else I'll lose myself down here in this dark hole. I've lost my brother, my mate, my friends, and family.

I have no one.

Chapter One

The Second Beginning

Hands sliding up my body, tightening their grasp as I fight against their hold. His lips on my neck, making my skin crawl. His hands grope me in a possessive hold, claiming me as his but I never will be.

"Zia..." His deep, dark voice whispers my name in my ear. My body shivers, paling as his hands continue their assault. His nails extend, digging into my body drawing blood from my skin that will only heal and be pierced again.

"Zia!" His grip on my neck tightens as he snaps my neck back, head slamming into his chest. "Look at me..." I try to fight his hold, but it becomes harder to breathe the longer I disobey him. I can feel the muscles in my neck strain and begin to pull as he forces my head back unnaturally to look into his eyes.

"ZIA!"

I wake with a fright as my mind fights between reality and nightmare. Every night it's always a new but old memory that plagues my mind, stopping me from sleeping. Every night it's a different memory of the man who kept me prisoner in my own pack.

Taking a breath, I look around the dusty cabin before I get up off the dirty floor. We found this abandoned cabin a few days ago as we came through the outskirts of this new town. Dusting off the dirt from my naked, sweaty skin, I look over at my brother's sleeping form beside me. He too naked as the day we were born which could only mean one thing. He was awake watching me as I slept. My nightmares keeping him awake as they usually do. We always fall asleep in our wolf forms and only shift back in our sleep if we have nightmares, or we sense one of us is in distress. Which means I'm always shifting back in my sleep from the nightmares and Alek shifts back because he wakes up to watch over me and make sure I don't hurt myself during the night terrors.

I take this time to sneak out, leaving him to get some sleep. It's still dark outside as the cricket's chirp in the night. But I can also smell the mildew coming in as the morning fast approaches. Closing the door behind me, the snapping of twigs between the trees in the distance catches my attention.

A rabbit.

I breathe in, squaring my shoulders and rolling my neck as I let my wolf come forward. My spine snaps painlessly out of place, my legs contort and bring me down closer to the ground. As my arms bend into place, my skin is replaced with fur. Shaking our coat, I talk inside my mind to my wolf, urging her to catch our early morning breakfast.

She hunches down, belly brushing against the grass as she zones in on the rabbit. Unaware of the predator stalking closer, the rabbit continues to look cute and nibble away cluelessly. I almost feel bad to kill it but we have nothing to eat. The only thing we've been eating the last few years is the food our wolves catch. Sometimes we cook the food, and other times we're just so hungry we stay in wolf form and completely devour the food raw.

I silence my thoughts, letting my wolf concentrate. She creeps forward, careful not to step on anything that could give away our position. Just as the rabbit pops its head up, smelling the sudden scent change in the air, it's already too late. My wolf has lunged through the air, jaw latching around the rabbit's neck, effectively killing it with one quick flick of her head. We trod back to the cabin, seeing the fire we tried to put out last night is still dimly lit. Shifting back is just as painless as shifting to wolf form. I pick the rabbit off the ground and head over to the fire. I stoke it before adding the extra wood we collected last night on and get to work on the rabbit. Picking up a pocketknife we stole, I skin and prepare it before placing it on the makeshift spit we made. Once the rabbit starts slowly sizzling away, I head inside to wake Alek. I make a beeline to our pile of clothes that we took off before bed to shift. We only have a few pairs of clothes that we have also stolen. I grab my black sleeved crop top and worn black shorts. I put my socks on that I cleaned in the river that we've been using to wash ourselves in before putting the one thing that I have left of my home. The old pair of now grey converses that I wore all the time at home. But I was fifteen when I wore them then, they were black not faded to grey. That was nearly three years ago. They're a tight fit and the front of the left shoe is duct taped with black tape to hold the front together, and the soles of the shoes have countless layers of tape to thicken the sole, so I don't feel rocks and twigs through them as we walk on all types of terrain.

"Ali?" I say as I bend down and tap my twin on the shoulder. He stirs but doesn't wake, making me giggle. "Ali, I've got breakfast cooking." At this he stretches out, groaning as his back cracks from sleeping on the hardwood floor.

"Shit...Damn floor fucked my back up." I laugh in agreement. Shifting this morning was slightly pinchy from sleeping on a non-comfortable surface in human form. If we stayed in our wolf forms, we'd be fine. But I usually shift in my sleep, so I'm used to the achy back aches. "What's for breakfast?" He says as he sits up, pulling his jeans on before slipping his black tank top on before wiping the dust off his shirt.

"A cute little bunny." I say waiting for his reaction and he doesn't disappoint.

"Stop doing that! It just makes it harder to eat." Laughing, I head to the door. I love teasing him because for a moment our lives don't seem so...lonely.

We eat in silence, letting the breeze blow around us while we ponder our thoughts. He's probably sitting there thinking of more ways to keep me safe while I sit here sneaking peaks at him staring into the fire. His shaggy natural platinum blonde hair with natural silver streaks, hangs in his eyes, covering the X looking scar I know that's hidden beneath. Just another reminder why I ruin everyone's life around me. If it wasn't for me, he wouldn't have that scar on his forehead or the ones on his ribs or the one jagged scar up his forearm. He still has the canine tooth of the rogue wolf that gave him that scar. That was his first kill. The first life he ever took because of me.

But for me, that wasn't my first death. No, the man who haunts my life killed his father right in front of me for trying to save me. Our Alpha.

"Do you remember what we spoke about last night?" Alek says after finally looking up at me with our matching aqua blue eyes. I can't help the feelings that take hold of me. "Come on, stop looking so sad." He urges softly.

I love my brother, but his constant happy upbeat attitude all the time drains me some days. He always looked happy, even when we had to move from place to place every day as our past kept catching up. But sometimes his faux happiness felt like it was put on or staged. I guess maybe he did that for my benefit seeing as I was the depressed twin and he the happy one. He was the one that smiled, the one that kept eye contact and the one that greeted and spoke to everybody. I was the quiet one, the one with eyes always on the ground, the twin that that never spoke and flinched with every sudden movement. He always had a smile on his face even as we moved further and further away from our pack, our home, our family, and our country. Now in America, our recent home in a secluded, abandoned log cabin is no longer home. It was the first time we ever spent more than a few days somewhere in the past year. The last time we stayed someplace longer was over two years ago, and I miss the pack and people that helped us. I wouldn't be alive today if it wasn't for them.

One deep breath in, I hold it until my lungs start to scream before I breathe out, letting the relief my lungs yearn for soothe them.

"I'm tired of running, Alek." I say looking sadly at the grass beneath my covered feet. Grass I will never tread on again because as always, we're running. Running from a past that should never have happened.

"I am too, but this is the last time, I promise." A promise I always wish we could keep but we always end up moving a day later because of his hunches or was it his fears? Alek is incredibly intuitive, and his gut feeling has never steered us wrong. But sometimes I see the way he looks at me like he's afraid we're going to be found. Afraid I'll end up back there in *his* room, chained and screaming.

I know he means well but being on the run is no life for a wolf. We're pack animals, we're supposed to be a part of a pack, contributing to pack life. Instead, we're rogues, forced out of our pack for my safety. I hear the nights he sighs heavily, knowing he's thinking of the same thing I am. The *what-ifs. What if* we never left? *What if* we never ran away? *What if* we faced my problems head-on? But we didn't, we weren't given the choice. He made the ultimate sacrifice in escaping our pack with me. To save my life, he gave up the chance to find his mate.

At fifteen we shifted for the first time, which is also the first time when you're able to smell and find your mate. That was the last whole day of happiness we had together with our family. The day before everything changed.

"I didn't want to take any chances last time." He says like it's something new but it's not. I've heard the same thing every time he moves us. "But something tells me this next place is the place we're supposed to be."

Yeah, *until it's not.*

"Really, Alek?" I can't help but roll my eyes at his optimism. "We're here because the werewolf government stated last night that '*Any and all rogues under the age of eighteen must attend school.*'" I say air quoting what we heard last night on our portable radio as we sat in around our campfire.

Though we were rogues, we still listened to the wolf radio stations that broadcast the new law. It lets us know which areas are off limits, which packs have pack wars going on and areas that were infested with the feral rogues. Alek and I were different from other rogues. We weren't forced out of our pack and made rogue by the alpha. We left of our own accord and that's a major difference. Those rogues that are exiled go feral. Their eyes go bloodshot, and their wolves become so aggressive they never have control over them.

Once the news broke that all rogues must attend school, no longer could we live in solitude and hide from our past like we have done for nearly three years. We had changed our names years ago when we became rogues. One less way for *him* to track us.

"We're only here because the next towns school is the only high school in the state that isn't on any pack land." I cross my arms against my chest, trying to keep my irritation in. I don't want to go to school, I don't want to deal with pack wolves looking down on us like we're complete trash. I don't want them looking at us as if we're like those feral rogues.

"Technically it's *bordering a pack,* but it's the safest one for us." He says matter-of-factly with his hands on his hips. "We're rogues, Zi." *No shit.* Like I don't already know that. It's made clear every time we accidentally come across said pack wolves.

"Yeah, well, just because it's *'bordering a pack',*" I air quote back to him, "doesn't mean those pack members won't be attending." I can feel that cold hand of anxiety creeping up my neck again as it always does when I start feeling panicked. "It's not like they'll be very welcoming either. You know how rogues are treated." I can't even begin to hide the nerves that threatened to take over my body. We haven't been to school or even socialized in years, then all of a sudden, we're thrown into society again, starting with a high school that will be overrun with pack members who will surely treat us badly. Who will make our lives a living hell and maybe even kill us?

"Rogues are treated like that for a reason, Zi. You know that. Most of the rogues we come across are feral and vicious. Rogues are treated that way because they've been kicked out of their packs for treason or much worse." He says calmly with his arms casually crossed against his chest. I can't help the fire that builds within, quickly expelling from my mouth, even as my eyes lock onto the jagged claw mark scars on his forearm.

"But we're not like that, Alek!" I say angrily before sadness takes over. "We left our pack because it wasn't safe...and even now it won't be. Not once they find out what we are."

We aren't the typical werewolf siblings, we're twins. Twins in the werewolf world are **extremely** rare and sought after. The last time we heard of twins being born was more than a hundred and eighty years ago. The reason twins are rare is because every set of twins are born with gifts from the Moon Goddess. We're called *The Moons Warriors*. Both Alek and I have gifts, gifts which we are hunted for if people were to find out. Alek was born with the gift of ***Serenity***. He's able to calm the angriest of alphas or savage rogues with just the touch of his hand. He can put them into a state of such calmness that they pass out from the euphoric feeling. He's how we escaped many rogues we've come across without fighting. But not all of them, not when we first got our gifts.

I have the gift of ***Last Sight***. I'm able to send people to the moon in a dream-like state to spend one last moment with their passed loved ones. Together with Alek, we can mend broken hearts and send lonely mates to the moon to spend one last moment with them. Those who have become malevolent are sent to someplace so dark and horrifying that they wish for redemption. I can send someone to the Forsaken Place to speak to whoever was sent there, but that is a betrayal of the Moon Goddesses gift. They are sent there for a reason, and it is forbidden to ever go near it. We can also draw strength from the moon in extreme instances, but we must be together to draw from her. Together we could become a weapon if people were to discover what we are. Which is also why we have kept running all these years. Not just because of my past, but because the rogues or packs we've come across have discovered what we are. All it takes is one look at our matching eyes, identical hair, the same eyes, nose, and lips. It's why Alek hasn't let us stop moving after all this time. Because I know *He* will be listening for any clues of us and if he hears whisper of twin wolves then he'll know it's us and he'll come for me. I just hope the family we left behind are okay. We don't know what happened to them the day we left the pack. Everyone waited for our fifteenth birthday when we would shift and get our powers. They all anticipated what we could do and how the pack could use us, but he got to us first...or should I say, me.

But he never cared about my gifts.

So, here we are.

On the run for the past two years and counting. The day we turn 18 will almost be three years of running.

"Come on, everything will be okay, Zi. I found us a nice apartment not too far from the school." He says assuring me as always. The one constant in my life is his ever-wavering assurance. His big bright smile that's hides his hurt as he puts on a brave face for me. *Wait a minute...apartment! We don't even have money!*

"How do you even have money for an apartment? Alek!" I question. I know for a fact he hasn't been selling drugs. Or was he? I squint my eyes at him accusingly as he laughs.

"It's called a credit card." He says rolling his eyes like I'm an idiot for not knowing. "I applied online last night. When the WG implemented that new rogue schooling law, they made like a grant thing. Any rogue under eighteen can apply for a fixed monthly allowance. So, accommodation, food, school supplies are all taken care of. I applied last night and got approved straight away. And there's an app that has a digital card on there so it's not like we have to wait for a card to come in the mail. We just have to go into town tomorrow and get money out so I can buy a new phone instead of using this stolen one. I don't want to steal anymore." He stops talking as he looks down at the ground. I can't blame him. We weren't raised to lie, cheat and steal but it's what we've had to do to survive being all alone all this time.

"Where are we staying?" I ask trying to take his mind off his plaguing thoughts.

"When I got approved for the grant they asked for our location and then a list of approved apartments came up and I just had to choose one. Then when we get paid monthly, they take part of that money out for rent. But don't worry I chose us a nice two-bedroom apartment. They're also furnished as well so as soon as we get there we can sleep on actual beds!" It's sad that the thought of sleeping in beds makes two seventeen-year-olds happy. We shouldn't have to worry about where we're sleeping every night or what we're gonna eat. Sometimes we go weeks without bathing. Our wolves run through a river stream and that's our bath for however long it is until we find another bed of water. "Now come on, you, silly sausage, we have a short walk before we reach the neutral zone and our new town." He says walking off into the forest line.

"Ew yuck, don't ever call me that." I repel in disgust.

All I can hear is his laughter booming from the trees as I begrudgingly follow after him.

That short walk Alek said we had, turned into a ten-hour walk trekking through dense woods. I needed to reapply duct tape twice to the bottom of my small old shoes because they wore down again and I could feel every sharp stick and stone I stepped on. I know we were just moving to the next town over, but I was thinking it'd be a two-hour walk at max. NOT TEN HOURS! I'm damn little and starving as it is. Alek said we couldn't shift so we didn't have any time to catch food. He wanted us to look presentable when we walked into town in case we come across any of the locals. But it wouldn't have mattered anyways. By the time we arrived, it was already late and there wasn't a soul in sight. We smelt bad, looked worse and we were coming out of the forest. I'm not sure what type of greeting Alek was thinking we'd be giving anyone, but I can assure you little kids probably would have run off screaming about the two monsters emerging from the forest. Luckily for us, everyone was already in bed as we emerged and to make matters worse, the idiot was lost.

"I think it's down this way." He said for the fifth time now as he looked ahead curiously, squinting at street signs from afar. *Clearly lost.*

"You *think!?* How about you *know*! We've been lost for an hour now trying to find this stupid apartment. You said this was a small town! Not a city!" I screech out as exhaustion and frustration start to muddle together as one.

"Town, City, same thing. What else should I call it when it's bigger than a town but smaller than a city?" He shrugs. Shaking my fists angrily at my sides behind his back, I contain the anger wanting to dispel out and tackle him to the ground. I may only come up to his chin but with the Goddess as my witness, I can take his ass down if I want to.

And I *really* want to.

"Come on, I think it's over here." He says walking off down the now sixth street we've been down. Taking a deep breath, I try to calm myself before I start shooting daggers at his receding back. *This boy is asking for an ass whooping.*

"I found it!" His distant voice yells out, echoing down the quiet street. If I wasn't a werewolf then I wouldn't have been able to hear it if he whispered but the idiot didn't whisper. He all but screamed it out and I'm surprised I didn't see any lights switch on from the apartment windows that littered the brick buildings up and down the street.

"Now he finds it." I mutter under my breath, tiredly following after him like a zombie.

By the time we climbed the three flights of stairs and pushed our way inside the apartment door, we were so drained that we immediately fell asleep on our beds once we found them. The beds didn't even have any sheets on them, and I thank the Goddess there was no stains on the mattress's either. They're new. I can still smell the crisp factory-made plastic smell deep within the mattress as if they were just unwrapped. Alek headed one way and me the other. I didn't care what the bedroom looked like; all I cared was that my tired ass hit that bed as quickly as possible because the ground started looking real comfy.

And for the first time in a long time, I fell straight asleep. Too exhausted for the nightmares to plague my mind.

Chapter Two

The Moon

ALEK

The day we turned fifteen I knew we weren't normal. Given we had heard the stories of werewolf twins our whole life, but when we woke up that morning, we felt strange. We could feel this new strength and power in us. I laid on the bottom bunk in our bedroom staring at the springs from the mattress above me. As wolves, we would shift for the first time today. We were always told at some point in the afternoon on your fifteenth birthday your bones will start cracking and contorting. Then you'll drop down on the ground and after the crunching stops, your wolf will have emerged, and you'll take your first step as a wolf.

But when I woke up around four a.m., I felt something else. It felt like my whole body was vibrating with this pure energy. I couldn't describe it even if I tried. Laying on my bed almost felt like I was floating, hovering above it. When I laid there taking in the strange new feeling, I saw a pair of tiny legs dangle over the side of the top bunk before a body dropped down.

My twin sister Zia.

She looked at me with the same wide-eyed curious look. She could feel the power too. I could see it in her bright aqua blue eyes that matched mine, but I could also see that she was scared. I knew because I was scared too. It wasn't anything like we were told we were going to feel when we woke up. I remember when she crawled onto my bed and sat beside me not saying a word. We didn't have to say anything to each other. Being twins we always had this special bond. I could always feel her, and she could always feel me. We could finally mindlink each other now that we were getting our wolves, but we were able to link each other since the day we were born. It always creeped our parents out that we could mindlink before fifteen. They always laughed and told the story of when we were four and were eating dinner and would randomly start laughing out at something that we linked to each other. Scared the living shit out of them until they realised what we were doing. Our parents always told us that when we were born, we'd cry if we weren't next to each other.

We shared everything together, all our toys, our room, our friends and sometimes our bed. Zia still wasn't used to sleeping in the dark. Even though we were both fifteen, I thought it was time we turned the night light off. She always said she hated the dark because she thought there was something watching her. No matter how many times I told her there was nothing hiding in our room or outside our bedroom window, she never believed me. But I could feel her worry and fear through our bond. So, she'd bring her pink fluffy blanket down from her bunk and cuddled her lilac-coloured stuffed unicorn plushie and took over most of my bed. I never minded because that's my little sister and I'm her big brother...by mere minutes but still, I'll always protect her.

"Ali?" She said in her small voice she used when she was scared.

"Yeah, ZyZy?" I said as I sat up next to her.

She went to grab my hand like she always did when she was afraid of something, but the second she did, we felt it. It was like we created this electric bond that was just between us. Our breaths were ripped from our bodies as the room around us disappeared.

When we could finally breathe again, we gasped in shock. What we saw was incredible. The atmosphere around us felt like we were being hugged, and the air almost shimmered like there was diamond dust floating around. The ground, if you could call it that, looked like clouds. We couldn't see our feet, but we could feel that we were standing. As we looked in the distance it was like we were standing on top of clouds during twilight. There were so many shades of pink, purples, blues, orange and yellow hues. There were stars sparkling high up in the sky, but these stars were different. They were so close to us. They were bigger and brighter than we've ever seen before in the night sky. We tightened our grips on each other's hands as we looked around amazed. Then we felt her.

The Goddess.

We couldn't see her, but we could hear her, feel her walking around us. She didn't speak psychical words, but she spoke in our minds. She told us that we were special, that we were her warriors who were born to help her. She told us that we each had powers to help wolves in need. That Zia had the gift of Last Sight. That she would be able to send people here to the moon to see their lost mates and loved ones. I had what she called the gift of Serenity. I had the power to calm anyone down. The angriest alphas or the wildest rogues, I would be able to calm them with just one touch of my hand. She said together with Zia, we could mend the broken hearts of wolves and send anyone to the moon who needed our help, who needed to heal. She also told us we have the ability to pull strength from her if we needed it, but she also gave us two warnings. One was for Zia to be careful. She said she gave Zia another power because she would need it. She was very cryptic about it and wouldn't explain why but the other one was anything but cryptic. She showed us the ***Forsaken Place****.*

Just as quick as she said it, a wild arctic wind blew around us. Zia's hair whipped around in the wind as the change in temperature was so sudden and chilling. The bright twilight sky changed with the wind. The vibrant colours were replaced by every shade of black, grey, and dark blues. Every breath we took you could see the puff of breath crystalize in the air. I looked at Zia to see her lips had gone blue. The temperature was so cold here we couldn't move. There were no stars in the sky, only darkness. What was even more chilling than the temperature was the howling and cries from all the wolves trapped there. We could see glowing eyes from wolves who were sent here after death as punishment for the way they lived their lives and treated others of our kind. We could feel their pain, their regret, and some of their anger. I didn't realise we were crying until a warm wind circled around us and we were back in that warm, starry skied place. Our tears felt so cold against our now warm skin. The Goddess told us we were not to take living wolves there. That place was only for the punished. The moment wolves die the Goddess decides which place their souls are taken too. She also warned that people would abuse our gifts. They would try to take advantage of us. Which is why she made us as strong as alphas.

"Why us?" I spoke out before I realized I had.

Just before she spoke, I could feel her hand being lightly placed on my cheek. I still couldn't see her, but I felt her. I felt the power she held. She said we came from a long line of strong wolves. That she gifted our mother with twins because she knew we could handle the power and responsibility of being her warriors. She said we would face hardships, but our bond will only strengthen us as we grow older. We felt so proud to be chosen by her.

We knew we were special before our fifteenth birthday. But now we knew why. I felt her place a gentle kiss against my forehead before I looked over to ZyZy seeing her beaming with the biggest smile I've ever seen. When her eyes opened, she lightly touched her forehead. We just looked at each other and knew we could do this.

We were born to do this. And just as we accepted our fate, our breaths were taken from our bodies once more. The ground beneath our feet gave out and we were falling. Then, just as quickly, we were back in our bedroom, sitting on my bed. ZyZy tackled me in a hug as we both cried tears of joy. That whole experience was incredible. As we basked in the glow of feeling the Goddess and speaking to her, her back cracked and snapped forward just as my shoulder dislocated and contorted to a new shape.

Then our screams started.

We held onto each other for dear life as our screams filled the room. I barely registered papa running into the room looking panicked. I could feel Zia's spine snapping in and out of place under my hand. Her screams and whimpers were ringing in my ears. Her head lay on my shoulder as we continued holding each other. Her tears were soaking my shirt with my own were falling on hers. The pain of shifting for the first time was excruciating. Everyone told us it would hurt but they never said just how painful and scary the whole ordeal would be. Papa squatted down beside the bed and rubbed our backs in encouragement.

"It's okay, my pups. It will be over very soon. You are doing so well!" And he was right. Just as he finished talking, Zia's shirt started to stretch and rip with mine following suit. As my hand felt her bare back, I could feel her small one reach for my hand, pulling it away from her back. Then we both gasped as our skin was replaced with fur.

"ZyZy?" I said but no words came out. Only a strange sound.

I looked down at my hands only to discover I no longer had hands. They were paws. My head popped up to look at Zia and I saw her wolf. She was sniffing around her paws before she looked up at me and barked. Then her tongue stuck out and I could feel my wolf surge forward and tackle her. Our wolves started playing with each other, growling, and yipping as they tumbled all around the bed before they rolled, thudding against the floor. Papa stood up and laughed watching our wolves play together. We heard a gasp come from the bedroom door and stopped seeing mama standing there with her hands covering her mouth in shock.

"They shifted already!?" She said to papa as our wolves tumbled over each other, fighting to see who can get to mama first.

She laughed as she crouched down and caught the two pups that jumped towards her. The second she lost her balance and fell to her side was when our wolves pounced, attacking her with licks and kisses. Her laughter filled the room and soon our little wolf bodies were being picked up in two large hands. Our papa placed a kissed on each of our furry heads before he announced that it was time to run with his wolf. The whole way out of the house our wolves were yipping and barking in excitement, legs dangling as they kicked in the air. They were so excited to see their papa wolf. As he opened the front door, our mama's cream coloured wolf ran out and waited for us in the thick layer of snow. Our wolves' fur was so white that Zia and I almost blended into the snow. Our wolves were the size of four-month-old puppies. But we were told that after our first shift our wolves were going to grow quickly. And In a few short months, we will nearly be the size of our mama's wolf, and in a year's time after that, we would be the size of our papa's wolf. To a human, mama's wolf would be the size of a large German Shepard. Papa's wolf and pretty much the average of every wolf would be the size of an Irish Wolfhound dog. Alphas were slightly taller than that. After papa shifted, we all went for a run around our pack land, bounding through the snow. It was the best day of our lives. Our wolves had so much fun running for the first time and spending time with their parent wolves. Papa's large black wolf stood tall ad proud. He was almost as large as the alpha wolf, considering he is the pack beta. The alphas second in command, the right-hand man.

Just a few short days after that everything changed.

Everything.

We were no longer in the pack, no longer with our parents. We were rogues, on the run for our lives. The new alpha of the pack had become deathly obsessed with Zia and would stop at nothing to get her. I was already too late once, and I wasn't going to let that happen again.

We spent months running through Russia trying to escape our pack who now hunted us. Zia was hurt, she took weeks to heal and that was only the psychical wounds she had. It wouldn't be until nearly three years later that her mental wounds finally had the chance to start healing.

A year after we escaped Russia, we spent another year just trying to get to another country that we felt was safe enough for us. Other countries always felt too dangerous for us or too close to home and to *him*. The day I saved Zia was the day I vowed that I would never let her down again. I vowed that I would always be there for her, that I would love and protect her until the day I die. I no longer cared about finding my mate. I gave that dream up the moment I took my sister and ran from the pack. I alone made the decision to make us rogues, but it was the only one that would have saved her life. We miss our family greatly, but we know we can never go back. That we can never contact our parents ever again.

There were so many clues, so many fucking clues that if I had only just paid more attention to them then none of this would have happened. Zia wouldn't have gotten hurt, she wouldn't have lost her spark, she wouldn't have lost her will to live anymore. Everything is always linked back to me. If only I was a better brother, then I could have saved her sooner.

Everything that happened was because of *me*.

Chapter Three

The Present

Two and a Half Years Later

We had just spent another night sleeping in an abandoned log cabin. The wind howled all night and did nothing to cover the silent cries coming from Zia. Every night was the same. She'd have those nightmares again. The ones where she's back there in the pack, being forced to love a cruel man who was once our friend. Be forced to do things she was too young to do. Every night she would scream in her sleep. She would scream from the nightmares that were her memories. She would shake and whimper, cries echoing around the room. Just like what she was doing now.

I laid there looking up at the cobwebs swaying from the wind, her nightmares would flash through my mind. Our link showed me everything. Our twin link made me feel the pain she went through, the terror she felt, the loneliness and the heartbreak she felt thinking I had left her. That I had forgotten about her and left her to that monster. My regret and guilt replayed every time she had those nightmares. I could easily block our link and choose not see them, but I won't. I'm the reason she has those nightmares in the first place. I'm the reason for everything. I ignored the warning signs and dismissed all the creepy feelings she had. I'm the one that said there was no monster standing in the shadows watching her at night.

It's all my fault because there ***was***.

I laid there for hours on the dusty dirty floor of the cabin listening to the crickets chirping and the wind rattling the unhinged door. Zia had finally calmed down from her nightmares after I let my wolf push against her mind to calm her down.

When everything first happened, we were completely locked out. Both Zia and her wolf were both so taken by the fear of their nightmares that we couldn't breakthrough. But as the years went on, Zia's wolf was able to heal with our help. But Zia...She couldn't heal. She held a psychical reminder on her neck from those painful days. She's in constant pain from the scar on her neck as it burns. That is a wound I couldn't heal.

Sighing, I get up, careful not to wake Zia and make my way outside. I remember seeing a small stream of clean water not too far from the cabin when we got here. I needed to get away and have some time to think. I let my wolf keep his senses trained on Zia in case she needs us.

We spent the past days travelling and trying to get out of the last town that was taken over by a pack. We just needed to ~~buy~~, *steal*, a few clothes, and some food but the first wolf we ran into wasn't so kind. I used my powers to knock him out before we ran out of the store through the back. I felt bad about not paying for our stuff but being labelled a rogue comes with a risk. You're forever seen as a feral, deadly wolf that will kill the second it gets a chance. Rogues can be detected easily because they smell different from pack wolves. They don't have the smell of a pack on them. They usually have a rotten smell to them. A build-up of dirt, sweat and blood linger on them making them stand out. And though we are rogues, we bathe every chance we get and always clean ourselves. We smell more of the woods than anything else. But pack wolves smell us without a pack and immediately group us together with the bad rogues. So, they always attack unprovoked. It takes a toll on our sanity especially when we didn't have any other choice but to become rogues. It was either I lost my sister forever or become rogues. So, I chose rogues.

I can hear the water trickles as it glides over the rocks and pebbles scattered along the riverbed. I crouch down, sitting on my knees before I cup my hands together scooping up the cool crystal water. After a few splashes to my face, I finally feel a bit more energized. Leaning back, I stretch my legs out before bringing them up close to my chest. Placing my arms across my propped-up knees, I open the temporary phone I had. Courtesy of the pack wolf that tried to attack us two days ago. We were in desperate need of a phone, and it was the only one available at the time. So, I thought *fuck it*. The internet still works on it, so, I scan through the local wolf news on the secret websites. Humans are unable to find the website unless they're a wolf or supernatural themselves. The werewolves that work in the governments all around the world unanimously agreed we need a news outlet of our own to get the news out. Which comes in handy now when the new countrywide policy was just announced the night before.

"All rogue wolves under the age of Eighteen MUST attend schooling. You are legally required by the newly stated law to attend the nearest school. That includes packless, lone wolves. All wolves will be fined and charged if they do not comply with the new law." I sigh and pause the video, looking out at the forest surrounding me.

I've watched this video so many times since last night

weighing the pros and cons. We could have skipped this shit, but I had to get fake ID's and papers made for us when we got to the country. It was the only way I was able to have paperwork for us if we ever needed it with the authorities or packs if we were caught. But because I got these papers, we were now in the system. We can't escape this new law even if we tried. But I couldn't stand not having a safe place to live anymore. I couldn't stand the guilt that I was the one holding Zia back from living her life. She doesn't remember anything that happened that day but the more we run into rogues and her PTSD gets triggered, the more she remembers.

I pocket the phone and go to stand up but my reflection in the moonlit water stops me. There was a dirt mark on my face from sleeping on the floor that didn't wash off. I dip my hand into the water and use the rippling reflection as a mirror to clean my face. Once I'm satisfied, I find myself staring at the guy looking back at me. My bright almost glowing aqua blue eyes that match Zia's look tired, but the cold splashes of water have erased any evidence of a bad night's sleep. I look at my hair, studying the tangled ashy-blonde mess that looks like a bird's nest. I run my hands through it, trying to tame the locks that hang over my eyes and ears. Then I trace the jagged X looking scar on my forehead. The scar left from the first rogue I fought when I was fifteen.

I still remember the first time I ever killed someone. The memory was sealed into my body and mind. We were only sixteen and no matter how much we tried to talk to the rogue, he wasn't having it. His wolf was looking at Zia, drooling like she was dinner. She was and still is, tiny. There was no way she could have fought that rogue or any of the ones that proceeded after. That was the day we decided to leave Russia. We were constantly on edge thinking *He* was always just around the corner. There was always that fear in the back of our minds that maybe the next rogue would kill me and take Zia back to him.

Rogues are notorious mercenaries. Part of the reason they're so feared is that some alphas don't care about their souls and hire them to do their dirty work. I was also tired of having to fight off rogues. But I'd do it every day of my life if it meant that Zia would be safe. There are other scars littered on my body, but I don't care them. My appearance isn't my top priority. My main goal now is to make sure we are safe. *Always safe*. I stood, whirling around, quickly making my way back to the cabin. Turning the wobbly doorknob slowly, I successfully make my way back inside without waking Zia, chuckling at the little bit of drool that's started leaking out of her parted mouth.

"Zi..." I go to wake her but think otherwise. It was still dark outside and since she was currently sleeping peacefully, I decided to get some more sleep. Stripping off, I shift and sleep in wolf form for protection and warmth.

Laying on our side, we get sleepy looking at the half sleeve tattoo on Zia's arm. I remember the day she got that. A man had gone for a run through the woods when he came across us. We could smell he was a pack wolf, and I was ready to fight him, but for once we were told it was okay and that he didn't want to hurt us, that he meant no harm. Zia and I shifted back to our human forms once we felt safe. Naked as the day we were born, she stood behind me covering herself from the man in front of us. He immediately took his jacket off and gave it to me for her. After I agreed it was safe to do, she took the jacket and put it on. He asked us how old we were and was shocked that we were rogues so young. He said he knew we were different from the ones he's come across before. He took us back to his work which turned out to be a tattoo shop. He was a tattoo artist which explained why he was covered in tattoos from head to toe. He gave us something to eat and a place to stay for the night. His shop was a studio underneath his apartment. He said he often fell asleep downstairs after drawing designs late at night or tattooing so his apartment was barely lived in. We gladly accepted, and as we looked around his store, we found a photo of him with a beautiful dark-haired woman at his station. He told us that was his mate and that she had just passed away when a drunk human driver hit her. We could feel his hurting soul and one look at each other, and we knew what we had to do. We sat him down, held each other's hands and sent him to the moon.

That was what the Moon Goddess told us we were born to do. It was the first time we actually got to do her work and it felt amazing. When he came back, he started crying. He was so grateful that he could see his mate one last time and could say goodbye to her properly. He wanted to repay us any way he could, and this time we didn't have to look at each other to know what we wanted. A tattoo. I mean come on; any 17-year-old given the chance would get one. Zia chose a half sleeve design. From her left shoulder down to her elbow were beautiful black and grey skulls with deep red roses delicately placed through and around them. She said it symbolised our work. Bringing beauty to death. I, on the other hand, opted for a smaller, simpler tattoo. Four little bluebirds flying across my collarbone. Symbolising our journey so far. We were still in flight, looking for a place to call home. And thinking about tomorrow, there was a feeling somewhere deep down inside me told me this next place would be the one.

We had one week before the new school year started. Which meant we had one week to settle in and make ourselves home before our senior year commenced. And the first thing on our *To Do* list was to enrol into the neutral zone school.

The next morning after waking up in our apartment, I walked to Zia's room and slowly opened the door, tapping lightly as it moved. She was still sleeping, so I decided to get some work done before she woke up. I cleaned the apartment and swept up the dirt and dust. Then I aired the old couch cushions out before putting them back on the couch and plopping down onto it. Pulling out the phone that only had 10% battery left, I called the school to enrol us.

"Thank you for calling Dawn High, this is Maria speaking, how may I help you?" The cheery receptionist said.

"Human?" I ask. Saying human will do one of two things. The first, she will either be confused and that will let me know that she is unaware of the supernatural and I will have to use our fake papers to enrol us. Or the second, she won't be human and will help us greatly.

"No, sweetheart. How can I help you?" Thank Goddess. That will make the process so much easier.

"My sister and I need to enrol because of the n-"

"The new law. What are your ages?" She cuts me off.

"We're 17."

"Okay, you and your sister did you say? Will start next week as the new school year will be starting. You will need to come by the school sometime this week to pick up your uniform and books." Okay, easy enough. "Now I am going to assume you and your sister are rogues, yes?"

"Yes, ma'am." She's quiet for a few seconds before she speaks again.

"Okay, so you won't have any documents on you." She says more to herself. "Which is fine, the new law included all of this. All we need is a name from you."

"It's Alek and Zia James." I say giving our fake last name. Even though we kept my real name and shortened Zia's, if we ever used our real last name we wouldn't be hidden anymore. I mean one description of us, pared with my name and her shortened one is more than enough to convince *him*.

"Alright, sweetheart. All that's left for you two to do is pick up your uniform which is supplied by the government. So, there won't be any charge for your uniform or books. On your first day, you will just need to pop over to the reception desk here at Dawn High to pick up your class schedules."

"Thank you so much."

"No problem, dear. Have a good day now." I smile. She won't ever know how much her kindness means to me. It's been a long time since the tattoo man. The last person who showed us kindness. But I don't have time to wallow in self-pity. We have a new life to live now.

And we did just as she said. First, we went clothes shopping to buy a new wardrobe for the both of us. We only have about three or four articles of clothing to our name. Then we headed over to the school to pick up our school uniforms. And just like Zia predicted, there were werewolves from the pack just outside of town that attended the school. Some were there picking up their uniforms too, and of course, when they smelt our scents, the same usual threats were spat out and growls were released. There's really nothing we or they could have done. Everyone is aware of the new laws now and unfortunately; we don't have any say about who gets to attend the school.

After that incident, our days seemed to fly by. We settled in nicely to our new home and found a new daily routine. No more nights of sleeping on the ground or in our wolf forms. We could finally sleep on a proper clean bed, finally have hot showers, and wrap ourselves in blankets or not go to bed starving. To say we were having the best time of our lives would be an understatement. But everything must come to an end. Because all too soon it was our first day of school.

Chapter Four

Dawn High

ZIA

When we enrolled into the local high school, we had to take this special test the werewolf government assigned all schools for rogues like us to take. To see if we were competent enough to join the rest of the kids in the whatever grade we were enrolling into. Having already completed the test, we were able to join the senior class without any issues. We didn't have that much to catch up on, seeing as we were smart enough to wing the test, but even if it was difficult, the school said they offered new tutoring programs to help get us up to speed.

Alek bought a few flowerpots to liven up the apartment and bring some colour to the dulled grey walls. Which those said grey walls were chipped, cracked, and had paint peeling off, the wooden floors looked like they've seen better days and the only part I liked about the place where the windows. Massive windows lined the left wall, showing a view from our third-floor apartment. The right side of the apartment was the little kitchen area and straight down the little hallway was two doors to each of our bedrooms and one to the bathroom with the toilet and shower in it. We were living on the poorer side of town. These apartments didn't look too great from the outside and honestly, they weren't any better on the inside. The apartment was barely furnishable, but it had everything we needed. Couch, beds, fridge, dodgy lamps, and a small box TV, not that we ever watched TV in the first place. It had a table behind the couch that was in the middle of the room that had a broken, wobbly leg. All we needed to get were the basic kitchen utensils, plates, and necessary food to fill the fridge.

It was hard doing grocery shopping because the food didn't appeal to us as much as it used too. Living in our wolf forms for months on end, hunting rabbits, deer, even fish had us get accustomed to that way of living. When we were shifted, we still changed back into our wolves to eat because we had nothing to cut, gut and cook the food with well...before we stole that pocketknife Alek carries. The grocery shopping showed the sad reality of the life we've been living. We got a sheet for the couch, new bedsheets for our beds and new pillows. Again, the pillows were a foreign item. Every night we slept in our wolf form because it was easier than sleeping on the cold hard ground. Our wolves were built to sleep on such terrains that our human bodies were not. Alek even let me splurge and buy fairy lights to hang up in my room. He knows how much I miss seeing the sky filled with stars like the ones from back home.

We came from a very traditional pack. We had bonfires every night during the winters, and we lived hours away from any human settlements. So, the stars were so much brighter without the city lights that sometimes we didn't even need any torches to see in the dark. All our homes were built out of the trees surrounding our pack. We had no internet and no electricity. It was simple living, but it was kept very close to the way our ancestors lived.

The shopping wasn't so bad, and it was rather nice being able to let our guards down just for one small moment. But all that fun ended when we had to go pick up our uniforms from the school. Even though we still had three days before it starts, there were other students picking up their uniforms. It was hard holding our wolves back from attacking. Living outside of a pack has made us more aggressive. We've had to survive on our own for years. I've escaped many of our encounters with rogues because Alek had always stepped in front to save me. It's even worse when I have to stare at those reminders every day on Alek's body. It's live or die out there and you do what you have to. So, when we have wolves growling and baring their teeth at us just because we're rogues who are minding their own business trying to get a uniform, it's hard not to growl back and show them who they think we are. But we're trying not to draw attention to ourselves. We have to go to school with these wolves for a whole year and I'd rather not start it off on the wrong foot.

I just hope our senior year is bearable.

A persistent knock woke me up from my dreamless state.

"Hey, sis, wake up. We start school in an hour." Alek said cheerfully from the other side of the door. *Great, first day of hell starts.*

"Time to get ready I guess." I mutter to myself before yawning. I stretch my arms up above my head and arch my back, smiling at the satisfied cracks. Then I get up and walk towards the bedroom door, swiping my towel off the hook on the door before I practically skip to the bathroom, exciting for a shower. No river, no little waterfalls or rain. A *shower.*

After a quick hot shower, I dry myself off and put my new uniform on. I pulled navy-blue plaid skirt up to my hips, straightening the hem out with my fingers that stopped mid-thigh. Next was a white quarter-sleeved dress shirt that went underneath the navy-blue cotton blazer with the school emblem embroided on the chest. The blazer dipped down my chest in a V neck cut, leaving plenty of room to see the school tie that must be tucked into the blazer. I put my socks and new formal black heeled ankle boots before I grab my new maroon backpack. I stepped in front of the mirror studying the girl looking back. We were always home-schooled growing up. We never had uniforms or anything of the sort. I felt weird and I looked foreign, like I was out of place. Shaking my head, I walked out of my bathroom only to stop as I near the kitchen. The smell of fresh cookies assaults my nose, making my stomach rumble and wail. Following the invisible steam line like a cartoon character, I stop in the kitchen and see a plate of fresh hot cookies on the bench. *Don't mind if I do.* I spin, cooking in hand and caught red handed as a chuckle sounds from the couch.

"I see you found the cookies." Alek mused, lounging on the couch already dressed for school with his bag sitting by his feet on the floor.

"Of course." I hold the cookie up proudly before devouring the delicious, circled slice of heaven. I love when Alek cooks. He was always watching mama in the kitchen when she whipped up whatever goodness was on that day's menu. Meanwhile I was always outside shadowing papa when Alek and I weren't glued to each other's hip.

"Come on fatty, time to go." Alek teases as he makes his way to me and pokes my belly and reaches for two cookies himself.

"Hey! Save some for me!" I say while flicking hair out of my face, panicked as I watch him finish those two cookies off in record time and before he goes back for two more.

"Don't worry, I made a second batch. They're wrapped up in the fridge for after school." He says proudly while tapping me on the head.

"Good cause these are bomb as fuck." I say, swiping his hand away from my head before snatching the last cookie off the plate.

"That's why you're my favourite sister. Who else would love my food as much as you do?" He says, clasping his hands together in front of his chest stupidly.

"I'm your only sister." I blanch.

"True. Let's go, trouble." He says turning towards the door and I giggle running after him.

Goddess, I love him.

The walk to school was only about fifteen minutes, ten if we didn't walk slow to take everything in or gearing ourselves up for when we step through those big wooden school doors. We walked down our street, leaving our dodgy neighbourhood and made our way through the suburbs. They all had white picket fences and beautiful looking houses. Their gardens were so green and full of flowers. I couldn't help but slow down and let my hands brush against the trimmed bushes just inside the fences. I've always imagined having my own home. Always imagined doing the gardening, planting fruit and vegetables like mama did in her garden patch. After the suburbs we came up on the school. They had massive trees all around the front, casting beautiful, shaded spots that I could see myself sitting under. The school was one big, bricked building that kind of looked like a mix between a brick mansion and a courthouse.

As we stepped onto the paved path heading towards the building stairs that lead right up to the front door, Alek's hand suddenly grabbed my arm stopping me as he turned me around to face him.

"Zia, just wait a sec." I face Alek, watching him breathe out before he looks at me with slight worry to his bright aqua eyes. "Remember what I said about masking our scents?" He asks nervously.

"Yes. That the first day we will mask our scents fully and then slowly release them little by little every day." I state remembering the words he spoke to me last night as we sat on the couch after dinner.

"Look," He sighs. "I know it seems extreme but how those people treated us the other day I..." He stops to take a deep breath. "They weren't so friendly and I just think it's safest for us to let them get used to us first. You know, before we let our scents out fully." I hate seeing him so worried. I've already accepted that we were gonna be outcasts but I'm starting to hate the people of this school already for the amount of stress they've given him.

"It's okay, Alek. I get it. Although we don't smell like normal rogues, we still smell like them. Just not as foul." I say trying to assure him that everything's okay and I understand the plan.

"I love you, Zi. We'll be alright here. My wolf feels it as well." There's that optimism I hate to see. But he's right about one thing...

"I love you too, Al. And...to be honest, my wolf has been so energetic this morning. She's overwhelmingly excited." He laughs as I rub the back of my neck shyly.

"See! Everything will work out, you'll see." He says brightly before leaning down and kissing my forehead.

"Time to go in." I state nervously looking up at the doors that seem to get larger the longer I look at them. He nods taking my hand in his as he leads us up the terrifying steps and through the doors.

Chapter Five

The Unexpected

Just as expected. I knew this was going to be hard, but I had hoped that I was wrong. I hoped the moment we walked through those doors our last year of schooling would be bearable. But I was wrong. The second we walked in and made our way down the long hallway lined with hundreds of lockers; the laughing started. I stopped, awkwardly scratching my arm while trying not to show any emotion as the bottled blonde stood in front of her brunette friend and laughed at us. Her judgemental eyes roamed up and down my body before deeming me worthless. Her scratchy irritating voice spoke, not caring that she wasn't whispering.

"I can't believe they're allowing rogues into school now. They better not infest the school with fleas." She says as the tall brunette sidekick laughs at her lame joke. "They're probably riddled with them." The snarky bitch continues making them both laugh.

Taking a big deep breath in, I try to push down the feeling of defeat as I knew this wasn't going to change. This is what we will have to deal with for the whole school year. Judgmental looks and hateful comments. "Ignore them." Alek said from behind me. His soothing tone helps control my own feelings enough to school my face from the hurt. But I think it was also thanks to his wolf that I could feel rubbing up against my mind. I think Alek thinks I don't know that he does that, but I've always known. I've known he's been doing that from the start.

The day we shifted on our fifteenth birthday and went running with our parents, my wolf had run over a thick pile of snow that concaved in on me. My wolf fell down a hidden fox hole. We tried to claw our way out of the snow, but it was getting darker, colder. Our whimpers and barks were being concealed by the endless snow that seemed to never stop falling on us. Soon we were buried. We tried to howl through the snow, but nothing could break through that cold barrier. Just as the air became less, light suddenly appeared from above us. Alek had found us, and our father was digging us out of the hole. I was terrified. I thought I was going to be buried alive. I couldn't stop freaking out. We were forced shifted out of our wolves back to human form. I was shivering, limbs and lips turning blue, body trembling from the cold and the snow touching and coating my bare body. No matter what I tried to do, I couldn't calm myself. But then I felt *serenity*. It felt like I was finally able to breathe again. It was then I realized it was Aleks wolf pushing up against my mind, calming me down and allowing me to shift back into my wolf for warmth. Since that day I've always been able to tell whenever Alek was there in my mind. I never said anything to him, so he doesn't know that I know he does it. I'm thankful for it. He's constantly helping me, but it makes me feel like such a disappointment that I can never help him back like that.

Clearing the memory from my mind, I stand there in the slowly crowding hallway as students started to walk in, heading straight to their lockers. I calmed my breathing and rising anxiety when a smell caught my attention, making my heart skip and wolf lift her head in my mind. "Do you smell that?" I whispered to Alek.

ZIA: *[It smells so good! Like smoke from a wood fire mixed with fresh grass clippings and a hint of vanilla and berries!]* I mind linked Alek as the scent smelled euphoric. My body started to hum as every nerve came alive at the smell.

ALEK: *[No way, I smell boysenberries, nougat, and chocolate!]* I don't know what's going on with Alek's nose, but I don't smell anything close to that. As we stand there breathing in the heavenly scents, I follow the direction it came from.

ZIA: *[It's coming from over there.]* I flick my head to Alek, eyes following the direction I was looking in.

A group of four guys stood next to their lockers talking. From here I could smell the wolf on them. The guy standing on the right side of the group nods as he listens to the conversation. Of Japanese heritage he is really attractive, but he's not where the godly smell is coming from. The guy standing opposite him with his hands crossed against his chest, stoically listening to the conversation. Again, this guy was extremely attractive with his dark chocolate skin and shoulder-length dreadlocks. I'm not surprised how hot these guys are, seeing as all werewolves I've encountered have been blessed with both looks and height. Thanks to the wolf gene of course, making each one of us look like Gods and Goddesses. Thought I didn't get lucky in the height department. I'll blame mama for that.

ZIA: *[Oh my Goddess, who is that guy in the middle?]* I exclaimed to Alek through our link as my eyes lock onto the tall exotic dark tan-skinned, black-haired guy standing in the middle of the group. He looked angry with his strong arms crossed against his chest, hands gripping his arms and jaw clenching. He's the tallest and most muscled guy out of the whole group and just one look at him made my heart double its beating. He radiates alpha energy.

ALEK: *[Um, you mean, who is that sexy blonde beside him...]*

I tore my eyes off that God and focussed on the sun-kissed

skin of the guy Alek spoke of. His blonde hair, slightly short on the sides but longer on the top hung down the side of his face with a curl to it. He is beautiful but I can't stop thinking about the wolf beside him. I've never seen a man so attractive before. Shaved sides with his black hair tied up in a bun of the top of his head gives him a casual but so damn sexy vibe to him. Even from here I could see his striking hazel eyes. I can't stop the pulse beating through my body as I continue to burn him into my brain. Just his scent alone is sending me into a frenzy but his body...Goddess his body. His arms are bigger than my thighs, stretching the fabric of his uniform. He's a complete head taller than me and his face is so chiselled and sharp that I can't believe he's a high school student. He should be a damn model with his looks. *Oh no!* I thought as the realisation hits me. At that exact moment, I could feel the same thought click within Alek.

ALEK & ZIA: *[Mate!]* Both our thoughts shout out through our mindlink as our wolves jump forward. Our bright eyes that always looked photoshop because of the rare blue they were, shift to bright orange-gold, showing our wolves fronting in our minds.

ZIA: *[Alek! We need to calm down! Our wolves are surfacing and letting our scents out!]* I rush out panicked just as the group of guys stop talking to smell our scents that have started releasing into the air. Breathing in as fast and calmly as we could, we succeed in pulling back the reins from our wolves and cover our scents again just in time before they realise who we are. But it was too late.

ZIA: *[They're coming over here!]*

By now my heart was beating so fast I'm sure they could hear it. I could hear Alek's, but his heart was slowly calming down, whereas mine was beating wildly with no intention of slowing. Standing frozen in place, time slowed as I watched my mate walk towards us looking disgusted and angry. The moment he stopped I was hit with his scent at full force. I could feel my insides heat up just from the intensity of his scent being so close. My knees start to buckle and just in time, Alek grabs the back of my shirt holding me up. My mate's eyes finally lock onto mine, a mysterious look flashing through his gorgeous eyes as his brows furrow. I thought we were having a moment, but he suddenly sneered at me, popping the little bubble of hope forming within my heart.

"*Rogues.*"

I know I shouldn't feel disappointed but I am. He has no idea I'm his mate because he can't even smell my scent to know, but I'm devastated not with what he said, but the way he said it. He *sneered* at us. Nose crinkling as he spoke the word to strangers. I'm disappointed that my mate can't even overlook the fact that we're rogues and greet us properly. Disappointed that my mate is so blinded by anger he can't even feel the attraction that's already forming between us. I look to Alek's mate, watching as he blushes while looking at Alek. His heartbeat spiking. Looking back at my own handsome mate I see nothing. Just a mask of anger and a calm heart. He doesn't feel anything when he looks at me.

Breaking out of his trance from staring at his mate, Alek growls out in warning to mine. His blatant disrespect towards me, his unknown mate, aggravates Alek. Being twins we've always been overly protective of each other, trauma or not, and when we're in situations like this he won't hesitate to warn others against hurting me. Most wolves are tall, well-built, and beautiful. But I'm one of the rare wolves that don't have the wolf height. Standing at five foot four, my six-foot-something brother stands a head taller than me as well as the other three males in front of us. My unnamed mate standing inches taller than Alek, making him seem more threatening to my tiny self. So, in situations like this, Aleks protectiveness is doubles. To his wolf, my mate looking down at me with the expression he has right now is not going to end well unless he changes his face.

"This might be neutral ground, but I won't hesitate to kill you, mutt." My mate spits out at Alek and suddenly all of my weakened composure broke. Fuck his beautiful face and his big muscly body. No one treats my brother like that. Before I even got the chance to growl at him, Alek's mate growled a deep rattly sound that resonated down the hallway, shocking everyone in sight, my mate included.

"Keiran! What the hell is your problem?!" My mate demands as he whirls around. *Keiran*...the name suits him well. I could hear Alek's heart flutter at the stand his mate took against his friend. I don't even need to look at Alek to know he's smiling. His little beating heart is all the confirmation I needed.

"I...I don't know." Keiran said rubbing the back of his neck, gulping as a harsh blush spread across his face. The guy with stunning alabaster skin and silky black hair looked at Alek and Keiran curiously. I could see him wondering what was going on and by the look on his face, I'm assuming he's close to figuring out what we're hiding. He scanned my mate, then Alek's, then us with a curious scrutinizing gaze and if he's smart like I think he is, he's gonna figure out were all mates and soon.

"Whatever. You better stay out of my way." My mate says turning back to us. "I'm not particularly happy with *rogues* in my school." Now it's my turn to growl. I'm sick of his attitude towards us who he's just met and I'm not gonna stand here and let him dictate our school year because of his shitty thoughts and feelings about rogues.

My growl draws his attention to me and I almost fault in continuing to speak when his beautiful hazel eyes lock onto mine. His black hair makes the colour of his eyes pop along with his dark-tan, honey toned skin making them seem even brighter. With being so close to him I could see the details in his face better. Light stubble line his strong jawline that's enhanced by sharp cheekbones. He is everything beautiful as he is pissed. The irritated, disgusted look on his face successfully puts me back on the wrathful path. "This is not your school; you do not own it. And if you ever threaten my brother again, I won't hesitate to put you in your place." I say angrily as the fire in my veins starts to cool, and a feeling of sadness quickly takes over.

Turning away from my mate's curious and furious gaze, I look at Alek with tears brimming my eyes.

"Can we please go?" I ask so quietly I'm unsure if he heard me as silent tears start to fall. He breathes in deep before he tries to wipe them away.

"Alright, let's go." I nod and walk past Alek back the way we came as his next comment hits my ears. "You're such an asshole. You're gonna regret the way you treated her, trust me." He says to I'm assuming my mate who really was the only one being an asshole. "And you...I'll see you later handsome."

I don't need to look back to know he just outwardly flirted with his mate and most definitely winked at him.

The last thing I hear as I reach the doors was my mate's deep angry growl at Aleks retreating back, which made my body shiver. I clutched the strap of my bag and push through the doors, skipping down the steps as I sniffle, and trying and failing to contain the tears that threatened to spill.

This wasn't supposed to happen.

I wasn't supposed to find my mate. Not when I will have to spend the rest of my life on the run from a past I can never escape.

ALEK

On the way to school this morning we were both quiet the whole way there, both deep in our thoughts about everything that could go wrong on the first day. *We could be called rogues.* That's a given. We've never not been called rogues. *Be outcasted, shamed, picked on and threatened.* We're ready for it. Just like we always are.

We would have to leave again.

I sigh at that last one. I don't know if the Goddess can hear me but I'm praying that the last one won't come true. I finally got Zia to laugh and smile again today. It's been months since I last saw her spark for life come back, even if it was for a few seconds that time.

When we reached the school, there weren't too many people hanging around outside. Given we were nearly twenty minutes early, but we figured we could lessen our image if we were on time. Now there was only one thing left to do. Remind Zia of our conversation last night and as I was hoping, she completely understood.

"We'll be alright here. My wolf feels it as well."

"I love you too, Al. To be honest, my wolf has been so energetic this morning. She's overwhelmingly excited." She said almost embarrassed. I couldn't help but chuckle. If I didn't then I would have cried. I could see a peek of my old sister back. The one that loved life, the one that laughed and smiled every day.

"See! Everything will work out, you'll see." I only wish that was true. Because the second we walked through those doors the laughter had started. The snickering and the insults pierced their way to our ears. The tall blonde, fake-tanned looking snobby bitch was the first to comment. I could feel her words were hurting Zia and although I would never show it or let Zia feel it, it was hurting me too. I was disappointed this school was no different.

"Ignore them." I said to Zia gripping her hand in mine. Suddenly we both froze, bodies going rigid.

"Do you smell that?" She asked. And I did. I really, *really* did.

ZIA: *[It smells so good! Like smoke from a wood fire, mixed with fresh grass clippings and a hint of vanilla and berries!]* Zia said mindlinking me excitedly.

ALEK: *[No way, I smell boysenberries, nougat, and chocolate!]* Fuck, it's like I can taste it.

We breathed in as much of the strange addicting scents as we could, the chatter in the hallway seemed to disappear as our eyes landed on the group standing by the lockers. Then, my eyes landed on *him*. He was standing between two other guys, but I couldn't focus on them. My eyes were glued to him. He was lean and muscly, light honey-toned skin and golden blonde hair. He had the most perfect, beautiful smile I had ever seen before. *He is so fucking beautiful.* I could hear Zia ogling the taller guy beside the one making my heart beat like crazy. I couldn't focus on anything but the handsome blonde. His face was soft but toned, beautiful blue-grey eyes, his hair looked so silky with those cute little curls dangling around his face. I was so lost in him I almost missed it when they all stopped and looked over at us and when his eyes connected with mine, I knew. He was my mate. My wolf had claimed him only seconds ago.

Suddenly, I could feel Zia's panic course through our bond. After realizing our wolves had come to the front and had taken over our eyes, a clear sign that a wolf has found its mate, they started letting our scents out. We quickly took back control. I could feel my wolf softly whimper at not being able to let our mate see that he has found his mate too. But I couldn't do that to Zia. She was petrified. I could feel her starting to hyperventilate from the realization that her mate was right in front of her. As much as I wanted to take my mate into my arms and mark that sweet honey coloured neck of his, I couldn't, wouldn't do that to her. What kind of brother would I be if I threw my happiness in her face while she suffered from my mistakes? While she still suffered from the past. I was trying to calm myself down in order to help calm her wolf, but her dipshit mate just had to open his mouth.

"*Rogues.*" He spat.

Growls

I couldn't stop the low growl that slipped from my lips. I don't care how he treats me, but I will not let him, or anyone else treat her like that.

"This might be neutral ground, but I won't hesitate to kill you, mutt." Her mate spews out and what surprises me the most is *my* beautiful mate. His own angry growl tore from his lips at the threat. I almost feel bad because his cute little face was so confused why he growled but his wolf knows. His wolf knows we're his and fuck if I'm not hard just from that. This is definitely *not* the moment to get turned on by our mate's possessiveness. Even if he doesn't know why his wolf is being possessive.

"Keiran, what the hell is your problem?!" Zia's mate turns his glare on our mate.

His name is *Keiran*. I have to silence the purr that wormed its way up my throat. He's so adorable and confused. I can't wait for the moment he realises we're his mate. But then Zia's dipshit has to go and ruin the moment, again.

"Whatever, you better stay out of my way. I'm not particularly happy with rogues at my school." He says staring me straight in the eyes. He's challenging me. Fucking game o-

****GROWLS****

"This is not your damn school. You do not own it." Zia growled out, shocking everyone, me included. "And if you ever threaten my brother again, I won't hesitate to put you in your place." She threatens her mate before turning to me. I could feel her anger was being quickly replaced by sadness and sorrow. "Can we please go?" She begged so quietly that I had to stop my wolf from lunging at hurt her mate.

"Alright, let's go." I know we shouldn't be cutting school on the first day, but she was hurting.

And I couldn't blame her. Who knew we would ever find our mates on the run? We thought we said goodbye to our chance at mates when we left our pack. We spent nearly three years telling ourselves we would never find our mates. And now we have! What is the Goddess doing?

Everything goes quiet as I watch Zia walk down the hallway to the door. I could feel she was barely holding on. She hates showing weakness. So, I know she's trying to put on a brave front right now, but her mate has thrown her.

"You're such an asshole. You're gonna regret the way you treated her, trust me." I say turning back to her mate. He looked pissed off but oddly quiet. I guess Zia's already started to affect him. Breathing out to calm myself down, I turn my charming blue eyes on my mate. "And you..." I draw out as I see a blush creep up his neck. "I'll see you later, handsome." I say before I winking.

Then I turn and leave and I almost trip over my damn feet when his arousal hits me. *Fuck, fuck, fuck!* As if this day wasn't hard enough.

Chapter Six

The Dream

I found Zia waiting outside the school looking up at a tree. She was watching two hummingbirds darting through over the branches together, weaving in and around one another. I could feel her heart hurting from finding out what a dick her mate is. And as much as I want to be angry at him, I can't. Because I found my mate too. He was so handsome with his boyish good looks. He looked so innocent like he had never known a day of struggle in his life. He had deep smile lines from constantly showing people his gorgeous smile.

I sighed; eyes closed before looking at Zia. With her head now looking down at the ground, I need to help her. Need to get her mind off her mate for a few hours because unfortunately, her mind won't ever be clear again. Not now after finding her mate. Not now, after he revealed himself to be the biggest prick there ever was.

"How about we get some take out for lunch?" I ask.

"I don't care." She shrugged sadly.

"Well, why don't we go grocery shopping and get something for lunch and dinner. Then maybe this afternoon we can go for a run around the place." I suggest but again, her mind is elsewhere. She shrugs again, before turning without speaking a word. I follow her a few paces back, knowing she just wants some space right now. She needs time to sort through her whirling thoughts and process everything that just happened.

Things just became difficult. We were only going to be here for a few weeks until we turn eighteen. Then we were going to drop out and leave. But now we've found our mates and leaving seems impossible now.

I tried to crack food puns while we were in the grocery store trying to make her laugh, but she never did. I bought her favourite food and ingredients for her favourite dinner, but she wasn't bothered. And after dinner and after the jokes continued to fail, she finally had enough and said something.

"Alek, stop. I'm not in the mood for jokes. I know you're just trying to help me but right now I just need some alone time." She said standing up from the table as she took her dirty plate to the sink.

"Okay, sorry..." I sighed.

"Don't do that, Alek." She said slamming the plate on the counter before she whirled around. "Stop blaming yourself. You didn't do anything wrong. I'm just..." She stopped to breathe. "Look we never expected to find our mates. Then on the first day of being forced to go to school, we find our mates together. That was a surprise. Then my mate disclosed his displeasure for rogues and on top of that threatened to hurt you. You did nothing wrong. He did. That big fucking handsome asshole. So, you just enjoy the rest of your night. I need to go and think about what I'm going to do with him." She finished and dried her hands on the hand towel before briskly walking over to me still sat at the table. Being a head shorter than me she only had to lean in a tiny bit to kiss my cheek.

"Goodnight, *brat*." She said pulling back, calling me brother in our first language. Sometimes when she's tired or emotional she'll slip back into Russian. I mean I do it too, sometimes it's easier not to translate everything. But we promised we would try to speak English first, always. It was safer that way. Less to track us with.

"Goodnight, *sestra*."

Unfortunately, this day was more draining than I thought it was going to be.

Not long after I cleaned our two plates and showered, I was face planting the bed. I was so ready for this day to be over. Rolling onto my back, I could hear tiny taps on the window from the rain. The night was as gloomy as this day had been and with the rain softly pattering against the window, I let my mind think back to my mate. Goddess, he smelt so good. I longed to step forward and pull him to me. Longed to shove my face into his neck and breathe in that magnificent scent right from the source. Longed to trace my tongue across the place where my mark would be. Longed to kiss those lips that belonged to *me*. I groan feeling myself stiffen. I've had a semi all day ever since I saw Keiran. My wolf itched to run back to school and claim our mate.

My hand slides slowly down my body with a mind of its own, down towards the waistband of my boxers as I remembered the way his body moved when he walked towards us. It was playing on a loop in my head along with the sight of the blush that stained his honey-toned skin when he looked at me. I remembered the way he licked his lips as he checked me out. Which only made the blush stronger. My hand slipped under the band as I remember calling him handsome and winking before I left. My hand strokes slowly up and down remembering the way his pupils expanded and dilated when they were nearly taken over by his wolfs. I moan going faster when I remember the smell of his arousal. I thrust my hips in time with my hand and imagine his mouth on mine, tongue dancing with mine. I moan again as my breathing comes to a pant. I want to feel his tongue on me. I want to feel it trace the sweat drops that are sliding down my chest. I want to feel him trace his tongue up my abs before he kisses the sweet spot on my neck. I want to feel him line his canines up against my skin. My hand starts moving in a punishing rhythm. I want my mate to mark me. I want him to bite down on my neck and claim me as *his*. I want to feel his tongue trace the mark as I bite into him. I want to feel his moans against me when he kisses me.

"Fuck...fuck..." I can't get him out of my head.

But I don't want to. I want him so fucking bad my balls hurt. I want to push him down on my bed and mark him over and over again. I want to taste him. I want to taste that scent I smelled, and I want to worship that body that called to me like a sirens call. Then I remembered hearing his name for the first time. ***Keiran***.

"Fuck!" My hand stops as I explode. My hand and stomach get coated as I lay panting and sweating in the aftermath. I need my mate now more than ever. I can only jack myself off for so long until I can have the real thing.

Until I can have my mate.

I woke up the next morning all sticky with my hand still shoved down my boxers. I mean I can't blame myself for passing out last night. I couldn't believe how much I came just from the thought of my mate. And if just thinking about Keiran had me exploding like that, then I can't imagine what completing the bond would be like.

Gingerly sitting up, I stretch, hearing a crack before I get up, slowly making my way to our shared bathroom. I pass Zia in the hallway, but she won't make eye contact with me. Hey eyes darted everywhere so fast that I could almost hear the pinball machine sounds. *Shit, did I forget to block our bond last night when I masturbated?* I made myself some breakfast and ate it quickly before getting dressed in our school uniform. I sat on the couch drinking some orange juice as I waited for Zia to finally appear.

"Morning, Zi. How did you sleep?" I ask eyeing her from the kitchen trying to decipher if she felt the sinful deed, I did last night.

Again, she looks anywhere but me as she says she slept okay. Then she blushed and her face went red as a tomato before she started coughing, trying to cover up the guilty blush. After she composed herself, she replied again and said she slept fine. But little miss forgot we shared a special bond. So, when she thought back to the dream, *she* had last night of kissing and marking her mate, I know why she couldn't look at me. She was afraid she did the same thing I thought I did. Deciding to have some fun, I tease her about her dream.

"Were you dreaming of your mate?" I ask as I throw my weight into the couch as I sit down beside her. Her panicked response was quick to spill out of her mouth making me smirk.

"No, I wasn't!"

"Oow, was it a *naughty* dream?" I tease and can't help but chuckle evilly at the look on her face right now.

"I will tackle your ass right off this couch if you don't stop." She warns but I'm not one for listening.

"What did you do in this *naughty* dream?" I pretend to be disgusted before the act is up and I break out in laughter. I miss what she says before I find myself tackled to the ground, ass stinging from the sudden smack.

"Owe, my butt!" I complain because the little shit really tossed me aside. I forget how strong she can be sometimes. Her little sight is so deceiving.

"Did I not warn you?" She says proudly and smirking.

"You know, for being such a small person, your tackles hurt." I state to which she replies,

"You're just weak." She flicked her braid across her shoulder which hit me in the chin.

"You just caught me off guard, that's all." I say flicking the braid back over her shoulder where I know she likes it.

"Pfft, yeah right." She mumbles which only spurs me on more.

"I'll show you weak." I say before I flip her over me and pin her to the ground tickling her. She screams out in laughter, trying and failing to tell me to stop. The more she laughs the more I do. When her face goes red from laughing too much, I finally stop to let her catch her breath. "Time for school, giggly one. No more skipping." She continues to catch her breath as I pick her up and throw her over my shoulder. Probably not helping the catching her breath part. But she laughs, wriggling around until I'm piggybacking her out the door.

She giggled most of the way to school while hanging onto my back as I jogged, making her bounce up and down, braid whipping her back. She finally demanded I put her down once she couldn't take the little whips anymore. Suddenly she took off running the rest of the way to the school saying the last one there is a loser. *Oh, it's on!* I take off fast, making sure my feet hit the pavement extra hard so she can hear me coming. I just catch up to her, but I don't overtake her. She hasn't been this carefree in months. I don't want to take away from her happiness any more than I already have.

Once we reached the school she celebrated, jumping up and down on the spot as I pretend to catch my breath. "You are too slow, *printsessa*." She said cheekily with her hands on her hips.

"I am not a princess!" I say stomping my foot dramatically. "I'm a prince." I flick my imaginary long hair over my shoulder the way she does when she's being sassy. She starts laughing again, not noticing the group that just approached us as they all stopped behind her.

"No, you are such a princ-" She stops when the smell of her mate clouds her.

She breathes in, deeply as her mate stands there looking at us annoyed. I swear this fucking guy only has one facial expression. He stood looking like king shit with my sweet mate who looked hella nervous. His other friend stood beside my mate looking at him and me curiously. The same as the girl who stood beside the guy with the dreads who I assume is her mate. He's standing next to her protectively with his arms crossed against his chest. The longer Zia stayed facing me instead of the group, the more her mate's jaw ticked. He looked like a ticking time bomb, only two seconds away from exploding or breaking his jaw from all that pressure. *He really is going to make this year difficult.*

Not wanting to draw an even bigger crowd, I mindlink Zia to turn around. Before she even says anything, I could feel the anger rolling off her in waves. She can be such a stubborn little ass sometimes. Apparently just like her mate.

***ZIA:** [I am not turning around.]*

***ALEK**: [It's not just him! It's the whole group.]* I warn.

I was slightly annoyed because come on, Zia. Why does she have to be stubborn today! And right now, in front of these people!

She breathes in and out before rolling her eyes. Then she slowly turns around, crossing her arms against her chest defensively staring at her mate. The seer girl stares at Zia curiously. I could feel Zia's defence waver as she looked at her mate up and down. The bond was already starting to affect her more strongly. But like I always say, she's stubborn. So, her fighting the inevitable bond will do nothing but hurt her further. That and his poor attitude that definitely needs to change.

"Can we help you with anything?" I ask breaking the silence between us.

"As a matter of fact, you can." He replies snarkily. "Release your scents."

Chapter Seven

The Rogues

THE DAY BEFORE

CAIRO

"Cairo! Are you listening to me?!" Mum said snapping behind me. It's hard to concentrate when you've had a shit night's sleep.

"Sorry, mum. What were you saying?" I asked tiredly, rubbing my forehead wishing the headache would go away as I face her.

"I was saying!.." She starts angrily before her tone switches drastically. "Have you had breakfast yet, baby?" *Always so dramatic.* One minute she's about to rip me a new one and the next she's a sweet angel. *Lies.* Rolling my eyes at her antics I try to speak through the pounding headache.

"Yeah, I had a bagel earlier." I say but she watches me carefully, scrutinizing every inch of my face for a lie. After a minute of watching and observing, she speaks.

"What's wrong?"

"Why do you think there's something wrong?" I counter defensively.

"I'm your mother! I always know when something is wrong with my son. Now tell me." Damn, she's good. I knew I'd get a lecture if she saw I was out of sorts, so I tried to school my face the moment I heard her voice. Breathing out defeatedly, there's no point in hiding now. She already knows. A mother always knows.

"I don't know. My wolf has just been restless the last couple of days. I haven't had much sleep because of it." I say crossing my arms across my chest tiredly. Her eyes roam over my body until she zeros in on my eyes. Squinting a little, I guess she can see the dark circles that formed.

"Hmm, do you think it's an alpha thing? You are the next alpha. Maybe you've been training too much." She says composed but I can see the slight frown starting to mar her face and her heart skips a beat.

Now I feel stupid for not having my shit together. She doesn't need the stress of worrying about me. She's been through too much in her life and I don't want to be another reason for her to be medicated again. The last time she had to be medicated and put into an induced coma was my fault. I never want to see my strong mother and the packs Luna, the way she was. She stopped eating, she lost weight and muscle mass, her wolf lashed out and attacked anyone that would be a potential threat to us. I don't want her to ever go through that again. Because of me, we almost lost her once. I won't be the reason that happens again. So, whatever I need to say or do to get her to not worry then I'll do it. Starting with reassuring her mind.

"I don't think it's that. I am doing a lot of training but it's nothing I've never done before." That probably didn't help reassure her.

"Ask your father, he should know." She says thoughtfully.

"Okay." I agreed, hearing her heart begin to steady.

"And get ready for school. I don't want you late on your first day of your senior year. I'm going down to help out the pups at the orphanage today, so give your mummy a kiss before I leave." She says as she leans in ready to receive a kiss on the cheek. I'm an eighteen-year-old werewolf. There's no way I'm kissing my mother, especially in the pack kitchen where anyone could walk in and see. I watch as she stays in the same position for a few more seconds before her head snaps back angrily. "What are you waiting for?" She snaps. Rolling my eyes, I do a quick scan of the room, making sure no one will witness this atrocity before leaning down, quickly pecking her cheek.

"Happy?" I say crossing my arms back against my chest as my cheeks heat up in embarrassment.

"Very." She says smugly. "Alright, bye baby. Have fun at school." I nod and watch as she leaves. *Thank goddess, no one saw that.* I'd probably die of embarrassment. Future alpha of the pack being babied by his mummy.

Dressed in the dark navy blue checked trouser pants, white button-up with the school tie tied around my neck and the navy school blazer on top, I knock on my father's office door before walking in. "Father?" With his back turned, his muscles bunch up as he speaks sternly to whoever's on the other side of his phone call.

Standing in front of the large floor to ceiling window, he looks out across the pack land as he continues his heated conversation. Our pack sits right along the border of the neutral zone, also known as Columbia Falls. The town is neutral land with the school sitting on the edge of town before our pack land starts. This small town is home to many humans, vampires and wolves that wanted to live in town instead of on our pack land and houses. The summers are perfect, and the winters are beautiful. Our pack takes over miles and miles of land near the base of the mountain and the mountain itself. We're not the biggest pack there is in the country, but we are known to be fierce and loyal. Thanks to my father. He's the best alpha we could have, and I only hope that I can live up to his standards. I just wish he would still be the man he was. Ever since *that* day, the day that haunts me with regret, my father wasn't the same. Watching his wife and mate, be induced into a coma to save her life is one thing but his kid...That changes a man. He used to be a family man. He used to play with me every day, he'd let me ride on the back of his wolf as a child and said he couldn't wait for the day I shifted, and our wolves could run side by side together, present and future alpha's leading the pack. He used to smile, used to joke around and banter with pack members. Now because of me, he doesn't. He doesn't joke around with the pack, he stopped playing with me and stopped being the man he used to be. Now he's just an alpha. He's not the father he once was. The only time I ever see glimpses of the dad I remember is when he's with my mum and...

"Let me call you back." His controlled voice breaks my thoughts. Hanging up and placing his phone back in his suit pocket he turns to me. Dressed in his usual business suit, I see the comparisons that everyone always talks about. Our matching skin tone, same hazel-coloured eyes and black hair. The only difference between us besides age is his full beard and body riddled with scars from years of fighting battles and rogues. "What can I do for you, son?" He asks with no emotion in his face. Breathing in I forget the ache in my heart that misses the old him. But I can't go back to the past, if I could, well, everything would be different. I'd still have my father; I'd still have a *brother*.

"Mum wanted me to speak to you." I say professionally. So many times in the past I've tried to bring forth emotions and get back the father I used to have back but it's like that part is dead inside of him. So, now I no longer try to entice those emotions from him because I know they're not there, especially for me.

"What about?" He asks looking thoughtful.

"My wolf. He's been restless the last few days. I don't know why and mum thinks it's too much training." I say still exhausted from the previous night's sleep or lack of but not showing him that I'm being affected by it. He would think even less of me if he saw a restless night sleep made me less of the strong alpha blood that I am.

"It's not that. Let me know if he continues to play up. Anything else?" He asks stoically, already ready for the conversation to end so he can go back to his pack work. It hurts but there's nothing I can do. I've spent too many years trying to get his attention.

"Nah, that's it. I better go. I'm meeting the guys earlier before class starts." I say excitedly. Though I'm tired, I am excited about the last year of school. I should have graduated last year but when I turned fifteen and shifted for the first time, I spent a year off school rigorously training with my father. He said alpha's need to be ready to take over from the moment they shift. In case anything was to happen to him, I would be ready to take the next step and lead our pack.

I turn to leave but he stops me with what he says next. "Son, I forgot to mention there are two new rogues that have enrolled in your school this year. They'll be in your grade." He says watching me closely. The fire that erupted from within my chest explodes out with a damning sound.

"What?!"

"You know the rules, son." Yes, that stupid fucking werewolf government ruling.

"Yes, I know but I didn't realize we'd get rogues enrolling so soon." Crossing my arms against my chest, I try to contain the rage coursing through my veins. I hate rogues. I fucking loathe them. They ruined my life and took my brother from me.

"I want you to keep an eye on them. Rogues are horrid things that should never be allowed into our schools and towns." He says with anger. The only emotion I ever see from him regularly.

"I couldn't agree more. Don't worry, I'll keep an eye on them. They won't do anything without me knowing." I state. If they think they're gonna waltz into my school without being watched then they have another thing coming.

"Good work, son. I'm proud of you. Have a good day at school." He says shocking me. He's too busy already getting back on his phone to see the shock and surprise on my face. I've never heard him say that he's proud of me before. I can't even remember the last time I saw him look at me with love and admiration. So, to hear the man I look up to is proud of me makes me feel like I wasn't a mistake.

Like he does still loves me.

Breathing deeply, I ignore the ball in my throat and exit the office briskly while trying to hold back tears as a smile threatens to show the world just how happy I am. My father said he's proud of me.

I jog to school like I normally do, getting my blood pumping and working myself out to keep in shape. Naturally fit and athletic, it's extremely hard for wolves to gain weight, but that doesn't mean we shouldn't work out. Our wolves become pent up and tend to lash out if you don't let them work out.

Reaching the school, I jog up the steps before pushing through the doors and head over to the lockers where Caleb, Keiran and Zack are already waiting. I stand next to Keiran with Zack on my left listening to their conversation, I can't help but think of these new rogues coming to school. My hatred for rogues goes beyond the typical amount of hate wolves usually have for them.

"Cairo?"

They're disgusting creatures who hold no value to packs. They come in, kill and destroy families for sport. They don't care who they hurt, they don't care how old you are. They will always kill first. So, rogues coming to this school is something I will not let happen. I will not tolerate it. I don't care if I have to force them out, I will. I will always protect my pack.

"Cairo!"

"What Zack!? Stop shouting in my fucking ear."

"Ugh, well if you'd actually listen when someone calls you, I wouldn't have to yell, asshole." Zack says snapping back just as quick, forcing me to calm down. I never snap at my friends, and I don't want to start now. It's just this rogue shit has me stressed the fuck out already.

"Sorry, what were you saying?" I ask him before looking at the other guys giving them my attention.

"We were just talking about the rogues coming to the school. Caleb said not to worry about them." Keiran said before looking at Caleb to continue.

"Kitty had a vision of the rogues this morning. She said she couldn't see their faces but that they were good. She didn't get the dangerous threatening feeling she always gets from warning visions. And..." He pauses looking at me warily. Kitty his mate who's this packs second Seer.

"What else, Caleb?" I don't like how silent everyone has become. He clears his throat before he continues.

"She said we need to protect them."

"WHAT! I don't fucking think so! I would rather die than protect some fucking rogue. And there's two of them! I'm not protecting shit!" My school bag flies out from my hand before I can even stop it, smashing into the lockers behind Keiran, resonating down the hall. There is no way in hell I'm putting my life on the line for traitors.

Caleb sighs out, rubbing his face before looking back up at me. “Look, I’ve gotta go meet Kitty. But Cairo, if the Goddess showed her we have to protect them, then we have to protect them. You have no say in the matter. None.” With that he bends down grabbing my bag before shoving it back to me. I feel like shit disrespecting his mate but I can’t believe it. I don’t want too. I watch as he walks off down the hallway leaving with my thoughts crashing inside of my head like waves during a storm.

I get what he’s saying but every fibre in my body is refusing to accept it. How could she, the Goddess want *me* to accept protecting these rogues without question after what happened to Siron? How could I willingly protect any rogues when they were the ones that killed my brother. They ripped him to shreds right in front of me and I’m supposed to just accept what the Goddess says?!

Fuck. No.

I was so in my mind I didn’t notice the hallway had gone quiet, but not from my outburst. I didn’t notice the lack of conversation in the hallway had disappeared, the presence of laughter or students gossiping had ceased. What drew my attention to the two students standing just in front of the school doors was the lack of scent my nose picked up. “I didn’t know the rogues were gonna be siblings.” Zack said quietly, more to himself but also confirming that these were the rogues everyone’s been talking about. I don’t even say anything. My feet moved on their own, straight to the rogues with the guys hot on my feet.

Once I reach them, I was truly stunned but I refused to show it. I stared down at the male rogue, making clear who the alpha and one in control is. Platinum ash-blonde hair hides a nasty scar on his forehead. I could clearly see the anger and protection in his eyes as his hand goes behind his sisters back protectively, ready to pull her back and out of harm’s way if needed. But his hand only draws my attention to her, the reason for my stunned composure. I couldn't deny she's the most beautiful wolf I've ever seen. Her eyes are so fucking aqua they can't be real. They have to be contacts Her long matching platinum ash-blonde hair that mirrors her brothers, sits over her shoulder in a loose braid. She's at least a head shorter than me and one of the shortest wolves I've ever met. She looks so tiny and frail, and her defined cheekbones and jaw don't help. They both look like they haven't eaten in weeks, maybe longer. Starved and almost on the verge of malnourishment, I can't help but look at the deep scar on her cheek and wonder what happened for such a young girl to get that kind of scar. As werewolves we have super healing, so for either of them to have the types of scars they have, that means they were deep wounds. But something else surprised me looking at her cheek and the scar that will forever mark her face. I was feeling anger. A new type of anger I've never felt before. It felt like slowly burning bubbles starting in the pit of my stomach, alighting something I could never foresee coming. Which confused the fuck out of me because I don't know anything about her, and I shouldn't care about her because she's a rogue. But that scar and the thought that she was in pain and hurt unsettles me.

But no matter my feelings, they need to know where they stand in this school. They need to know they're at the bottom of the food chain.

As I sat at my desk, I looked out the window and down the path which I assumed the rogues took home. That meeting went differently than I thought. I was expecting a few growls, a fight, maybe even a brawl. What I wasn't expecting were the strange feelings that came over me. I don't know if it was because the Goddess may have been influencing me or if I had genuine feelings for them... for her. While their bodies may have looked weak, their determination was not. They were fiercely loyal and protective of each other. It made me angry that I was never that protective of Siron. I should have protected him better, shouldn't have taken his life for granted. I never thought that living in a pack could mean we lose that fierce sense of protection for one another. We just assume we're protected because we live in a pack. But seeing those rogues, seeing how there was no hesitation between them protecting each other, it made me hate myself. I should have been like that for Siron, but I wasn't.

"Cairo! Are you paying attention?" I was abruptly pulled from my thoughts and view from of the window by the teacher staring from the front of the classroom.

With glasses sitting atop her head, she gives a not so impressed look. But the longer she stares and keeps eye contact, the more my wolf begins to enter the forefront of my mind. Though she's one of the wolf teachers, she still needs to respect pack hierarchy. And right now, she's challenging an alpha. Even if I don't have the official title yet, once you're born with alpha blood, you have the same air and respect of the true alpha until the title is officially handed down to you. So, this teacher seems to have forgotten her place.

The class goes deadly quiet as she continues to fight for dominance. I let my wolf come forward, glowing sunset eyes shine through, melting with my hazel ones as they mixed for a split second before his are shown. I bare my teeth in a low growl, warning her to back down. Now she doesn't hesitate. She suddenly looks down, angling her head slightly to the side in submission. It's probably killing her to do this in front of the class but she and everyone needs to remember who I am. I hold my stare, dragging this moment out because right now taking my frustrations out on her seems to be letting some of my stewing steam at those rogues out. I hear someone clearing their throat before Zack's voice enters my mind.

ZACK: *[Cairo, come on, man. She gets it, we all do. Please, stop it.]* I'm lucky to have my chosen Zack and Keiran to be my beta's. While Keiran is the quieter one of the two, Zack is the jokester of the pack. The one that doesn't care if I snap at him, or when someone needs to pull me in check, that's him.

I lift my head, pulling my wolf from my mind as he feels satisfied by her submission. Orange melts and swirls with hazel before my eyes are back to their birth colour. I can see the shift in her shoulders when she senses my wolf has gone. She dusts off her pencil skirt and fixes her glasses back on her nose before turning towards the board to hide her flushed cheeks. She resumes her lesson, talking about whatever chapter in supernatural history she has to teach as I go back to looking out the window.

This school isn't like the regular ones. The humans that go here know about the supernatural world. They know werewolves exist, vampires exist and the rare hybrids. They're either children of mated supernatural's and humans or they themselves are mated to one of them. So, everyone in this school knows who exactly I am and who I will become in the next five years.

It's not long before everyone's packing up their books and heading out the door after class ends. "Cairo? You coming?" Zack says stopping by my desk as I turn from the window to look at him.

"I'll meet you outside." Sighing, he shakes his head, muttering something under his breath. He already knows what I'm going to do and doesn't approve. I leisurely pack my bag before heading to the front of the class where the teacher stands timidly waiting.

"I. Cairo..." She stutters out, audibly gulping.

"Ms Mark." I stare at her expectantly.

"I...I'm sorry. I forgot my place. It won't happen again. Please don't tell the alpha. I love my job and I don't want to lose it. Please, Cairo!" She quickly rushes out and I almost think she's going to drop down on her knees and beg.

"Don't let it happen again. I'll see you tomorrow." I go to

turn but stop as I think of something. "Tomorrow the rogues will be joining this class. You will make sure the girl sits next to me." I don't give her a chance to reply before I spin on my heels, swiftly exiting the classroom.

Just as I thought, Zack was waiting by the door looking annoyed, foot tapping the tiles, still shaking his head. I don't need to hear it but he's gonna say what's on his mind anyways. "Was that necessary? To do that to the teacher in front of the whole class? You're damn lucky Jordan wasn't there or else she would have texted the whole damn school and ruined that poor teacher's life." He says pointing at me angrily. It's always amusing seeing him get angry as he hardly ever does. "You're lucky the rest of the class has a little fear for you and won't say shit." He continues.

"Since you always like counting things, I'll do the same. One, I don't give a shit who hears what happened. They should all know not to fuck with the fucking order of the pack." I end up snapping. Not only am I still reeling from the rogues but my wolf hasn't stopped being on edged and that little show of defiance in class has pissed him right off. "I'm not sorry for what I did because she needs to remember I am no ordinary pack member. I will be the alpha one day and if one wolf won't give me the respect I am earned, then the pack won't see me as the alpha they need. The whole hierarchy and pack will fall. They won't come to me as the alpha they need for protection. Their wolves will begin to go rabid with no alpha to lead them if their humans don't respect me. I am sorry I snapped at you." I finish.

"Seems to be happening a lot lately." He mutters under his breath but of course with me standing right next to him, I hear it.

"It's my wolf. This past week he's been angsty and restless. Then this morning we find out rogues are coming to school, they growl and threaten me in the hallway and that fucking teacher challenges me in front of the whole class." I rant. He then sighs, tucking a strand of his fallen fair behind his ear.

"Okay, okay! I get the whole hierarchy thing. And the challenging parts from both rogue and teacher." He relents.

"What, nothing else to add? You usually have more to say." He laughs, rolling his eyes.

"What can I say, Cairo. You made good points I didn't think about." He chuckles and shakes his head. "Come on, I'm starving, and the rest of the gang are probably already at the table by now." He finishes already making his way towards the cafeteria.

If he's not laughing and cracking jokes or putting me in my place, then he's eating. This damn guy is always hungry.

When we got to the cafeteria and to our usual table, the conversation dropped the second I got there. No one said a word, they all glanced at each other awkwardly, like none of them wanted to speak. Kitty, sitting on Caleb's lap looked like she wanted to say something but her shyness and like everyone else, hesitancy stopped her. But I didn't have to wait long until Zack spilled the beans that the male rogue might be Kieran's mate. The table exploded in a series of scolds, groans and sighs as Zack sat there smugly like he just won a bet. As much as I wanted to explode and demand they were lying, not wanting those rogues to ever enter and join our pack, I can't deny Keiran his mate. Though he's never said it, I always see him searching. He desperately wants to find his mate, desperately wants to find the one he'll grow old with.

Keiran pulls me from my thoughts, asking shyly how he could tell if the male rogue was his mate if he couldn't smell his scent.

"Tomorrow when they get to school, I'll demand they release their scents. Then you'll know." Was all I said. It was time they stop playing.

Chapter Eight

Fate

PRESENT

ALEK

It's times like these I'm grateful to the Goddess that I have patience. Because if I didn't, I would have decked Zia's mate by now. I can't stand his fucking attitude and right now he's not good enough for my sister. He doesn't deserve her. I don't know what he did the rest of the day when we left yesterday but I have a rough idea he probably sat and let his hate for rogue's fester, for *us* fester. It would explain why he stormed right over to us and demanded we release our scents. He couldn't even ask nicely. While I stand here watching his usual pissy looking facial expression not change, I fail to stop myself from riling him up more, so I probe.

"And, what would happen if we do release our scents?" I say looking in thought so I don't laugh instead. If he could, I'm sure he'd have steam coming out of his ears considering the small vein pulsing in his forehead. The guy *hates* being talked back to and even more so given he's of alpha blood. This must be killing him not to be able to command us.

"We'll cross that bridge *if* we come to it." He snaps, arms crossing defensively against his chest, but I can see he's trying to hide the claws that have descended from his fingers. Interestingly enough, he's trying not to show it. Trying to hide that he's in a dangerous mood right now. But I get it when his eyes flick to Zia before coming back to mine, when they lose the sharp edge they held for me. *Ah, the mate bond playing its mind games already.*

Since the moment he asked us to release our scents, Zia's had a permanent scowl on her face. I could feel her annoyance and anger through our bond. She thinks her mate is an asshole as well. Which is true, he is. But I can also feel fear. This is the first time we've ever released our scents since we left our pack. We were so driven by fear that for nearly three years our scents have been masked. It's gotten to the point where I don't remember *how* to release it.

When I made no move to change, he looked down to Zia. I don't know how long their little staring contest lasted, but it wasn't long before Zia sighed out and gave her back to him. A sign of disrespect to the alpha and given the shocked looked from his friends I would say we maybe should tone down how much disrespect we give this guy.

She breathes in and out before looking up at me with her sad puppy dog eyes that I've gotten so used to seeing.

ZIA: *[Do it, Alek. I want you to be happy.]* I look at her sadly because I already know the answer to my question before I ask it.

ALEK: *[Aren't you going to do it too?]*

ZIA: *[No. He hasn't proved himself to me yet.]*

My inner turmoil was suffocating me. My head wants to oppose her and wait until she is ready. We were born together, and we'll die together. We've always been inseparable. And the one time we weren't was when everything changed. When her light was taken from her because I didn't do my job right and protect her. Instead, I was off flirting with the pack hottie because puberty had welcomed arousal. When puberty hit, I was no longer a boy. I was becoming a man. No longer had I just had crushes, now these crushes turned into more. Wet dreams became my life and masturbation was the next best thing. It was new and exciting, and Yuri was driving me and my body haywire. And imagine my surprise when he cornered me in the woods one day and confessed his attraction to me. That whole year I had fantasised about kissing him every day when he walked into class fashionably late. He always had girls hanging off his arms and I couldn't blame them. They were like bees to honey. His shaggy brown hair accentuated his bright brown eyes. They drew everyone in, and I was infatuated with him. He became my biggest crush. He took over my mind and my fantasies. After that day he found me in the woods, we met up there every day after and made out with each other. We were each other's first kiss. I thought he was my mate up until the day we had a new girl transfer to our pack. The second he laid eyes on her I was nothing but a memory. I never got to see his eyes shine and glow towards me. Now he only had eyes for her, his mate. I still went to our spot in the woods and hopefully, stupidly, waited that he would show. But he never did. Then I fell into a dark hole of depression where I snapped at my parents and ignored Zia. I pushed her away because she was so happy with *him*, that I was jealous of her. If only I had just opened my eyes, then I would have seen that she wasn't happy at all.

She was terrified.

I sighed as Zia pushed her feelings onto me from our bond. She really was okay with me releasing my scent. She wanted me to be happy.

ALEK: *[Are you really sure? I can wait, Zi?]*

ZIA: *[I am sure, Alek.]*

ALEK: *[I love you, Zia.]*

ZIA: *[I love you too, brat.]*

I gave her one last look, making sure she didn't change her mind at the last second. She gives me a smile and nods, encouraging me to go on before she turns back around. I watch my mate intently as I let my wolf do his thing. Waiting to see his beautiful blue-grey eyes shimmer as he and his wolf recognise me as their mate, and I don't have to wait long. The second I release my scent he sniffs the air before excitement takes over, eyes shimmering when they connect with mine. Liquid gold makes a seamless transition as they take over his eyes signalling his wolf has come forward to claim me as his.

"He is!" He exclaims so happily my chest puffs up in pride. The rest of the group smile and look from him to me and back again as though they already knew he was mine. All except Zia's mate. If anything, he looks more annoyed at the outcome. Annoyed that he now has to accept us. He looks down to Zia with a yearning but confused look across his face before it's quickly replaced by that pissed off look again. My quick observation is cut short when my mate speaks.

"H..hi.." He just manages to squeak out as his face is taken over by a raging blush. To make matters better, I wink and smirk, causing his arousal to become thicker in the air. I try not to laugh as he realises what's just happened and blocks his scent. Besides the *sour one*, the others look amused. That is, until said sour one speaks again.

"I do believe I said scents, plural." He states.

Zia's conflict rose tenfold as she battled with her wolf. Her wolf wants to release their scent, but Zia isn't ready for that just yet. So, like the best big brother I am, I come to her rescue. "She doesn't need to do that. I have found my mate within your pack, that should already be enough." I state clearly. He's about to reply when the other mated girl, the seer, stops him.

"What is it?" He asks annoyed. Her mate with the dreads

shoots him a look before he rolls his eyes and looks down at her impatiently.

I could feel Zia freaking out, rushing through her words through our mindlink. I know what she's worried about. The seer. The only one out of this group that could put the puzzle of us together.

I tell Zia to calm down and wait to see how this plays out. No need to cause a scene until we know what she wants.

"I just need to see something." She says before walking over to us. She studies our hair, eyes, and our faces. I know what she's looking for and it doesn't take long before she finds it.

"What is it? What do you see, Kitty?" Zia's mate asks.

"They've been touched by the moon!" She gasps.

ZIA

The temperature feels like it dropped two degrees as I watch the seer slightly inch closer to inspect us more thoroughly. I could see her violet seer eyes studying the silver streaks in our hair that match her full head of silver hair, and our unnatural aqua blue eyes and the uncanny resemblance between our faces. I see the moment it clicks in her head that we're twins. As she goes to announce it she's stopped suddenly as her eyes change from violet to white. She was getting a vision from the Goddess and the second her eyes changed back made my heart stop.

"Omg! He's your-" I cut her off before she says anymore.

"Yes, he is." I look down at the ground wishing it could swallow me up whole as I try to reign in my sorrow. *Damn, Goddess. What a snitch.*

"Aren't you going to tell him?" She asks but I answer her honestly.

"He hasn't proved himself. When he has, then I will." She looks conflicted as she watches my face. I can see the fight within her. He's her friend and future alpha but she's also not obligated to tell him anything.

"I don't know if that's a good idea. He-" She goes to speak further but the school bell cuts her off. The tension in the group lifts as my mate says we're saved by the bell. Assuming he means from this interrogation.

ALEK: *[Literally.]* Alek says making the both of us laugh.

Although I'm sure Alek was laughing at how miffed my mate looks. He doesn't know what was said but I'm sure he's thinking of something completing different with his hatred for us impairing him. He turns without another word, storming to the large wooden doors. His friends awkwardly nod or wave before they turn and follow him inside. I look to Alek, he smiles and nods his head in encouragement. This is our first official day of school, and my first-class Alek isn't in. I'll be all by myself and it's a strange feeling.

I find my class and stop at the door, taking a breath before I walk in, shoulders back and head held high. There were still students coming in and finding their seats, so, I stood to the side, waiting until there was a seat available. I didn't want to steal anyone's seat. I could smell many different scents circling the room. Wolf, vampire, human, *mate*. But he wasn't currently in this class. His scent was flowing from a few doors down. His scent was so strong it lingered everywhere he went. Like he's coated the entire school in his scent. Giving myself a mental pep talk, I walk over to an empty seat and sit next to the only human girl in the class. With beautiful orange auburn hair and big blue eyes, she smiles brightly as I ask if anyone was sitting there. After inviting me to sit down I wondered why a human of all creatures was in this class and not hating on me. She was the only one not shooting me daggers or watching me curiously. She was the only one that smiled. I'm sure she doesn't know I'm a rogue or else she would be treating me the same as everyone else.

"Excuse me...If you don't mind me asking, you're not a-" I go to say werewolf, but she cuts me off as if she expected me to ask.

"Werewolf?" She laughs. "Nope, I'm human!"

"I know humans are allowed to be here, but it seems to be a predominantly wolf school. Why are you here?" I ask curiously and hope I'm not stepping on anyone's toes by asking.

"My mate is a werewolf. He finished school two years ago. This is him." She says happily while pulling her phone out. She presses the home button and I watch as the screen lights up and a photo of a man appears. Wearing an all-black outfit with lace up boots and a silver dagger strapped to his thigh, I wonder what the outfit means.

"That's interesting, what he's wearing." I smile.

"That's his uniform. He's a pack warrior. Well, he's one of three head warriors. Meaning he leads a group of warriors."

"That's really impressive." I say honestly. He looked not much older than her and for him to be a head warrior must mean he's an impressive fighter.

"So, you're new here?" She asks, looking at me curiously probably trying to guess what species I am.

"Yeah, I'm Zia. Nice to meet you?..." My voice trails off as I wait for her to answer.

"Somner."

"Somner? That's a unique name. I've never heard of anything like that before." She starts laughing and nodding her head at the same time. I feel almost stupid for saying anything, but she doesn't seem bothered by it.

"I know! You wouldn't believe how often I get that. When I was born and my father was filling out the birth certificate, my mother said Sommer but his hard of hearing self thought she said *Somner*. Which we all find hilarious still to this day but at the time my mother was mighty pissed. But after a while she loved the name and loved the story behind it. So, she never changed it and I stayed Somner." I giggle at her story. She must have a great family. I wonder how they took her being mated to a werewolf. "Oh, also. Welcome to Dawn High!" She says excitedly. I know I should be excited but what we've experienced already has made me dread coming to school. But meeting Somner has slightly changed things. *I've made my first friend.*

"So, I'm assuming you're a werewolf? Giving how much you know." I nod and she continues. "Do you have a mate? I don't see a mark on your neck. Or have you not found him?" She asks staring at the part of my neck that isn't covered by my hair. I look around awkwardly as a few students linger around the door or by their desk talking.

"I've recently just found him." I guess I must have been very vocal facial expressions because she asked if things aren't okay between us. I take a few calming breaths before I answer. Somner just has a calming presence about her. It doesn't feel like she has any secret agendas or malicious intent behind her calm demeaner. "Let's just say it's a work in progress." Already way too many people know who my mate is.

Cairo.

I literally can't take two steps in this school without someone whispering his name when he walks by. Even the teachers. Apparently, there was an incident yesterday with Cairo and his teacher. I overheard two women at the reception desk talk about it. They said something happened between Cairo and his teacher in front of the whole class. How she disrespected him. Whatever happened all I know is that she asked to transfer out of that class to another.

Somner smiles at me and begins talking again. I'm glad she's human. If she wasn't I know she wouldn't be talking to me right now.

"Ohh, have you had the *Who's Who* tour yet? Created by me

of course." She said with an excited glint in her eye. I shake my head as she laughs. "The Who's Who tour. A tour or more like gossip tour of who everybody is at this school."

"Oh, like the food chain. Well, in that case no. I haven't had the tour yet." I say shyly although I already have a feeling who's on top. She claps her hands and bounces up and down in her seat.

"This is my favourite part. I mean we don't get many new students, and I'm sure Cade is so sick of me gossiping and talking about people at school that he has no idea who is who." She laughs with not an ounce of guilt. Sounds like they have a great relationship. Something I only hope to have with *Cairo* but I don't...I don't know what's going to happen there. "Okay, so, I'm gonna tell you about who's who when they walk. But first I need to make sure they can't hear me. Some of these wolves can be snappy." She said quietly which makes me laugh at the description. "But um, please don't freak out. I'll explain everything." Okay...now I'm slightly worried.

I watched puzzled as she reached down into her bag on the ground beside her and unzip it. Her hand goes in, and she ruffles around the very bottom making it look like it's deeper on the inside. Like that Poppins lady. Then when she's found what she's looking for, she pulls her arm back out and smiles awkwardly at first then reassuringly. My eyes nearly bulge out of my head when I see what's in her hand. "What the hell!" I say staring down at the pure solid silver ball sitting in her hand. It's slightly bigger than a tennis ball but that's not the worrying part. It's the silver part.

All supernatural creatures have a natural disability. Something that can harm and kill us. Just like humans have sickness and disease and vampires have wood and vervain, werewolves have silver. It psychically burns us to the touch. Our skin blisters and burns, it melts the skin and it's the only thing that can scar a werewolf. That and deep wounds. Just like the one on my cheek. I felt when it was cut open straight down to the bone. Some feral rogues rip their claws out and replace them with silver claws. They become even more dangerous. And some alphas use liquid forms of silver to kill or torture rogues.

"Please don't worry! I don't use it to hurt anyone, I swear. It's just for privacy. I got into too many fights with wolves from gossiping too much. Cade ended up making me this so that I can protect myself at school when he can't be with me." She says hurriedly like I might flip out if her reason isn't justifiable. But I'm not like other wolves and I'm not quick to judge. Unless it's that bitch from yesterday that made the stupid flea joke. Her I'll judge any day.

"W..well how does it work?" I say unsure but I give her the benefit of the doubt, but I do scoot back a little further in my chair. I've had more than my fair share of pain in my seventeen years of life and if I can help it, I'd rather not cause myself anymore pain.

"The ball omits like a ring of protection, of sorts." She places it on the desk in-between us. She looks like she's struggling with how she to describe it. "It's basically like a wall that stops wolves from hearing. Unless you're in the hearing proximity of a human, then the wolves won't be able to use super hearing to hear. So, now when I gossip with you, they won't be able to hear what I say and get offended." I softly chuckle. I had no idea silver could be used like that.

"That's so smart."

"Right! My mate is a genius." She laughs proudly. "Now, let us begin." She says scooting her chair closer to me and turns to she face the door.

A guy with short dreads walks in and takes his seat. He's followed by a beautiful girl with long black hair, ivory skin, and the reddest eyes I've ever seen. Like the colour of rubies. I look down at her mouth and see fangs poking out when she smiles. Somner introduces me to them from afar. The guy's name was Danny. He's the school flirt. Apparently, he's caused plenty of fights from flirting with mated men and women. Even though he's a werewolf and knows exactly who is mated by people's marks, he still does it. A flirty troublemaker. Then Somner moved on to the vampire. Her name was Lina. She said she was born a vampire, so she has incredible control over the blood-lust. Somner said she was our age and that everyone thinks just because she's a vampire she must be like a hundred years old or something. She said they're both really nice and that if she's never here I can always sit with them.

"Isn't that right, Lina." She say's normally as silver doesn't affect vampires. She smiled over at us with her sharp fangs sparkling in the light. She nodded and winked.

Just this one class and I already feel so welcome. That was, until the flea bitch walked in. Somner said her name was Jordan. Her friend that followed after and the one that laughed at her joke yesterday was Beth. They're the school mean girls. Well Jordan is. Somner said Jordan treats her friend like crap and that she's actually nice when she's not with Jordan. Then, Somner really dropped a mother of a bombshell on me. She said this bitch, *THIS BITCH*, was in love... *WITH MY MATE!*

That this whore, has gone around the school telling everyone that she's mates with Cairo. And what's worse is he isn't telling them otherwise! He's letting her tell everyone they're mates, and he doesn't care. I ran from one alpha just to be mated to another. The human part of me is hurting from this new revelation, but the wolf side of me is fuming. So much that I had no choice but to let her front in my mind. I didn't have the strength to stop her. With eyes as orange as the sunset, she pierced Somner with a hateful glare as she demanded she tell us everything she knows about *Jordan*. She gulped and nodded quickly, seeing the obvious change in my demeanour and eyes. She knows my wolf is fronting and knows how dangerous this situation could get.

Their *relationship*, started when they were sixteen. They all grew up together so they both know full well they aren't each other's soul mates. It was a whole year after turning fifteen before they even began whatever they are. By the way Somner says it, everybody knows or are certain they aren't mates. He's never marked her although she tries her best to get him to. She said from what she heard from her mate Cade, that Jordan was always after the Luna position. She wormed her way into Cairo's life and when they were sixteen, she successfully took him to her bed. Ever since they've been...intimate. Somner says Jordan is dangerous and extremely jealous when it comes to Cairo. A human girl once spoke to him and Jordan saw this as a threat. She clawed the girls face up so bad she went blind. She had to transfer schools and the Alpha had to pay for the girl's medical treatment and hospital bills as well as a settlement for compensation. Jordan was warned personally by the Alpha to keep her jealousy in check or else she'd have to face the consequences. She was the school bitch, the popular girl who was in the prime of her life. She is what I call a Peaker. Someone who will only ever peak in high school. And with me arriving in town and realising that I'm mated to Cairo and would take the Luna position, I have a feeling all hell will break loose when she finds out.

Once Somner finished talking she sat looking at me with a worried almost anxious expression on her face tracking my every breath and I couldn't stop taking breaths because I was trying to calm myself and my wolf down from all this dreaded new information. *Cairo willingly laid with another, lied about another being his mate...* I know he has no clue who I am but what kind of man does that when he knows every werewolf has a soulmate. I longed for the day I could meet my mate and our relationship would blossom and bloom as we grew with each other.

My train of thought stopped when I heard someone obnoxiously sniffing. I looked up into the shit green eyes of Jordan herself. She sniffed and scrunched her nose up, looking around the room before her eyes landed on my now aqua-blue ones. She then laughed as if she found the foul smell. "Oh, I thought someone stepped in dog shit but it's just the rogue." She laughed and her minion beside her giggled. I continued to stare, imagining what her death would look like. I bet it would be so satisfying to see. *Especially if my wolf was the one killing her.*

"He's your mate, isn't he..." Somner said whispering.

I turned, seeing the guilty, sorry look marring her pretty face. I guess my reaction to the revelation about Cairo and Jordan gave myself away. I'm glad I kept my scent hidden; glad Cairo doesn't know I'm his mate. Who knows what he would have done if he knew? He's already treated me like shit, rubbed his fake mateship in everyone's faces and clearly hates rogues with a passion. Goddess, I don't know what I'm going to do. This whole thing is a shit show.

"Y.." I go to speak but I stop eyes flicking around the room, making sure no one can hear. "Yes. Sorry if I scared you before. My wolf she just...got super angry." Apologising, she raised her hands and shook her head.

"No, please, don't apologise. I know sometimes you can't control your wolves in times of high stress. I know I'm only human but being mated to a werewolf, I see when his wolf takes control. I've loved him and known him long enough to know nearly everything about wolves. I don't hold it against you when that happens. It's completely natural and it's in your nature." She finishes with a smile. Making me feel relieved and grateful.

"Wow, you're just a breath of fresh air." I say honestly as she laughs.

"We should have a sleepover sometime! The weekend maybe?" She wants me to come over for a sleepover? I've had a sleepover with someone that wasn't Alek or *him*. But I'm excited at the thought. She's my first friend I've made in a long time and my first ever human friend. I'm excited to see what her home is like, what her parents are like. I think it will be fun.

"I'd like that." She claps her hands excitedly before giving me her number and her address. I'm sure Alek would be more than happy to have Keiran over to get to know each other.

Somner left the silver ball on the desk hidden just inside her opened pencil case as the teacher started the class. When it was time to read our textbooks, I couldn't concentrate. As much as I tried to study, I couldn't stop thinking about Cairo. I couldn't stop thinking about how far they had gone. Did they only make out? Or did they go all the way? Knowing I'm probably being stupid wishing it wasn't the latter. Of course they went all the way. She's obviously very easy going and he's a hot young guy with both of them having hormones raging through their bodies.

I brush those thoughts from my mind just as Somner speaks again.

"Did you hear it's taco day?!" She says and it's perfect timing because her stomach rumbled. I laugh. She can't hear it with it being so subtle, but with my wolf hearing I hear everything.

"No, but I do love a good taco." The last time I had one it was a Peri-peri fish taco when we were in Portugal. Since we left there, it's either been raw meat or sometimes cooked on the fire.

"Did you want to sit with me at lunch?" She asked but I have to politely decline. "I usually eat outside because Cade comes and has lunch with me, but you're welcome to join us."

"Oh, I'm sorry, I would but I have to find my brother. He found his mate today, so I bet he's dying to tell me all about it." I smile. I couldn't wait to find Alek. He's gonna be so happy.

"Omg, who's your brother mated to?"

"Uhm, his name is Keiran." She gasps excitedly.

"Kieran is so sweet! Your brother is super lucky. There's no one sweeter and more caring in this school than Kieran. He's going to be Cairo's beta when he becomes Alpha." I'm glad. Alek deserves nothing but the best.

When the bell rings the class quickly starts to pack up.

"I'll see you tomorrow then," Somner said zipping her bag up, "and I'll text you the deets about our sleepover." I nod and say goodbye as I don't have any more classes with her until tomorrow. Swinging my bag over my shoulder, I'm the last to exit the classroom.

Now, where would Alek be?

I eventually find him in the cafeteria. The schools' hallways are so long and big I got lost a few times. But after a while I figured out that the large body of noise was actually all the students in the cafeteria having lunch. So, all I had to do was follow the sound. Like a bee to honey, it led me straight to him. There were tables and students everywhere, and sure enough those tables were filled with delicious smelling tacos Somner had mentioned. I stood by the doorway for a couple of minutes scanning the crowd until I find my matching pair of aqua eyes watching and smiling at me. Gently making my way through the crowd, I see who Alek was sitting with. When I first found him, I only saw him. I didn't see anyone else at the table until I got closer.

Sitting on the left side of the small round table was Zack, then a spare seat before Kitty, sat on her mate Caleb's lap. Keiran sat beside the happy couple and Alek right beside him. There were no other spare seats beside the one next to Zack, so I got to that one. Just as I bend to sit down, Zack stops me.

"Just letting you know, that's Cairo's spot." Throughout our lesson Somner told me about the rest of Cairo's group and told me a bit about them. All of them seem to be nice with my mate being the only ass of the group. Rolling my eyes, I look to the seemingly innocent chairs that sat against the back wall of the cafeteria. "And the spare chairs are broken." He finishes. I sigh, frustrated as I walk over to Alek.

"Move over." He nods, sliding over to make room on his

chair for me. But the chair ends up being too small to share so I end up sitting on his knees instead.

Kitty laughs saying she likes how I think. I try to smile at her, but it drops almost instantly. I felt so awkward being around people I didn't know. And it didn't help that the moment I came over everyone stopped talking. The table went silent, and it almost felt like they were talking about me by the way they continued to be silent after I sat down. No one said a word. I was ready to stand up and leave when Zack spoke again, sending a chill down my body.

"Cairo!" He smiled at him before he turned back to us and waited for Cairo to sit down. "Great! Now that everyone's here, we can finally learn more about you two." Zack claps his hands together once, but the table remains silent. Neither me nor Alek wanting to talk. "Okaaaay then, how about your names?" I'm sure he knows, but I can tell he's just trying to get the conversation started.

"I'm Alek, and this is Zia." He says not saying anymore or any less. Just enough.

"Ah, beautiful name for a beautiful girl." Zack said making me smirk and raise a brow when his eyes flashed to watch Cairo's reaction at the flirty comment. And when Cairo grunts and shoots Zack a warning look I can't help the extra beat my heart does. "Something wrong, Cairo?" Zack asks innocently as he smile widens. After a moment Cairo rolls his eyes and turns back to the group annoyed, eyes looking anywhere but in the direction of Alek and I although I know he wants too.

"Do you know?" I say softly to Zack. I have a feeling he knows Cairo and I are mates. He's studied us long enough every time we're near each other.

"Yep!" He says proudly. "I suspected."

"Um, Cairo, what happens now?" Keiran asked looking nervous. He's probably got a million emotions running through him right now and his main concern is if his mate will be accepted into the pack. He's probably thinking Cairo will say no and ban us, but I'm surprised when he speaks.

"They'll both participate in the pack Trials. Only once they succeed in defeating their opponents will they be able to join the pack." I feel Alek about to protest but I speak first.

"Fine." I didn't have to turn to see Aleks surprise or Kieran's anxious look. I don't know what the trials are exactly, but it sounds like a simple fight. One I vow to myself to win. It's the least I can do for stopping Alek from living his life with his mate. I'm done being a burden for him. "When and where?" I ask Cairo.

"In four days, Saturday, at the pack." I guess I will have to reschedule my sleepover.

"Zi, are you sure?" Alek whispers with his uncertainty is coming through our twin bond.

"I'm sure, Ali. You deserve this. For everything you've done for me, I...I just want at least one of us to be happy." I say, sadly looking away from his eyes.

"You can be happy too." He whispers back and I know he's meaning me letting Cairo know I'm his mate. But I can't.

"Not while he's alive." I say this time barely above a whisper. I should have linked that last part, but I didn't.

"Don't cry, Zi. Remember, you're *moya vtoraya polovina*." He said calling me his other half as he always did. "If you cry, I cry." He said, accent so thick it made me laugh and because it was also true. Doesn't matter if I'm happy crying or sad crying, I always look over at Alek and he's there with the same fat tears rolling down his cheeks.

"What's your story? How did you become rogues?" Cairo suddenly asks curiously. I didn't peg him for caring about anything we have to say which shocked me. "What did you do?" His simple question if you could call it that and not assumption, ignites a fire within me. I feel my wolf surge forward, eyes taking over mine as she pushes me from the forefront of my mind.

"We did nothing wrong. You *vysokomernyy mudak*." She says angrily, calling him a fucking asshole from my suggestion of course. My fists were clenched against my side as my claws started to extend. She's always been protective of me, always seeming to sense something I could never. Then when everything happened, she became more protective. She knows nothing was my fault and what happened I had no control over, but our mate suggesting it had made her angry.

"Zia! *Uspokoysya*." Alek snapped telling me to calm down. "*Day mne skazat'.*" *Let me talk* he says as he grabs my hand reassuringly, trying to coax my wolf back. We take a deep breath as I let my wolf know it's okay for me to come back. That I'm okay to front.

"We were born in a pack. Had a great life up until we shifted. Then we left." Alek says matter of fact.

"Left?!" Cairo says disgusted like he can't imagine why anyone would leave their pack. "You chose to leave your pack and become rogues? Why would you do that?" I couldn't stop myself.

"Because we had too! If we didn't, he would have killed my family and eventually me!" I say as my rage simmers just under breaking point. I'm sick of him looking at us like we chose wrong. Like becoming rogues was the worst choice we could have ever made.

"Who? Why?" He says remembering that I mentioned a *he* being the reason we left. He could see the hurt and pain in my eyes when he asked, his own softening as he come to realize something. He knew whatever happened to us was bad. Bad enough to leave everyone and everything behind. But my fire was still burning.

"Because I was born! Because I'm me!" I spill out making everyone but Cairo gasp.

"What does that mean?" Cairo said as Kitty sighed, knowing she's the only one with a brain.

"Seriously! It's not that hard to figure out now. They're

twins." She says turning to face him like she's figured out that was the reason why we left. Because we have these powers that's the reason whatever happened to us, to me, happened. But she couldn't be more wrong. Besides Kitty, every single one of the guys looked stunned, even Cairo. I could see all of them comparing our features and seeing the evidence right in front of their face confirming what she said was true.

"Wow, we're so stupid." Zack says before he laughs. "I mean they even look the same. Same skin tone, same hair colour with the weird ashy streaks that look real, the creepy almost glowing aqua eyes and everything. They're literally a carbon copy of each other.

ZIA: *[Alek, I'm freaking the hell out!]*

ALEK: *[It will be fine, just deep breaths.]*

"What are you doing?" Zack says as Cairo stands up from the table, chair suddenly scraping against the tiles.

"My father needs to know about this." Cairo says speaking of the Alpha.

"NO!" I scream out in panic. *No one can know we're here! No one!* I get off Alek, running to Cairo as fast as I could. I warn him not to tell anyone but that only agitates him.

"I don't take orders from you." He spits out. "If I want to tell someone then I will. You have no damn say. Pack member or rogue, I, outrank, you." My body was shaking, bristling with anger as he spoke and the second he finished, I swung.

My hand flew out so fast I didn't have enough time to pull back before it was too late. My hand slapped him right across the face and for the split second that our skin touched, it was enough for the soulmate sparks to fly. My hand zinged like it was just electrocuted. I gasped and I stared up at Cairo, waiting for him to realize what I had just done. What I had just *revealed*. Sparks shot straight up my arm the moment my hand connected with his face and there's no going back for me now. I royally fucked up. The whole cafeteria went silent, everyone in the room stopping to watch the event unfold. He suddenly grabbed me by the collar of my shirt, swinging me around and slamming my back into the wall. I heard Alek's chair fly back, crashing into the table behind as he attempted to come save me, but his mate and Caleb held him back with struggle. Cairo spoke so low that if I wasn't inches from his face then I wouldn't have heard.

"You will never do that again." He said so calmy, but I could see the white-hot rage burning within his eyes. "Disrespect me again and I'll kill your brother." I gasped, tears instantly springing to my eyes at his threat. I could see the truth in his eyes and he meant it.

"Please..." I beg looking into his hazel eyes as tears fall down my face, dropping onto his hands holding my collar. "I..I don't want to go back there...I don't want him to hurt me again." The tears continued to fall. I watched his eyes drop down to the scar on my cheek.

They softened as he followed a tear drop over my scar and down my cheek before he looked back up to my eyes. I try to show him my fear, pleading with him to have some compassion and not tell his father we're twins. Once one person knows it will spread like wildfire until it finds its way back to *him*.

He gently lowers me until my feet touch the ground. I didn't realise he had held me up in the air against, dangling me against the wall. He still didn't make any connection that I was his mate. Maybe he thought the electric feeling from the slap was me just hitting him hard and not it being the mate sparks? He nods once, letting go of my shirt before he spins quickly, walking towards the exit. Soon after he disappears the cafeteria erupts in chaos as every student starts talking about what the hell just happened. Then I'm spun around as Aleks crazed eyes look everywhere, making sure he didn't hurt me.

"What did he say!? Did he hurt you?" I shake my head and breathe in, trying to stop the tears from falling but they won't obey.

"He won't say anything." I say low. Alek pulls me into his chest, hugging me. His heart is beating so hard I could feel it against my own and his breathing was erratic. I look over his shoulder to his mate and Caleb. Both looking exhausted like they've just ran a marathon. Then I see Zack panting and realise all three of them were holding Alek back when Cairo pushed me against the wall. It would have taken a fourth person to restrain him if he had used his powers, but he restrained himself.

"Did he hurt you?!" Alek said again, shaking me roughly to get my attention back to him.

"I'm fine, Alek! Just let go." I snap back and get out of his hold to push past him.

"Where are you going?" He says to my back but I can hear the hurt in his voice. I know he just wants to protect me but I'm sick of feeling like a helpless little girl. I'm not as weak as everyone thinks. I can take care of myself.

"I just need some air, Alek." I say and I continue walking to the exit. I mindlink him that I love him just before I walk out of sight.

Chapter Nine

Babushka

Cairo

I can't believe she hit me.

I saw her hand swing out and I could have stopped it easily, but I was so shocked that she was actually going to do it. No one has ever dared lay a finger on me but this tiny little five-foot something wolf was gonna try. And try she did. She smacked me so hard across the face my cheek vibrated, and sparks shot up my face. I could still feel the stinging now as I sit at a bare desk in an empty classroom. Everyone's either in the cafeteria or outside sitting against the trees under the shade. I slipped in here from the quiet hallway to escape. I needed time to think. Needed time to re-evaluate what the fuck just happened.

My wolf was eerily quiet the second Zia slapped me. I thought my wolf would flip out and lose his shit on her, but he didn't. Even Zack, Keiran and Caleb expected to me to lash out which is why they held her brother back when I slammed her up against the wall. My human side was the one that reacted. She publicly hit me in front of the whole school. You could hear a pin drop the second she did it. Once I had her pinned against the wall her tears started falling. I could see the fear in her eyes. She was so terrified I could feel her body shaking from just the thought of someone else knowing she's a twin and the fact that she hit me. Clearly, they're running from someone, and everyone knows the story of twin wolves and how they have special gifts from the Goddess. There's only one set of twins with these gifts almost every one-hundred years. With her tears burning my hand as they landed on me one by one, they seemed to ease the burning rage inside of me. When they glistened and glossed over the deep angry scar on her cheek, I started to connect the dots. With her fear, the person they're running from and her not wanting me to tell my father she's a Moons Warrior, I understood then. Once word gets out that we have a set of twins, it will get back to the person they're running from.

I felt bad for her in that moment. I've never seen such fear in someone's eyes before. I studied the scar as the tears glided over it. I could hear her brother snarling behind me, thrashing against the restraints holding him back. I think in that moment if Keiran and Caleb hadn't grabbed him in time then he would have tried to kill me. His body is riddled with scars just like my father's and I'm sure he could beat me easily if he tried. I've never had any real experience fighting rogues, but he has. But he did nothing wrong. He was simply wanting to protect his sister from a threat. I spoke to her low enough that only she could hear. I knew every wolf and vampire in that place was straining to listen. She knew I was serious, but I could see her pleading with me in her beautiful eyes and for some weird reason, I wanted to pull her into me and hug her and tell her everything was going to be alright and that I didn't *really* mean it...Did I?

My body and mind feel like it's being pulled apart. She's a rogue, something I have hated for a long time. But she's also different. She's got this sadness to her that makes you want to protect her, but also this hidden fury within her. One minute I want her and her brother out of my school and the next I *want* her. I want to see a smile on her face that's always hidden. One minute I want nothing to do with her and the next I want to know her stories, know what she's been through, where she's come from. I haven't heard her speak much but the few small times she has; I've heard an accent. It's not strong but when she says certain words my ear catches it the way I hear my mums accent sometimes. Alek speaks almost fluent English with no hint of an accent. Like he's always speaking for the two of them. But I did think I heard one when he spoke to her. And I really couldn't deny that she didn't sound hot when she was cursing me out in another language. And I know she was because she was spitting those words out like they were fire.

I could feel a nagging in my mind, someone's trying to mindlink me. Usually that nagging comes from one person only. Jordan. It feels like just this last week I've been getting sick of her. Getting sick of the clinginess and the neediness. She used to be one of my best friends when we were young. But then as we got older, she started to change. Started to want different things. She became the worst type of person and when we were sixteen, she tried everything to get into my pants and I let her. She was easy and always wanting it, always wanting to show off to everyone that she was fucking me. I never even had to try. I just laid there and let her suck me off or fuck me till she came. But I never did, and she never cared. She just wanted to get herself off and claim me as her mate. I never corrected her or anyone when they called us mates. I never planned to set her straight but after the rogues came, I started thinking maybe I should. Zia started plaguing my mind and I started picturing what it would be like if Zia was the one in my bed. I should be repulsed at the thought but I'm anything but. If I stare at her too long, I start to find myself looking at her body. Feel myself getting harder as I picture her beneath me. I even had a dream about her the other night. I woke up in a puddle of sweat and hard as a rock. Had to go and jack myself off in the shower. Then I got mad all over again that I was masturbating to a rogue.

As I sat there annoyed, a flash of blonde-ash hair passes by the window on the classroom door. I know that two toned hair anywhere. I get up, striding quickly before swinging the door open.

"Rogue." I say standing next to the door and watch the retreating figure stop.

I could hear her heart skip a beat the second I spoke. I wonder what she's thinking. Maybe that I've come for revenge for that *slap*. I should be but I don't know why I came after her. My feet moved on their own like they were influenced by my wolf. I think he feels bad the way I had her pinned up against the wall when I threatened her. But she was the one who chose violence first. So, his little pity party can end right there. She stands still with her back to me, irritating me as she refuses to turn around.

"Look at me when I speak to you." I say trying to reign in my irritation that's slowly turning into anger from her disrespect. Luckily no one's in the halls right now to see *this* interaction.

"Why?" She says suddenly turning around and glares at me. "You've not earned my respect. Why should I respect you?" She says defiantly, tipping her little head up at me. I hold in a smirk.

"Because I'm an alpha. Whether you're a rogue or not, you should respect me and you will if you want to join this pack with your brother." If we were in a cartoon, she'd probably have steam coming out of her nose. But for now, her eyes are the ones shooting daggers.

"I will never cower to another alpha. I've done my time being beneath an egotistical, psychopathic alpha. I won't be subjected to another one. Especially *you*." I couldn't stop myself as I strode forward. She took a step back as I stalked closer until we were almost chest to chest. She was a head and a bit shorter than me, so I had to look down at her to keep eye contact. If she stared straight ahead, she'd be looking at my chest. But she wasn't, she was looking straight up at me with that same fire in her eyes. "What are you gonna do? Shove me against the lockers this time?" She snips with a tilt to her cute little head now making me smirk.

"You'd like that wouldn't you. Get to slap me again." I say with a condescending smirk, seeing her irritation rise.

Her chest rises and falls with her quick angry breaths. Both of us stand with our arms crossed against our chests just inches from each other. As the silence stretches, I find my eyes scanning down her body. I stop at her chest, watching as the buttons stretch against their restraints everytime she breathes in. I go back up to her face but stop at her plump lips. They're slightly parted, breath escaping and gently fanning my crossed arms. When I look up to her eyes my own breath hitches slightly when I realize she's staring at my lips. *She wants to kiss me*. I could see it in the way her cheeks slightly tinted from a blush. Then I noticed her breathing had changed from quick angry puffs to aroused exhales. I found myself mirroring her when I felt myself harden at the thought of fucking her. I could tell she would be just as wild and fiery in bed.

I lose all restraint when her arousal hits me. She's just as turned on by me as I am of her in this moment. I grab her by the waist and pull her against me as her hands land on my chest. I push her into me more so she can feel how hard I am. I slide my hands from her waist down to her ass. We're both still staring right into each other's eyes when I feel her back arch.

Her pupils begin unnaturally expanding as her arousal makes itself known in her eyes. The second I start to lean down, she gasps, eyes widening as she pulls out of my grasp. She spins around, running towards the doors leading outside.

I growl from the rejection. She's the fucking rogue not me! I should be the one repelling from her not the other way around!

My fist flies out and crashes into the locker, indenting my hand as I watch the door slam behind her. What the fuck was that? One second we were on the brink of another argument fight and the next we were about to make out. I stood there for a few more minutes seething as I willed my hard-on to fuck off. Lunch was about to end, and my next class is about to start. Which she so happens to be in, and I know I planned on having her sit next to me, but I think that's going to be a bad idea right now. I turn and head the other way, feet pounding the ground as students start to fill the hallway.

I sat in my usual spot at the back, sitting like a sentry in the classroom, observing everything. It's one of the alpha tendencies I can never shake. Zack enters the class with Alek behind him. He looks around the room for Zia and when he can't find her his eyes land straight on me. They harden and shoot me an accusatory look. I smirk in return, pissing him off as his knuckles go white from the pressure of his clenched fist. He sits at an empty desk off to the side with a clear view of the classroom door and me. I watch his eyes glaze over and can only assume he's mindlinking her. When he's finished, he looks at the door and waits for her to appear. When she finally does his shoulders visibly relax as he watches her walk over and sit down beside him in the empty chair. She avoids looking at me and he asks her where she went. Both of their eyes glaze over, and I find myself angry that they're having a private conversation that I can't hear.

"Stare any harder and you're gonna burn a hole in them."

Zack jokes from beside me making me roll my eyes. "So, what did you do?" He asks.

"Why do you think I did something?" I scoff and turn to look at him.

"Maybe cause he's shootin daggers and she's avoiding you like the plague."

"Nothing that concerns you." I turn back to her...them.

"Something else happened, didn't it? This isn't from what happened in the cafeteria." He questions. How very observant of him.

"Maybe." I say but I'd rather not divulge what nearly happened in the hallway or her *slight* rejection to me.

"Alright, keep your secrets. Just know I'll find out one way or another." He says sooking but I doubt he ever will. With Alek still looking like he's quizzing her through their mindlink, Zia's gonna take what happened to the grave. I doubt she wants her brother knowing I was rubbing my crotch up against her. That would also explain why he shot me a look when she walked in. He could smell me on her and sitting so close it must be torture for him.

"Afternoon!" The teacher that disrespected me greeted as she walked into the room. *Ah, so her request to transfer was denied.* She stopped by her desk when she spotted the two new students in the class. She knew they were the rogues I mentioned and when she flicked her eyes towards me I know she remembered what I said.

I was going to shake my head and let her know not to worry about making Zia sit next to me, but I changed my mind. I want to see how this plays out. I continue to stare at her before she clears her throat and looks away. I slouch back in my chair with my legs spread and arms crossed against my chest as I wait for the teacher to speak. She doesn't take long in making up some bullshit reason for the *rogue* to sit next to me but it does the job.

"We have two new students joining us today! Alek and Zia.

N..now I thought you Zia, could sit up the back and Alek you can stay right there. That way you two can interact with the other students and get to know the best class in the school." She laughs nervously to cover up how much she's obviously lying but Zia buys it.

She's shy and looks back at Alek sadly like she doesn't want to leave him and he looks just the same. I almost feel bad for separating them until she scans the room for the empty seat up the back and spots the only other empty chair in the room is next to me. I see her nostrils flare and her jaw clenches as she realizes who she has to sit next too. I get a sick pleasure from making her angry and testing her. I don't know what it is about her that draws me to her like a moth to flame but I do. My eyes always find her in the hallway, my wolf always wants to be close to her and wants to know everything about her and my dick... well let's just say he's attracted to her.

She grips the strap of her bag and heads towards me with much reluctance. I catch a slight change in her eyes as aqua melted with sunset orange. I watched, intrigued as her wolf fought to come to the surface but she slammed her eyes shut so quick a cute little frown marred her forehead. When she opened her eyes again, her bright aqua eyes were back. No hint of wolf anywhere.

Interesting.

She gingerly sat down beside me breathing in and trying to calm her rapidly beating heart. I love that I make her nervous. Apparently, another sick pleasure I have for her. She places her bag on her lap and awkwardly tries to get her books out in a hurry but in the process her pen flies out from the bag and falls to the ground. I catch it mid-air easily and tuck my arms back into my chest. She didn't see me move, too focussed on trying to get her books out without all of them spilling everywhere. The teacher begins teaching the class. Zia looks all through her bag for her missing pen and frowns again when she can't find it. She looks under her chair and around the surrounding area for another minute before she stops disheartened. She places her bag on the ground beside her feet and turns to me. She looks annoyed and reluctant but speaks anyway.

"Do you have a p..pen I could borrow just for the class?" I smirk and hold out her pen and watched as her mouth popped open. Then she looked at me with that fire again. She snatched the pen out of my hand again without touching me and turned back to her desk, angling herself so that she gives me her back. A sign of disrespect but for some reason it makes me smirk.

She's so feisty and doesn't give a shit what my title is or who I am. It's refreshing considering everyone in this school who aren't my friends walk around me like they're walking on eggshells. My friends don't care but they can get like Zia sometimes when they're upset or just pissed off. But she doesn't care. I see her brother trying to pull her back in line sometimes reminding her I am still an alpha, but she ignores him. For the rest of the class, I continue to watch her. I know she knows because her shoulders have been tense since the first time she sneaked a peak at me and realised I was watching her. At one point she muttered *"Do your work"* under her breath which made me laugh because I know it was aimed at me. I didn't need to do anything in this class because my dad made me read every textbook of werewolf history since I was a child. Part of my alpha training with him. I need to know the history of werewolves, being an alpha and pack leadership skills.

As the class ended, everyone packed up quickly and headed for the door. Alek followed Keiran out and stood by the door as he waited for Zia. She had pages and books sprawled everywhere from jotting down everything the teacher said. When she finally zipped up her bag and stood up from her chair, I grabbed her by her sleeved arm, stopping her from walking away but she ripped her arm back and out of my grip like I burnt her.

"Don't touch me!" She said panicked but I caught the wanting in her eyes. *She didn't want to pull away.*

"Don't touch you? You let me touch you earlier. Don't you remember?" I said standing. I stared down at her, both of us in the same Mexican standoff we were in earlier.

"T..that was different!" She stutters, and blush heats her face making me smirk.

"Why? Because you were turned on?" I say leaning down close to her ear. "Do you want me to touch you again?" I say, my breath softly caressing her ear making her shiver. Toying with the end of her skirt, I pull back slightly so I can look into her stunning inhumanly aqua-blue eyes. Her breaths coming out in hot pants hits my lips from our close contact.

Suddenly her hands came up, softly landing on my chest. She begins to push at me but stops, feeling my body through my shirt. Even through the school blazer she could feel my physique. I've trained every day since I got my wolf, so I was more muscled than any other wolf my age. Plus being the next Alpha, I was already gifted with a strong body. I just had to tone it and build myself up to be stronger. Her spread hands slowly slid down my chest, down my abs and stopped at my waist. She looked up with her bottom lip caught between her teeth. Goddess, she looked so sexy right now. That need to taste her washed over me again and I had to kiss her. I closed the gap between us and just as our lips were about to touch, she was roughly pulled away.

"What do you think you're doing?!" Her brother said pushing her behind his back and looked at me like he wanted to hit me. I growled at him, trying to hold my wolf at bay. He surged so close to the front that I almost lost the control I had. It seems he wants Zia more than I do and he's starting to become possessive of her, even towards her family.

Without replying, I shoulder past him and storm out. I really don't know what's wrong with me and I'm starting to sound like a fucking broken record. Keiran who's still standing by the door, watches me with angst as stride past him and walk down the hallway. I need to blow off some steam and maybe even jack off because my dick is painfully hard and being trapped in my pants is killing me. Zia and the thought of kissing her and touching her body had mine reacting tenfold.

Reach the forest line behind the school, I quickly strip off my uniform and leave them in a pile before I quickly shift and run off into the woods. I don't know how I'm going to survive another day seeing her around school and not being able to touch her. She pulls away just as I'm about to touch her and it's making my wolf go right to the edge. He's one more rejection away from completely pushing me out of my mind and demanding her to kiss him. I sigh in our joined mind and watch as my wolf pushes through foliage and jump over fallen trees. *I need to get laid.*

ZIA

I was exhausted by the time we got home from school. Cairo fucked with me all day and my sanity was hanging on by a thread. I had so much adrenaline coursing through me from every time he came near me. He came so close to touching my skin and feeling those lightning bolts from our mate bond. It would have instantly let him know I was his mate but I'm just not ready for that yet. He hasn't proved anything to me other than he's a cranky horny bastard. Alek was pissed when he saw him all over me in the classroom. He said he couldn't hear what we were saying but that he could smell Cairo's arousal and saw what we looked like and came to either stop us or rescue me. I haven't discerned what his actual reason was yet. All I know is Alek is not Cairo's biggest fan. If anything, Alek looks like he wants to deck him every chance he gets. Probably from the incident in the cafeteria.

After school we went for a run through the woods in the

neutral zone. Our wolves always love running, especially when our human sides have had a big day. They're the ones that end up with pent up emotions that they need to get out of their system. We had hot dogs for dinner and then worked on some assignments so that we could be ahead of the class and not fall behind. After that, Alek ended up going to his room and I could hear music playing from the little radio he bought. I headed up to the roof of our apartment building. There was an access door that led to a big, opened space with a few air-conditioning vents. Being five levels up now, I could see much more of the city. The lights from other apartments and houses were twinkling like little stars. Far off to the right I could even see our school building and somewhere beyond that would be the pack.

I shiver from a sudden chill in the air. Wolves are naturally hot-tempered creatures in both emotions and body temperature. So, we never really notice the difference in air temperature until it's clearly obvious. Humans can tell instantly but for werewolves it's a bit harder. But up here I could feel the seasons changing. It was like the cold front decided to start rolling in on this particular night. I sigh, thinking about everything that's happened in just a short amount of time. I'm so tired...of everything. I miss my parents greatly and what makes it worse is that I don't even know if my father is alive. The last time we saw him he was bleeding out when the *Alpha* tried to rip his throat out. He was my best friend, the man I always looked up too. Through everything in life, my papa was always there for me. Just like Alek. They're so similar in that way. Their love for me is so strong. But now with the uncertainty of not knowing whether he's alive or dead has been slowly killing me as the months went by. I'm thankful every day that I have my brother with me, but he just doesn't understand me these days. If it wasn't for me, we would have never left our home. We'd still be in our pack with our family and friends. We'd be sitting by a bonfire every night with the other pack members as we ate what our hunters caught that day. Our wolves would be running with our parents in the thick snow, and we'd prank papa by blending into the snow making him panic from not being able to find us. The colour of our wolfs fur is determined by the colour of our hair and since our father has black hair, his big black coloured wolf always stood out in the snow. So, we always saw him coming. All Alek and I had to do was lay down in the snow and make our wolves cover their nose then he wouldn't be able to find us.

But now we're in a foreign country, thousands of miles away from home, only to end up in a small town that's occupied by another pack. My mate, the future alpha of this pack has taunted me, teased me, been rude, ignorant and has threatened us multiple times. While the mate bond has started affecting him little by little, he still doesn't know me or Alek. Doesn't know what's happened to us or what we've been through. He treats us like every other rogue.

I face away from the direction of the pack, not wanting to think about it. I don't often use my gift for myself, but right now I need a piece of home to comfort me. I breathe in, drawing strength from my core and mentally picture releasing energy from my body. As I do, the air around me shifts and changes. Darkness is splintered with every colour of a sunset. I'm standing on the ground but the space around me is like I'm standing in the middle of a cloud. I can see through the colourful clouds and see the darkness of the night, the rooftop and the ground I'm standing on. I'm in two places at once. This is what it's like sending someone to the moon when they're awake. But this usually freaks people out like the people wearing VR headsets for the first time and they fall in the game but in real life they're just standing still. That's why Alek puts them in a calm, sleep-like state.

Right now, I've come to see someone special to me. Someone who might give me answers. "*Babushka*?" I call out softly to my grandma. She has never appeared before but as soon as I called for her, she answered. I watched her appear as though she just stepped through a wall of clouds. She gasps, seeing me before her. She looks me up and down, looking concerned as she stares at my defined cheeks, collarbones poking out and my skinny figure. I know how I look starved. Just like all the other rogues but it's not like we feasted every day. We've gone days without food and with a high metabolism that werewolves have, sharing a rabbit with Alek does little to help us gain weight or muscles. We're skinny and lean. Those few special meals give us just enough energy to make it to the next hunt. I start crying as she smiles reassuringly at me. I wish for anything to feel her big warm hugs again, but I would feel nothing but tiny tingles from contact with her.

"Don't cry, my child. Tell *babushka* what's wrong." She says calmly and waits for me to stop crying. For the heaves to settle.

"It's everything," I say wiping my eyes as I sniffle. "Everything feels out of control, and I don't know how to stop things from spiralling. And my mate he-"

"I know, dear. I'm always there with you, watching. Remember that. You can get through anything. You come from a long line of men and women in our family. When others would break, our ancestors never did. We never do. You and your brother will get through anything as long as you're together." She says smiling and Goddess I missed her.

"It's just so hard it feels like everything is piling up on top of me." I say now exhausted. My emotions are all over the place and I blame Cairo. Just today alone I've never been so exhausted.

"I know, dear. But everything happens for a reason. You will get your happily ever after." She says making me feel better before she continues. "But first you need to do your Goddess given job and help other wolves in the world." She says in that stern grandma way making me nod. I know she's right and we have helped a few wolves along the way but Alek and I both know we were meant for more. That we were meant to help hundreds and thousands of wolves. "I must be going now, baby." She says as her figure starts to fade. Her time on Earth is coming to an end. I can only hold her here for so long.

"Wait! Have you seen Papa there?" I ask and look at her with eyes full of hope. We can't always see people that are in the moon. Those souls can choose whether they want to be brought forward or not. I always worried maybe papa was dead and just didn't want to see me because he wouldn't want me to be upset. And we could never call babushka before to ask her because we were and still are learning about our powers and how to control them. But as the days go on, our control is getting stronger.

"No, child." She says shaking her head. I breathe in relief knowing our papa is still alive. "I love you and tell your brother I said I love him and remember this," She stops as her face is taken over with concern and worry. "He is coming, baby. You must prepare and trust your mate. Let him in. You are only hurting yourself." She says forcefully. I go to object, but she holds her hand up, silencing me. "Trust in the bond." She says before she disappears. The clouds around me disappear as the night seeps back in. Her words replay in my mind as Alek stops behind me asking if that was finally her. I nod as I turn to face him.

"Did she give you another lecture?" He asks as I laugh. She always lecturing us when she was alive.

"When didn't she?" I say as we both laugh. "She said to say that she loves you and she also gave me a message."

"What message?" He asks as my breath comes out all shaky.

"He's coming, Alek." I say afraid as my heart starts beating rapidly.

"How?! We've been so careful, and he doesn't even know where we are!" He says angrily and I understand where his anger is coming from. He's worked hard covering our tracks all through Russia and more so when we left. He spent days running around leading our scents away from the freighter ships that we used to escape Russia in. He ran long and hard, making sure to mark our scent everywhere before he secretly made his way back to the port and onto the boat that I was hiding in.

"I don't know. She didn't say when either. It could be sometime within the future but...she said that my mate can help. She said that I have to trust him and let him in" He scoffs and looks at me pointedly.

"I told you, you know."

"I know, alright. I know I'm the one stopping him. I just...I just need to know he's not gonna be like...like *him*." He nods sadly, understanding.

"Are you going to tell him now? Let your scent out?" He studies me as he waits for my answer.

"Yes. I think I will tell him tomorrow. Babushka is never wrong." He laughs and nods his head in agreement.

"I'm proud of you, Z." He says pulling me in for a big brotherly hug.

"We should head back inside and get to bed. I have a big day tomorrow." I say against his chest. He nods, head bopping my shoulder before he pulls back, tucking me into his side and walks us back inside. I find myself excited about tomorrow. Excited at watching Cairo's beautiful hazel green eyes flash orange as his wolf comes forward and recognizes me as his mate. I know we have some ways to go with the state of our current relationship, but I know with our mate bond it will help mend our cracks.

Chapter Ten

Him

UNKNOWN

As the months passed her scent slowly disappeared. My sheets no longer smelled like her, my room and clothes no longer smell like her. The only source I have is the lock of hair I took from her one night when she was *pretending* to sleep. It was cute. She shivered when my clawed finger scratched her shoulder when I picked up the lock of her hair that was draped over her shoulder. When we slept in our sleeping bags with our backs against the fading bonfire. I leaned forward and licked the sweet blood as it started to pool against her cut. She held her breath as I wrapped her hair around my finger until it stopped at my claw. Then I twisted and sliced through the silvery-blonde hair. I wanted a piece of her, many, pieces of her.

I got mad when I came to see her that day. She and her

brother would be shifting for the first time, and I would finally mark her as my mate. Her eyes would flash a colour I longed to see, and she would give me her big bright smile she always shone my way. I couldn't have been more wrong. By the time I got to her house she had already shifted, but her scent never changed.

She was not my mate.

It would have made things easier if she were my mate, but not much changed. I watched her as she came to the realisation and kept her mouth shut. She didn't look at me with love anymore. That was the day she started looking at me with fear. But she was so clever at hiding it. She made it too easy to take her and claim her.

She screamed when I marked her that night. I held her mouth shut while I bit into her neck marking her as mine. She will never belong to anyone else, only me.

But then someone had to interfere. Her pathetic brother, heartbroken by a closeted slut had come running for his sister to console him. To make him feel better. But she was no longer his. When my father tried to interfere after he started nosing around, I had to kill him. I watched the pure fear in her eyes as she watched the Alpha power transfer to me. I laughed, feeling my muscles bulge and tighten as they grew. I felt the air around me change with power and the cowering of her body told me she felt it too. It made it easier for her to submit.

Just as things were getting good, her brother took her away from me. When I find him I will skin him alive. She will wear the fur from his wolf around her shoulders as a reminder that no one will take her from me again.

She will always be mine.

And I will find her.

Chapter Eleven

Heartbreak

ZIA

The morning started like any other. I woke up, showered, got dressed for school and came out to eat whatever breakfast Alek had cooked that morning while I slept. I brushed my hair, tied it in a loose braid over my shoulder and put my shoes on. We walked to school, watching the birds dart in and out and around each other, dogs yapping as they ran up to the fence to greet us and the friendly human neighbours watering their lawns greeting us good morning. We got to school, we hugged and parted ways as Alek went to hunt down Keiran and I headed up the few short steps and entered the school. I liked being early to class. It took the unwanted attention away. I hated walking in and feeling everyone's eyes on me as they watch me take a seat. Today was just another typical day in our new life. But I should have known nothing is ever that easy. Not for me. Because what I saw when I walked through those large wooden doors broke my heart in two.

Time slowed down. I looked down at my feet, every foot fall felt sluggish. Like I was in slow motion, my wolf was refusing to let me move. She was trying to stop me from walking and when I stopped and looked up, I saw why. Jordan, the school bitch, the one that's actively tried to steal my mate for herself, was leaning against her locker. Her skirt was pulled up way too high, her shirt and blazer were two sizes too small so that when she took the tiniest breath her tits would stretch out the shirt, drawing attention. She twirled a lock of her piss-yellow hair around her finger and battered her eyes at my mate. He had his arm up near her head, holding his weight against the lockers. He was looking her up and down hungrily. I watched as her hand landed on his chest and travelled down, just like mine did the day before.

"What are you doing later, Jord?" Cairo asked as he licked his lips. His eyes travelled down her legs and slowly back up in a heated stare. She giggled and asked what he had in mind but with a look that said she already knew what he wanted. "Wear something sexy." He said toying with the hem of her too high skirt.

I was barely holding back tears but when I smelt his arousal from across the hall, the dam broke. Tears streamed down my face and my heart clenched tightly in my chest and my throat went dry from trying to hold in my whimpers. I willed myself to stop but my heart wouldn't stop hurting. Hearing is one thing but seeing your mate flirt with another is completely different. I knew they were fuck buddies but now it's clear that they are. I'm sure if there were less people in the hallway they would probably fuck right up against the lockers. I felt my heart start to crack and shatter from the pain but I had no one to blame but myself. Babushka was right. I'm only hurting myself. My stubborn stupid self is the reason why I'm in this pain. If I had just let my scent out when he asked, then none of this would be happening right now. But I didn't. I had to be fucking stubborn and make him earn the right to know I'm his mate. I just... needed to know he wasn't the person he had shown us. I needed to see that he wasn't like *him*.

"Why are you crying, mutt?" Jordan's screechy voice was so close I jumped. I looked and saw the two now standing in front of me. I didn't even hear them walk over. She laughed as I tried to erase all evidence of tears from my face. "Don't tell me you were crying over us?" She said while Cairo stood idly by behind her not showing any interest on his face. "I'll let you in on a little secret, rogues don't get mates. Look at her, Cairo. I bet she wishes she had a mate bond like ours." Again, not one flicker of emotion crossed his face but mine? All hell was going to break loose if she didn't shut her mouth right now.

"That would be true but he's not your mate. I guess it would be easy to pretend to have a bond like that. I mean, I could pick anyone in this school and proclaim we're mates. But that wouldn't be the truth, would it." I said pointedly as I looked into Cairo's eyes. Now he was looking curiously, probably wondering how I would know she wasn't his mate.

"Really? If he's not my mate then why does he fuck me every night?" I should have lost in then but all I could think of was how pathetic she is and sounds.

"Because you're easy." I say and didn't that make her mad. She screamed down the hall as her fists shook from her temper tantrum. Cairo on the other hand thought it was funny and laughed, causing her to get more enraged.

"That's it! You need to be taught a lesson." She screeched and pointed a manicured finger in my face.

"What? A lesson in how to be a slut?" I retorted and again, Cairo laughed. Probably at the accuracy.

I saw it in her eyes the moment she decided to hurt me. Time slowed down as she reared her fisted hand back. I looked up at Cairo, wondering if he was going to stop her. Now was the best time to see what kind of man he was. Would he let unnecessary violence happen? Especially to someone who's not fighting back? I stayed still with my hands by my side, watching his face and I saw the heartbreaking moment when he crossed his arms against his chest and decided he was going to let this happen. I think that hurt more than hearing them talk about their sexual relationship.

Her fist made contact with my cheek, making my head snap back with an audible crack. She used her wolf strength on me. I'm surprised my cheek didn't split open from the force but I'm glad it didn't. If I bled right now Cairo would smell my scent from my blood and know I'm his mate. But him letting her hurt me just proved he was exactly the man he showed me he was. My cheek throbbed as I felt is swell up. The vision in my eye became clouded as the swelling constructed my eyesight in one eye. I'm sure the blood beneath my skin was already spreading over that side of my face, bruising instantly.

"What's wrong? Can't take a hit?" She laughed before she swung her fist out again. This time I caught her wrist and held her in place, watching as she struggled to get out of my grip. But my next words were only for my mate.

"What's wrong with you? Why would you let her hit me?" I said as pain splintered down my face when I blinked hard to clear the welling tears. He didn't move, just stood there listening before he finally spoke.

"You're a rogue. Why would I help you?" I let go of Jordan's wrist and stepped back. In this moment my heart hurt more than my throbbing face and my knees threatened to buckle from the heartbreak. I knew I was right to mask my scent. He doesn't deserve me. If this is what he's like to someone that isn't his mate, then what would he be like knowing I was his mate...a rogue. I breathed in and out, calming my heart before I spoke.

"Some mate you are." I said before turning around and walking out the door.

"What a freak." Was the last thing I heard before the doors closed behind me. I wanted the satisfaction of seeing the realisation hit Jordan that I was actually his mate, that I would be the one to claim his mark and bare his children.

But she won.

She can have him.

ALEK

I said goodbye to Zia and hurried off to find Keiran. I know I said to myself I wouldn't do anything without her moving forward with her mate, but I still want to be around mine. I want to learn everything I can about him.

I caught him standing against a tree looking off into the distance watching every student that walked closer. *Is he looking for me?* My heart beat at the thought. As I got closer to him, I watched him suddenly stand up straight, angling his head to the sky slightly and breathed in. He could smell my scent but not where I was coming from.

The walk to school was beautiful, but the sky had begun to change the moment we got here. The wind picked up and swirled around us as we parted ways. Now as Keiran tries to figure out which direction I'm coming from, I use it to my advantage. I sneak up behind him and when I get close, I wrap my arms around his waist and pull him back into me. He gasps in shock, jumping but the second he feels our mate bond sparks he leaned back into me. He rested his head against my shoulder. My nose instinctively pressed against the spot where my mark would be. I inhaled his overwhelmingly addictive scent. I could spend forever in this moment breathing him in. He giggles cutely and shimmy's around in my arms, hugging me back. I hold him there, loving having him so close that I could feel our hearts beating together through our chests. When he looked up at me his blue-grey eyes stopped at my lips.

"I wish more than anything that I could kiss you right now, Keiran." I say tucking one of his long curly golden strands of hair behind his ear before I pushed his head up with my finger under his chin. "But I just need a little more time. I need it to be perfect. Okay?" He nods and breathes me in before pulling himself back. It's probably for the best as my restraint was dwindling by the second.

Suddenly a loud clap of lightning and thunder cracked across the sky. Keiran and I both dropped to the ground, clutching our head in pain from the sudden loud noise. Our supernatural hearing made that clap sound ten times louder. My ears were still ringing when we got up from the ground. Other wolves and vampires around us were groaning and holding their ears from the sudden pain. I try shaking my head my head, hoping my hearing would come back quicker. I see Keiran mouthing that we should head inside before the rain starts falling. Nodding, I follow him, rubbing my head from the massive headache that's spreading across my forehead.

My hearing came back during our first class together. Me and the others had blocked our wolves so that we wouldn't go deaf again when the next loud thundering strike hit. With now normal human hearing, all we could hear were the usual murmurs in class and the rain splattering on the windows. I texted Zia asking how she was going but she didn't reply. Without being able to mindlink her, I figured she was just busy in class and that I'd see her at lunch. It felt refreshing not being able to hear people's conversations. I should block my wolf more often when we're at school. But something was definitely a hot topic of conversation today. Everyone seemed to lean in and whisper as their eyes quickly glanced to me. I figured it was the normal *'rogue this'* and *'rogue that'*. But when I walked into the cafeteria and that bitch Jordan was looking smug as she watched me walk over to the table I sit at with Keiran and the rest of his group, I knew something was wrong. Zack sat in his usual seat next to Cairo looking awkward and worried, Keiran mimicked him and Kitty sat in Caleb's lab almost hyperventilating before she looked up at me with caution. Every time I've seen them look and act like this, Cairo was involved.

"What did you do? Where is Zia?!" I say facing him as he breathed in with his arms across his chest.

"I didn't do anything. It was Jordan. She.." He looks away as he speaks. "She hit her. I guess Zia left." I growled as I spun, storming back through the cafeteria to the exit.

Jordan stood in front of the cafeteria door, blocking my exit but it wouldn't have mattered anyways. I'll deal with her later. I shouldered past her, hearing as she dramatically dropped to the floor screaming that I attacked her. Ignoring her scene, I pick up my pace, running through the halls. I need to get home and make sure Zia's okay. Need to make sure she's not hurt. The rain was still pouring as I ran all the way home. I race up the steps, finally coming to stand in front of our doorway soaking wet as I struggle to get my key out. I trip over her school bag that's next to the front door and hurriedly make my way to her bedroom. I swung her bedroom door open, finding her sitting on her bed, clutching her legs in comfort. When she looked up at me with her big sad eyes my heart stopped. Her whole cheek was swollen purple. Already showered and in her pyjamas, she sighed looking away as she spoke.

"It looks worse than it is. I can see out of my eye now." She tries to reassure me but I'm anything but reassured. I'm gonna kill that bitch.

"What the fuck happened?" I say with my fists clenched trying to keep my cool long enough for her to talk.

"Nothing-" She tries to shut the conversation down but I won't have it. I need answers.

"Don't give me that bullshit. Jordan's walking around the

school like a smug little bitch and not one person said anything. And if you've forgotten that something has happened, then take a look in the fucking mirror. Half your face is still fucking purple!" I say and almost laugh hysterically when I overhear her thoughts. "Yes it's still there! Answer me, Zia. Why do I hear Jordan hit you?" She sighs before shrugging.

"I got in a fight." Is all she says which shit me off.

"Then why did you get hit?! You know full well how to fight. I taught you how to defend yourself enough so that you can dodge any hit coming towards you."

"You done?" *Fucking-!* She knows how to push my bloody buttons.

"Don't take that tone with me!" I cross my arms against my chest.

"Do you want me to tell you what happened or not?" She says mimicking my posture. I sigh out, trying to contain myself. She can be such a sarcastic shit when she wants to be. I love her but fuck she can rile me up like no one else can.

"Go on then."

"Well Cairo-"

"He did this?! That fuck said Jordan hit you. I'm gonna kill him." I turn towards the door, but she suddenly shoots up out of bed.

"No! You idiot let me finish." She sighs before shooting me an annoyed look. "He let his *suka* hit me. I know I could have dodged her but I wanted to see if he would stop her." I don't have to look down to know my knuckles are white from pressure. "And he didn't." She looked down as a single tear fall down her face. The crack in her voice made all my anger disappear. I quickly brought her into me for a hug.

I hold her tight, telling her I'll always be there for her. Always. She hugs me back, repeating the promise as she sniffles against my chest. After a while her sniffles stop and her breathing becomes even again. I brought her out into our little living room and sit her down on the couch and turn the TV on.

When Netflix popped up, she looked at me curiously and I wink, heading to the kitchen to cook the popcorn.

"What are you up to?" She asked, eyes squinting in question. I eventually made my way back over to her with a big bowl of popcorn for us to share.

"I thought we could have a movie day since we're home already and that storm outside makes perfect movie watching weather." She laughs and shoves her hand right into the bowl making popcorn spill out everywhere.

"Well, you're not wrong. So, what are we watching?"

Zia had just said goodnight and went to her room. I stayed back to clean up the dishes from our dinner. I filled the sink with hot soapy water which to a human, their hands would burn from the temperature but to a werewolf it's not that hot. I grab the sponge and start scrubbing the plates as I sink into my thoughts.

I'm so torn. On one hand, I'm really worried about Zia. Worried about this game she's playing with her mate. I know it's not on purpose and I know she's only protecting herself by making sure he won't hurt her like *he* did. But I'm worried she's doing more damage to herself then she realises. I can feel her emotions so strongly ever since we came here. Usually, I would have to push and use our twin bond to see what she's feeling but here I haven't needed too. Meeting her mate has thrown her through a loop. She's happy but extremely sad. I mean that prick let that waste of space hit her! Even if she wasn't his mate, he should never condone such violence towards someone as sweet as Zia. Let alone an alpha. What type of pack does he plan on running? I may be biased when it comes to her but she's my everything. I was born with two soul mates. One belonging to Keiran, and the other, Zia. Keiran is my other half, but Zia is a part of me, my twin. We were born together, we share the same face, the same everything. Which brings me to my next problem.

Why I'm feeling so torn.

I found my mate and he's so goddamn beautiful. His golden skin, golden hair, and stormy blue-grey eyes. He should be a God with how beautiful he is. Not to mention he's so kind and sweet. Nothing like Zia's mate. Which is why I feel so conflicted and so torn. While she's over there shedding tears, I'm feeling happier than I ever have. Keiran makes me laugh, he makes me smile, he makes me happy. And that kills me because I can't let her see my happiness. It will only hurt her more and she'll only blame herself for being the reason I can't be with my mate. Even though I was the one who promised not to do anything until she's happy too. I can't force her to do anything but what I can do is sit with her in the dark until her light is ready to find her.

I finish rinsing the clean dishes before laying them out on a dry tea towel. I wipe my hands on my sweatpants before walking over to the window. Looking out into the street, the night sky was still raging with thunder and lightning as the storm refused to leave. A dark figure below caught my attention. They were looking up at our building and when I followed their line of sight, I let out a low growl. They were looking straight into Zia's bedroom window. I stretched my hearing out, listening to see if Zia was asleep but she wasn't. She was still awake and walking around her bedroom. The dark figure was watching her. And when a clap of lightening thundered through the sky, it lit up the dark figure, letting me see his identity.

And when I saw who it was, I snapped.

Chapter Twelve

The Storm

Cairo

The rain pelted down against my back, soaking my hoody as I stare up into the apartment window. I know it's her window because I saw her stand there and watch the rain fall for a long time. If she looked down, she probably would have saw me hiding in the shadows across the street. I had this overwhelming need to see her. I had to make sure she was okay. I've never condoned violence, ever. But I just got so in my head about the fact that she was a rogue that I never considered that she was an actual person. Until Jordan hit her. I still hear the sound of her fist hitting her cheek while she stood there and took it. She could have easily dodged the hit, but she didn't. It was almost like she was testing me to see what I would do. And I failed. The moment she looked at me with her reddening cheek and said, *"some mate you are"*, I felt a knife pierce my heart. I don't know why she said that, but it changed everything because she was right. Some mate I am. How could I be a mate to anyone, an alpha to anyone if I can't... won't stop unnecessary violence. Is that the type of alpha I want to be? No. I want to be an alpha that anyone can come to. Young or old, male or female I want my people to feel safe enough to come to me without hesitation. Without fear of what I would do or what my reaction would be. This was a lesson I never should have learnt.

Nothing made me hate myself more when I watched Zia through the window gently touch her cheek before she shuddered from the pain. I touched my own as if I felt her pain. Then she wiped a tear and turned away, escaping into the darkness of her room. I wanted to climb up the fire escape and tap on her window, wanting to ask if she was okay but I don't. I've fucked up any chance of a friendship with how I've treated her. Her brother is my betas mate. She's going to be in my life for a long time whether I like it or not. But now I've ruined that chance of mending what little friendship we have or could have had. I doubt she'll ever want to be around me again. I'm such a piece of shit. As I continue staring up into the stormy night watching her window, I didn't notice the figure approaching me until a fist flew out, cutting my view until I was on the ground with blood spilling from my mouth and nose. The assault continued, hit after hit rained down on my body and I could do nothing to stop it. I could just make out the scent of the person now that they were close, and the rain couldn't muddle his scent anymore.

It was Alek.

And I know why. He saw the bruises on her face. I know he would have consoled her and asked her what happened. I know she would have told him everything. Honestly, I expected this onslaught to happen at school tomorrow, but I guess he saw me here. Just like Zia, I could easily block each hit, but I don't. I deserve this. This was my punishment for letting Jordan hurt her. I could feel blood pooling in my mouth from my busted lip. My eye started swelling and my cheek I'm sure looked worse than the bruise that marred her face. I heard a rib crack as Alek focused on my body. This would take a while to heal as my wolf has upped and left. He's shutting me out ever since he saw the tears pool in Zia's eyes when she cupped her face and walked out of school. He was the one in control when he grabbed Jordan and shoved her into the lockers and told her to never touch Zia again.

It was only after Alek felt I wasn't fighting back that he stopped. He pulled himself off me and stood above me panting, bloody knuckles going white as his fist remained clenched while he stared at me. No words were needed as I looked up into his eerie glowing aqua eyes that always matched Zia's. I could see deep in their depths that he'd kill me if I ever hurt her again and I believed it. He stared at me long enough for me to get the message before he turned around and walked back inside. I laid there on the ground letting the rain cool my throbbing face. *What the fuck is wrong with me?* I begged my wolf to come back to the surface. Begged him to heal me and only when I said if father saw these wounds and found out that the rogue did it, it would be war, that he surfaced again. He'd kill them not caring if they're mated or not. After a minute the throbbing in my face lessened and I could see again in my now not swollen eye. I could breathe again without pain. I'm sure the bruising will stay but by morning it will be gone.

After a while I gingerly sit up before I stand. I breathe in before looking up at the window one last time. I see Alek slowly open her bedroom door, not moving as he checks on her. He doesn't speak which means she's probably asleep. Then he turns and watches me. I breathe again, feeling healed enough to walk. I don't look anymore as I turn and walk down the street, heading back to the pack.

I walk through the rain, not being bothered by the cold as my wolfs temperature keeps me safe from human colds. With the rain clouding my sense of smell, I'm still able to catch the softening break of a twig from the tree line ahead. Zack appears, slowly heading towards me as he looks me up and down. Standing under a tree, shielding away from the harsh rain, he's able to study me as I get closer. I'm sure my face looked black and blue and with the slight limp to my step I'm sure he's trying to figure out what the hell happened. He's always so observant which is the reason why I chose to have a second beta. With Keiran being level-headed, Zack was the one who always noticed everything. He had almost a photographic memory, so he was perfect to help counsel me with Keiran.

"What happened?" He asks watching every ache and pain in my body that makes itself known.

"Nothing that wasn't warranted." I shrug and stopping in front of him sighing.

"I heard what happened." Zack said before he continued. "Jordan's told everyone. The Alpha heard but he looked like he didn't care. The Luna on the other hand was pissed. Sent Jordan to the pack kitchen for cleaning duty as punishment. I'm sure you're gonna get an earful. What were you thinking? We all know Jordan's a self-cantered, stuck-up bitch who loves to prey on the weak. But you? What the fuck, man?" As if I didn't feel like shit already, seeing the disappointment in his face was just the cherry on top.

"I don't know. I guess I just...I just wanted to see what she'd do. I wanted to see if she was like other rogues and would attack back. But she didn't do anything. She just let it happen. It was like she was waiting for *me* to do something." I say exhausted hearing him.

"Look I don't know what's going on with you lately, but you need to sort your shit out. You're getting a reputation that's not the kind you want. You're making people nervous."

"That's the last thing I want!" I stop and breathe. Breathing seems like the only thing I've been doing lately. "I'll do better, be better." I promised.

"To them as well?" He questions with an eyebrow raised.

"Yes. It was out of my hands the second Keiran found his mate. I've just been angry and in my own head making everything worse by overthinking and thinking about Siron. But they will have to compete in The Trials, Zack. Those are the pack rules." He shakes his head before I finish talking. He stays silent for a while before he finally nods and turns, heading back inside.

Why is everything so complicated now?

I just hope Zia will be at school tomorrow. I must make things right. Starting with apologising to her in front of everyone. Get rid of this reputation Zack spoke of and I finally need to sort Jordan out. She's been a problem long enough; one I should have ended a long time ago.

Chapter Thirteen

The Trials

ZIA

The last two days Alek had me training with him. The pack trials were coming up and he wanted me to be prepared. From what Keiran had told him, both of us would be fighting a group of warrior wolves in a trial by combat. Only when our opponents or us are dead will the trial be over. Or if we make them submit. But making wolves submit especially in a fight is almost impossible. Alek wanted me to train, and he trained me hard. He didn't go easy on me and knocked me on my ass more than a handful of times. We've hardly been home at all.

We were currently on top of this hill that had the perfect view of the town. It was part of the neutral zone, so we were undisturbed here. Dressed in work out gear, Alek held his hands up, making me punch at them with my strength. When he wasn't happy with them his brows would furrow and he'd watch my face instead of my hands. I could tell he was annoyed, and he was starting to annoy me too. Just this morning he had me doing ten laps around our neighbourhood before he allowed us to stop and have something to eat. From lunchtime well into the afternoon we spent our time sparing on this hill. I thank the Goddess I have werewolf stamina and energy or else I'd be in the hospital right now from severe dehydration.

Being a head shorter than Alek and most wolves who are blessed with height, when we encountered feral rogues on the run, Alek always pushed me back. He was the one who always fought them. The one with the scars. He taught me basic defensive fighting techniques, but I've never really had to use them in an actual fight before. Let alone a life-or-death fight in front of a whole pack. Being able to doge a hit here and there wasn't the only trick I had up my sleeve. Everyone always misjudges me because of my small height. They think I can't defend myself. Alek taught me defence with my body and strength, but that's not the only thing I can do. Unlike Alek, I've never had to use my powers before in a fight. But if I had to then I will. Alek said if we're in trouble we might have to use a small amount of our powers. Fighting a group of warriors won't be easy and there's no way we're going to come out of this unscathed.

"Alright, you can stop, Zi. I think you're ready."

"Thank Goddess! My arms are literally about to fall off." He laughs as I take in a much-needed breath. My lungs are still burning, and my clothes are drenched in sweat. "Well, I guess we better head home now. We need something to eat and an early night sleep, I think. I know tomorrow is going to be difficult and I don't want to be impaired. We need our sleep and strength. If we had a bathtub, I'd suggest we each take a bubble bath before bed." I finish as Alek bursts out laughing.

"Such a child." He teases shaking his head making his shaggy hair sway from side to side.

"Plus, my body needs to heal after the beating it got today." I say stretching out on a yawn.

"It wasn't a *beating*," He quotes me, "you baby. You just haven't been training lately. So, slacking won't help. Hence why you're sore and tired." I roll my eyes at his response.

"Blah, blah." I say doing the little hand motion.

He laughs and wraps his arm around my shoulder, pulling me along as we head down the hill. Tomorrow will be one of the most important day of our lives. I know we'll succeed in the trials but it's not us I'm worried about. It's the warriors were fighting. I have a feeling they're going to fight extra dirty just because we're rogues. And if that's the case then I fear we won't succeed like I hoped.

Saturday morning was finally here. I slipped on some gym shorts, a crop top and tied my hair up into a high ponytail. I needed my hair out of my face and with the thick straps from my top covering the red scar on my neck/shoulder, I feel confident enough to walk out and shut my bedroom door behind me. Just as I come step into the hallway, a Gatorade bottle flies straight at my head. I shoot my hand up, catching it as a droplet of water sweating from the bottle hits me square in the forehead.

"Good, your reflexes are on point." Alek says standing in front the little kitchen counter proudly.

"What the fuck kind of test was that!? What if I wasn't paying attention?? I'd be showing up to the pack with a black eye already." He laughs and walks to me, bringing me in for a hug when he reaches me.

"I love you. Remember everything I taught you. Lean into your instincts and listen to your wolf. These are her basic instincts so if she pushes you to do something then do it. She'll keep you safe. And drink the Gatorade. We need our energy up and hydrated to the max. Now, are you ready?" He says pulling back to look at me.

"I am. I'll drink this on the way there." He nods his head, eyes dropping down to my neck where the nasty scar lies. I'm sure being this close he can see it peeking out from underneath the strap, but he says nothing. Just a flash of sadness crosses his eyes before he turns around and walks to the door. I exhale a breath I didn't know I was holding from watching the way his shoulders tightened from the reminder on my neck.

I see an apple and protein bar sitting on top of the bench and grab them as I follow after. I was finished the drink and protein bar by the time we got to the pack line. There weren't any markers indicating that it was pack territory, but any supernatural creature can feel it. It's like you're stepping through this invisible ward. Like the pressure in the air doubles. We stopped and looked at each other, entwining our hands before stepping onto the pack land. There was almost a ripple in the air as we stepped past the pack line and continued on. Soon enough there will be pack members on their way to 'escort' us. I'm sure they won't be happy to see us, let alone let us join their pack. We slowed when they arrived. One greeted us, the other just grunted. With one in front of us and one behind, they led us further into the pack. Soon we heard the mumbles of conversation from members up ahead. When we came into view we paused. There were hundreds of people everywhere. It was the biggest I had ever seen. Our pack back home just barely scratched a hundred members. But this? I wasn't prepared for this. Wolves of all ages, stood around on one side of this big open field. At the front of this so-called pack, was the alpha family. The tallest man in the middle dressed in a crisp dark navy-grey suit stood the Alpha. His face was stern, stress lines mark around his brows and a trimmed beard covered the bottom half of his face. He didn't smile when people spoke to him. The only affection I saw was when his eyes softened at the stunning woman beside him. His mate and the Luna. She had gorgeous golden light brown hair that was twisted and pinned up at the back. She wore dark red lipstick and a stunning suit that flattered her so well but still made her look professional. They looked like the ultimate power couple in the middle of a board meeting. In fact, the whole pack looked like they dressed up for the occasion except for the ten men that stood off to the side of the crowd. Bare footed and only wearing pants and a black fitted tee-shirt, my bet would be these are the warriors we're fighting. They're the only ones not dressed up beside Cairo. Which confuses me too because looking at his parents, he should be dressed to the nines just like them.

ALEK: *[Hey, just breathe. We'll be okay.]*

ZIA: *[There's just so many people he-]*

I didn't get to finish before I was flung forward. The grunting warrior that guided us here pushed me forward to continue moving but I wasn't expecting the sudden movement. I quickly held my hands out in front of me to catch my fall. Alek instantly helped me up before he turned to the man, growling as his eyes shifted to his wolfs. The one who pushed me stepped up into Alek, puffing his chest out as they both growled at each other, teeth baring in threat.

"That's enough!" A loud voice boomed across the field. I didn't have to look to know the Alpha just spoke.

"Alek, I'm fine. Let's just get this over with." I whisper tugging on his shirt trying to pull him back. With one last growl he relents, turning back to me as he grabs my hand and storms us towards the Alpha in strong but slow steps.

If he walked any faster with his current attitude it would be considered a threat or challenge against the Alpha. We stopped the safe distance in front of the alpha family and waited for them to speak.

Cairo

I don't know what the hell is going on with me anymore. My wolf has been punishing me. He won't let me shift and the worst part, is that I don't even know what I did wrong. I've had to pull out of alpha training this week because of him. How embarrassing is that? The future alpha of this pack can't even shift because his wolf is throwing a tantrum. He's punishing me for a multiple number of reasons, and I think all of them have to do with the rogues. He shut himself off the moment Zia got hit. Wouldn't even come to my defence when Alek beat the fuck out of me. I had to beg for a little assistance afterwards and even then, he hesitated and what doesn't help his prissiness is that the twins never showed up to school the next day after everything happened. Or the day after that. They didn't show up the rest of the school week. My wolf was on edge, itching to run back to their apartment and see if they were okay. If *she* was okay. But I didn't, my mother warned me to leave them alone for now until the trials that were happening on the weekend. And when said weekend fast approached, I didn't understand why I was anxious. As the time got closer, I found myself having cold sweats and unable to sleep or eat. My wolf was extremely nervous and worried about something.

I missed seeing Zia at school. She's the most beautiful wolf I've ever seen. Her gorgeous blue eyes are so bright they always call my attention when she looks at me. And her tiny height makes me want to protect her. I don't even know why I feel that way. I haven't spoken to her long enough to know anything about her. Alek on the other hand I know that he's been in countless rogue fights. He's shown Keiran some of the scars on his body not including the one on his forearm and forehead. He was transparent about them but when Zack mentioned the scar on Zia's cheek, they both shut down. He wouldn't speak and she wouldn't look up from the ground and both of their shoulders tensed from the question. She hardly ever speaks. Alek's the one who answers for her and even though she's quiet on the outside, I always see their eyes glaze over. She talks and answers through their mindlink and I find it irritating. And what aggravates me more is not because I want to know what they're saying, but I find myself wanting to hear her speak. I just want to hear her angelic voice that holds so much sadness yet can spit fire in an instant like she's a flame thrower.

On the days the twins didn't show up, my mind was playing on a loop. Replaying that moment with Jordan, replaying the moment tears sprung in Zia's eyes as she spoke directly to me. Replaying the pain I felt when Alek's fists rained down on me in the street. But I'm still plagued by the whys. *Why did Zia let Jordan hit her?* I could see the fire in her eyes and knew she wasn't going to let Jordan belittle her. I could see the way her body adjusted and got ready to attack. But she didn't move. *Why?*

Goddess, I wish I could read her mind. It would make everything easier.

I probably got like ten minutes of sleep last night. My wolf was restless, doing fucking laps in my head while I was trying to sleep. If I feel him pace one more time, I'm gonna snap. He still wouldn't talk to me which only made my shit night's sleep worse and he still wouldn't give me any answers. I just don't know what his damn problem is. All I can do is hope he sorts his shit out soon.

Getting out of bed, I notice that bad feeling is still there. Like something bad is going to happened today during the trials. I shake off my thoughts, stripping as I walk to my bathroom. I don't know how long I stood under the hot spray of water for but it wasn't until I saw my reddened skin in the chrome shower handle reflection that I knew it was time to get out. Wrapping a towel around my waist, I swing the door open and suddenly jump backwards as my mother stood in front of the bathroom door, had raised in the air about to knock. With my wolf shutting me out I have no super hearing at the moment and no way to tell when someone is close.

"Fuck, mum! I could have been naked!" I say grabbing the part of the towel that's tucked into my waist. No fucking way am I risking that coming undone.

"Cairo, it is not the first time I have seen your penis. I birthed you remember?" She says crossing her arms looking at me pointedly.

"For your information, it's a lot bigger now than the last time you saw it. So, this situation is different." I say shooting back facts, but I probably should have just kept my mouth shut because what she said next made me gag.

"If you are anything like you father than that's to be expected."

"Goddess! Can we stop talking about my dick! What do you want??" I say exasperated as she laughs like a villain from one of those Disney movies. I roll my eyes, shouldering past her to the draws beside my bed.

"I came to wake you up and to make sure you dress in formal attire. This is a formal event." She reminds me.

"Why do I have to? Half the pack isn't even showing up to watch the trials." I say spinning my finger in motion and looking pointedly at my mother to turn around. She sighs and does what I ask.

"Only the Alpha family is required to be there during the trials and the warriors participating. *WE*," she says emphasising her words, "dress up. We are the leaders of the pack. So, we are expected to look professional." She says still with her back to me. I quickly dry myself before wrapping the towel back around my waist and let her know she can turn back around.

"I will wear what I wear. And don't come into my room like that again unannounced. I could have wolfed out on you." I say because if my wolf wasn't ignoring me and he did get spooked then he would have acted first. She laughs and rolls her eyes dramatically.

"If I can handle your father than I can handle you. Oh," She says stopping as she looks deep in thought. "There was one more thing I needed to tell you. Now what was it.." She taps her finger against lips and I almost think she was pausing for effect. "Oh yes, that's it. WHY AREN'T YOU DRESSED YET?! THE TRIALS START IN AN HOUR!!" She screams out and I'm so glad my wolf fucked off long enough for me not to go deaf by her screaming. She's always so dramatic and goes from one to a hundred in the flash of an eye.

If I wasn't awake before I am now.

"Be sure to dress quickly now, baby. Everyone will be arriving shortly." She says turning for the door and leaves as quick as she arrived.

"Why do I have to have a crazy Hispanic mother?" I say only after I wait a few seconds to make sure the door is properly closed. Damn woman gives me whiplash every damn day. She just waits for a reason to reach down and grab her *chinelo*.

Walking to my wardrobe I grab the first pair of faded jeans I see and a quarter length sleeved top. With my sneakers quickly laced up, I head out my bedroom, quickly walking down the hall, turning, and skipping past Jordan's room so I don't get stopped by her and jog down the stairs to the back door of the pack house.

The field isn't far from here so a quick jog and I'm there. I can already see my mother's bright browns eyes scrutinizing my outfit from afar. I looked across the field searching through the sea of eyes for a pair of glowing aqua blue ones, but I come up empty. All night I couldn't sleep, worrying about today and how she's feeling about the trials. But then, again, I find myself asking why I care about her. I feel like I'm cursed to be drawn to this rogue. Maybe out of punishment. Maybe the Goddess saw how I treated her and her brother and decided I needed to learn a lesson.I passed by Kitty who looked extremely nervous and uncomfortable and Caleb who as usual showed no sign of emotion on his face. He always kept to himself, kept his cards close to his chest. He is the most unfazed wolf I've ever met. The only time I've ever seen any emotion from him is when he talks to Kitty. Zack was standing next to Kieran who were standing behind my parents. My father as usual looked passed me and my mother was waiting for me to get closer before she let me have it.

"Cairo! You are the future Alpha of this pack!" She said pointing her manicured finger at me as her accented voice thickened. "Why are you dressed so poorly? This is a formal event. I thought you saw the suit I hung up for you in your closet." She said crossing her arms against her chest in annoyance.

"I did. But if I need to shift, I'd rather destroy these old clothes than my suit." I say as my eyes search the crowd behind her.

"Why would you need to shift?" Because I have a feeling my wolf will force a shift if things don't go well today. Every time I even think of Zia's name, I can feel him rearing his head listening in. "If the rogues die, they die. No one, not even your father is allowed to interfere until the trials are over. That includes you too, Cairo. Keep your wolf in check. We all know the rules, so do they." Yeah, I'd love to keep him in check if he would stop ignoring me.

My father suddenly looked past me as he studied something. I thought maybe he'd say something to me but as usual it was about anything else.

"So, this is them?" He asks and I follow the direction he was looking.

Fuck me, she's hot as hell. Long ashy-platinum blonde hair pulled back in a high ponytail makes her look taller than she is but it also opens up her face. She always had her hair loosely braided down which always covered parts of her face. She was dressed appropriately for the trials today but seeing her out of her uniform and seeing more of her, it changed something in me. I couldn't explain it, but I could feel myself longing to smell her scent now. Why is she masking it? A part of me thinks she's hiding it from me. I see the way she tries not to look at me and I saw the way her body responded to me in school that day. She wants me yet she's fighting so hard not to let me win. Her light golden skin makes her eyes pop more. At school she's this sweet little innocent quiet rogue with a secret fiery side. I never could have seen this coming. From shoulder to just down past her elbow was a full half sleeve tattoo. Beautiful roses laced around skulls lay on her arm and it just seems so right on her. It matches her sweet and sometimes salty personality. I'd love to know the story behind that. Even Alek had a tattoo. Four or maybe five bluebirds flying across his collar bone.

"Zosar.." My mother warned my father as the wolves that were guiding Alek ad Zia to the field approached behind them and pushed Zia. The second she fell my wolf instantly came alive in my head.

A growl rippled from my throat and forced my feet forward. My father's large hand grabbed onto my arm and pulled me back in line. When my now orange-coloured eyes looked into my fathers, I felt his power pushing against my mind. He was making my wolf submit. He could feel the change shift within me and seeing my wolfs eyes only confirmed it. He called out to the group, stopping a brawl from happening as they turned around and walked towards us. I didn't need to look at my father to know he was watching Alek. The way he was walking towards us even had me a little worried. He was pissed off and didn't show any sign of stopping his attitude from showing through. They stopped a few meters, but I couldn't hear a word my father said. I couldn't stop looking at her. I feel like a broken record saying how beautiful Zia is but seeing her face clearly without hair obstructing my view, I could see just a little of what she's been through. That angry scar on her face tells a big story that I hope one day she will tell me. They look healthier than what they did when they first arrived. Before they looked like rogues but now, they're starting to look like pack members. And soon will be if everything goes okay today.

"Let the trials begin."

Chapter Fourteen

What Could Go Wrong?

ZIA

The alpha explained the rules before letting us get into position for the fight. We thought it would be a simple fist fight, but we were wrong. Five of their warriors would be in human form and five in wolf form. Alek has more experience fighting in wolf form, so I knew he'd take that group. That leaves me with the ones in human form, and as I stood studying each of my competitors, I recognised one of the warriors. He was Somner's mate. He stood out from the other warriors because he was the only one not looking at me with disgust or hate. The others? Well, let's just say I know they won't be going easy on me, and they won't stop until they hear my heart give out.

"*Ya voz'mu volkov.*" Alek said saying he'd take the warriors who just shifted behind me like I knew he would. I could hear their soft growls as they start circling us.

"*Bud' ostorozhen, brat.*" I say telling him to be safe. He nods and walks behind me, leading the wolves away as I hear his own clothes start to rip from him shifting. I look behind me, watching as his wolf now joins in on the predatory circling before my attention is drawn back to the group in front of me.

"Well, well. Looks like the rogues are trying to join our pack." The leader of the group speaks. His dark orange-auburn hair and cream skin tone do nothing to lighten his black eyes. I can see every intent in them, and I know he'll be going for the kill.

"We can't have that." The warrior on his left says.

"You made a mistake coming here." The leader says confidently.

"We won't be going easy on you." The third warrior on the leader's other side says as he joins in with these pissy threats.

"She won't even get the chance to fight back. I mean look at her, she's tiny." This warrior seems to be the leaders second in charge. He stands closer to him than the others and his demeanour is similar to the leaders. Both men wanting to end my life instead of making me submit.

"And you are?" I say, sick of calling them thing one and thing two in my head.

"She wants to know our names, Jaxon." Leaders number two says smirking before he flinches when the leaders voice snaps to him.

"And now she knows mine, *Brady*. I don't need that bitch knowing my name." I try hard to hide my smile at these idiots, but they see it anyways and growl.

"Alright! That's enough. We have a job to do so let's stop fucking around and do it." This one I recognise. He's Somner's mate. "I'm sorry I have to be one of the guys to fight you today. Somner's told me a lot about you, and she calls you a friend." He says apologetically as he turns to me. I smile and nod, understanding that he has orders he needs to follow no matter his own feelings.

I spread my feet apart, strengthen my arms and get ready for the first hit. He misses my head by mere inches, but I can tell he was pulling his punch. His momentum slowed before he even reached me. He gave me enough time to turn my head to the side, missing his fist before I step forward, both hands landing square on his chest. I look into his eyes, watching his face scrunch in confusion. He wasn't expecting me to do this, and I know he's not expecting what I'm going to do next. "Sorry for this." I say just before the air ripples around my hands as I pushed forward against his chest.

Letting my white light energy flow into him, his eyes widen in shock before they roll back inside his head. His head drops down, body slouching forward as I catch his weight, slowly lowering him to the ground as shock erupts from the crowd. I can imagine the confusion seeing this irregularly small female wolf knock a full-grown man out with one touch. I guess the Alpha kept our secret.

Jaxon and Brady throw out slurs and threats as they watch their fellow man being laid on the ground. They're scared but are unwilling to show their fear. I hear a yelp suddenly and turn my head to Alek. I sigh with relief that the yelp didn't come from him. He had his wolfs mouth clenched around a warrior wolfs neck, lightly shaking him into submission. The wolf wines out and Alek lets go. His hackles go back up when the next wolf steps forward. All of a sudden my head snaps to the right from a surprise blow just as I was turning back to my own opponents. My cheek throbs as I stumble back, catching myself before I steady. *Brady likes to fight dirty.* The winds suddenly shifted; loose strands of hair blow across my face as I catch sight of Cairo. He stood next to his father; hands fisted at his sides with a worried frown marring his face. He was watching me intently. The bond already weaving its hands around him. When his eyes flicked to the man in front of me, I had just enough time to pull back. A fist flashed past my face that would have made contact if I wasn't watching Cairo. His eyes widened and I knew I was about to be in trouble. I stepped back once, twice, trying to regain my foot from moving back too quick. I duck my head, feeling my platted ponytail rise and fall as it slaps against my back as I dodge another quick hit. I could use my powers, but I want to prove to myself that I'm more than them, that I don't always need Alek to fight my battles.

Brady was pulled back by the other warrior. His hits came hard and fast. I dodged them with skill but towards the end of our match they were getting harder to miss. He was a skilled fighter, but he fought like a pack wolf. Pack wolves fight with consistency. You can come to predict their movements. But fighting rogues is much harder. They are inconsistent. They fight feral. I barely managed to knock this warrior out before Brady was back with a vengeance. He hit harder and faster with every second hit connecting with my body and face. I could feel the swelling in my face already and the tenderness of my ribs as I lurched forward. Yelps and growls sound from behind me but I have no time to check. Brady won't give me a second to rest. But with everything we've been through, I know Alek is an extremely good fighter. So, I know he'll defeat them all soon. By the time I landed the last hit to Brady, I was physically exhausted. My face throbbed, ribs burned, and my legs were cramping. When I finally caught my breath and looked up, I realised one of the fighters was missing. Jaxon, the leader was nowhere to be seen. Figuring he bowed out after seeing his fellow warriors drop, I finally let myself breath and relax. Everything stung but I smiled through the pain, relishing my win. Alek and I did it. Which means we're accepted into the pack.

"Are you okay, Zi?" Alek asks as he circles me, looking at my wounds before stopping in front of me, face clouded in concern.

"I'm alright, bit tender though. How are you-" I stop talking when a flash of wolf catches my eye behind Alek. *Jaxon!*

I screamed at Alek to look out, but Jaxon's wolf had already lunged through the air with spittle flying from its mouth. I had just enough time to push Alek out of the way. Gasps and screams filled the field. I could see the look in the wolfs eyes and I knew he wasn't going to make me submit. He was aiming for Aleks throat. He planned to kill Alek before trying to kill me. In the seconds that I pushed Alek out of the way, I had no time to move myself. All I could do was brace myself as Jaxon's wolf came crashing down on me. My face burned like white hot fire as my vision went red. I could feel blood drip out in a constant flow, leaking into my eye and down the side of my face as my body went numb. Screams tore from the crowd and Alek roared as I laid staring up at the sky. Thunder clouds were rolling in quick, but it wouldn't do anything to stop the wrath coming.

Am I going to die?

A gut-wrenching howl echoed through the air, circling me as everything faded to black.

"ZIA!"

Chapter Fifteen

Mate?!

Cairo

I watched the twins fight gracefully. They were incredibly perceptive of their opponents. It was like after a few hits they both knew how their opponents fought or where they were going to step next. I looked to my father and saw how impressed he was. Head nodded as Alek had made every wolf submit to him. To be honest, I was expecting the both of them to fight like rogues, to go straight for the kill. Instead, they fought with honour and enough precision so that their opponents were hardly hurt. The wolves lost very little, if any blood, and Zia's hits were all to points in the body to knock them out instead of hurting them.

"They fight well." My father stated, eyes shifting from Alek to Zia now that he had finished his fight. He shifted back and sat on the ground catching his breath before he reached for his discarded clothes.

"They fight how our warriors should. Look at them, they're the ones trying to kill them." I say and I can't help the rising anger. I could see the way they all looked at her. They wanted her dead.

Zia's movements had slowed. My fingers ached from the being clenched so hard the whole time I watched her. I hardly looked away. I hated seeing her fight. Hated seeing her in pain. Her breathing was laboured and on the verge of panting and gasping for air, her hits were getting sloppy, and she was barely able to stand straight and still without swaying. I flinched, quickly hiding my reaction as the warriors last hit connected with her already bruised cheek. Again, it was like I felt her pain. My hand lightly trailed over my cheek as if I could feel the swollen contusions on me. I frown and shake my head, crossing my arms against my chest, feeling a tightness taking over. I feel like I'm on the edge of a shift. Like my wolf and I have been backed into a corner. If I was shifted right now my hackles would be up and if you looked closely, you could probably see the fine hairs on my neck raised.

"She's good." My mother states as Zia lands the final blow. The warrior drops to the ground like a sack of potatoes, with no control left in his body. They were both exhausted, but Zia managed to pull through. "What is he doing?" I hear mum just as I was about to step forward and congratulate them.

I look over, Jaxon, my father's head wolf for the warriors started shifting off to the side. He was hidden in the forest line, away from the twin's eyes. Once he shifted and stepped out into the open, I gasp and watched his wolf lower to the ground, ready to lunge. "He can't do that!" I say stepping forward this time to stop them, but my father's hand clamps around my arm, hauling me back to his side.

"Rules are rules, son." Our eyes connect in challenge. Fuck

the rules. The twins aren't even aware of the wolf getting ready to lunge at them and he's doing nothing to stop it.

Just as I go to yell out, Zia, beat me to it. She saw Jaxon just as his wolf lunged into the air, aiming straight for Aleks neck. His back was turned but Zia saw him just in time. She pushed Alek just as Jaxon was inches from his head. The crowd went silent as everyone watched in horror as Jaxon's wolf came down on Zia. He snapped at her face, blood spraying everywhere as his wolf licked his blood-stained lips and looked down at her ready to finish her off. The second her blood spilled I smelt it. Her scent was now released into the air, and it was the final piece to my puzzle. Grapefruit, lemon, Honey, and the smell of rain filled the air. My eyes shifted instantly as my back snapped out of place. The shift happened so quickly I couldn't stop my wolf from taking control. He leaped forward, bounding across the field as fast as he could go. The second he reached Zia's body, he latched onto Jaxon's wolf's neck and shook him like a rag doll. I could hear the crowd screaming, women crying as his wolf yelped and howled in pain. My father, Zack and Keiran yelled as they ran towards us. I could feel Jaxon's wolf trying to shift beneath our jaw, but my wolf wouldn't let go. Refusing to let him shift. If he did, his throat would be torn apart. So, he stayed in wolf form. All we could see was red. A red haze covering our eyes, the sight of blood on his fur, the iron smell in the air that came from Zia.

My father tackled my wolf to the ground as the others grabbed onto Jaxon and pulled Zia back from my writhing, snarling wolf. My father hit my wolf in the stomach and commanded us to shift back. My wolf snarled at him, spittle flying out as he snapped towards his face. When my father jumped back my wolf twisted his body around and stood up before running over to Zia. He needed to see she was alright. But when he saw the now shifted Jaxon with Zia's blood dripping down his face, he lunged at him. Zack and Keiran both dived for my wolf and held him down as my father commanded people to take Jaxon to the infirmary. Then he turned and grabbed the fur at the back of my wolfs neck and pulled him up to face him.

"I SAID SHIFT BACK!" He roared as my wolfs eyes began to get a red ring around the glowing orange. He was on the verge of going feral.

"She's okay...She's okay..." I heard Alek whisper to himself as he held Zia close to his chest and rocked back and forth, whispering his relief repeatedly. That was enough for me to take back control from my wolf. I finally shifted back; my father's hand wrapped around my throat as he walked me backwards away from Zia. If his hand wasn't wrapped around my throat my wolf could force another shift.

"What the fuck was that!" He said squeezing my neck tighter as the veins in his arms protruded. I ripped his hand off my throat and shoved at his chest.

"Get the fuck off me! She's my mate!" I say before running over to Alek.

I reach for her, but he pulls her away, tucking her unconscious body into him as he looked up at me with hatred. I watch his tears run down his face, falling onto her arm, mixing with blood and dirt. I close my eyes and breathe in, holding for five seconds then breathing out. "Please, my wolf...I *need* her." I say opening my eyes and looking back at him, begging. My whole body feels like it's being ripped apart at the seams just from the need to hold her. I look down at her, tears welling in my own eyes as I look at what I've done. I'm the reason she's hurt, the reason she's laying there bleeding out. I'm the one the made them do this. I could have easily gone to my father and convinced him to just accept them into the pack. But I was angry. I held onto my hatred for rogues and punished them just because of the label. "Please..." I beg Alek.

He looked down at her, brushing a red stained strand of

hair away from her face. His hands were shaking as he finally handed her over to me. I gasp as little currents of electricity buzzed in the spots where her skin touched mine. These are the sparks mated wolves always talk about. The ones I thought I'd never get to feel. My eyes snap wider, suddenly realizing I have felt these sparks before. The day she slapped me in the cafeteria. She didn't hit me hard; it was the sparks I felt.

I look to Alek about to ask him why, but he cut me off, answering for me.

"She said you didn't deserve her." He sneered angrily. "Haven't proved yourself to her. And she was right." He said shooting me a look before he stood up and faced Keiran. He pulls him into a hug as I look back down to Zia's soft face and cry. My chest is burning and feels tight as I realized she's known I was her mate the whole time. She had to watch me flirt with Jordan, watch as I treated her like scum. Now I know why she never released her scent. Why would she? From what she's seen I'm a complete asshole with a God complex. That's why she fought herself every time I was around. Why she always looked so torn. *Why she never touched me.*

"Cairo," My mother gently touched my shoulder. I look up at her with tears in my eyes. "Baby, she needs to see the doctor. We don't know how bad her injury is." She nods her head encouragingly and helps me up as I keep Zia close against my chest.

Alek turns back and takes her out of my arms before I realized he's done it. My eyes instantly flash to my wolfs, clawed hands reaching out as I go to take her back. But before I can, Aleks hand slams into my chest, flinging me back with a strength I've never seen before. I was thrown meters away but that wasn't all he did to me. One second my anger was quickly rising and the next I was on my ass and the anger was gone. I couldn't stand, couldn't even try to get up. My legs felt like jelly and my body felt heavy. I stared up at the sky and watched the clouds swirl around like they were dancing in the air. What the fuck did he do to me? I feel like I'm high.

"Are you okay?" Zack said as his face appeared above mine. "Bro, your pupils are like fucking massive right now." I blink but it feels like I'm blinking in slow motion.

"I d..don't knnnow.." I slur as I try to speak but even my tongue feels heavy. He laughs and sits down beside me.

"I'd love to do that. Be able to throw your ass anytime with just one touch of my hand." He says as he re-enacts what Alek did. I'd roll my eyes if I could. "Just relax. I've been doing some reading. Apparently when twin wolves are born, they're given gifts when they reach shifting age. They vary from gift to gift, but from what I saw from the both of them during their fights, I think I have an idea. Zia can knock anyone out with the touch of her hand and Alek can basically make them high." He stops in thought. I think it's probably a special combination of both. Zack said my pupils were blown out and I don't feel angry anymore. "What are we, no, *you*, going to do now that you finally know she's your mate?" *Finally?*

"You knnnew?" I turn my head to his...Picasso face? Whatever Alek did that was some strong shit.

"It was obvious if you just watched her." He says shrugging his shoulders before looking in thought again. "While she tried to fight it, she was always looking at you. Always checked you out then blushed when she realized what she was doing." I smile, that's cute. "Then when she absolutely refused to let her scent out it clicked. Also explained why she threw daggers at Jordan every time she saw her." I groan. This is such a fucking mess. I need to make things right with her, need to apologise to her.

The foggy drug infused state slowly started to clear. The clouds stopped dancing and Zack's face was back to being ugly again. I grin at my joke and slowly but surely sit up. Zack starts nodding and I don't need to ask as I see the glazed-over look in his eyes. He's mindlinking someone. I take the time to look around, seeing it's just us in the field now. No scared crowds, no screaming, crying females, no one. I don't remember seeing anyone leave or what happened with the twins once Alek threw me. Everything stopped when I saw the pool of blood coating the grass as it slowly seeping into the soil. I frown, still unable to feel anger just yet from the linger feeling of calmness.

"When Alek did what he did, your mum took them to the pack infirmary. Once you attacked Jaxon everyone ran. Your mum just linked me. Aleks fine, Zia got some stiches and will scar but other than that she will be fine. Doc says she's absolutely exhausted though. Says she'll probably be asleep for a few days." He says filling me in.

"I want her in my room. She needs to be near me."

"You mean *you* need her near you." He says teasing but I shoot him a look. He holds his hands up in surrender before continuing.

"I figured you'd say that. Told the Luna and she and the doc both agreed the bond will help Zia heal quicker. They're moving her to your room once they change her." My head snaps back but he cuts me off before I can growl out. "The Luna! Your mum, she's changing Zia. This ain't her first rodeo you know. Your mum teaches the young shifting pups. She knows how quick jealousy can set in with mates." I breathe out before standing up. I still a bit wobbly but I feel fine enough to walk.

"I'm gonna kill Jaxon." I state as I look down at Zack still sitting.

"While he dabbled in the grey area of the rules, he was still in the right." Zack says as he stands up and faces me. "The Alpha wants to see you."

"I'm seeing Zia first. He can fuck off." I turn and head back towards the house.

"Cairo, he said if I don't bring you to him as soon as you can stand, he'll send guards." I feel like a caged wolf, pacing a cell with my father rattling the bars. I want to be with Zia but I know my father will be true to his word. He'll send guards to come fetch me and he'll give them free range to bring me in, however way they can. Rough or soft, easy, or hard they'll get me to him one way or another. Going to him will get me to Zia quicker. I growl in annoyance but continue on to the pack house now with a new destination in mind.

The top level of the pack house is my mother and father's suite along with their separate private office they each have. The next level below is where my master bedroom is, as well as Zack, Keiran, Caleb who shares with Kitty and Jordan's room. Kitty used to live with her parents but when she shifted and found Caleb, she pretty much moved into his room. Once we graduate, they'll get a house built somewhere on pack land and someone new will move into their rooms. The level below mine is the conference room with a media room, game room and a bar. Ground floor is where the combined kitchen and dining room is, a lounge room, a foyer near the front door and a mud room that's attached to the side of the house that connects and leads into the kitchen. It also serves as a back door to the pack house. We stock the mud room with spare clothes for when we come back from runs or if our clothes get shredded when we shift without taking them off first. There's no actual door connecting the mud room to the kitchen. Just a big empty doorway. It's big enough for three or four of us to shift back inside and it's usually covered in muddy foot and paw prints. There's a building a short walk from the pack house that has a massive industrial kitchen and dining area where breakfast, lunch and dinner are served every day for the pups, shifting wolves and anyone who wants to come. Most of the mated wolves with family don't come as they have dinner with their families in their homes. I usually eat there since the Hall as we call it, is so close to the main pack house. Plus, the kitchen there is hardly ever used. There are other pack buildings on the property, one is the orphanage solely for orphaned children with the guardians living there. They have their own dining hall, but the kids are always welcome at the big hall.

When the pack house came into view, I jogged the rest of the way and entered through the mud room. Grabbing a pair of pants, I quickly put them on before jogging through the house and up the three flights of stairs. I was naked as the day I was born when I force shifted on the field during the Trials. Everyone would be in the main hall by now eating lunch as they gossiped and talked about what happened out there. I could hear the deafening silence in the pack house. Even though all rooms are soundproof with extra sound proofing in the bedrooms, I hear no running footsteps down the halls, feet stomping down the stairs or chattering and laughing from the game room or the bar. Just my own footfalls as I head to my destination. My father's office door is located on the left side of the hall right next to their bedroom door that sat right at the end of the straight hallway. I stop in front of the large mahogany door, hesitating to knock.

"Don't just stand there, boy." My father's deep, rough voice calls from behind the door that was cracked open slightly. He could hear my footsteps and knew from the sound it was me.

I grab the door handle and open it hesitantly stepping in. My father had his back to me, large frame and shoulders tensed as he looked out the window at the vast pack land. He always stood there when he was deep in thought or troubled by something. Sometimes I think he just likes seeing what he's accomplished. He took over this pack from his father who had immigrated here from Egypt. The pack started out small but when my father took over, he helped it grow into one of the five largest packs in the country. And when I take over, I plan to grow it even more. But I can't think about that just yet. Right now, I need to sort things out with my father.

"You don't have anything to say?" He questions still facing the window.

"Not really, no. I don't regret what I did. She's my mate." I say standing tall.

"That is no behaviour for an alpha. You put your mother and pack members at risk."

"Sorry. It won't happen again." I say but he laughs as he turned around.

"Lie. You'll always lose control when it comes to her. *If* she's your mate."

"What the fuck do you mean *if?*" I say stepping forward as my eyes shift to my wolfs.

"Watch your tone with me, boy. I'm alpha first, father second." He says as his own eyes shift. I turn my head, hiding the hurt flashing through my eyes. He should be my father first, alpha second.

Ever since my brother died, he's always blamed me. He stopped looking at me like he used to. He changed after that fateful day. He shut himself away, hardly spoke to me unless it was about alpha duties, or my mother instructed him too. He stopped treating me like a son and started treating me like a pack member. Everytime, we interact it's always so formal. I'm getting to the point where I don't care if I disrespect him. I'm sick of him treating me like this.

"Why do you say if? I told you she was my mate." I stand my ground.

"I only ask because you've known her since school started and you never once mentioned that she was your mate." *Yeah, because she's been a pain in my ass.*

"It's complicated. She..." I look away before continuing, "she had her scent masked the whole time." I look back at him as he laughs again. I don't think I've heard him laugh so much in years. Even if it does feel disingenuous.

"She's perfect for you. Alpha's need Luna's who will keep them on their feet. You don't want a docile mate. Your mother is tough when she needs to be. I know I could trust her fully to take over if I ever needed. So, today was the first time you smelt her scent and only because she bled." He states thinking back to the trials. "Why would she mask her scent from you? I'm sure you would have gotten close to both twins by now or at least got to know them enough for them to trust you."

"I don't think they trust any of us yet. Even Keiran. He hasn't been marked yet."

"He hasn't been marked?" My father questions further.

"I don't think they trust easy. They're both covered in scars, just like you. But they're so young. They become rogues not long after they shifted and they're not from here. They have an accent." I say that last part more to myself because I'm still trying to figure out what that accent is.

"Interesting." My father muses. "I want you to stay away from her for the time being." He says giving me his back once again as he faces the window.

"I won't be doing that."

"You put one of my men in the hospital, Cairo. You can't control yourself right now." He says as if the conversation is now starting to bore him.

"I'd do it again." I say proudly before turning, opening the door and slamming it behind me. He lets me go, not bothering to call out as I head to the stairs and jog down to my level. Zia should be in my room by now.

When I open the door, I have just enough time to see a flash of blonde before my body is pushed out into the hallway and the door is softly closed behind us. Alek stood in front of the door, guarding it as he crosses his arms against his shirtless chest. He still has dried mud caked across his chest with specks of blood still staining his jaw. His eyes seem deadly blue right now. As if they didn't look like they were glowing before. Now they were creepy.

"She's my mate. This is my room, and I won't ask again." I say looking down at his arms and chest at the healed scars that lingered across his skin.

"I don't give a fuck who you are to her. I'm her brother, I

get to decide who sees her and doesn't. And you have no right to call her your mate when you go about fucking every *cyka* in the pack." He says spitting out a foreign word that I don't understand but I'm sure I don't need to know what it meant to understand the insult. I go to speak but he cuts me off. "Enough. *Idi nahuey*." He says before turning around and slamming the door in my face.

When I hear the lock click in place, I raise my fist to bang on the door but stop. I don't want to wake Zia or make this situation worse by fighting with Alek. He may have beat my ass last time but that was because I deserved it. I'll wait here until she finally wakes and wants to see me. *If she wants to see me*. I sigh, leaning against the wall before sliding down until I'm sitting. I can't believe I found my mate and I can't believe I almost lost her to the trials. Woman stopped participating in them years ago because they all kept dying. Zia did say she would fight but I was the one who insisted and convinced my parents otherwise. I was the one who twisted the rules so that she would compete. I need to make this right, I need to see her, need to say how sorry I am and how much I regret the way I acted. I need her to trust me, want her to trust me. I need to apologise, and flowers just won't cut it with her. She's my mate, she deserves only the best from me. She deserves a mate she can trust, and I vow to be that for her. Vow to be the pillar that holds her up when she can't stand. Her protector, her rock, her knight in shining armour. I will be all that for her and more.

I sit in silence, playing over the day's events that led up until now. Aleks words played in my head and how protective he is of her. I think back to the words he said to me before he left, *idi nahuey*. I fish my phone out of my pocket that I had left in one of the drawers in the mudroom near the pants I grabbed. I had a feeling I would shift so I left my phone in there and I was right. I did shift. I click open safari and search up google translate.

"Idi...na..huey," I say out loud as type the words in as I remembered them. Then I laugh as the page loads.

Alek told me to fuck off, and in Russian it appears. I wouldn't have guessed these two were from Russia but then again, I really don't know anything about them. They're still a mystery, one I plan to solve.

Chapter Sixteen

He Knows

ZIA

I moan and cuddle myself into the thick quilt covering me. It smells mouth-wateringly amazing, but I can't think of where I've smelt that scent before. Then I gasp, eyes snapping open as I realise it was Cairo's scent and I'm in Cairo's room. On his bed! *What the hell am I doing here? What the hell happened?!* I try to move but my body refuses. I've never felt so sore before. Sure, I've felt excruciating pain, but this was like an achy pain in my bones. Like I've been non-stop running my whole life and only now have I come to a stop. My joints hurt and my muscles scream. My head feels like it's throbbing, but I can feel it's the healing type of throb. Like you can psychically feel your own body weaving itself back together. I try turn my head, but it still feels too heavy to move. The headache still screaming in my head forbids it. I know the bruises I got from the fights would have healed by now, but I don't know about my head. I can't remember anything that happened after I pushed Alek out of the way.

"Alek!" I yell as I shoot up. "Owe..." I cup my face from the headache that just transformed into a migraine spreading like wildfire across my whole head. I move a finger aside, peaking out into the room as I squint from the light, trying to see where he is.

"I'm here, Zi." His solemn voice speaks from beside me. "Goddess, I've been so worried about you. You've been out for nearly two days." He says as I gingerly turn to face him. I breathe in, internally checking that I have the strength to stand up. My head feels lighter now and the killer migraine has already lost some of its juice. "What happened?" I grabbed onto the bed pushing myself up, but I wobble, ready to fall back but he catches me by the arm.

"Careful." Alek reprimands me. "Firstly, I just want to say," He stops to add some dramatic flair, "don't you ever do something like that again! I can protect myself, Zia. I'm the one who taught *you* how to fight, not the other way around." I roll my eyes at his outburst.

"For someone who knows how to fight, you sure did miss the big fucker of a wolf headed straight for you." I blanche back.

"This isn't the time for jokes, Z." He says exhausted.

"Why? What happened? Did something happen?" I ask.

"Well...When you pushed me out of the way of that 'big fucker'," He says quoting my words back to me, "came crashing down on you. He was aiming for my neck but because of our height difference he got your head...or re-aimed for your head, I don't know. You were bleeding everywhere, and you weren't healing as quick. It's pretty much healed now but you'll have a scar." *Great, another one.* "But, as you bled out, Cairo smelt your scent and realized you were his mate and freaked out. He force shifted and started attacking the warrior that hurt you. The Alpha, Keiran and Zack had to pull his wolf off the warrior. Cairo put him in the hospital." I gasp. I should have thought about what would happen if I were to bleed and Cairo would smell it. I'm so stupid. It's my fault that warrior got hurt. I could have prevented it.

"Then what happened?" I asked afraid.

"I took you to the infirmary with the Luna. They stitched your head and said you just needed to rest and that you'd be okay. So, the Luna suggested you stay in here. Cairo's scent would help you heal faster."

"Cairo just let you take me?" I always heard mates did anything to protect what's theirs. Especially if his wolf was in control then no one would be able to get through to him.

"I politely told him that you needed medical treatment and that I had to take you. He understood." Alek said as he smiled reassuringly. Probably to let me know that Cairo didn't abandon me or something.

"Oh, okay. W..where is he now?"

"He's outside. He hasn't left since you were brought in here. He's been waiting to see you. He's worried." Alek says and I could see he didn't give two shits what Cairo thinks or feels.

"Wow, I didn't expect him to care." I mutter honestly. I can't picture it. All I can think is how he's been since we arrived. Alek sighed and rolled his eyes before he spoke.

"Of course, he cares, Zi. He's your mate. He knows your mates, and nothing will stop him from wanting and caring about you now."

"So, a scar you say?" I ask changing the subject.

"Yep! My tough little cookie." He says making me laugh. I look around the room before seeing the object of my desire and walk towards it.

"Where are you going?" He says watching me.

"Mirror. I want to see this scar. Now that I'm awake and walking around, I feel all my wounds have healed fully." I see Aleks goofy smile in the mirror reflection. "Oh Goddess."

"What's wrong?" He says while trying to hide a smile.

"Now I look even more like you." I grumble and turn to him. He cracks up laughing and I know he would have been thinking the same thing.

"Hey now, we shared the same womb. It's only fair we share the same scar." He says touching the scar across his own eyebrow.

"Alek! We share the same face! I don't need to look more like you than I already do." I say annoyed. Same eyes, same nose, same mouth, same hair colour, and now same scar across the exact same eyebrow. This just can't be a coincidence. The universe is trying to make it even more obvious that were twins.

"Maybe I can get the same tattoo." He says eyeing off my half sleeve.

"I will kick you in the face. Just try me." I warn.

"Wow," I jump from the sudden deep sultry voice that spoke. "I've never heard you speak so much before." I spin, finding Cairo standing by the door. I didn't even hear him walk in.

"Alek, *ne ukhodi*!" I beg Alek not to go, giving him my best puppy dog eyes. I'm not ready for this conversation with Cairo yet. I'm not ready to be left alone with him. But my wishes fall short as I see the smirk cross his face.

"Well, I think I'll let you two have some time alone. You have a lot to talk about." He finishes and winks at me before walking towards the door.

"Kooshay govno sooka." I say to his back which only makes him laugh as he closes the door behind him, successfully closing me in with Cairo.

"What did you say?" Cairo asks with a mixture of awkwardness and shyness.

"Nothing nice." I smile tightly making him chuckle.

The silence stretches between us. I stand there awkwardly trying to make sure I look decent in front of him. I don't have the same clothes on that I wore to the Trials. Alek would have refused anyone coming near me to change me, but he must have let someone. Which I'm thankful for because me in a hospital gown, nothing on underneath and Cairo standing mere meters from me knowing I'm his mate is a recipe for disaster. I'm not ready for that personal step yet. I wasn't ready for him to know I'm his mate, but I can't turn back time. He knows and the conversation that's about to happen will be interesting to say the least.

We both step forward at the same time and falter. Mentally agreeing to meet halfway, I'm glad he thought the same. Now in the middle of the room with his bed behind me and the door behind him, I don't know whether to feel scared or worried. He's blocking my exit unintentionally and I know a part of me with past trauma should have slight fear from that thought, but all I can focus on is the bed behind me burning holes in my back and the scenes playing in my head are definitely not helping the situation. *Damn bond.*

"What do you want?" That came out harsher than I meant but I was angry. My heart wasn't ready to forgive the hurt he put me through. He breathed in, nodding as he understood my tone.

"I know that we're mates. I..I could smell it when you..." He stopped and breathed in again. "I just want to say s..sorry. I was going to say it when I saw you next at school, but you weren't there. I'm sorry for-"

"When I was verbally attacked the second you saw us?" I say cutting him off. "When you made me compete in the trials? Or was it for when you let Jordan beat me and did nothing to stop it?" I snap as I feel my anger rise. He crosses his arms against his chest looking uncomfortable. "Rogue or not, Cairo, you shouldn't let anyone beat someone up for something so petty. I have no control over being a rogue. If I could I would be back home with my *mama i papa*. Some of us have gone through more shit than you could ever imagine. Some of us still bare those scares today. And some of us, don't go around letting our pack members beat and attack other wolves just because of their title! A pack is supposed to be a family!" I finish with my fists clenched against my sides as my chest heaved up and down. It felt so good to get all of that off my chest.

"You were a rogue!" Cairo fires back. "Rogues can't be trusted!" *Oh! He wants to talk about trust!*

"I never gave you a reason not to trust me! I literally stepped one foot through those fucking school doors before you claimed me as an enemy." I yell back as my body vibrates with anger.

We stood there staring at each other in an angry stance, our wolves' eyes front and centre and our breathing all haggard. I had never hated anyone more than I did right now. He doesn't think about anyone but himself. Just looking at his stupidly handsome face made me even more pissed off. I could feel my skin bristling with anger. I wanted to hate him so much in this moment but the heat from his glare and the tension stretching between us was becoming unbearable. The bond was fucking with us in more ways than one. I wanted to hate him, wanted to attack him but at the same time I also wanted to kiss that stupid sexy face of his that haunts me every day and night. The need to touch him burns my skin.

My eyes suddenly widen.

Cairo's eyes turned black. When we get aroused our pupils expand until there's no colour left in our eyes. We have one sole focus and that's our mate. A visual sign that werewolves are turned on and are about to basically fuck the shit out of their mates. What shocked me more was the realisation that my own eyes were deceiving me. I could smell my own aroused scent filling the room and mixings with his and once I saw his pupils expand further I knew that was it.

One moment we were in a Mexican stand-off, glaring each other to death and the next we were devouring each other. I was raised up on my tippy toes, hands gripping his muscled shoulders as his large frame bent down to kiss me back. One hand was on the back of my head, the other on my waist pulling me into him. Goddess it felt so right. The sparks were flying and my body was buzzing with a need and want so strongly. My body felt like it was lit on fire with every nerve vibrating from excitement. The moment I stepped forward Cairo grabbed me by the waist and hauled my small body into his. He slammed his lips against mine making me to moan. He took that moment to slide his warm hot tongue in and I shuddered. It was like his tongue was the key and he just unlocked the floodgates between my legs. I kissed him back with just as much vigour. His hand at the back of my head grabbed a hold of the tie holding my hair up and pulled until my hair curtained around me. Then he grabbed the backs of my thighs and pulled me up into him, wrapping my legs around his waist. I rubbed my chest against him, wanting to feel some friction as he moaned and slowly began walking us back towards the bed. Suddenly there was a loud knock at the door. Cairo's lost his footing and tripped from the sudden sound but managed to right himself just in time.

"Ahh!" Me on the other hand, had no time to do anything. The idiot dropped me.

"Fuck, I'm so sorry!" Cairo rushed out as he bent down to help me up. Once I was upright and standing, I dusted myself off and ran my fingers through my hair quickly. I'd rather his parents not see any evidence of what we were nearly about to do. "Come in." He said as he looked like we weren't doing anything except talking while my flushed face is a major giveaway.

"Afternoon, Cairo, Zia." A young woman a little older than

us said as she bowed her head in respect. “The Luna has sent me to fetch you for lunch.” She says just as she stops and looks at us both in question. “You two look *cosy*. Did I interrupt something?” She says smirking. We both cough out and scramble to say something.

“No! I gotta go!” Cairo rushes out before he runs out of the bedroom.

“I’m gonna take the raging blush as a sign of yes. But also, you might want to crack a window open in here.” Oh my god kill me now. I don’t need Cairo smelling my arousal let alone anyone who dares to open the bedroom door.

“I don’t know what you’re talking about.” I say turning around and picking the hair tie up off the floor. She laughs and watches in amusement as I do a loose braid before tying the up the end.

“I’m Sienna. It’s a pleasure to meet you.” She says kindly. I introduce myself, using our fake last name which she doesn’t seem to question. “We better get going or else they’ll eat all the food and we’ll get the shitty scraps.” I laugh and nod my head, following her out.

Damn, she walks fast. I had no idea where we’re supposed to go to eat and apparently, she forgot that. She just disappeared around a corner before I could yell and ask her to wait. Figuring there’s some stairs that way, I start to walk but stop when I hear Cairo’s voice. Thinking he must have waited for me; I head to the end of the hallway but stop just before turning the corner and coming into view. I heard a fake laugh and knew who he was talking to.

Jordan.

The hallway was shaped like an L. Cairo’s room was at the end of the hall with two doors on each side of the hallway. That’s probably Kieran’s and the other’s rooms. Just around the corner from what I could see were two staircases. One leading up and one leading down and an open door beside them where Jordan stood. Scantily dressed and standing just inside her door leaving a gap wide enough for someone to enter. Cairo stood outside, looking like he was annoyed with his arms crossed against his chest. *Must be his go-to pose.*

"Come on, Cairo, just come in for a little bit. You haven't touched me in ages. I *need* you." She said as her manicured hand reached out and caressed his arm. My wolf slammed so quickly to the front of my mind I almost missed when he said no. I had just enough time to stop my wolf from fully taking over. I didn't want to let them know I was listening in on their conversation.

"I'll suck your dick just the way you like it." I caught the growl just in time. My hands were shaking from the words she was speaking. I wanted to rip her hair out and make her watch as I mark Cairo. Show her who his mate really is.

"I said NO." My ears rang as his loud voice boomed down the hall. She gasped before she screamed. Her heals slammed down on the wooden floors as she growled out.

"This better not be because of that bitch!" She screeched but was silence when Cairo's hand slammed against the wall beside her.

"You don't ever call her that again. You don't come near her, you don't speak to her, don't speak *about* her, you don't even fucking look at her! She is **mine**. My mate, my only one. Stay the fuck away from her, I mean it Jordan. Raise a hand to her again and I'll personally see to it that you are punished." My heart skipped a beat at his words. She screamed again as he retreated down the stairs, feet stomping as he quickly disappeared. Her bedroom door slammed soon after before her heels smacked down the stairs as she ran after him. But from what I just heard I don't think he'll be giving her the time of day anymore.

I giggle and relish in what just happened. I love that he put that bitch in her place. I've been wanting to do it for a while but now I don't think I need to anymore. My words could never hurt her or get through to her the way Cairo's could. But I do know something that will get to her. Something that will really rile her up. I smirk and turn the corner, walking straight over to her door before twisting the knob, checking to see that it's unlocked before I walk in and close the door behind me.

"This is going to be so fun."

Chapter Seventeen

Fuck

Cairo

I can't believe I found my mate. I can't believe she's a rogue out of everything I could have gotten. I remember longing for a mate when I was a child. Longed to find the girl I'd spend the rest of my life with. But then my brother died and I punished myself. Said I didn't deserve to have a mate when I couldn't even protect my brother. I slept with anyone who wanted me, I disrespected the bond and I turned into an asshole. It wasn't until Alek and Zia came that I realised just how much I had changed. Zia changed me before I even knew she was my mate, before I even knew she was changing me. Then I got to touch her, got to feel the mate sparks everyone talked about.

"Hey, Alek. Where's Zia?" Kitty asked Alek who sat next to Kieran across from Kitty and Caleb.

Shit.

I forgot about Zia. She doesn't even know where to go. I'm hoping Sienna, the pack member who interrupted us will bring Zia here since I ran.

The dining hall has ten long wooden tables situated in the middle of the room all evenly spaced out. The buffet is to the back of the room with the entrance/exit on the opposite side of the room. The table I always sat at was closest to the doors encase I ever needed a quick exit if I was called on which is pretty often. On one side of the table was Kieran, Alek, a gap, then me, Jordan who hasn't taken her scorned eyes off me since we got here, and her best friend Bethany. Although I don't know how much of a best friend she really is though. Jordan treats her like shit and orders her around. Kitty sat opposite Kieran next to her mate Caleb, then Zack who sat in front of me. There were other pack members who sat further down the table with their own friend groups.

"I don't know." Alek said thoughtfully replying to Kitty before his eyes glazed over mindlinking.

"Has anyone told her about lunch?" Zack asked looking around the room for her.

"She knows." I say before I go back to eating the homemade pizza the cooks made for lunch today.

"Oh my god!" Kitty says gasping as she draws our attention. "She didn't!" She exclaims enthusiastically with a glint in her eye as she looks towards the entrance. Alek turns and begins to laugh.

"Oh, I cannot wait for this." Zack says smirking as his eyes flick to a curious Jordan and me before they look beyond me.

Finally turning around to see what has everyone gasping, my own breath hitches as I look upon Zia. Time slowed down; my eyes turned with a fraction of their speed before connecting with hers. My wolf and I battled for control, both wanting her as much as the other and both wanting to be the first to experience everything. Her long lashes blinked away our connection. The room went silent, conversations hushing and the only sound that could be heard besides the door behind her closing were the beating hearts in the room. One throat cleared and another coughed as we all stared at Zia. Dainty feet strapped in black stilettos, toned bare legs, thighs and hips covered by a tight black skirt that clung to her like a second skin, black lacey bralette covered her ribs and held her generous tits in place. Her silver tinted hair was loosely braided which I'm now only realising is how she always wears her hair. It hung over her shoulder, resting against her chest as she fixed the strands of hair that hung in front of her face. Her plump lips were coated in a vixen shade of red, eyes dusted in black eyeshadow that made her eyes glow even more earie. Once she stopped primping herself, she stood up straight and locked eyes with me. I felt my mouth pop open on a silent gasp, transfixed as she made her way straight to me. All I could do was watch and listen to the clicking of her heals the closer she got to me. My heart beat so hard I jumped when Jordan screamed at the top of her lungs. My ears rung as my head shot towards her direction. *What is her problem now?!*

"Is she wearing my clothes?!" Jordan screeches out like nails running down a chalkboard. Before anyone can reply, the clicking heals stopped as that addictive scent hit me at full blast. *Oh shit, she didn't.*

"Move over, *suka*." Zia said with her foreign word easily rolling off her tongue. She looked down at Jordan, challenging her and her wolf. Jordan screamed again, slamming her hands on the table before she pushed out and stood up against Zia, accepting the challenge. Both girls squared off. Jordan with her manicured hands down by her side fisted as her nails broke the skin on her hands before they healed and were broken all over again. Zia on the only hand stood there casually, smirking at Jordan.

"I don't take orders from you." Jordan finished with a hmph.

"Just remember I asked." Zia spoke with a hint of amusement before she turned to me. "Hey baby," she said batting her eyes at me and I know she's only doing this to bait Jordan but I was so weak. I couldn't help but fall under her charm. I inched over, making room for Zia to sit down but she surprised me and took my breath away when she landed in my lap.

I gasped again and held still as her ass moved and made itself comfortable. I looked up at the roof, breathing in and out as if a bucket of cold water was just thrown on me. *Goddess,* I thought. *Why here? Why now? I'm hard as a fucking rock and nearly the whole pack is here watching the show.*

"Mmm," Her breath hit my face from our close proximity, "your lap is so much comfier than a chair anyways. But I think it may be a little *hard* for you." I hear chuckles and shoot a look at Zack to shut the fuck up.

"Are those my clothes?!" Jordan said as her healed foot slammed against the glossed wooden floor.

"Oh yes! I'm glad you noticed! I needed a change of clothes and you had so many to choose from. But I definitely think I wear them better. Don't you agree, baby?" Zia said joyfully which only made her ass wiggle more. I place my hands on her hips, stopping her from moving so much or else I'm gonna have an unhappy accident right here in the dining hall. She turned her head, lips stopping inches from mine as I feel captivated by her. I wanted to kiss her again, wanted to feel her lips against mine, tongue teasing and dancing with mine. I couldn't stop looking at them, couldn't stop remembering how they began to swell from our first kiss.

"Hell yeah." I breathed out before leaning forward to kiss her. Just as our lips were about to touch, Jordan ripped Zia away from me. I could see a red mark forming on her shoulder where Jordan grabbed her, nail marks deepening as Zia's face went still. She blinked once before a smile curved across her face and she continued talking.

"This morning was so good...When you pulled me against

you, took my breath away as you gave me yours and let's not forget that thing you did with your tongue." She says leaning forward, tracing a droplet of sweat up my jaw with her tongue. I shuddered and gulped, feeling my body heat skyrocket. Not only did Jordan gasp, but several other unmated males in the hall did as well.

The feel of her hot tongue made me purr, a clear sign that not only am I aroused, but my wolf is as well. We can also purr when happy but it's different in this moment. Zia giggled from being tickled by the low growl vibrations in my chest that caused the purring. Her hands toyed with my shirt, feeling my muscles beneath before her small hands grabbed the back of my head and pulled me into her. Our lips crashed against each other in a hot passionate kiss. My hands on her hips tightened their grip and pulled her body against mine as close as I could get with her sitting across my lap like this. After seconds of pure bliss, heals smacking against the floor as Jordan walked away broke our spell. Zia pulled back as she breathed me in with her eyes closed as she relished in the moment. Then they snapped open, like she suddenly sensed something before she looked past me. I followed her gaze and immediately rolled my eyes at Caleb, Kitty, Zack, Keiran and Alek all watching us amused.

"I can safely say on behalf of everyone..." Zack said interrupting the silence, "wow." He says as everyone breaks out in a laugh. The tension in the room finally cleared as the conversations started back up again. People will be talking about this for the next few days to come.

"Oh, Zi. *Takoy smut'yan.*" Alek says confusing the group to which Zia replied back saying she knows. *What does she know?*

I sigh. I really need to learn Russian.

Zia

I giggled at Alek calling me a troublemaker and slid off Cairo's lap to sit next to him where Jordan used to be. I know I put that whole show on to make Jordan angry and show her Cairo is not hers anymore, but I'm not ready for all this mate stuff yet. I wasn't ready to release my scent but that was taken away from me when I got hurt. Then we kissed for the first time and that was because our emotions were so high during our argument, and it didn't help that our wolves were rubbing up against our minds influencing us. Then this show, I didn't mean to kiss him. I was only going to tease the both of them but then I felt how turned on he was and how hot his body was against mine and how his mouth was mere inches away and I could feel his breath against my lips and I just...couldn't hold back. But I need to. I need to trust him first. I can't just jump into this just solely based on the fact that he's my mate. I can't be stupid and get my heart and body broken again. Last time I ignored the warnings blaring in my head. Last time I was scared, backed into a corner with nowhere to go. I was scared into submission. But this time I won't be naïve. This time I will make sure I see every red flag before they turn to into alarm bells. I'll make sure I trust this man with my whole heart and soul. When I know I would jump off a cliff for him then I will give myself to him one hundred percent. I'll let myself fall for this man harder than anyone has done before. But before all that, I need to know he will protect me, be the man the Goddess intended. She wouldn't have chosen him if he was anything like the man in my past...

Right?

"Are you okay? You're sighing a lot.." Cairo asked watching me with his brows furrowed.

"Uh, I..I'm fine." I say clearing my throat but not turning to look at him. If I did he'd probably see the turmoil in my eyes. Alek always said my eyes are so expressive that he didn't need a bond with me to know what I was thinking. It was always in my eyes and written all over my face and like he often says, *'I can read you like a book.'*. "Oh, there's garlic bread!" I say excitedly like an idiot trying to change the subject. I lean across Cairo to get to the basket of garlic bread.

Pulling back, I quickly finish the two pieces in no time before I lick the buttery garlic off my finger. Wiping my hands on a napkin, I finally look back up, finding Cairo's eyes having a mind of their own as they stare down lower than where my pretty aqua-blue ones are located. *Is he seriously staring at my tits?* I thought and followed his train of sight and yep, he's staring exactly where I thought he was. I let out a low growl in my chest, warning him to lift his damn eyes because the tension in the room has gone and I'm not about to let him start it back up again. I've lost control once already and I won't lose it again. When his eyes don't leave my chest, my hand swings out faster than his peripheral vision can catch. It stings connecting with his cheek as he repels back in shock.

"What the fuck was that for?!" He says crossing his arms against chest defensively, cheek brightening a light shade of red from both the slap and being caught ogling me.

"Stop looking at my girls!" I say making everyone laugh. "Ugh! I mean my b... my ti...UGH! You know what I mean! Keep your damn eyes up." I say mimicking his defensive stance which only pushes my boobs out more in this too small top. Clearly Jordan's chest isn't as big as mine or else I wouldn't be failing at this argument right now.

"My eyes will go where they damn well please." He said smugly.

We end up in a glaring contest. Me holding his eyes just daring him to look down again and him staring back at me not wanting to lose and do exactly what I'm daring him to do. I can feel my wolf jump around in my head excited at this challenge with her mate. I'm a hundred percent positive Cairo's wolf is doing the exact same since I can see his pupils dilate every time he talks to his wolf. Before long we turn our backs on each other at the exact same time and I'm fairly positive I heard a little defiant *hmp* after he turned. I can just see him inching his head up like he won.

Once I feel like I've cooled down a bit, I reach for the last slice of pizza on my plate. Zack just shoved his last bite in before he started he started eyeing off my slice.

"Hey, girl." A voice spoke from beside me. There was a gap between me and the woman who looked in her mid-twenties sat looking smiling at me. With beautiful long black braids and a dark complexion, she was stunning. Werewolves really are attractive. I don't think I've ever seen an average looking wolf yet. I smile and nod my head shyly to her in reply.

"Loved the show." She said with a twinkle of amusement in her eyes.

"Thank you." I said flicking an imaginary strand of hair over my shoulder making her laugh.

"I've been waiting for someone to knock that bitch down a peg or two. Just...with her relationship with *Cairo*," She whispered his name low enough that only I could hear, "I'm glad you were the one to do it. With you being his actual mate just makes this so much more sweeter." I smile happy to help out a fellow pack member. "But," *Uh oh, but?*

"What is it?" I ask curious.

"Well, I'd just watch my back if I were you. I heard in their freshman year Jordan scratched a girl so bad she went blind. The Alpha had to pay off the girls family." She said again whispering.

"What!?" I whisper back. *She blinded someone?* What the fuck.

"Yeah, she's a real witch. Not actually a witch but you get me?" I nod. "She's not as possessive anymore or doesn't show

how possessive she really is since the Alpha really scared her, but she holds grudges like you wouldn't believe. She *will* try to find a way to hurt you back." *Great, fucking pack drama already.* Why can't she just accept that Cairo isn't her mate and let him go? Will it really come down to a fight between the two of us? I really hope not.

"Thank you." I say as she nods and turns back to her food.

ALEK: *[Hey, Zi?]* Turning I see Alek walking up to me.

ZIA: *[Yeah?]*

ALEK: *[We should get going. We have school tomorrow.]*

I nod, remembering that we still live outside the pack in our own apartment. Placing my dirty napkin on my plate and pushing it forward, I stand up and go to follow Alek but Cairo stops me.

"Where are you going?" He asks looking uncomfortable with an uneasy look swirling around in his eyes.

"I'm going home. I don't live here." *Yet,* I don't say as I reply awkwardly.

"You're not going anywhere! THIS is your home now!" Cairo said slamming his hands against the table as the chair or bench as it is, scrapes against the floors roughly, hurting all of our ears.

I jumped, looking into his eyes to see them taken over by his wolf. Our wolves have different levels of possessions that they can take over our bodies. The first is our eyes, showing everyone that our wolf is close to our mind and can take control in a split second if they need too. The second is when our eyes and voice have changed. That means our wolves have possession over our human bodies without us being able to take it back. This level is the hardest to control because we are not the ones in control. Our wolves could do anything, and we wouldn't be able to stop them unless our wolves gave up their control. The third level is when we shift in our wolf forms. They control their wolf body and are in control. They will listen to us in this level, but they ultimately have full control. But they're more lenient when they're in their form because they feel more relaxed so it's almost like 50/50 control over the body and right now, Cairo's wolf is fully in control of the human mind and body.

"Woah, man, calm down!" Zack said standing up slowing with his hands out in front of him showing his wolf that he means no threat. "It's okay, she-" Zack goes to speak again but I cut him off.

"I've already had one controlling alpha in my life, I don't need another." I say fuming. I hate being control, especially by someone of alpha status. "Now," I say stopping to calm myself down. "I *am* going home, back to my apartment. I will see you tomorrow at school. Okay, Cairo?" I say holding myself firm and trying to get Cairo back in control but his wolf won't have it. He growls low in his chest, still looking like if I take one step away from him he'll pounce. "Do not growl at me." I let my wolf come forward in my mind, eyes switching from blue to orange. He whines seeing his mate's eyes.

I breathe out deeply. *Great, now I've made his wolf sad.* I stand up on the bench, coming face to face with Cairo now that he's standing and way taller than I am. "Listen," I call to his wolf and place my hand on his cheek reassuringly. "You be a good boy for Cairo. You'll see me at school tomorrow, okay?" I say sweetly to him and he whines again not wanting to see me go. "That's a good boy. I'll let you have all the licks and kisses you want tomorrow." I promise before kissing him on the nose.

When he breathes in, I see the change in Cairo's eyes as he takes back control from his wolf. Alek grabs my hand helping me down off the bench before we walk towards the door. I don't look back not wanting his wolf to come forward again. Not that I didn't love meeting his wolf, but I know everyone watching Cairo lose control like that so easily isn't a good thing. If they don't think their future Alpha can't control himself then they won't be able to trust him.

"Are you okay?" Alek says as we step out into the open and walk towards the forest line.

"I'm okay. I need a long ass run, a hot shower and then the best sleep of my life. But if I can't have all three then two will be fine." I say making Alek laugh.

"I don't know about a shower but I can make one of those wishes come true. Race you home?" He says making me laugh and smile before he sprints off. I giggle to myself and jump into the air as my body twists and morphs into my wolf. I can feel my wolf smile a big toothy grin as the sound of Jordan's clothes shred to pieces and fall to the ground. We're glad not to be wearing those skanky clothes anymore.

Chapter Eighteen

Him

Zia

Standing in the Alpha's office, I can smell the cedar wood burning in the fireplace behind me. The heat licks at my body, making me shiver. I don't know why I shiver. I look around as my eyes adjust to the dimly lit room. There's a big brown bear skin hanging over the large wooden throne like chair behind the mahogany desk.

Wait...I know that chair...

My skin prickles, breath hitches as my chest starts to restrict. My hand goes to my chest, feeling my heart pounding as my ears pick up the sound of heavy but slow footsteps behind me. I'm back in this office where everything first happened. Back at my pack.

No... I can't be back here...I can't...

"Zi, Zi, Zi..." He sang darkly with his voice so close to my ear that I could feel his breath fan against my neck.

"Vladik...please, stop.." I say, body shaking from fear of what he'll do to me.

His body heat encases me as he stands behind me. I can feel his chest at my back, moving up and down as he breathes me in. His hand is on my neck, gently tucking my hair behind my ear. He leans down, mouth inching closer as he speaks, "I've missed you.." His canines push against my skin before his hand clamps around my throat, claws digging in as he pulls my head back roughly and-

A clap of thunder and a flash of lightening have my eyes snapping open. But it wasn't the whether outside that made me release a blood curdling scream. It was the cold hand on my cheek and the dark figure appearing above me.

"It's me! It's Ali, look!" Alek said quickly removing his hand to switch the lamp on.

"Alek..." His name was a whisper. I couldn't speak, couldn't move as fear still gripped me. He enveloped me in a hug, holding me tightly as he slowly rocked me back and forth. He started humming a song our mother always sang to us when we were children. I couldn't stop the tears from falling, couldn't stop the heaving. It felt like I was back there again, back in that office where all my pain began.

"Nightmares." Alek said. It wasn't a question, and he didn't have to ask. He already knew. I could feel him probing into my mind, looking at my memories and seeing what I dreamt. "That one felt different. Like there was a red filter over your dream. The colours were weird..." He muttered more to himself.

"What do you mean?" I ask sniffling before pulling back and looking at him.

"Oh, d..don't worry." He stuttered. Alek is always so sure of himself and he never stutters. He's hiding something from me. He shut his link off to me before I could even look into his mind and hear his thoughts. All I know is he's worried about something because he's frowning and spacing off as he thinks. I'm too exhausted to question him further.

"Will you stay with me? I-"

"Pshhh, you don't even have to ask. Let me shift and you can cuddle my wolf." I giggle and sniff one last time before wiping the stray tears off my cheek and out of my eyes. Alek turns the lamp off just as something moves in the corner of my eye. I look to the window, rain gently tapping against the glass as a nasty storm rolls in.

I watch for a few more seconds swearing that I saw something move but in the end I figured it was just my jittery brain making me see things. The lightening continues to blanket the sky and thunderclaps here and there in an almost soothing way. Shaking my head, I try expelling the nightmare residue that still plagues my mind, or the prickles on my skin where I can still feel Vladik's touch and lay back down. I scoot backwards until my back touches the wall, making room for Alek's big white wolf. He rolls onto his back, panting happily before he licks my face making me laugh. I push him by the shoulders, making him roll his big ass body over so I can wrap my arm across him and cuddle into his fur.

"Goodnight, you two. Thank you." I whisper before my eyes begin to get heavy. Sleep finally takes over and with Alek beside me, the nightmare is gone.

For now.

Hours after I fell asleep cuddling Alek's wolf, I ended up in that rare dream state where you know you're dreaming and find you're able to control yourself in it. I was in this beautiful meadow covered in snow. It reminded me of home when the snow would come in overnight. The air smelt so fresh and crisp, there was a beautiful breeze and my body shivered from the sudden warmth. I closed my eyes and smiled, lacing my hands with the warm ones that wrapped themselves around my waist. His strong arms tightened around me as he leaned into my neck and kissed. I shivered again but not from the cold. I hummed out, enjoying the safe embrace before I slowly turned around to face Keiran.

"Keiran!" I said suddenly springing awake from my dream. *Ugh, gross. Alek was projecting his dream on me.*

Slowly not to wake him up, I gently slide down the bed. Alek must have woken up at some point because he was back in his human form and dressed in his tracksuit pants. He was dead asleep, laying on his back with his hands clasped together on his stomach like mine were in my dream. He had a big sleepy smile on his face. Then he let out a soft purr making me gasp. His dream must have taken a happy turn because a tent was quickly rising in his pants.

"Oh gross!" I quietly rushed out of the room before his mind tried to push more of that dream on me. I'm lucky I woke up when I did or else I would have had to experience that.

I wash my face in the bathroom sink before walking out and sitting on the couch in the living room. The lights were still off but it was still raining outside. The sky had that dark pink tone it always had when it rained during the night. It lit up the room enough for me. Tucking my legs against my chest, I open my mind and connect with Alek. Pushing past his dream, I look into his mind. Feel what he's been feeling these past few days and hear his thoughts. He misses his mate. He wants that connection; he wants to complete the bond with Kieran. He wants to see him every day, feel his hands on him, kiss him anytime he wants. But then I feel his sadness at not being able to have that. Because of me. He's repressing his feelings so he doesn't hurt me. It only makes me feel worse. He's done everything for me ever since we ran away. He's constantly on guard, constantly on the lookout for danger, constantly protecting me and putting me first. I feel like the bad guy stopping him from his happiness. I sigh, turning my head, I look out the window and watch the rain fall. I think it's time I put his happiness first. I can endure whatever happens to me as long as he gets his happiness.

"We need to see the Alpha."

Chapter Nineteen

Alpha Zosar

The next morning, I woke to Alek banging and clanging in the kitchen. He was making breakfast and he looked as fresh as daisy's while my back felt out of place from falling asleep on the couch.

"Pancakes." Alek announced just seconds before I asked. I laugh and stand up, making my way to the bathroom to brush my teeth and get ready for the day. I come back out just as the pancakes are being plated. "Why aren't you dressed for school?" He asks placing two plates on the small, wobbly legged table and sits down across from me.

"We're not going to school today." I say before grabbing my cutlery and start cutting away small bites to eat.

"And what exactly are we doing?" He questions curiously as I swipe my piece of pancake through the yummy syrup before bringing it up to my lips.

"We're moving into the pack house today." I swallow the dripping piece.

"What?!" He says shocked.

"I think it's time. We passed the Trials; both found our

mates within the pack and if I have to suffer through another sex dream of yours then I'm gonna kill myself. I cannot go through that again." I finish as he starts choking on his breakfast. He smacks his chest hard and goes bright red in the face. I laugh as he finally composes himself enough to speak.

"C..come again?"

"Yes, you heard correct. You pushed your dream onto me last night. Which is how I came to the conclusion that we should move."

"Are you okay with that?" He asks unsure.

"I am. Cairo is my mate and I have to learn to accept the bond. I think living in the pack house will help me with my trust issues. Help me accept my own mate bond." He's quiet for a couple of minutes. We ate in silence, him thinking about everything and me waiting for him to speak.

"Okay, if you're sure. Then let's go see the Alpha." He smiles and for the first time it's a genuinely happy smile. Not a put on one more my sake.

The walk to the pack was fairly quick. I think we both had a skip in our step from excitement. Though be both tried to hide it, I could feel myself buzzing at the thought of being in a pack again. Our wolves missed being a part of a pack. They're pack wolves. Plus, with everyone in the town, at school or work right now, it made little traffic to slow us down. We stopped once we crossed the pack lines. The invisible wards rippling in the air again before they disappeared. Even though we were technically part of the pack now, we still felt weary. We were still seen as rogues, still getting side eye glances or whispers when we walked past.

After a couple of minutes, two different warriors arrived at the border this time. They were different to the ones that escorted us on the day of the Trials. Both men were as tall as Alek, more built and looked like they were siblings. They had a few resemblances between each other but one looked a few years older. They didn't say anything, just led us through the woods, across the open field where the Trials were held and to the main pack house. The one where I know Cairo's room is because that's where I woke up after the fights. We followed one of the warriors up the stairs while the other stayed on the ground floor near the front door. We stopped in front of two large wooden doors. The warrior knocked once before he turned, briskly walking past us. Alek and I watched as he turned the corner and descended down the stairs. We weren't quite sure what was happening until the doors opened and the Alpha stood tall in front of us. Again, no words were spoken as he turned and walked to his desk before he sat down and gestured for us to follow. Alek closed the doors behind us before we both walked forward, sitting down in front of the large desk.

"Welcome. I was expecting a visit sooner or later. Not during school hours but I suppose you two haven't really been in school for a while." He spoke firmly with an edge of calmness to his voice. But something told me everything could change within a split second. Like the tension in his body could snap.

"Good morning, Alpha." Alek said politely as he reached over and grabbed my hand in support. I threaded my fingers through his, feeling my hands shake within his. The last time I sat in front of an alpha my whole life changed. I couldn't help the memories that were slowly over taking my mind.

Alek gave my hand a squeeze, letting me know he's here with me. I breathed in deeply, calming my nerves before looking up at the Alpha. He was already watching me and from our close proximity I could see just how similar Cairo and he were. Both had strong ethnic features, dark hazel-coloured eyes, similar dark golden skin tone, both had jet black hair. Although the Alpha had silver streaks on the side of his head and a full trimmed beard. He had almost a military style cut but the hair on top of his head was longer and had a natural wave to it. He was handsome. I could see Cairo will definitely age well when he's that age. But the Alpha had small scars littered around his face, hands, and I'm sure he had more all over his body. From what I've seen, Cairo's body is unmarred. The Alpha was half a head taller than Alek and was built like an Alpha. You'd have to be living under a rock to miss that this man is an Alpha. His build and the air of power that surrounds him alert any supernatural to his power.

"What can I do for you two today?" He asked as his eyes flicked back between Alek and me. He was studying us, looking at the subtle differences between us and he was probably even thinking about the powers we hold.

"We want permission to move into the pack house." Alek said getting straight to the point. I nod in agreement, watching as strong hazel eyes flick to me for confirmation.

"To move in here you will have to officially join the pack through the ritual. And since you have found your mates, you will be moving in with them. You won't be getting your own room. Are you fine with that?" He asked but his question was pointed towards me. I breathed in, thinking about the consequences of moving in with Cairo so soon but this wasn't about me. It was about Alek and his happiness.

I can deal with Cairo.

"Yes sir." I say standing up. Alek joins me and soon the Alpha smiles, nods and stands up before he walks around the desk and stops in front of us.

He raises his hand in the air, already clawed, and turns his other hand palm up. With his clawed index finger, he pierces the flesh of his palm, dragging his nail down and cuts deep. As blood begins to pool in his hand, Alek and I do the same. The Alpha grabs my hand and mixes our blood together, holding my hand in a strong grip. His wolf comes forward in his mind drawing mine out. We share a silent vow before I feel a wave of power wash over me. My breath hitches as I feel like I'm part of a family again. When he releases my hand, I look down and see through the blood that my cut has disappeared. There's not even a scar. I step aside and watch as he takes hold of Aleks hand, their blood mixes together and within a couple of seconds, Alek's hand is released and again, within the blood there's no scar. We look at each other and smile brightly before I jump at him and hug him tight. We forgot this feeling. The feeling of being a part of a family again. We could feel a current run through us of every pack member. If we wanted to, we could mindlink anyone.

"I look forward to getting to know you both. Especially you, Zia James. My son might be a handful now but I have no doubt you are his match. We should have a dinner soon. My wife will want to get to know you as well."

"I. Yes, sir." I say shyly. I was thrown by him using our fake last name. We still weren't used to hearing it.

"Now, do you need help packing your apartment?" He asked as he made his way back behind his desk. He pulled a handkerchief from his pocket and used it to wipe the blood off his hand.

"No, Sir. We don't own much. We will be packed within the hour. It will just take some time to bring our stuff over." Alek said.

"Do you know how to drive?" He asked us.

"N..no." Alek faltered. "Our old pack was in a rural area. We had deliveries made to us. We had no reason to drive anywhere."

"I see. Wait by the front door. I will have someone drive you to and from your apartment. It will make moving your boxes easier. I will have the chefs prepare a feast in celebration. I'll also have my son arrive home earlier."

"Actually, Alpha." I said butting in. "If you don't mind, can you keep this a secret from him? I want to surprise him. I made a promise to his wolf and I intend to keep it." He smiles at that, nodding his head before he dismisses us.

I was surprised that went well. I thought the Alpha would surely be weary of us but he was anything but. He was so welcoming, didn't hesitate to slice his hand open and welcome us into his pack officially. His pack ritual was more modern than ours. When we grew up we saw a few new pack members join to the pack. But the ritual our pack held was far more traditional. Both wolves would shift, the Alpha would have the new pack member submit to them before the Alpha wolf would bite down on the new member's neck. As blood was spilt, the Alpha would lick the wound and it would be healed. Not many packs follow traditional rules these days but our pack was deep in the wilderness, far away from any human civilizations. Our pack didn't even have electricity.

We all but raced home. Our driver understood we had too much adrenaline and happiness to burn off. We gave him our address and agreed to meet him at our apartment. Then we stripped, shifted, and picked up our clothes in our mouths before we sprinted off. Our paws hit the ground hard as we jumped, ducked, and weaved our way through the woods on our way home. Once we shifted back, we spent the next few hours packing everything we bought since we moved to town, cleaned the apartment, and left the keys in the landlord's mailbox. Then we sent the driver and car off to the pack as we decided to walk back. We needed that last bit of clarity and peace before we officially started acting like pack members again. We weren't by ourselves anymore.

"Are you sure you're okay with this?" Alek said for the millionth time.

"Yes, Alek! Oh my Goddess, stop asking me. I wouldn't have suggested it in the first place if I wasn't one hundred percent sure. I want you to have your happiness. I still gotta work some things out with Cairo but you and Keiran are perfect for each other. He's so sweet and kind and let's not forget cute!" I say making Alek blush and before he smirks.

"Damn straight. He's a God." He says making me laugh.

"Come on, lets jog the rest of the way. Schools nearly out and we spent so much time packing and cleaning that the hours have flown by. I smell and need to shower and change before everyone gets home from school.

"Mmm, I could get used to this." I say to myself as I stand under the extremely amazing water pressure. Cairo had his own private bathroom in his room and the shower alone was huge.

Well, I guess it would have to be considering how tall Cairo is and once he becomes alpha he's only going to grow more. But this shower, instead of having one shower head he had four. One straight above, one in front of me, and two to the sides. I felt like I was being massaged by all angels. Using his shampoo and conditioner made me blush. I could feel my cheeks heat once I lathered my hair and breathed in. It felt like I was being intimate with him without actually being with him. I was in his bathroom, in his shower, naked and using his soap and shampoo and conditioner. When I got out of the shower I used his towel and my knees almost buckled once his scent surrounded me. It was strong but it wasn't like the real thing. I changed into one of the new tops I bought. A pink sports bra/crop top and a pair of cute dark grey jeans that had a tinge of navy in them. I wore my new black and white high-top converses because my old ones were falling apart and were way past their use by date. No amount of tape could save them now. Once my hair was dried enough I loosely tied it in a braid and laid it over my shoulder.

Alek and I sat on the front steps of the pack house for about half an hour before we heard conversations in the distance. The wind was on our side, blowing towards us which carried our mates' scents. We stood up and walked to the end of the path in front of the house and waited. We were brimming with excitement. We couldn't wait to see their faces when they saw us. Couldn't wait to tell them we moved in.

"I'm a bit nervous." I said whispering to Alek as I rubbed my arm nervously. "What if he doesn't want me here? Let alone in his room." Alek scoffed from beside me.

"Zia, don't be stupid. He wolfed out on you yesterday *because* you were leaving. Do you really think he'd want you to leave if he acted like that? If he didn't want you as close to him as possible?" Alek said making me sigh at my stupidity.

"Why do you always have to be so smart?" I say annoyed.

"It's because I'm older, more wiser." *Wiser my ass,* I thought to myself making me giggle. "Look, here they come!" He whispered excitedly making me look ahead.

The group appeared through the trees. Keiran, Zack, Cairo, Caleb, and Kitty all stopped as they spotted us. Keiran looked shocked and happy before he ran to us. Alek nudged me out of the way and caught Keiran in his arms as he dove in for a hug. I zoned them out, looking ahead at Cairo as he looked sadly down at the ground. I felt guilty knowing I was the reason he was sad. He was expecting me at school today to live up to my promise.

"Cairo, look!" Kitty exclaimed finally making Cairo look up. He was confused at first but then he saw me. He smiled so brightly before his eyes were suddenly taken over by his wolfs. His head turned up to the sky and he release a howl. After the beautiful happy sound was released, he dropped down on all fours and shifted as his uniform shredded away. I laughed watching his wolf barrel through his mind and take control. I only stopped laughing once I saw him bound towards me.

Oh shit.

"Wait!" I yelled, swinging my arms out in front of me but it was too late. His wolf pounced off the ground and leaped through the air right towards me. His big black paws landed square on my chest and sent us both flying to the ground. "Cairo!" I laughed out as his wolf panted and purred above me. He licked my face over and over again and I couldn't stop laughing. He laid his big body above mine and his weight made me gasp out. He was so damn heavy. Werewolves are big to begin with which is why humans always run the other way when they see our wolves coming. They come up way past our hips and are bigger than any large dog bread.

So, Cairo's wolf laying on top me right now is taking my breath away. I could barely get a sentence out but I had to or else I was going to pass out. The others all stood back and laughed.

"Y-you're getting s-slobber all over m-me." He licked my face again and shifted his body so his hind legs were now beside me but his top half still rested on me which honestly, I don't think did much difference. I rubbed under his chin, across his jaw and behind his ear. I could see his back leg shaking every time I scratched one particular spot. My hands stopped at his shoulders and pushed the top half of his body off me. He whined until I sat up and reached across to hug him. Then he started slobbering all over my back with his tail whipping me in the leg. I laughed again, not caring as we rolled in the dirt, his drool making the dirt and grass stick to me and dirty my clothes.

"Okay, guys, break it up! Save it for the bedroom." Zack said and I know he meant it as a joke but his words seemed to annoy the big wolf above me. His head whipped to Zack and growled as his lip rose, showing his teeth in warning. "Okay! I won't mention the bedroom again." He said raising his hands and lowering his head.

"Hey, handsome boy." I said trying to coax him back to me. It worked and once his teeth were hidden and his hackles went down, I scratched his favourite spot again. "Who's a good boy! You just love those ear scratches don't you?" I say to him and he barks happily.

"So, you guys moved in today? I figured that's why you guys weren't at school today. Where are you staying?" Zack said as I stood up and dusted my pants. *Oh, that's right. I need to talk to Cairo about that.*

"Hey, boy. Can you go and shift back to Cairo please? I need to talk to him about something." His wolf lowered his head and whined. "I promise I'll play with you again later, okay?" He whined once more before he lifted his head and nudged my hand with nose. "That's a good boy. Now off you go. I'll meet Cairo in the kitchen once he's dressed." I watched his wolf slowly trod off towards the house before he turned the corner.

"That's amazing how you can do that." Zack said stopping beside me. "No wonder Cairo couldn't sleep last night. But then again, his wolf kept calling for you and no one got any sleep. He ended up going for a midnight run just to give us all a break." I laughed feeling slightly guilty.

"Well, that won't be a problem anymore because I've moved into his room." Zack looked shocked before he laughed out loud.

"Oh man, don't be surprised if he marks you tonight." *What? N..no I'm not ready for that!* "He's been wanting to do that ever since he found out you were his mate. He even wanted to do it when you were hurt after the Trials but the Alpha and your brother wouldn't let him near you. Plus, that little show you did yesterday didn't help."

"Heh, yeah...whoops." He chuckled while shaking his head.

"Sorry, I have to go work on this assignment. Can you remind Cairo we have training this afternoon? I have a feeling with you around he may forget."

"Will do." I giggle. He jogs to the front door and disappears inside. I look around and notice I'm the only one left. I didn't see Caleb and Kitty leave but they probably left when I had a wolf on top of me. Alek and Keiran had also disappeared.

"Guess it's time to speak to Cairo. Let him know he has a new roommate." I giggle shyly. *One who's sharing his bed.* That will be a fun surprise, but there's going to be some ground rules. Maybe even floor sleeping.

I opt to walk around the back of the house where the mudroom leads into the kitchen. I told Cairo's wolf I'd meet him in the kitchen and I'm sure he was in there listening. I heard his voice before I entered the room. But there was a second voice, a female voice. I didn't want it to seem like I was hiding and listening in on their conversation, so I headed towards the door opening only stopping once I realised the woman's voice belonged to his mother. I haven't met her yet besides seeing her during the Trials and I don't feel prepared to meet her right now. It doesn't help that their conversation stopped the second I walked into the room. *Best get this over with*, I thought.

Breathing in deeply, I square my shoulders and exhale. Walking with more confidence than I have, I stop next to Cairo and greet the Luna. "H..hello, I'm Zia. It's nice to meet you.." I trail off once I realise I don't actually know her name. I only know the Alphas name because I heard pack members calling him Alpha Zosar. She doesn't say anything, just studies me as her bright brown eyes look me up and down.

"*Então esta é ela?*" She says in Portuguese and as luck would have it, I actually know it.

When we were able to escape Russia, we boarded a cargo ship that was headed for Portugal. We were trying to find a place to hide when we ran into a group of rogues. We barely escaped but not without serious injuries. They fought dirty using silver. I was dying when we stumbled across a small pack. They took us in, cut the silver away from my burning flesh and saved my life. We befriended the pack and became close with the Alpha family. They had a daughter our age who shared her room with us, taught us Portuguese in our few short months of staying with them. We never got to learn how to speak it properly but we can understand most of it. After a while Alek got that feeling again, like we weren't safe anymore. I'm not sure what made him feel like we weren't safe, but the next day we were packing up and running again. Eventually when I asked him why he made us leave, he said it was because he overheard some pack members talking about how we were twins. He had a feeling that word may spread. So, we left in the middle of the night. We left a note on our bed and that was the extent of our goodbyes. We had to leave, the sooner the better.

I missed that pack. It was the first one we came across that accepted us, didn't cast us aside or attack us because of our status. They saw how young we were, how hurt I was and they immediately took us in. Fed us, dressed us, and gave us a place to stay. They started to become a second family to us. It got easier once we started understanding them. They spoke English but it was a second language to them so they didn't always remember to speak it. Right now, I am thankful for our time there. It's coming in handy when Cairo's mother asked if I was her. Assuming she means his mate.

"*Sim.*" Cairo replied saying yes.

"*Ela é bonita.*" She said calling me beautiful. I could feel myself blush at his mother's compliment. I really should let them know I can understand but I also want to hear what they're saying when they think I can't understand.

"*Entao e o que e que vais faze rem relacao a Jordan?*" She said and I didn't need to know the language to know she's talking about Jordan. "*Eu avisei-te para não te meteres com ela. Isto nao devia ser permitido, a relação entre companheria é algo precioso.*" I wish I could whole heartedly agree with her when she said the mate bond is precious. I'm also interested in hearing Cairo's reply in asking what he's going to do about the Jordan situation.

"*Ja estou a tratar disso. Mas Podemos falar em ingles agora?*" *Oh, he's working on it is he?* Thankfully he asked to switch over to English. I was starting to feel like a third wheel here.

"Sim, claro." She says giving him a look before she turns to me. "Nice to meet you, Zia. I am afraid you have caught me at a bad time. I am needed down at the orphanage. I would like to have lunch with you soon to get to know my daughter in law."

Daughter in law?! We haven't even marked each other yet. Not only was I shocked, Cairo, started coughing like he had food caught in his throat. Both of us just as embarrassed from the statement as the other. "I..I'd like that." I say shyly. Cairo's composed himself and she looks amused as she gives me a fair well nod before turning and heading for the front door.

"Oh, and Cairo? *Eu quero grandbabies.*"

"Mother!" Cairo scolded her quickly and I couldn't help but laugh. It didn't take a genius to know what she just said. Plus, Cairo's cheeks are as red as a tomato. He rubs the back of his neck and looks down before he clears his throat, eyes meeting mine.

"S..so you moved in.." I nod.

"Yeah, um...intoyourroom." I blurted out quickly. I was hoping he didn't hear me but his head whipped back in shock before a shy smile crossed his face.

"Did you say my room?" He looked like he was trying to hold himself back from an excited YES! My heart skipped a beat at the thought that he was happy to be sharing a room.

"Ye..yeah, is that okay? The Alpha said we were to move into your rooms. Alek moved in with Keiran." He laughed loudly.

"Oh, man. I'm glad these rooms are soundproof." My cheeks heated at the statement.

"Are you sure?" I said butting in. "Sorry, it's just Zack said you kept everyone up last night." I really hope the rooms are one hundred percent soundproof because no way am I doing any mating with everyone in the house being able to listen in with their super hearing. He gave a shy smile before rubbing the back of his neck again. A nervous tick of his.

"Oh, that. I uh, forgot to block the mind link." I giggle as silence falls between us. He looked like he wanted to say something but he never did. We just stood there staring at each other as the minutes stretch by. "Yes," He, says finally speaking. "I..I'd be happy to have you move in with me. I uhm, I missed you." My heart thumped so hard in my chest and my cheeks heated. I didn't think he could be anything other than an asshole but he has a soft side I'm only just now seeing. *Could this be the real him?* Not the mask I see he puts on for everyone else.

"I missed you too." I said honestly because I did.

For the first time since we met, I couldn't feel the hate between us. The strain that started to stain our short relationship or the thick hateful tension wasn't there. Ever since we did the joining ceremony with the Alpha, I could feel Cairo more. I could feel his link in the pack bond. If I wanted too, I could finally mindlink him. I wouldn't be able to read his thoughts or feel his true feelings as only marking would let us do, but I could feel him as part of the pack. I could feel everyone. And when I saw him this afternoon and the pure happiness that came over his face, I just wanted to kiss him. To put my hand against his chest and see if his heart pounded as hard as mine did every time I saw him. Under all of my apprehension about moving in with him, I couldn't deny to myself that I wasn't excited to stay with him. His mother was right. The mate bond is a precious thing and I could feel fate weaving its threads around us trying to stitch us together.

I never thought I would get a mate, not after what my *Alpha,* did to me. He took my chance of having a mate away from me. I thought I didn't deserve a mate. I wasn't strong enough to stop him. He took everything from me. But most of all, he took my soul and my dignity. But being here now and feeling this happiness fill me, I couldn't help but feel guilty. After running for so long I gave up. Gave up on love, on life. And when I did find my real mate the first thing I did was test him. I feel horrible for pushing our mate bond away because of my own pride and ego. I don't know who he is or what he did before me. I haven't given him the chance to tell me who he is. To let him in. Let him show me the man behind the mask he wears. I shouldn't have gotten jealous. I had no right to be angry at him when I hid my scent. He had no idea I was his mate. Had no idea he was breaking my heart by hooking up with Jordan. He wasn't really hurting me. I just couldn't accept it. But my babushka was right. I need to let him in. Especially if what she said was true.

I breathe away my darkening thoughts. I need to focus on the present. "Oh, I was meant to remind you about training this afternoon. Zack said something about it but never said where." He laughed and I only now just took in his appearance. He wasn't wearing a top and at a closer look I realise he was wearing training pants. I unfortunately didn't have time to ogle his well-defined muscles because he was already grabbing my hand and leading me out the door.

"Ah yes, training. We'll we better go." We said stepping outside.

"We?" I ask stopping him. He turned and faced me, standing so close I could feel the heat coming off his body. He hooked a finger under my chin and gently lifted my head up so that I could look into dark hazel eyes.

"Can't have the future Luna of this pack slacking, now can I?" He asked in a deep sultry tone. *Goddess he smells so good.* His scent was captivating me, clouding my mind, and stealing my words. I couldn't speak. The only sound that came out of my mouth was a purr. My vision tunnelled and I knew my eyes had gone from bright blue to black. His touch was literally electrifying. The buzz was circuiting through my body, making my nerves go haywire at his touch.

"You shouldn't do that or else we won't make it to training." He said leaning in closer until our bodies touched. I gasped, feeling his hardness against my stomach.

That was all it took for the tension between us to snap. He inched down more as I stood up on my tippy toes trying to meet him halfway. Our kiss was hot and heavy. Hands roamed each other's bodies as our tongues dance together. I moaned as he groaned, grabbing the back of my head, and pulling me even closer. We were fused together with passion and I felt like I wanted to take things further. My gums ached; my wolf was trying to elongate my canines so that I could mark him. I was just inches away from his neck, I could do it. I could bite down on his skin and join us, join our souls together the way they desperately want. Our souls call to each other like a moth to a flame. We couldn't resist each other even if we were fully marked and mated. The universe was pushing us together whether we liked it or not. Our lips parted; he leaned his forehead against mine and inhaled as I exhaled. Our breathing came out in pants. I wanted more, we both wanted more but we had to stop. We had training...I smiled to myself as I used training as a weak excuse.

"I hate training." He said annoyed making me laugh as he grabbed my hand again and lead us off to wherever the training was being held.

When we finally reached a small opening in the woods, our group came into view. Jordan and her friend stood off to the back with Jordan staring daggers at me, Caleb and Kitty stood next to each other, Alek and Keiran beside them and Zack at the front. He had his typical smirk on so I know by now nothing good is going to follow.

"And just what have you two been up to? You are late for training." He fake scolds us as he looked us up and down in a disapproving manner.

"Sorry, couldn't help if my mate's lips are so kissable. I just needed another *taste*." I said emphasizing the word just to see the look on Jordan's face when certain scenarios ran through her head. I'd have holes in me by now with how many daggers she was throwing my way with her little evil eyes. I laughed and stepped back into Cairo, making sure to rub up against him.

Cairo's hot breath was suddenly at my neck. His mouth grazed my ear as he spoke softly, not wanting the others to hear. "Now now, behave, little one, or else I'll smack that ass in front of everyone. Don't make me punish you." He threatened as his tongue darted out and teased my earlobe before he placed a hot kiss on my neck. Goosebumps immediately covered my skin, body shivering as it wanted more. I turned to face him; black lust filled eyes stared down at me.

"Maybe I want to be punished. Maybe I want to see your alpha side." He grunted and gave me his back suddenly as he spun around. The hell? "What are you doing?" I asked so thrown by his sudden movements. One second we were teasing each other and the next he was ending the conversation weirdly. He breathed in and out multiple times before he composed himself. When he turned around again it was like our moment never happened.

"Alright guys, time to train." He said looking past me. I thought that was it, until his hand smacked me on the ass as he walked past. His hand swung back so fast I didn't see it coming. I laughed, realising he turned around to hide a certain member that arose to say hello. It does make me wonder, what would he be like when there's no one around to interrupt. Maybe this shared room predicament isn't as bad as I thought it was going to be. *I wouldn't mind ruffling his feathers some more.*

Chapter Twenty

The Intruder

I don't know if these training sessions are always this brutal, but my body was burning. I couldn't feel my legs and if I had to do one more squat then I don't think I'd be able to make it back up. I could feel sweat dripping down my back and front, loose hairs stuck to my face and neck, and I needed water like my life depended on it. My lungs were screaming from the dryness. I was huffing and puffing and when I went to step forward my knees gave way and sent me crashing to the ground. Cairo laughed and bent down, grabbing me by the waist and lifted me up effortlessly. I will never not swoon at how strong he is. He can lift me up like he's picking a pillow, like I weight nothing at all. But if a human were to try pick me up like that, they would definitely have some trouble.

"Do you always go this hard?" I asked him, looking around at everyone else who seemed to be in much better condition than me.

He leaned down, mouth stopping inches from my ear, "I can go hard, soft, whatever speed you like." His deep voice was like silk, cascading over my body heating me. I shivered, the pictures in my head playing a scene that I really shouldn't be picturing but that's exactly what he wanted to happen.

He tucks a sweaty strand of hair behind my ear that was covering my eye. A silence falls between us. We stare into each other eyes, bodies both naturally gravitating towards each other. I could hear the symphony his heart was playing in his chest, the heated stare of his beautiful darkening hazel eyes, the way his chest rises and falls with each breath. I was so attuned to him it scared me. I never thought I'd experience any of this but here I am, feeling and see every little nuance in his body. We were in a weird stage of our relationship. Our minds wanted to fight each other, pull away and almost refuse the bond just from our stubbornness. But our hearts, they beat for one another, calling to each other and our bodies were wired the same way.

"So," I clear my throat trying to break the rising tension. "Where is everyone else? I thought they'd be training with us?" Growing up our pack would train together except for those few that were on patrol but even then, that was only a small handful. Our pack was so remote we had very few threats against us.

"Well, everyone does train at the same times for the most part. But we're separated into six groups. The first group is my fathers. He trains the head warriors first thing in the morning. Then the head warriors each train a group in the afternoon." He says breaking it down for me because he can probably see the gears turning in my head as I try visual it all. New pack, new rules. "Then there's my mother who trains the pups and newly shifted wolves. She's great at handling kids and add that with her Luna position, there's no one better for the job. The last and sixth group is mine. This one. I train Keiran and Zack, my betas, and Caleb my delta, then the girls. I train them at the same standards, so when it comes time for you to choose your betas and delta, they'll already be trained at the expected level."

"You have more than one beta?" I ask. It's not often you see alphas with two betas. My old pack only had one beta and that was it. It's even rarer for packs to have deltas too. *Wait, he said choose your betas and delta?* Who would I even choose? I don't know anyone here enough to have my back besides Alek. He would be my beta. There is no one more fitting for that position than him. Jordan can go fuck herself if she thinks I'd ever choose her, Bethany is a no and Kitty is a Seer so she literally has more important things to do. Maybe Zack's mate can be my second beta when he meets her.

"CAIRO!" A voice came shouting from the tree line as Jaxon appeared. The same wolf I fought in the trails and the one I later learned Cairo attacked. The same one who I recently just found out was also one of the Alpha's head warriors. We all turned as he spoke. "A rogue has been spotted crossing the border." A chill ran down my spine as the air shifted. Everyone became tense. I watched Cairo's face change into one I saw the first time I met him.

"What?!" His hands fisted by his sides, knuckles turning white as his breathing changed. "Which direction are they coming from?" He spoke with so much anger and hatred that it scared me. He first met us on our first day of school, I shudder to think what he would have been like if he met us crossing the pack border. I fear his hatred could have blinded him to the point of rejecting me or worse.

"The North." Jaxon said turning to face the way he came. Cairo turned to the group, face stoic as he spoke commands.

Kitty kissed Caleb goodbye, Jordan and Bethany nodded and ran towards the pack house along with Kitty. Alek, Keiran and Zack got into a fighting stance, ready to face anything as our ears picked up rusting of leaves and crunching of branches and twigs as the footsteps got louder. They were heading straight towards us. Cairo looked down at me, hatred and fear mixing before his warm hand softly touched my shoulder. I could feel his panic through his touch, and the worry showed in his eyes. "Please stay behind me." He said before wrapping his arms around me. "I would never forgive myself if something were to happen to you. I can't go through that again." He said as his voice broke.

"Cairo, they're approaching." Zack announced. Cairo straightened up as he let me go. The worry still evident in his eyes. He turned around, placing his hand on my waist as he gently guided me behind him. He was shielding me with his own body.

I looked over at Alek panicking, but he was already looking at me. He knew the fear I have from rogues. He had the same fear, but he was always good at hiding it because he was always the one that had to protect me from them. He never had time to let his fear cloud him. The first few months running through Russia, Vladik sent rogues after us. They were like bloodhounds, so relentless to catch us and get paid. Alek gave me a small smile and nodded, telling me it would be okay. I breathed in, steeled myself and placed my hand on Cairo's tense back. I could see some of the tension leave. I needed him to not worry about me but I also needed to feel him. I needed to feel the sparks and bond to calm my own nerves. The physical touch from your mate was like adrenaline, crack, and ecstasy but it could also be super grounding. It was a two-way street for your emotions.

"Stay back, baby." His words were soft, but his voice was steel. We all watched the direction the intruder's sounds were coming from.

The rustling stopped.

"WAIT!" A feminine voice shook with urgency and a note of familiarity. "I'M NOT A THREAT!" The rogue begged to be believed.

"Show yourself now!" Cairo growled back.

I frowned as I replayed the words the rogue spoke. There

was an accent to them. I frowned harder as I searched my brain for why this voice sounds familiar. Then it clicked. I looked at Alek the same time the lightbulb went off in his head. He looked at me, both of us stunned to hear this voice again. We know it! We know that voice!

"Maya!?" The both of us exclaimed at the same time she stepped out from behind the trees.

She gave a small smile before looking back at the alert men in front of her. Her pants were torn and dirty, shirt ripped along the edges and her short shoulder length brown hair was tangled with little twigs and leaves in it. She had a small knap-sack bag in her hands which she slowly placed on the ground before raising her hands in front of her as she lowered her head and showed her neck in submission. Alek and I stepped forward. Twin sounds of slapping could be heard as Cairo and Kieran's hands both landed on our arms to stop us. They held us back, still wary of the rogue in front of us. Unaware of the history between us.

"Take her." Cairo said sternly.

"What? No! She's not a threat!" I said fighting to get out of his grip.

"Zi, it's okay. I'll go willingly." Maya said breathing out before Jaxon stormed up to her.

"Move it." He said going to grab her arm but she quickly side stepped.

"Don't touch me. I said I will go willingly. Tell me where to go and I'll go." Jaxon spoke, watching her with disgust as she walked. He followed close behind her, giving directions when she needed to turn.

Cairo finally let go of my arm as he faced me. "You know her?" I nod, breathing in as this situation could have gone a hell of a lot worse.

"I-we do. She wouldn't hurt anyone. She saved my life. I wouldn't be here today if it wasn't for her." And it's true. She was the one that found me bleeding out and brought us back to her pack where they saved me. Her pack and family were the ones who housed us in Portugal. We will forever be grateful to her and her Alpha and father who let us stay.

"Look, she's a rogue. Which means we need to interrogate her regardless of your friend status. It's pack rules."

"I was a rogue! You never interrogated me!" I said heatedly. I saw the way that wolf Jaxon looked at her. I knew he wouldn't go easy or gentle. Maya would have bruises on her arms by now or bleeding from his claws if he had gotten a hold of her arm. Cairo looked annoyed, angry that I was yelling.

"You never crossed the border. You skirted the edges in town. If you did, you'd be sitting in that cell." *Cell?*

"Please, don't hurt her." I beg. He breathes in and out before he pulls me towards him. His arms wrap around me in a hug. My hands land on his chest ready to push him away but I don't.

"If she really did save your life then I owe her mine." He said making my heart beat. "You can be in the room when I question her."

"You? W...what about your dad?" I fear his dad wouldn't be so kind. He doesn't give off the impression that he would listen to me unlike Cairo.

"He's visiting another pack signing a treaty. Come on," he says pulling back and smiling reassuringly, "let's not keep her waiting." I nod and follow behind him as he leads us in a different direction from the pack house.

A small stone like building appears as we get closer. He opens an old looking wooden door with iron hinges. There are two more similar doors inside. One straight ahead, and one to the right. The one ahead of us has a hook holding a large ring with old keys dangling from it and an unlit torch sitting in place beside the keys. "That door leads to the dungeon." Cairo speaks making me shiver. The pack dungeon was underground, deprived of light and air. The thought sacred me. A wolf needs land to run around and fresh air to breathe. Being locked up underground was the worst type of punishment. I never saw our old pack dungeon, but my father once told us about it. He said from the outside you could see little barred windows near the ground and when you crouched down and looked inside, you could see some of the dungeon cells. It was built out of stone and silver, long corridors underground led to the cells which he said were hardly used because we never had anyone to throw in there.

"This way." Cairo says walking towards the door on the right.

My heart stopped the moment I stepped into the room. The dirty ground had old blood stained into the concrete. On the side wall held ropes and rusted silver chains of different sizes, hooks, knives, and muzzles that looked like torture devices. They had dried blood still on them and fresh wolfsbane hanging up all over the place. Wolfsbane and silver separately burn us but put together they are a deadly combination. The smell in the room was strong. I looked at Maya, she sat in the middle of the room tied to a wooden chair with wet ropes restraining her. I could hear her skin burning and sizzling from the wolfsbane soaked rope. She had a pained look etched across her face and her lips wobbled like she was holding back a cry. Tears welled in her eyes as she looked at the same wall I did. A female wolf stood tall behind her; face riddled with battle scars. Her sharp eyes were trained on Maya like a bloodhound. Everything in this room made me feel sick and I struggled to swallow at the thought that Cairo could be capable of hurting an innocent rogue in this room solely based on the fact that they're a rogue.

"Lane," he addresses the wolf behind Maya, "anything?" He questions and she nods once before speaking.

"She came from the *lua de Prata* pack in Portugal. Travelled alone, looking for Alek and Zia, sir. We searched her person and bag, no weapons or anything of harm were found. She had a week's supply of food rations in her bag along with some memorabilia. The trackers followed her scent for miles outside of the pack lines, no hint of other rogues have been detected. From my findings she is harmless." She finished speaking like she reading from dot points. She was very straight to the point.

"Good. Untie her." Cairo said shocking Jaxon and her.

"Sir, that is unwise to do so. It's not part of protocol. My findings indicate she is harmless but she could still be dangerous." She spoke angrily but still respectful of him.

"Oh, bite me!" Maya snapped making the warrior behind her growl in warning. I laugh, out of any situation she could be in, she chooses this moment to be sassy.

Cairo sighed, telling the warrior to untie her again. The second Maya was free, we ran towards each other. I held her so tight against me. "Jaxon, Lane, you may leave." Cairo says as they nod before leaving. "I'll give you two a minute." The door closes behind him as the room falls silent.

"I missed you, Maya! I never thought I'd see you again." I say holding back tears.

"Me too, me too." She says squeezing me.

"What are you doing here? How did you find us?" I ask pulling back. "Why are you a rogue?" I had a bad feeling in the pit of my stomach. She loved her pack; she would never willingly leave it. She looked at me, tears welling in her eyes again as she spoke.

"He came, Zia. The alpha you were running from. He found out you were in our pack and he..." Everything stopped in that moment. Because what she said next was my greatest fear. The reason we stayed hidden as long as we have, the reason we kept running all these years. "He killed everyone, Zia. Everyone. Even the children." Her voice broke as she started crying. Tears fell as I pulled her to me.

"W...what happened?" I was afraid to ask but I needed to know. Needed to know how he found out we were in a different country let alone her pack. I needed to know what he did.

"He had trackers following you. Ever since you left your pack. He said they followed your scent to the docks. The workers were tortured into giving away the ship directions. He said when they arrived they lost your scent. But then as they ran from pack to pack, they smelt your blood. When you were injured and I found you, they tracked you from the blood that dried in the dirt. He ordered rogues he hired to round up the pack and restrain us while he was on his way. When he got there he demanded the Alpha, my father, to give you to him. When we told him you weren't there he..." I started crying. I shook my head, not wanting to know anymore but she continued. "He lined us all up and went down the line, asking if anyone knew where you were, where you and Alek went. If they gave him the wrong answer he killed them. Father was screaming saying he didn't know where you were because you had left but he wouldn't hear of it. He..." She stops, breathing in and out, tears pooling in her eyes as she looked at me with guilt. "He saw my face, Zia. He knew that I knew. I was the only one that had the answer he wanted. Instead of coming straight to me, he killed everyone until there was no one left but me." My breath hitched; I couldn't imagine the horror of seeing your whole pack killed in front of you. "When he asked me where you went, I couldn't answer. I couldn't remember which way you and Alek went. That's when he screamed and stabbed me. I laid there bleeding out and watched as he lit my pack house on fire. Then he left. I would've died but a scout from a neighbouring pack saw the smoke and came to investigate. He found me, took me to his pack doctor. I had to feel them cut away the flesh from my wound that wasn't healing from the silver. I took off the next morning. I needed to find you, tell you that he knows where you were."

"How-" I begin to ask but she cuts me off.

"A Seer found me; said I need to come to this pack in America. It was hard at first, I spent months travelling around the packs in Portugal before she found me. Then I had to get here and then find out where this pack actually was."

"I'm so sorry, Maya. W..we should have told you where we were going. You could have saved everyone." I say feeling more guilt than I ever have.

"No, Zia." Maya said angrily. "You didn't see him. He was unhinged. Everyone could tell he wasn't going to let us go alive. He came there to kill us and that's what he did." I drop to my knees as the pain, sorrow and guilt overcome me.

"I never...should have..run away." I said between heaves.

"Don't you dare say that!" Maya said pulling me up from the ground roughly. "You did the right thing running away when he..." she stopped speaking. Unable to bring herself to repeat the words, about what he did to me. "Listen, what's done is done. We can't change anything now. But just know that you did the right thing in running away. I will forever mourn my family and my pack. That is just something I will have to overcome. Now, let's stop these tears and go talk to the Alpha about letting me join this pack."

"Y..you want to stay?" I asked through tears.

"Zia, you and Alek are the only people in the world that I know now. The only ones who hold memories of my home. No one else could understand what I miss besides you two. So, yes, I want to stay. You are the last piece of home I have." I sniffle and wipe my tears away. I can do that for her, I can be that rock that helps her heal. Alek and I can also let her see them again.

We can take her to the moon.

Chapter Twenty-One

The Tension

Cairo

These past twenty-four hours have been such a rollercoaster ride. Everytime your wolf suddenly takes control of your mind, you lose a big chunk of energy and become very lethargic and tired. Usually, I can control him but when Zia said she was leaving to go back to her apartment, he lost it. We still haven't marked her or completed the bond and ever since the Trials he's been on edge, worried about her getting hurt again. Not being marked we can't tell if she's hurt or in danger. And again, last night we couldn't sleep. My wolf wouldn't stop whining until he saw her. I wanted to see her too after some of the things she said when my wolf took over. I needed to make sure she was okay and I missed her. The bond was slowly driving me crazy with a need to see and touch her. I threw the blankets off me and got dressed. Black hoodie and sweatpants later, I headed to my door, cracking it open and listening for anyone awake outside. My mother saw the lingering bruises from my fight with Alek and ordered me not to sneak off at night anymore but she doesn't understand how I feel.

I jogged all the way to the city, down the main street before I stopped in front of Zia's apartment building. I walk around the back, heading towards the fire escape and quietly made my way up to her window. *Goddess, I feel like a fucking stalker.* I lean in and listen, no other sounds come from the apartment besides Zia's shallow breathing. I watch her chest slowly rise and fall. She looks so peaceful, so beautiful sleeping. If she's not mad, annoyed, or teasing Jordan, then she's frowning. She constantly looks like she's stuck in her mind, replaying whatever makes her frown. I wish I could hear what she's thinking, see the reason that makes her unhappy. I think a part of me just hopes it's not me that makes her feel like that. But too many times now she's said things about an alpha that hasn't sat right with me.

She whimpers softly, catching my attention. She's frowning again but this time there's a tilt to her brows. She looks scared. Her chest rises and falls in a quick fashion. She's having a nightmare. I don't wait. My hands grab the bottom of the window and ever so slowly, lift the window up. I hate that her window wasn't locked. It's not safe. I quietly slide through the opening, careful not to knock anything and wake her up. I'd rather not see a pissed off Alek come out of nowhere again. I take my shoes off, socks helping me stay silent as I walk to her bed. She shakes her head lightly, more whimpers sounding in the air. I lightly touch her shoulder, unsure if I'm trying to wake her or comfort her. I think I'd just scare her more by suddenly appearing right beside her. She tosses her head to the side, hair falling over her face as her breathing becomes labored. Softly, I move the hair out of her face, revealing the scar that lay on her cheek. I've only seen quick peaks of it because her hair is always covering it. It's a nasty deep scar, marring her stunningly beautiful face. I touch it, feeling the soft healed tissue. My chest rattles softly as my wolf becomes angry at the thought of her being hurt. Wolves heal incredibly well and hardly ever scar, so for this scar to be on her face means she went through something bad. Something we don't want to think about or we may lose even more control of ourselves and right now we aren't in the best place to do that.

"...please, stop.." She begs in her sleep. I repel, thinking it was my touch that made her speak but her eyes flickering back and forth beneath her eyelids tell me otherwise. Not even my touch is enough to wake her from this nightmare.

I hear rumbling in the distance and rustling of sheets coming from Aleks room. The night sky is changing to match her dreams, waking him. But I think he's more attuned to Zia than anything else. He seems to know her better than herself. I often find him watching her at school. Always watching, studying everyone around her for a threat. What made them this way? I can't stay and think. I only have a few seconds to open the window and get out before he comes into hearing distance of the window. Grabbing my shoes in one hand and lifting the window with the other, I successfully get out and close it behind me without being caught. The rumbling of thunder that was getting closer by the second shielded the sound of the window closing. I ducked down just as Alek opened the door and walked over to Zia. Slipping my shoes back on, I leaned back against the brick wall underneath the windowsill. He spoke to her, trying to wake her but she wouldn't. It wasn't until a crack of thunder and flash of lighting lit up the sky that I heard her gasp. Then she screamed. Every hair on my body stood up in alert. My heart was beating hard as I shot up, ready to slam the window open and climb back in. The light in the room flicked on as I peered through the window. He managed to calm her down, even to the point of shifting to make her feel safe. I ducked just in time as she turned to look out the window.

I was soaked through by the time I climbed down the fire escape and made my way down the street. The weather was usually great here but the last week it's been weird. We've had more storms in a week then we do in our wet season. I stopped at the corner of the street and studied the sky. The sky always has a pinky tone to it whenever it rains, but tonight it looked like there were bright red streaks through the sky. I've never seen anything like it before. It felt ominous almost.

"It's an omen." A cloaked woman said suddenly appearing behind me. I face her, seeing her study the sky just like I did. I didn't hear her because of the rain.

"An omen?" I question. I could hear slight jingling of coins or little wind chimes under her cloak. She had long dark hair, eerie eyes, and pale white skin and when she looked at me, they shimmered in an unnatural way. Like cat's eyes when they reflect in the dark.

"Someone has been cursed. The elements are reacting to it." *A curse?*

"Who are you?" I've never seen this woman before and I've seen everyone in this town at one point, but I've never seen her. Something about her makes her unforgettable.

"I'm being called here by the spirits. Someone is in danger."

"What are you?" I asked as she went back to looking at the sky.

"I am a Priestess. This dark cursed magic has disrupted my coven." I've heard stories of witches but I've never seen or met one before. We all thought they were myths.

"You're real? I thought witches were just stories."

"Says the werewolf." She smirks.

"Heh, right." She got me there. If werewolves exist, who's to say all the other magical creatures don't?

"Your kind became comfortable, same as the vampires. Others of the supernatural kind are not so trusting. We hide."

"Is...do you know who's cursed? What will happen? Can't you do something since you're a witch?"

"No. I can only determine that someone around here is cursed. That's where this dark energy resonates from the most. But this is powerful dark magic. Neither I nor other witches can stop what's coming. Only the caster can stop it." I don't like the sound of this one bit and there was a small part of me that feels like it's Zia who's cursed. There was something Alek said about Zia's nightmare that's been bothering me. It started playing on a loop the second this priestess spoke about the red streaks in the sky. There's a feeling in the pit of my stomach that tells me she's connected.

"If a dream has a red filter like appearance-"

"You know who's been cursed." She said, head snapping towards me. Her eyes glowed in the light, making the hair on my arms stand up in alert. My wolfs eyes replaced mine, telling her she needs to be very careful right now. She laughed, cackling in the air before she turned around, cloak swaying behind her.

"Wait! What's your name?" I call out to her. I know when I tell my father about this, he'll want to find her.

She laughed again, before she turned her head, eerie eyes staring right at me, "*you,* can call me Glinda." She said as she continued laughing before she raised her hands and disappeared before as they came back down. I'm pretty sure she lied about her name. She found it too amusing. She laughed before she said it and laughed again after. The only thing I could take away from that was her telling me she's a good witch. I've seen the movie, the only thing she was missing was the big puffy pink dress, sparkly wand, and foot tall silver crown.

The next morning, I got ready for school, anxious to see Zia after the whole priestess encounter. I needed to calm myself down, see her to make sure she's okay. But she never showed, neither of them did. The whole day I kept looking towards the classroom doors, out the windows at the pathways leading into school and in the hallways. Everyone kept trying to cheer me up but nothing would work. My mind was a mess and my senses were so out of whack I didn't hear the excitement when we got home. I looked up when I was called and saw Zia standing in front of the pack house smiling brightly. She looked happy and that was enough for me to lose it. My wolf held onto the promise she made him and he pounced. I let him surge forward and shift. I laughed on the inside watching them interact. She was so sweet and gentle with him. He kept trying to nuzzle his nose down into his neck to try and mark her. Eventually we shifted back and began our training for the day. I pushed her hard, annoyed that she constantly makes me hard in front of everyone and loves to tease me. She looked so hot being all sweaty and panty. The more time we spend together without completing the bond, the harder it gets to stop ourselves.

When I walked into my bedroom after dinner, I decided to make my room more presentable since she moved in. But what I was not expecting was to see her standing next to the bed, freshly showered. When I opened the door and gasped, she jumped and dropped her towel. Her beautiful, sweet scent hit me like a ton of bricks. There was no clothing barrier dulling her scent anymore. She stood there, eyes wide in shock, mouth parted and frozen. The water droplets still clung to her naked body. Her hair was down, half over her shoulder, wet and sticking to her ample chest. When my eyes slowly roamed down her glistening light golden skin, I couldn't help but admire her. I pushed her hard today during our training session. But who wouldn't when you could make your mate drop a squat or ten in front of you? The need that's been building inside of me ever since the day I laid eyes on her had finally reached its boiling point. I've been wanting to mark her ever since I found out she was my mate and right now, I want to do just that. My gums ached and burned, canines wanting to come down and help me do the job. I strode forward in a quick pace, eager to reach her. She still had not moved and still had that cute, shocked expression on her face. Once I reached her I pulled her to me, she instantly melted against me as I leaned down, mouth connecting with hers. She tasted sweet, moaning into our kiss as I grabbed the back of her head and pulled her into me more. I wanted to feel her body against mine. I just came from a run so I didn't have a shirt on. I could feel her breasts pushed up against my chest. The heat from her body making me groan. My other hand stopped at the small of her back, holding her in place while our tongues danced together. Her hands roamed up my stomach, gliding effortlessly over the rigid muscles.

"...Cairo.." She said breathlessly against my mouth as she pulled back ever so slightly.

"Fuck, Zia." My body was going haywire. Her breathy voice, hot lips and naked body moulded against mine, had me so hard it hurt. "Let me mark you," I begged. I kissed along her jaw, down her throat and stopped at the junction of her neck. I teased my canines against the skin, letting her feel them. "Please.." I watched her shiver as my breath fanned across that special spot.

I could feel the moment she gave in. Her head tilted back slowly, revealing her neck as she panted out her consent, "Okay..". I kissed her soft delicate neck once, twice, three times before I lined my teeth up against the right spot.

Suddenly we jumped, breaking apart from the loud banging on the door. Zia bent down and grabbed her towel before she snapped back up and covered herself quickly. We both smiled awkwardly at each other, feeling like we just got busted by our parents.

"I uh," I coughed, clearly my throat trying not to draw attention to my raging hard on, "I need to have a cold shower." I all but skipped to the bathroom that adjoined my room, hearing her giggle behind me as I closed the door. *Living with her is going to be harder than I thought.*

I showered quickly, letting the ice-cold water cool my defiant member. I hopped out and wrapped a towel around my waist before I walked back into the bedroom. Zia stood in front of the door, dressed in a short-sleeved shirt and underwear, and standing in the doorway was Lane. They looked at each other heatedly like they were in a Mexican stand-off. Neither said a word and neither realized I had come out. You could cut the tension with a knife it was that thick. I caught the end of their conversation when I shut the water off. Lane had asked Zia personal questions about herself and her pack. I had wondered myself where she came from and what her pack was called. She's said a few things before about running from someone, but she's never said who. The only thing she's spoke about was an alpha. I needed to say something before she felt like she was being forced to answer or backed into a corner and lash out. I wanted her to tell *me* when she was ready. When she felt safe and comfortable enough with me to share those parts of herself. And I hope that's soon. I can't wait to know everything about her. We didn't have the best start and I know I still have some making up to do in order to gain her full trust. Everytime, I see her all I want to do is bring her into my arms and never let her go. The mate bond is a strange and complicated thing. I never imagined feeling that way the first day I saw her but I guess those red strings of fate Zack always talks about really are real. I already feel so strongly for her but we're still strangers.

"Hey, Lane. What are you doing here?" The second I spoke; it was like whatever spell over them broke. They smiled at each other although I'm pretty sure they were fake smiles.

"Oh, hey, Cairo. I was just officially introducing myself to Zia." Lane said. Zia still with her back to me, replied.

"Yeah, introducing, getting to *know* me." She said and there it was again, that tension.

"Well, I'll be off. Good night." Lane said sharply before she turned around and was out the door in seconds. Zia made sure the door was shut tight before she turned around and stopped, finally noticing me in my towel. I smirked as she smirked. She was unabashedly checking me out and was proud of it. Her bright aqua blue eyes slowly roamed down my body, study every inch of my chest before she lingered on my towel and the knot at my waist. When her eyes flicked back up to mine, I had to bite my lip. She sauntered towards me with a swing in her hips and a glint in her eye.

"Ready for bed?" She spoke in that breathy tone again. That glint I saw in her eyes was pure evil. She knew exactly what she was doing to me. My eyes shot to the roof, willing myself not to fall for her games.

"Don't go talking to me in that tone. It... does things to me." I said shyly, swallowing the lump in my throat that wants to release a purr and look back down at her. She smirked again and winked at me. *Oh, she wants to play it like that, huh? Alright game on.*

"Turn around." The order and change of tone were so sudden she looked flabbergasted.

"What? Why?" She questioned.

"I'm gonna show you that alpha side you were begging to see." I said to her as I stared down at her heatedly. Her eyes blinked rapidly as she swallowed audibly.

"Heh, I..I don't think I begged.." She said laughing shyly while stepping back. She was trying to put distance between us but I wouldn't have it. I stepped forward, bringing us closer again.

"What's wrong? I thought you wanted to see my alpha side?" I said smirking. I knew I won this round before she even spoke.

"Y..yes, b..but I.." She stammered. "Iwasplayingwithfire-andgotburnt!" She rushed out before she turned and took off for the door.

I ran after her, reaching her before she could turn the doorknob. She screamed out and laughed as I carried her back, hand crashing down on her ass cheek before I tossed her back on the bed. She laughed and giggled as she bounced. I smirked and shook my head, turning and walking over to one of my drawers to grab a pair of sweatpants out. Can't be sleeping naked next to her. That would be a whole lot of danger right there. I watch her gravitate to the side I usually wake up on. I smile inwardly, hiding the blush heating my cheeks. Does she know she chose the side of the bed that my scent is strongest on? I switch the lights off and climb into bed. I grab my pillow, fluffing it before placing it on the floor.

"What are you doing?" She asked confused, head tilting to the side as her cute dark brows furrowed.

"I am sleeping on the floor?" I question, confused as well.

"Y..you can't. This is your bed, Cairo." I smile.

"I know but I don't want to rush this. Don't want to make any more mistakes. I want you to be comfortable. I'll sleep on the floor as long as you want me to." Her face went bright red before she looked away. She spoke so quietly I almost missed it.

"You can sleep on the bed. I..I'm fine with that." It was cute seeing how shy she was. If she's not sad, she's angry. If she's not angry, she's cheeky. I don't often get to see this super cute shy side. *It's adorable.* Picking the pillow back up, I place it on the left side of the bed. With her taking the right side it felt weird. But I can get used to it. Especially when being this close to her feels like I'm drowning in her dreamy scent. I just know tonight I will have the best damn sleep I've ever had in my life.

Chapter Twenty-Two

My Dream

Jordan

I stand in front of my mirror admiring my slim, toned body. I know I'm hot and I know I look sexy. My hands glide down the red lace bodice. Red was always my colour. It drew the eye to me, making me stand out among the boring crowd. Cairo always like me in red. It was the same colour I wore the day we lost our virginity to each other.

We were sixteen and I had been flirting with him for weeks, but my crush had started when I was thirteen. He was the son of the Alpha; he was going to be strong and powerful one day. Not to mention as we got older, he got hotter. When he turned fifteen his features were turning from boy to man. At sixteen he stood tall, his features were sharper and his body was to die for. We all had our wolves for a year. He had this new aggression about him that called to me like a moth to a flame. I wanted that power he had. I knew he wasn't my mate but I had heard him say multiple times he never wanted one. So, I knew I could get him but I had to work on it. It was the night of one of our pack parties the high school kids always throw when they graduated. There were no elders, no parents, or adults. Our friends were all occupied getting drunk. I dressed up in a tight red dress and took what I wanted and he gave in so easy. He was begging to let out all his newfound pent-up aggression from his wolf. After that he came to me willingly. Whenever he wanted me I was there for him. Willing to let him have me, take me from behind. When he turned eighteen a few months ago, I knew it wouldn't be long before he would take over as Alpha. My dreams were almost within my grasp. I just had to bide my time, then when it was time, he would look to me to be his Luna. He would have to eventually take a mate and I was ready for him. I had primed him for years. Whispering things here and there. But everything changed the second *she* walked in.

Zia.

That filthy fucking rogue. I saw him that day. He couldn't take his eyes off her. At first I was thrilled because he looked like he wanted to rip her throat out. But then his eyes trailed down her body in a way they never did for me. Their confrontation made me happy. She made him angry and who did he come to that night to let out his frustrations? Me. I still had him. But the more he saw her at school, the more they interacted, the more he pulled away from me. The more he got in my face telling me to *fuck off*. The day of the Trials I couldn't have been more excited. Even though he was older, I had started fucking one of the head warriors, Jaxon. He was going to be fighting against the rogues and I made a deal with him. I would continue to fuck him if he killed Zia during the trials. But then things didn't go as planned. She lived and what's worse was Cairo almost went feral. He attacked Jaxon, started attacking anyone who dare came near that pathetic rogue.

That's when I started hearing rumours that they were mates. It wasn't true, it couldn't be. So, I had to be sure. I tried inviting him into my room, tried enticing him with my body but he wouldn't budge. He looked at me with disgust! Me! As if I was some gross creature!

I woke up this morning with a plan. I would make him mark *me* first. I pulled out my sexiest lingerie set, put red lipstick on, curled and styled my hair, then I loosely tied my robe around me. I was going to climb into his bed, get on top of him and force him to make me his mate. I was going to take pictures of us fucking. I was going to send them to that mate stealing whore and run her off. But what I saw was my worst nightmare. **SHE** was in his bed! The sheets were covering their lower halves, his chest was naked and his hands were all over her. She was asleep on his chest, head tucker under his chin. I could see her leg wrapped over his waist under the sheet and her hand was on his chest. *I should be the one tucked into him, not her!*

I inwardly screamed as I stormed back out of the room. I slammed my bedroom door behind me as I let my scream out. Everything was wrong! Jaxon wouldn't fuck me anymore, my plans of becoming Luna were ruined all because of that slut.

"I HATE HER!"

Chapter Twenty-Three

Bunny

ZIA

The sound of a door shutting woke me. I regretfully rolled off Cairo onto my back onto the left side of the bed. I had no idea when or how we ended up cuddling each other in our sleep, but I had a feeling my grinning wolf had something to do with it. I yawn, stretching my arms above my head and relishing in the dreamless sleep. It was perfect. No nightmares, no memories, nothing. Just pure empty black bliss of sleep. For once I didn't wake up covered in sweat. I look over to Cairo after hearing a small puff of breath that doesn't quite belong to him and gasp, slightly jumping back. There was a little girl standing right next to his side of the bed staring right at me. She couldn't have been older than four at most. She had the same complexion as Cairo but her hair and eye colour were different. She had beautiful fawnygolden hair, large bright brown eyes, and a curious face. Her hair was short and curled behind her ears. She wore a white shirt with long pink pant overalls and to tie the outfit together, she had a pair of white fluffy bunny ears sitting on the top of her head. She smiled at me, a cute welcoming smile that warmed my heart.

"Uhm, Cairo," I said lightly tapping him as I continued to watch her. He murmured something before he turned his head away. "Cairo," I said nudging him this time. "There's a uh...bunny in the room."

"A bunny?" He said through a yawn as he began to stretch.

"There is a cute little bunny right next to the bed. Staring." I say sitting up and reaching for the sheet to bunch in my lap, covering my bare legs. He finally turns his head, seeing the little girl.

"So, there is. Good morning, bunny." He says greeting her. "What are you doing in here?"

"Morning, bubba!" She says excitedly right in his face. "I a bunny!" She almost screams in his face and I hold back a laugh as he tries to pull his head back but the pillow stops him.

"I can see that." He says gently pushing her back to get back some of his personal space.

"Who her? Mate?" She says in simple English. Still learning to form big sentences.

"Yep, this is her. Zia, meet my little sister." *Sister?* I didn't know he had a sister. No one ever mentioned her and I never saw her around the house or pack all the times that I've been here.

I push aside my confusion and greet her. "Hello, I'm Zia. What's your name?" She claps her hands excitedly.

"I Sasa!" She says dancing around making me giggle.

"Sasa? That's a pretty name." Cairo chuckles as he looks back at me.

"It's Sarana. She can't pronounce her name yet." I make an O shape with my mouth, understanding. That's true, I remember when I was young. My father said I could never say my name properly. Even after he helped me shorten it but I still ended up saying Yi-Yi instead of Zi-zi.

"How old are you, Sarana?"

"I this many!" She says holding up one finger. Cairo laughs and shakes his head.

"You're one?" I ask her and she smiles, nodding her head.

"You are not. You're three and you know it." He says holding up three fingers.

"Uh oh, Cairo. You've upset the bunny." He looks over at her, seeing her little hands balled into fists by her side and a cute frown on her face.

"Fine, you're one." He says sitting up and swinging his legs over the side while rolling his eyes. She's got him wrapped around her finger.

"Bubba," She says trying to say brother, "Sasa up." She says flicking her fingers in and out as she raises her hands at him. I laugh, hearing him sigh and roll his eyes again as he leans down and grabs her.

"Your wish is my command." He says tickling her. She laughs loudly and tries to pull his hands away but failing miserably.

He was making my insides melt. Watching him interact with her was so sweet. I could see the love he had for her even though he was acting annoyed. She really loved him. I could see it in the way her big eyes lit up when he looked at her. Seeing them together you could see they were siblings. Though there was a fifteen-year age gap between the two, they were really similar. He tickled her some more, making her laugh a big belly laugh. I definitely needed to capture this moment. I look over at the bedside table closest to me and find Cairo's phone. I went to sleep on the right side of the bed but woke up on the left. His phone had no lock on it so I got into the camera straight away. He spoke as I was lining up the frame.

"What are you doing?"

"What do you think I'm doing? I'm taking a photo of *bubba* with his Sasa." I said teasing him. He squinted his eyes at me making me smirk.

"I'm not liking this." He said crossing his arms across his chest as he glares at me.

"Bubba, shush! Eya taking picture." Sarana spoke from his lap, crossing her arms across her chest just like him. She wasn't even looking at him yet did the same gesture as him. It was cute seeing more of their similarities. It was even cuter that she tried to say Zia and failed successfully. I would happily be called Eya.

"You heard her, shush." I smile evilly as his jaw ticks.

I focus the camera, making sure they're perfectly in frame before pressing the button. I take a few more before smiling and nodding to myself for a job well done. The photos turned out great. Really captured the sibling bond I think.

I sit back, watching as Sarana clumsily stands up before she turns around facing Cairo, coming face to face with him as she looked at him with determination which made him frown in question.

"What are you doing, bunny?" He asks her.

"I not a bunny." She announces with her hands on her hips sassily. She raises her hands, grabbing the bunny ears headband off her head and places it on Cairo. She adjusts it, making sure the headband went behind his ears before she stood back and approved of her work. I held in a laugh, absolutely loving this.

"That is perfect. Stay still!" I say quickly getting the camera ready again snapping a pic. And he does, he stays still, arms still crossed against his chest, one eyebrow raised to really show off the glare he's shooting me. I smile behind the phone, making sure to take a couple zoomed in on his face.

"Youu a bunny, Bubba." Sarana announces. Cairo doesn't move an inch as Sarana smiles brightly at him. Then she stops suddenly stops smiling and frowns almost pained like. Her hands move down, holding herself as she looks at Cairo.

"What's wrong, bunny?" He asks unsure.

"Sasa, pee pee." I laugh as he repels back like she just slapped him.

"Oh Goddess, get off me!" I grab my stomach from laughing so hard as he scoops her up, holding her away from his body as he gets up off the bed looking absolutely ridiculous with the bunny ears still on.

"Where are you going?" I ask.

"I'm taking her to the bathroom before she pisses all over me!" He yells as he runs towards the bathroom door. *Damn. I should have recorded that.*

Laughter expelled from everyone's mouth as they took in the newly dyed hair on Jordan. No longer did she have that piss blonde, yellow colour. Now it was platinum...

"What are you looking at?!" She snaps from the end of our table in the cafeteria. The warrior wolf Jaxon sat beside her talking to someone beside him and her minion Beth sat in front of her glaring our way. I couldn't help myself, I just had to say something.

"You didn't really think that would work, did you? He's *my* mate, Jordan. He and his wolf will **never** want another. So, get used to it." I say bluntly.

"Who is this, Zi?" Maya asks as she turns to look at Jordan. Sat across from me, she studied her.

"A pack *shlyukha.*" I say calling her a whore. She laughs, understanding the word. When Alek and I stayed with her, as everyone does, we laughed and joked as we exchanged swear words in our languages to each other. It was fun learning the naughty words and it definitely came in handy right now.

"What did you just call me!?" Jordan screeched from her seat.

"You don't want to know, love." Alek inserted before laughing.

"Get up, Bethany! We're leaving!" She said stomping her booted foot down on the ground as she stood up from the seat.

"But I haven't eaten yet." Bethany said shyly from her seat. She hadn't had a second to eat her French toast before Jordan's demands came in. We were all dressed in our uniforms ready for school.

"NOOOOW!" Jordan screamed, making every wolf in the hall jump, hurting our sensitive hearing. "Fuck the food!" She threw her hands down angrily.

"Hey! Don't swear in front of the food." Maya said making everyone laugh.

"Jordan, wait up." I said shocking everyone as they went silent. I was the last person they expected to see talking to her.

She wouldn't turn around as I walked to her, defiantly giving me her back. "What do you want?" She sneered as I stopped behind her. I leaned in, whispering low so that only she could hear me. Noticing the silver earrings she wore, I knew no one would be able to hear us, even with straining their ears. So, I wanted to be honest with her.

"You can dye your hair all you want, but you will never be me. So, stop trying, bitch." She growled low, stomping away as she latched onto Bethany's arm who had come to her side and headed towards the door.

If she thinks she can dye her hair to look like mine just to get Cairo's attention, then she's got another thing coming. Every waking moment I spend with Cairo I can feel our bond strengthening. Sleeping on his muscular chest this morning felt amazing. Then seeing him with his little sister had me feeling all mushy inside. The longer we go without marking each other and completing the bond, the harder it will be for the both of us. It will make our bodies feel like they're on the verge of everything. On the verge of a shift, on the verge of our wolves taking control and marking us themselves. I never thought I'd meet my mate and I never thought I'd get to have a family or a pack again. But I do, I get that now. I do deserve it. No matter what happened in my past, no matter how much I punished myself for something that was out of my control, I deserve to have a mate. I deserve to have a *life*.

I look towards Cairo, watching him as he eats. He's so handsome, so perfect in every way. I'm seeing a different side to Cairo and this new side? It's making me fall in love with him.

"Hey, day dreamer." He says making me focus back on his face. I blush, feeling embarrassed he caught me dazing at his face. "Get your butt over here, there's something we need to discuss." He says not commenting on it. I silently thank him as I move down until I'm seated next to him. And by next to him I mean on his lap. I guess I've gotten used to his touch and my body really misses him when I'm not near him.

"You just love sitting on me don't you." He says more than asks. But it's not like he's pushing me off either. He placed his hand securely on my waist the second I slid into his lap.

"What can I say, it's comfy." I say winking at him as I wiggle against him purposely. He coughs, clearing his throat and breaths in and out as I feel him harden. It's crazy how reactive he is to me and I to him. I giggle before continuing to make things hard for him. "I love being *close* to you too." I say as he goes red in the face realising that I can indeed feel him against my butt. I hear a laugh come from across the table.

"Omg, you guys need to get a room. The air's getting thick in here if you know what I mean." Maya said amused.

"Right! All that sexual tension." Zack adds, making both of us blush and squirm uncomfortably. Forgetting that these werewolves around us can smell our scents, especially when we're letting out our arousal.

"You two just wait until you find your mates. Then you'll

understand our struggle." I laugh, absolutely agreeing with him. We grew up hearing about how your mate is irresistible to you but I never thought it would be so intense.

No matter what you're feeling that pull is always there. You could be mad, sad, happy, or bored one minute and the next, you're ready to rip your mates' clothes off. And this is only what I feel just from being near him. I don't know how strong it's going to be when we actually do mark and complete the bond.

I shake my head, remembering I came over here for a reason. I slide off his lap but keep our legs touching. I needed away from his happy member or else I won't be able to concentrate on anything else. He called me over here for a reason.

"What did you want to talk about?" I ask watching as he tries to discretely rearrange himself so he's more comfortable. I smirk and try to hide it as he shoots me a look.

"I wanted you to go to the shops tomorrow. You can take the day off school and take Maya with you too if you want." *Shopping?*

"Why? What's going on?" I ask, confused why he wants me to go shopping.

"We'll be having a ball to introduce you, Alek and Maya to the pack. We usually do this once a year but since you're my mate, I wanted it done sooner. I think it's time the pack meets their future Luna. *My Luna.*"

Those words.

Those two little words that have the power to bring me crumbling down.

My Luna.

"Zia?" Maya says seeing my instant change.

Those words...I thought I'd never hear them again. My heart started beating rapidly as I hurriedly breathed in and out trying to control myself. I could feel my hands start to shake, chest restricting as I went cold. I could feel the blood drain from my face as my body started tingling. I could see

Cairo saying something, but I couldn't hear him. The only thing I could hear was blood rushing to my head and a ringing in the distance. Those words...I can still hear his voice saying them. He said them, he said them when he...when he...

I can't breathe...

My hands became clammy as I grabbed at the school tie around my neck. It was too tight, too restricting. I needed air, I needed...I needed...

"What's going on? Baby?" I could finally hear Cairo speak but it wasn't enough. Wasn't enough to stop the panic attack that gripped me. I was caught in a vice, unable to escape.

Suddenly I was pulled up from my seat and spun around as Alek forced me to look at him as his hands gripped my arms, grounding me. "*Ego zdes' net. Vse horosho, ty v bezopasnosti.*" Alek rushed out, reminding me that the man who hunts me wasn't here, that I was safe. "*Sestra, poslushay menya! Ty v bezopasnosti, uspokoysya.*" Alek said repeating the words that I am safe and to calm down. He pulled me into him, wrapped his arms around me, rubbing my back as my body shook. I tried to steer my nerves, willing myself to calm down and listen to his words. Alek never lies to me, never. So, I know I can trust him. His touch helps soothe me. We've been together since the womb; we were born together and we'll die together. He's my rock.

"Stay home today. Take Maya to the shops and get your dress for the ball. I'll bring whatever schoolwork you have home for you."

"Okay..." I speak roughly. My voice feels horse like I've been screaming for hours.

"Have fun and don't forget what I said." He reassures me.

"I won't. And Ali?"

"Yeah?"

"Don't ever leave me." I say quietly. I can hear Cairo breathing in and out behind him.

"I won't, Zi. I will always be with you." He says kissing my forehead. I nod, letting his words soothe me.

"Baby? What's going on?" Cairo says unsure. I can hear a note of worriedness in his voice. I pull away from Alek, slowly turning back to Cairo. I give him a quick hug, unable to kiss his cheek even on my tippy toes because of his height.

"I'll see you this afternoon. Have a good day at school." Is all I say before I turn back and follow Maya out the door.

CAIRO

"Alek?" I ask him as he sits down beside me sadly. I've never seen Zia like that before. One second she was happy and the next it was like she was taken over by fear. I don't know what I did wrong...I don't know what I said to make her like that.

"Look," He says exhausted, "Zia and I both have our demons. But Zia more so. She's the reason we left out pack in the first place. Why we became rogues, why we lost our friends, our family, everything."

"What? Why? What did she do?" I ask. Both Alek and Zia have said things here and there but never the full story.

"That's not important right now. What is important is that you give Zia time. Time to open up on her own because once she does, you're stuck with her for life. She's fiercely loyal and will not go down without a fight. But we all have a weakness. And Zia's just happens to be her demon. So, don't push her for answers because if you do, she will never tell you. They can be triggering for her. This is one subject you don't want to challenge her on. We are no alpha blood but we are as strong as one being the Moons Warriors and all. If she feels attacked and overwhelmed by you wanting answers, by being pushed, I can't help you when she freaks. Because even then I can't stop her. Our powers..." He says and for the first time I start thinking about them. I completely forgot that they're not like normal wolves. They have these gifts and abilities unlike any we have ever seen. "I don't like to admit it since I'm the older twin, but Zia's powers are much stronger than mine. She can do so much more than what she thinks. When we first got our powers and she was put into a situation, she lost control of herself. We barely got her back and even then, she has no recollection of it. She still thinks I'm stronger but I'm not. So, I beg you, not to push her because I can't lose her. I simply don't have the power to save her anymore. She's grown too strong." He says looking at me with his glowing aqua eyes. I can see his heartbreak and fear within them shining brightly back at me.

"I'll wait for her as long as she needs." I assure him. I don't plan on pushing or forcing her to do anything ever. I'm still earning her trust; I won't do anything to jeopardise that.

"Thanks. I guess you're not all bad." He says with a straight face. I don't know if he was making a joke or not. I'm leaning towards not since it wasn't that long ago that he was pummelling me into the ground. "I guess we better head to school now." He says standing up from the table. "Keiran, babe. Put the donut down. You've had enough." He says to his mate, my beta making him laugh with a mouthful of doughnut. *So, that's Alek joking*. Well, that answers my question then.

Chapter Twenty-Four

The Mall

Zia

After we left the dining hall, Maya and I separated as we headed to our rooms to get changed out of our school uniforms. Finally, I was able to wear something cute and new that Alek and I bought when we first moved into town. I decided on a loose fitting light pink crop top that had beautiful lace detailing on it, a pair of light blue flared short pants that looked almost like a skirt, and a pair of brand-new white converses that I haven't got to wear yet. I loved the pastel vibes this outfit had going on. Maya waited for me and soon we were off. By the time we were changed and heading out the front door, everyone had already left for school. Maya and I spoke along the way as we walked to the mall. It wasn't empty but wasn't packed either. It was the perfect number of occupants for someone who gets anxiety from big crowds.

"Fill me in, Zi. What's been going on around here lately? How did you meet Cairo?" Maya asked as we passed a churro stand.

"Well, it was no walk in the park. When I first got here, I smelt his scent and discovered he was my mate. I was happy, but then I found out he had a fuck buddy who went around telling everyone that they're mates."

"She didn't!" Maya exclaimed angrily.

"You met her this morning, the dramatic one." I say confirming her suspicion.

"Knew it. I definitely don't like her. And Cairo's weak for letting her claim him when they aren't mates." She gasps, quickly looking to me as I take in a breath. Hitting a tender spot for me.

"Oh, Zia, I'm so sorry! I didn't mean you were weak, just that he is the next alpha so he should have put her in her place." She said as she looked like she was walking on eggshells.

"It's okay. I got what you meant." I say but it doesn't stop my smile from fading. I was weak too.

"Have you told him?" She said stopping to face me. "Cairo, about your past?" She asks quietly.

"No. You're the only person Alek and I ever told. You were the first person in a long time that we felt like we could trust and be open and honest with." I stopped speaking, noticing the pained look on her face. Her mouth opened and closed like she wanted to say something but couldn't. In the end she stayed silent, looking down at her feet as tears welled in her eyes.

"Those three months," She finally spoke, "we spent together were the best months of my life. I never connected with anyone so strongly the way I did with you. I didn't have anyone in my pack who was a best friend or even a close friend.

You were that and still are for me. I would help you repeatedly, Zi. I wouldn't have trekked halfway across the world in one outfit if it weren't for you." She said making me laugh but something in her eyes didn't feel like a joke. I think she was still holding back her pain.

"Speaking of outfits, this one you're wearing is cute. It's not the smelly one you were wearing when you arrived." She primped her hair, really rocking the boho style outfit.

"Thank you, the Luna came by my room with a welcome package of sorts. It had a bunch of clothes in it, so I made do. But I don't have anything for this ball on the weekend though."

"Well, there's a dress shop behind you I think we should go in. There's a dress in the window that I think will look stunning on you." She turned, eyeing the dress before nodding her head in agreement. The store was beautiful and looked very posh. The dresses on display looked so pretty and the ones on the racks were even more breathtaking. I couldn't wait to find the dress for me.

"Damn, this place looks expensive." Maya whispered. I agreed, it did but I had that covered.

"Don't worry, we have some money saved plus the Luna stopped me on my way to my room this morning. She gave me some money. So, pick whatever dress you want!" I said happily. She clapped excitedly as she turned, scanning the racks.

"Morning ladies, welcome to-" The lady who worked in the store said before she stopped. "You guys are not rogues?" She asked looking at us curiously.

"We recently joined this towns pack." I say explaining why our scents haven't fully changed from the rogue scent.

"Ah, that explains why you guys smell a little like rogues but my pack as well. Oh! Are you Cairo's mate?" The young woman exclaimed. I nodded. "I wasn't there during the trials. When I heard Cairo was forcing a female rogue to fight, I couldn't stand there and watch it happen. But from what I heard, you and your brother totally kicked ass." I giggle, feeling guilty that's what the pack thinks. I was the one who said we would participate.

"I taught her well." Maya said confidently. I scoff, giving her a side eye before replying.

"You did not. You taught me some Portuguese, nothing else." She primped her short hair again before laughing.

"What can I do for you girls today?"

"We're looking for something to wear to the ball." I said as she buzzed excitedly.

"Oh, yes the ball! You girls are lucky you got here first. By Friday all the good dresses will be gone. If you girls want to follow me, we just got a new shipment in fresh off the runway." She led us towards the racks with dresses that were still in their plastic bags.

We spent the rest of the morning going through each and every rack. There were so many beautiful dresses that made it hard to choose. Jane, as we came to know her, helped us tremendously. She was so kind and even showed me a handful of dresses that Jordan had put on hold. I guess even she doesn't like Jordan considering she offered to let me try them on. And who was I to decline? Jane led both of us to the dressing rooms. Maya went in one and me the other. After looking endlessly, she decided on the dress we saw from the window. She really did look amazing in it and announced that it was the one. Me on the other hand, I had a few to try on. I tried on the dresses I picked out, then the ones Jordan had on hold, and I hated to say it, but she has great taste. I ended up picking one of her dresses that was so stunning I couldn't see her pulling it off. But this dress felt like it was made for me.

"Goddess, you were in there for ages!" Maya said when I finally emerged from the rose gold curtains.

"Sorry, had a lot to try on." I smiled guiltily.

"What did you end up choosing? Something good I hope

because you took about fifty dresses in there with you." She said making me laugh.

"Uhm, it was like ten at most. But I narrowed it down to three, then I tried on the last one and knew that was my one. One of Jordan's." She laughed loudly, loving the drama to come.

"I like the way you think." She said winking at me.

"Jane said they have a delivery service here so; we don't have to carry our gowns all the way home since we walked here."

"Oh, that's smart! They'll stay in pristine condition." Maya said which is exactly what I thought.

"Let's go pay."

"No need. Everything is paid for." Jane said coming up behind us.

"What? How? I still have the money?" I said confused as Jane smiled.

"She paid." She said motioning with her head behind us. We turned finding a familiar warrior standing in the middle of the store watching us. It was Lane. *She paid for them?*

"Why did you pay?" I asked walking over to her.

"I didn't." She said crossing her arms against her chest, confusing me more. I waited for her to continue. "Cairo." Was all she said.

"What?...Why would he do that?" I said shocked.

"Because he cares about you." Lane said annoyed. "Enough to pay for whatever you want so that you'll be happy. Even if that means putting his happiness aside so that you'll come first." She said glaring at me.

"Why are you so hostile towards me?" I snapped back. From the second she saw me in that torture room she's had that same glare and look of annoyance on her face.

"I don't trust someone I don't know. You hold secrets, Zia. Ones that could cost the lives of OUR pack members." She said pointedly. “You aren’t alone anymore. You have a family within the pack now. You’ll be our Luna one day. You can’t put yourself first anymore. People in the pack are already looking up to you because you survived the Trials. Don’t let innocent people die because of your selfishness.” She said not holding back. She probably wanted to say this to me before Cairo interrupted us last night. “Tell him what he wants to know. Now come along, he’s wanting you back home safely.” With that she turned and stormed out of the store. I wanted to scream back at her, tell her things weren’t so simple and that I wasn’t being selfish. I was *protecting* everyone. Maya knew who Alek and I really were and now look at her. She’s the sole survivor of her pack because my demon, the man we ran from, heard we were in her pack and came. I’m stopping that from happening here but she doesn’t understand. But she was right about some things. I wasn’t alone anymore. I had friends, a pack, a mate.

“She’s intense.” Maya said stopping beside me.

“Yeah,” I said breathing out trying to calm my jittery nerves. “But I like that. She doesn’t beat around the bush that’s for sure.” She’s a great warrior, always looking out for the protection of her pack.

“I don’t want you to take this the wrong way, but maybe she’s right. Hasn’t Cairo proved himself enough yet to know about you and Alek’s past?” She asks unsure. “He adores you, Zia. I’ve seen it. Enough to pay for our shopping today and protection.”

“Protection?” I say confused. She rolls her eyes and shakes her head before she replies.

“He would have given you his money if he wanted but he didn’t. Instead, he sends one of the packs strongest warriors.”

“So, what’s that go to do with anything?” I say still not seeing it.

“He sent her to protect you. She’s here to be your bodyguard. She could have simply paid for our dresses and then left.

Yet she followed us here, stayed outside the store for hours while we tried on all of these dresses, and even now, she's still here. Waiting for us to leave." She said as if she was stating the obvious. "I'm assuming your PTSD attack has him and his wolf worried. So, Lane's right. You should tell him. He clearly cares about you and your safety."

"Yeah.." I say not knowing what to think. This all feels too much.

"Has he seen you having your nightmares?" She asks quietly.

"No. Last night was our first night together. I slept amazing." I blushed.

"Zia, we both know it won't be long until you have another one. Then what will you do when he starts asking questions?"

"Okay! I hear you, the both of you." I say exhausted. "I'll think about it."

"That's good enough, I suppose." She sighs out. "Do you think we have enough time to get lunch before grumpy pants outside drags us home?" She says making me laugh. Lane definitely is a grumpy pants.

Walking home from the mall felt different. I didn't feel happy like I thought I would be after buying a dress for the ball. I couldn't stop the conversation from Lane and Maya out of my head. Maybe they were right. Maybe it's time I tell Cairo about me and how we ended up here. The whole way home I thought of the pros and cons of telling Cairo. The positives being I wouldn't have to keep secrets anymore. I wouldn't have to dodge questions or hide myself. I could speak with him freely without worrying that I might slip up and reveal something I shouldn't. But the cons were piling up, overweighing the scales. What if I tell him everything and he doesn't want me anymore? What if he looks at me differently, with disgust and decides he'd rather take Jordan as his mate? Could I risk it? Do I tell him the truth and risk him rejecting me? Or do I not tell him the truth and risk losing him because of it? *Why did my life have to be so hard? Why did I have to be born with so many responsibilities?* I just wanted a normal life. But apparently a normal life was never meant for me. I drew different cards.

Chapter Twenty-Five

The Club

We finally made it back to the pack just in time for me to hear paws pounding on the grass behind me. They were headed straight for me and I knew it could only mean one thing. "Not again!" I turn, just as Cairo's large black wolf lunged straight for me. We hit the ground with a thud, breathing ripping from me as his heavy weight sits atop of me. His tongue seems to shoot out a mile a minute, licking me everywhere. I laughed as best I could and scratched him behind the ears, giving him all the scratchies he deserves. When he started trying to nudge my head aside and get to my neck, I knew it was time to get this big lump of fur off me. He was getting too...pawsy.

"You are so cute. Maybe you should stay in wolf form forever." I joked. His wolf was very excited at the thought, but Cairo was not. Their purring growl was wrangled like both tried to speak at the same time. It was such a cute sound.

"Okay, buddy," I tapped his wet nose with my finger, "time to let me up." He huffed, making me laugh as I reached down and rubbed his fur, scratched behind the ears again and kissed his furry forehead. "Alright, go get changed. It's Cairo's turn for kisses." I said and was almost barrelled over as Cairo's wolf took off.

"Hey." Kitty said bending down to help me up as the rest of the group goes on.

"Hey, Kitty, how was school?" I haven't properly talked to her yet but I've been meaning too. She was one of the first people here who treated Alek and me like we were people. She didn't judge us for being rogues.

"Boring as usual. You didn't miss much." She said shrugging. "But you did miss Alek and Cairo sulking all day. They missed you." I laughed shyly. "Oh, I hear we're going to the club tonight!" She exclaimed happily.

"Really?" This was the first I heard of any club plans.

"Caleb just linked me. He said Alek told him that Maya said we're all going out tonight. You'll love it!" She nods reassuringly as she sees the unsure look on my face. "Let's go get ready, the pack club opens in a few hours." I nod, following her inside before we go our separate ways.

I guess I need a shower and time to do my hair and pick an outfit out. I do have some really pretty outfits I haven't had the chance of wearing to clubs or anything. I push open the bedroom door and stop, seeing Maya sitting on the bed crossed legged with a grin on her face.

"Just the wolf I was looking for." I say squinting at her. "What are you up too!?"

"Whatever do you mean?" She says blinks her eyes innocently.

"Why are we going out tonight, Maya?" I question.

"Well one, I thought we could dress up. I know Cairo won't be able to keep his eyes off you, much less hands." She teases. I could feel my cheeks heat up at the thought. "And two, you need to have fun. Everything has been so hectic for the both of us lately but I know you more. When everything starts changing your emotions run high and you start having bad nightmares. You used to have bad ones when we first met. This will be a good chance for everyone to have some fun and let their hair down." She says making sense. I don't tend to take change well considering, but I guess she's right. We have the ball on the weekend but that's a formal event. This tonight is a chance to let us drink and not worry about elders or the Alpha or anything plaguing our minds.

"Okay, fine. You convinced me."

"Yes! Great! Perfect! Now go have your shower and get ready, you have two hours." I nod, watching as she walks to the door but stops as she leans into me.

"And happy birthday." She whispers. I don't have a chance to reply before she quickly closes the door behind her. This whole thing was just a ruse! She was planning a party instead of a spur of the moment get together. She remembered our birthday.

I breathe in, remembering the last happy birthday I ever had. It was the day we turned fifteen, the day Alek and I got our wolves. It was such a great day, we had so much fun running through the snow as a family. Our papa's black wolf running beside three white ones. I remember when I was younger, I asked papa why his wolf was a different colour to our mama's. That's when he told us the natural colour of our hair in human form is the colour our wolfs fur will be when we shift. I thought it was so fascinating. That was also the first birthday I hated. It was the day I kept a secret that would turn deadly. If only I had told someone, anyone! Everything that happened since wouldn't have. The tidal wave that crashed into my life may never have happened if only I had spoken up sooner. If only I wasn't taken over by fear.

I shake my head, dispelling everything from my mind and start to strip. I needed to get ready. The shower was quick. I just had to wash my hair then shave. Well, I guess it wasn't that quick because once I got out of the shower and saw the time on my phone I panicked. Time had flown by and I was now late. I ran my towel through my hair, ruffling up the bottom so my hair would dry with a wave to it. I swipe some ruby red lipstick on and exit the bathroom, beelining straight for my clothes. I have just the outfit in mind. Choosing a strapless baby pink coloured dress that hugged my body and shimmered and glittered in the light, I bent down, slipping on a pair of silver heels that laced up my calf. I look at my appearance in the mirror and nod. Tousling my damp, almost dry hair, I turn and head for the door. If I speed walk I may be able to catch up. I hadn't seen Cairo since this morning but I was hoping he was waiting for me. The second I close the door, a loud voice boomed behind me.

"BOO!" I screamed, jumping back as I turn around finding Alek laughing.

"Alek!" I scold. "You know I hate it when you do that!" I growl lowly as I storm to him.

"Well, little *sestra*. I'll stop doing it when you stop jumping." He said winking. I contemplated, then decided as he looked at me curiously. He didn't have time to react. I tucked my head down then ran, barrelling into him and taking him to the ground. His body hit the ground with a satisfying thud. I smirk at him. He never sees *that* coming.

"OWE!!" He says dramatically but I know he's fine.

"I'll stop doing that when you stop being so unsuspecting." I mimic his words back to him. "You had that coming."

"Okay, get off me, fatty." He cries out as my hand moves on its own. "Okay! You're not fat! Just ugly..." I raise my hand again and let my wolfs eyes show.

"I'M JOKING!!" He says eyes wide. I laugh, getting off him as I stand up.

"Stop being so gullible. You know my wolf would never hurt you." He sighs, falling for it before begrudgingly standing up.

"Come on, trouble. You took too long getting ready so we're meeting everyone there."

"Do you know where it is?" He nods before he starts walking towards the stairs. I follow, excited to see this pack club and excited to finally see Cairo. I felt guilty how I just walked away this morning without answering him and I missed him all day. This damn bond continuing the play havoc on me.

From the outside, the club looked like a normal building. You could hear the music through the walls, lights flickering through the curtains on the windows. There were a few pack members scattered around the gravelled area, some smoking, some in conversation with others. When we walked in, we paused, amazed at what we saw. We've never been inside a club before, only knowing from what we saw on TV. The hardwood floors were glossy, reflecting the strobe lights off the dance floor near the stage and the dim, magenta, purple and blue lights around the club. There were low coffee tables near the entrance along the back wall with dark purple leather cushioned seats. There was another exit, guarded by a pack warrior. Standing near the entrance in front of the booths, the stage was straight ahead, with live music being played on the raised area. The middle of the room was the dance floor with fairy lights lighting up the ceiling. It gave off such a magical atmosphere. To the far left was the large bar, alcohol lined the glass shelves with a mirror behind, three bartenders raced about serving drinks. There was a long glossy black bar with matching silver stools in front. The club was a perfect mix of biker bar meets fancy LA night club. The mix worked. I saw faces I didn't recognise and some I did.

"This is their pack club?!" I exclaim to Alek beside me who looked around in awe.

"I know! This is so much better than our pack club." I laugh if you could even call it that.

“Ours was just a wooden barn, with a second level that looked down on the dance floor.” He laughed and continued to look in wonderment.

“Finally!” Maya said as she weaved her way through the crowd. “We’ve been waiting forever for you two.” She says exhaustedly.

“You can blame her. She’s the one that took her time, then added more time by tackling me.” Alek said.

“You probably deserved it.” Maya said shrugging making him *hmph* and me laugh and nod.

“I knew you’d take her side.” He muttered begrudgingly. Kitty appeared on one side of Maya, dressed in a beautiful purple dress. Keiran stood on the other side of Maya in red maroon skinny jeans and a light grey button up shirt. His eyes widen, taking in Alek as a blush crept up his neck. Without even looking I know Alek’s probably behind me winking at him and checking him out.

“You guys look great!” Kitty exclaimed happily.

“They’re even matching! How cute.” Maya exclaimed. *Matching?*

I turned at the same time seeing Alek look down at my dress. I did the same before looking across at him. He wore a salmon-coloured tee and light grey jeans that had a silver chain hanging from his belt loop for decoration. We looked at each other in disgust, rolling our eyes as our outfits did indeed look like they matched.

“You can say that again.” Keiran said making the three of them laugh. He smiled sheepishly. “A..Alek? Would you like to dance?” He spoke shyly.

“With you, always.” Alek said making all three of us girl’s awe. They walked off together holding hands, finding a nice spot off to the side of the dance floor.

“Have you seen Cairo?” I ask Kitty and Maya. “Do you know where he is?”

“He’s at the bar getting some drinks.” Zack said coming up

behind me. "I was waiting outside for you guys when I saw you. I told Cairo you were almost here and he went to get a drink for you so you had one when you walked in. But the bars a bit busy at the moment so there's a hold up." I blushed, loving his gesture. I didn't see him in the sea of people by the bar but I feel like I can breathe again knowing he's close.

"Come on! Let's dance together!" Maya said already bobbing her head to the beat of the music. Kitty and I clapped excitedly, loving the idea. We walk to the centre of the floor, moving and dancing to the music. I was surprised at how much fun I was having. Never in a million years did I think I would be on a dance floor smiling away my troubles.

Cairo

When Maya approached me this afternoon just after I had shifted back and asked if we could go out tonight for Zia, I didn't hesitate. I know she's close with Zia and I know she knows about Zia's past. I see the way she looks at Zia the same way Alek does. With worry, always watching to see if she's okay. So, I said yes. All day I haven't been able to get Zia's panic attack out of my head. It's been on a loop, replaying the way her breathing changed, the way her skin went cold, and the blood dropped from her face, the way she was so paralysed that she couldn't even hear me speak. It fucked me up seeing her like that. I never want to see my mate like that, let alone anyone else I care about. I wanted her to have fun tonight and forget her troubles. If only for a moment. And when Zack said he saw them approaching, I ran inside beelining straight for the bar to get myself and her a drink. I wanted to be ready for when she walked through the door but apparently everyone decided they were thirsty. I could have pulled rank, pushed through, and got our drinks served first. But that's not the type of man or alpha I want to be. By the time our drinks were served and I made my way over to where I saw Zack standing, she was gone. He flicked his head forward. I followed his direction spotting her on the dance floor. I gasped, drinks slipping out of my hand as they crashed on the ground, alcohol splashing up from impact. I wasn't ready for what my eyes were about to see. I could do nothing to catch the plastic cups except stare at the hottest scene in front of me. Time had froze. The music slowed, the chatter disappeared and everyone in the club melted away. All except her, Zia. She was all I could see. She was dancing so sensually, letting the slow beating music move her. Her hands were running through her hair, mouth parted on a breath and her head tilted up, stretching out her delicate neck. Her hips slowly swayed, drawing my eyes. Her dress looked like it was made for her. She moved like she had not a care in the world. Her face looked so at ease, no frown lines, no twisted brow in pain, just a smile. Her lace up silver looking shoes clung to her legs and man did they do wonders to my overly imaginative mind right now. My wolf was in battle with himself. He was raging thinking about all the unmated males in the club staring at her, and then he was also fighting with how needy he was feeling, wanting her all to himself. At least we can agree on something tonight.

Goddess, she's so damn beautiful. I can't ever seem to take my eyes off her. Even when I sleep I see her and when I wake, she's there. I'm glad she moved in when she did. If she didn't I feel I would have camped outside her apartment window every night. She's constantly on my mind and I wouldn't have it any other way. I can't stand here and watch her anymore. I calm myself, quelling my thoughts before I make a promise to myself.

I'm going to mark her tonight.

Chapter Twenty-Six

The Attack

ZIA

Since I hadn't seen Cairo all day and I was missing him badly, I decided to pick this outfit specifically for him. I was hoping for a certain reaction out of him and I wasn't disappointed. I felt a heat come up behind me before large hands gently slide around my waist, guiding me back. I could feel the sparks, rippling up my skin from our contact. I moved my hips to the beat. I could feel his arousal as we danced together. He moulded our bodies together creating an exciting friction as he held my waist protectively. I'm glad for our height difference. If he wasn't over a head taller than me then his excitement would be rubbing against my ass and I would be unable to move. Too turned on for my brain to function. I loved this moment. I didn't want it to end but it was going to with his next words.

"We're leaving right now." His deep voice sent thrills down my body as he spoke inches from my ear. His head lowered, kissing up my neck ever so slowly making my breaths come out in pants and my body shudder. "If we don't," He continues, "I'm going to bend you over that bar and mark you. Over and over again until everyone knows you're my mate and their Luna." His hands slowly travelled up my body as he spoke, fingers brushing the undersides of my breast. Even through the material of my dress it felt like he was touching my skin, setting me alight. His scent was so thick in the air that I didn't need to turn around to know his eyes were black with lust. I could feel my own eyes change the moment he spoke. My body was so buzzing with anticipation I almost screamed out.

"Then what are you waiting for?!" I said spinning around when his hands let go of me. He smiled a toothy grin before he grabbed my hand, pulling me through the crowd and out the door.

"Wait.." He said stopping just as the doors closed behind us. "Why didn't you tell me it was your birthday?" He asked sadly as if it was on purpose. *Damn Maya must have told him.*

"I...we don't celebrate it." Was all I said. I couldn't find one ounce of happiness inside of me that wanted to celebrate turning eighteen. Something bad always happened when it was our birthday.

On our sixteenth birthday, the first year on the run we got attacked. That was the first time Alek killed someone. I could feel how overcome by guilt he was. On our seventeenth birthday we had just arrived in Portugal. The cargo crew found us hidden on the lower deck and chased us out. We ran as far as we could until we crossed onto pack land. We were captured and thrown into their prison cells. We could hear the screams coming from other rogues that were caught. They were torturing them. We knew we would be next so we had to escape. I regret not trying to save the other rogues but Alek was determined to get us out. He burnt his hands badly prying the silver barred door open. They blistered before they started bleeding but he didn't care. He pushed through the pain, siphoning power from me to break through the door. If we didn't have these gifts then we wouldn't have been able to escape. Aleks hands weren't healing fast enough. We shifted, running to the border as fast as we could. Once we crossed it we thought we were safe but they were coming after us. We ran for hours pushing through exhaustion just to be safe. Once we realised they were long gone we stopped running. As we shifted back, the exhaustion hit me like a ton of bricks and I came crashing down to the ground, but I didn't have enough energy to dodge the animal trap left by rogues as a sick way of trapping unsuspecting victims. The saw-like teeth snapped around my side, bladed teeth ripping through the skin on my ribs, cracking and breaking ribs as the metal contraption clamped down. I couldn't breathe, couldn't even scream. White hot pain shot through me, paralysing me as I began to bleed out. Alek screamed, feeling my pain through our twin bond. The blood drained from his face as he ran to me, prying the clamped saw teeth from my ribs. Then I screamed. He kept saying no, over and over again. He picked me up with one hand, clutching me close to his body as the other hand pressed against my side, trying to stop the bleeding. He ran as fast as he could on foot, running crazed trying to find the nearest town to save me. If Maya hadn't heard his scream that day and found us I would have died. My wounds were deep, I had a broken rib piercing my lung, making it hard to breathe and was bleeding internally. That's why we stayed so long at her pack when we never stayed longer than a day or two at any other place. Her father the alpha was kind. He homed us, fed us, dressed us, and made us feel safe. We maintained the story that we were attacked by rogues because in part we were. The real feral rogues loved their sick games and we fell right into one. We were just lucky that we left before any could find us.

Alek's hands eventually healed and he was okay letting us

stay a while. I think he was worried I wasn't healed enough to leave. But I saw the way he loved being part of a pack, loved making friends and having a home. Then after a while that frown appeared on his face again. The gut feeling that we needed to leave came back. Soon we were gone, leaving the country, and arriving in America. Which eventually led us here, meeting our mates.

"I thought you said you wanted to mark me?" I ask Cairo changing the subject.

"Yes but-" He says and tries to continue but I cut him off, letting my wolfs eyes flash through mine before I speak.

"You'll have to catch me if you want to mark me." I say, eyeing him in challenge. I could see the moment the predator inside him lit up. All werewolves have a need to hunt inside of them. And I just ignited his.

I took off like a rabbit, bounding through the trees and racing further into the forest as his growl rippled through the air. I could hear him laughing as he watched me run. My face was burning from how hard I was smiling. Adrenaline shot through me, making my heart double its beating as Cairo took off with the sound of gravel shifting, pebbles flicking up through the air. I thought this would be easy considering the head start I had but Cairo was fast. He was on me in seconds, growling at me as he caught up. I could hear him snicker and purr as I continued to run from him. He loved the thrill of the hunt just as much as I loved the chase. When he growled, he would slow down, letting me get ahead again and I laughed every single time. Everytime he let me run I would look back; seeing the alpha shining in him just as bright as his wolfs eyes in the dark. When he got close again, this time his hand reached out, brushing against my body. Lust shot through me, anticipating the moment he catches me. But I couldn't wait anymore. I was so turned on my footing was getting sloppy, heels wobbling as I ran my best with them still strapped to my feet. I slowed before I came to a stop. Turning around, eyes as black as the night, I let him see my arousal, let him smell the thick scent in the air. He stopped a distance away from me. Eyes like midnight, he watched and waited. His chest rose and fell with each breath. We were both panting, both purring just waiting for one of us to move to snap that thin thread of tension between us.

"Come on, Cairo. I thought you were going to bend me over...I thought you were going to mark me..." I said breathy, coaxing his wolf to stalk me and take his prey. He smirked, accepting the challenge as he stepped forward. Then he stopped, black eyes instantly widening as they shifted back to hazel. Fear etched across his face as he looked behind me.

"ZIA, LOOK OUT!" He screamed.

My body was suddenly thrown forward, weight crushing me as a feral growl tore through the air. I twisted my body, kicking my legs out and throwing the red eyed rogue above me off. He flew through the air, body thrashing around as he landed. He growled, spittle flying, paw dragging back, scrapping through the ground as he launched into the air again. I didn't have time to react. Cairo's painful howl tore through the air and the smell of iron quickly followed. Blood was seeping into the earth as two wolves fought savagely behind me. When everything went still, I feared the worst. I turned, finding a now naked, shifted rogue lying still on the ground as he bled out. *Lane* laid in front of him. Hand clamped against her neck as blood coated her hand. As her eyes widen before she fell back, body crashing against the ground. *Lane? She saved me?* I crawled to her, replacing my hands with hers as she watched me, face paling by the second. *Why isn't the blood slowing?* Something was wrong, we had to get her help now. But I couldn't lift her by myself, I needed to keep my hand on her neck keeping the blood flow at bay. Looking back to Cairo, fear had taken over. He was on his knees, staring at the ground as his eyes teared up, fat tears falling to the ground.

"Cairo!" I yelled trying to get his attention but I wasn't

getting through. “Cairo! Snap out of it! I need your help!” I screamed. His head suddenly snapped up, a tear streaking down his face as he gasped.

“I..I thought you were dead.”

“I’m hard to kill. Cairo, I need help, it’s Lane!” I said gesturing down at her. The blood was still seeping out, she was panicking making her heart pump harder, blood rushing out faster. She needed to calm down or else this wound could be fatal. I closed my eyes, pulling in my strength and power before releasing it, letting the power flow through my hands into her body. She went limp just as Cairo scooped her up. He stopped, fearing the worst.

“She’s okay, she wouldn’t calm down. I needed the bleeding to slow so I.. put her to sleep. But she won’t last much longer if we don’t get her to the pack infirmary.” He nodded, not saying a word as he turned, taking off towards it.

“What happened?” He asked confused how he could have missed her.

“I..I’m not quite sure. She came out of nowhere taking him to the ground. Her wolf was fighting him in her human form. That’s when she screamed as they both wounded each other. It wasn’t me you heard. But...Cairo, what about the rogue? He’s still there.” I say worried he might come after us.

“I heard him take off. Don’t worry, I linked the closest trackers. They’ll get him.” He said determined.

We didn’t speak again as we picked up the pace. I haven’t felt fear like that in a long time. As soon as I saw those red rabid eyes of the rogue everything stopped. I could still hear Cairo’s scream as he thought I was the one who got hurt. I never wanted to hear such fear in his voice again. Never wanted to see him on his knees defeated. Lane had come out of nowhere and jumped in front of me right as the rogue was inches from me. She tackled his body, bringing him to the ground as his jaw snapped at her neck. She screamed and growled, claws descending from her nails as she fought back.

The fight ended as both warrior and wolf fell to the ground, wounded and bleeding. I should have gotten up and helped, should have done something, anything to help. I should have reacted faster. I just hope we weren't too late in saving her.

I paced the hospital hall while Lane was in surgery. Cairo had to go speak to his father and help with the rogue situation. I looked down at my hands, there was so much blood. My dress was stained red. I couldn't stop seeing the blood on my hands well after washing them. Everytime I paced past the bathroom I ducked in to wash them again. My fingers were raw from scrubbing but nothing worked. I couldn't stop thinking this was all my fault. If only I had been prepared to fight, if only I wasn't scared, wasn't so blissfully unaware of my surroundings. She wouldn't be in surgery right now. *Everything is always because of me.* This is why we don't celebrate our birthdays. We're cursed. I'm cursed. Everyone I love, everyone I care about always gets hurt. Anywhere I go, chaos and death follow. I need to leave. I have too many people here I care about, too many people I could get killed.

I tracked down a nurse, asking for any updates on Lane. Her surgery had just finished and she was taken to a room to recover. She explained the wounds could have been fatal if we hadn't brought her in when we did. Then she led me to her room before the nurse left. She said someone will let us know how everything went in the morning. I stood there for I don't know how long, watching her chest rise and fall. Her neck was wrapped in bandages, her hands were also taped from cuts. She had an oxygen mask on and heart monitor clip on her finger. It was a comforting sound hearing the regular beeps from the machine. She saved my life when I thought she hated me. Why would she do that? I'm not worth saving. It was just one thing after another. Death surrounds me wherever I go and so does *He*.

Vladik.

My own personal demon and grim reaper all wrapped up into one sadistic bundle. He never leaves. He's there when I close my eyes and he's there when I dream. I can never get away from him. Because what I feared is true.

I will always be his.

Chapter Twenty-Seven

Inner Thoughts

Alek

It pained me this morning when I pulled Keiran aside and watched his face drop as I explained why I couldn't mark him. Tears instantly welled in his eyes although he tried to hide them. He asked if I was rejecting him with a crack in his voice that nearly killed me. I took his hand, reaffirming that he was my mate. I just couldn't mark him until Zia was ready to take that step with Cairo. She's had a rough, hard life and I didn't want to make that harder by shoving my love and happiness in her face. How I couldn't be happier with my sweet mate. Once I broke it down, he understood, seeing reason within my request to wait. But that didn't mean I had to wait on other things. Everyone saw her panic attack this morning, everyone saw her fear. It reaffirmed why I had to wait for her to be ready to take the next step with her mate before I could with mine. That's why I had to talk to him before any more time went by and questions went unanswered. I took his face in mine, telling him how gorgeous he was, how I love the way he laughs, the way he smiles, the way he always gets nervous around me. I leaned down ever so slightly as he stood a little shorter than me and kissed him. Slow and sensual, this kiss meant everything. His hands were on my waist, holding me still. I almost whined when I pulled back, seeing his parted lips calling for more. He was so shy, telling me that was his first kiss. I smiled, tucking a strand of hair behind his ear. I loved looking into his blue-grey eyes. There was a softness to them that could calm me instantly. Taking his hand, we walked all the way to school in silence. Every time I looked at him he was smiling harder and brighter than I've ever seen. We didn't need to speak; I could feel whispers of his emotions through our hands. If I wanted to, I could push into his mind and read his thoughts. It was a power of mine that nobody knew I had. I never told anyone, not even Zia. Although I had a feeling she knew.

Everything was great until we walked past the student desk where Zia and I picked up our class schedule. The same lady I spoke to on the phone the day we enrolled called out to me, saying hello, and wishing me a happy birthday. It felt like I was hit in the face. I repelled back as she said it, frowning before I turned, walking away. I could hear Keiran, Zack and Cairo behind me, whispering and speaking their confusion. Our birthday wasn't a happy day for us. Just the mention of our birthday and I went cold and numb, feeling that sickly feeling shoot down to my toes. I could feel sweat forming on my forehead. Once I turned a corner out of view from the guys, I took off. Running straight to the nearest bathroom, I slammed open the door, quickly running into a stall. I didn't have time to lock it behind me before bile rose up. I hung my head, throwing up everything I ate for breakfast as my body shook. This day was always so painful for me.

It was the day I really failed my sister.

The day the Alpha died, the first day that changed Zia's life forever. Just a week later I was carrying Zia's unconscious body as I ran away from everyone we ever loved. I could smell the memory of her blood the second I heard the words Happy Birthday.

By the time I washed my face and mouth and left the bathroom, our first class had begun. Everyone was already seated; the teacher had just arrived and began teaching. I walked in, ignoring the guy's eyes as they watched me walk to my seat. I couldn't even look at Keiran when I sat down, staring ahead at the teacher. My eyes flicked down to my hand, seeing the colour still drained from my skin. I knew they could see how off I looked. Thankfully nobody said a word. Zack looked at me curiously the whole class, Cairo looked back and forth from the teacher to me, frowning as he spaced out. You could read the guy like a book when he wasn't focused. He was usually so stoic, rarely laughing or smiling unless Zia was involved. Today he was plagued by his thoughts, questions swirling around his face. I felt bad for Keiran. He thought he was being quiet but I could hear his wolf softly whimpering. I couldn't bare it anymore so I reached back, grabbing his hand, and taking it in mine. He gasped from the coldness of my hand. My naturally hot body temperature was shot. But feeling those sparks in my hand, feeling our bond, my colour soon came back. My stomach stopped turning and the headache went away. It felt like I could breathe again.

The rest of the day went fine without a hitch. It was a little quiet during lunch time, no one wanting to say anything since my little incident this morning. Soon school was finished for the day and we were home, getting ready to go out. The guys were excited, not having gone out in a while. Apparently they had a pack club that the high school students used when they needed to relax. I could use the distraction. I told Keiran he could go ahead with everyone else; I was going to wait for Zia and then we'd come together. I chose a fitted tee that apparently matched Zia's light pink dress. I thought it was an off white or salmon colour but the club lights made it look pinker than it was. But it distracted us, got us out of our funk.

Keiran asked me to dance, face red as a tomato while he could barely keep eye contact. It made my heart flip, loving the shyness. I followed him to the dance floor but grabbed his hand and pulled him off to the side. I wanted a little corner of privacy, plus the music wasn't so loud there. I could tell he was still nervous, his body was tight and rigid, eyes looking anywhere but mine. I leaned in, taking his face in my hands as I looked into his eyes. He was perfect, everything about him was perfect. The way the long strands of hair twist and curl at the ends, his golden honey skin tone, and of course the matching honey-coloured hair. The long lashes that fan over his blue-grey eyes, the slight blush that stays on his cheeks, the way he looks up at me with puppy dog eyes. I love everything about him. He was made for me, exactly how I always pictured my mate to look like. It's crazy that I dreamed about him before I even met him. Though with a few slight differences, he was who I envisioned. I just couldn't believe I found him.

I closed the gap between us. Again, his lips tasted sweet, his moans making it even sweeter. His hands gripped my shirt, pulling me closer and he couldn't get enough. His golden hair felt like silk between my fingers, almost like water melting through. I opened my mouth, inviting him to deepen our kiss. He obliged, opening his mouth ever so slightly but that was enough for my tongue to weave its way through. He moaned, knees buckling at the sudden move. I tightened my grip on his head as my other hand dropped down to grab his waist, holding him up. He really was going weak at the knees from our kiss. I don't know how long we stayed like that. Mere minutes maybe but I knew I had to stop soon. I was painfully hard and so was he. I could feel him against me, slowly grinding against me as we got lost in our kiss. I had to pull back. This wasn't the place or the time. *Unfortunately*.

"Fuck, Keiran. Do you know how hard you make me?" I ask, panting as I lean my forehead against his.

"I..I have some idea." He joked, voice low and breathy.

"You are so addicting. You're making it really hard not to mark you." I say, staring into his lustful pitch-black eyes. "Are you doing that on purpose?" I say leaning in as my hand rests on the wall beside his head. I could see my own black eyes reflected in his.

"N..no. I'm sorry.." He said shyly as he looked down at the ground. I placed my finger under his chin, slowly lifting his head up so he could look back into my eyes.

"Never apologise. This face and this heart can never do any wrong. I don't want you apologizing for loving your mate. Your very handsome, very sexy mate." I said making him laugh.

"You are very handsome and very, very sexy." He said gaining some confidence.

"Don't stroke my ego, baby. It won't end well." I tease making him smirk. I kiss him again, wanting one more quick kiss before I pull back. "Dance with me." I say. He nods, raising his hands up to start dancing along to the rhythm of the beat but I have other ideas. I grab his hands, guiding them to my shoulders as he looks at me confused. I place mine on his hips, guiding him to sway left and right. I can see the moment it clicks; the moment he understands I want to slow dance. He blushes again, smiling as we stare into each other's eyes and dance slowly to the fast-paced music.

"You know this isn't exactly club dancing." He says amused.

"I know. I'm just getting some practice in before this ball on the weekend. But if it's club dancing you want...then we can club dance."

I spin him around, hands sliding down from his waist to his hips. He babbles out, trying and failing to ask what's happening. I chuckle, pulling him back into me and begin to sway my hips side to side, letting the music move me. The music almost muffles another moan but I heard it. We dance like this for a bit, his hands resting against mine, our fingers entwined as his back sways against my chest. My mouth flies open as he drops down, turning his head and looks back at me with a hot sultry look as he makes his way back up slowly. It was the sexiest thing I've ever seen. Especially coming from a man who's constantly shy, blushing and fumbling his words.

"How was that?" He turns, watching as I bite my lip. I bite down hard, drawing blood. I need to distract myself fast or else my itchy hands are going to move on their own. My wolf purrs, sending the forced vibration through my chest so his mate could hear it.

"That was-" I begin to say as his eyes glaze over. I stop, someone was mindlinking him. I watched, waiting for him to come back when he gasps, fear etched across his face. At that very moment everyone in the club goes silent. All panicking, some even running out the door scared like a shooter just entered the place and started firing. I didn't get time to ask until I felt it. Zia's fear shot through me like a white-hot rod.

"There's been a rogue attack!" Keiran yells out at the same time I do.

"Zia!" I don't think I just run. The last thing I hear before I slam the door open and jump into the air shifting as I go was Keiran calling for me.

"Alek!" It pains me but I can't think about him right now. I need to make sure Zia's okay.

I run as fast as my wolfs paws can take me. I skid to a stop, sticks and dirt flying up as we sniff the ground, smelling fresh blood. Three scents take off ahead, one went to the right. There's only one scent I care about and that's the one I follow. We take off, running ahead as wolves howl into the night. I don't focus on the calls, only focus on getting to Zia as fast as I can. Her scent leads me to a massive one level building. The pack infirmary. I shift, seconds before reaching the glass doors. I slam into them, losing balance as I shift from wolf to man without stopping. I brace myself against the glass, using it to slow me down and steady me. Her scent is stronger here. My heart begins to beat painfully, I turn left, running past a nurse as she screams at me.

Finally, I see her.

And she's covered in blood.

"ZIA!" The panic is evident in my voice. I race to her, spinning her around as I take her in. The heels she was wearing earlier are now gone. She has scrapes on her legs, the bottom of her dress is ripped and covered in blood and dirt. She has faded healing bruises on her arms and some leaves still in her hair. When she looked up at me her lip trembled, sadness and defeat overcoming her. I could hear her whisper my name sadly through our mindlink.

Shit.

Her voice sounded broken as she said my name. I don't know what exactly happened tonight but I felt it. I felt her fear, her panic, her sadness. Every minuscule feeling she had, I felt. Our bond is different from other sibling and family bonds. We are able to feel each other's emotions just like mates can. Pairing that with my gift to enter her mind, I can always hear everything she thinks. I could read any wolfs mind, just like they're mates could with a single touch. It came in handy on days when Zia was silent, never saying a word, never even moving. But I never had to touch Zia to be able to hear and feel her thoughts. Our twin bond and my gift make it easier for me to hear her. No matter where she is in the world, I'll always be able to hear her. Unlike mates who need to be a certain distance to hear their mates, I don't have those restrictions.

I pull her into me, taking the lone leaf from her hair. She was crying a river into my chest. Tears staining and dampening my chest as she cried and cried. Her thoughts were so loud it sounded like she was screaming them at me. And what I heard broke my heart. She thought all of this was her fault. She still thinks what happened to her and us in the past was her fault. But it wasn't. It was *his* fault. His sick obsession with her that ruined any chance of happiness for her. As long as he lives, he will always be inside her head. Whispering words of hate and fear into her sweet delicate mind. I know she puts up a strong front sometimes but I always feel her hidden emotions behind her tough façade, which makes me frown. And when Cairo marks her, he'll be able to feel it too. I don't think she even realizes she feels them. But I know in my heart that all she needs is Cairo. She needs to fully let him in. He's grown so much in just the short amount of time that we've known him. He went from hating us because we were rogues, to falling hopelessly in love with Zia. I know because he looks at her the same way I look at Keiran. Who, I haven't marked yet in fear that if I did, Zia would feel pressured into letting Cairo mark her when she's not ready. I don't ever want her to feel pressured from anyone again, especially me. I'm her big brother, her twin, her other half. Keiran is the best mate I could have asked for. He's understanding of what I want. Of how I feel. He told me he'd wait a lifetime for me to mark him if that is what I desired. I nearly marked him right then and there from the amount of truth and love I saw in his eyes.

But right now, I need to focus on Zia. Because I can hear her thoughts and I don't like where they're headed.

"Have you seen Cairo?" She finally spoke. She pulled back, looking exhausted as she whipped tears from her face.

"I'm sure he's gone after the rogue. It's where Keiran would have gone. If he wasn't then he would be here with you." I said reassuring her. "Come on, I can feel how tired you are. Let's get you to bed." I said but the second I finished speaking her whole body went rigid. She was no longer sad, no longer defeated. She crossed her arms against her chest, straightening her back as she spoke.

"I'm not going anywhere." I could feel the power in that

statement. Could see the luna she would one day become. "I want to stay with Lane." She said as her exterior broke. She turned, facing the large window behind her. Looking into the room, I saw this Lane person asleep on the bed. She must be important to Zia if she wants to stay.

"Okay, let me know if you need me."

"I'll always need you, *brat*." She says holding her hand to her chest. "But right now, I need to be here for her."

"You know it wasn't your fault, Zi." I said trying to calm her thoughts. She kept repeating guilty over and over again.

"It was, Alek!" She snapped making me jump, surprised. "That rogue came straight for me. I'm the one that froze, the one that didn't act quick enough. If I hadn't, then she never would have dived in front of me. She wouldn't be laying in that fucking hospital bed right now if it wasn't for me!" She was angry and hurt. Feeling like the world is always out to get her.

"Okay, you froze. But it's not only your fault." I say giving her some of the blame she's clinging too. "You didn't tell that rogue to cross pack lines and you didn't tell that rogue to attack you. Did you?" I ask the unnecessary question.

"No, I didn't." She said sighing.

"Then there you go. Not your fault. Sometimes these things just happen. Rogues like that just enjoy the thrill of entering pack territory and attacking. They love their games, remember. You were probably the first pack member they saw and unfortunately targeted you."

"You can go now." She says making me laugh. I was making sense.

"Very well." I lean forward, kissing her on the head before saying goodnight. I think I should find Keiran, make sure he's okay too and see if they need any help.

Chapter Twenty-Eight

Mates?

ZIA

Once Alek left, I opened the door to Lanes room and closed it quietly behind me. No one had come for her yet so I don't know if she has any family here. A lot of times pack members are orphans because their parents die in battle or rogue attacks. I sit down by the window, watching her as I grew tired. Soon enough, the adrenaline had completely burned from my system and sleep had taken over.

I woke with a fright. Opening my eyes this morning, I wasn't expecting to see a face right before me. It was a woman. She had short, shoulder length layered brown hair, a nose piercing, and large sunglasses that kind of reminded me of snow goggles. There was something familiar about her but I couldn't put my finger on it.

"Hii," she said happily. "You come here often?" She said

blanky waiting for me to reply. I heard laughter from the bed, noticing Lane was awake and sitting up watching us.

"Leave her alone, now, Sadie. Go annoy someone else." Lane spoke as she squinted her eyes at the woman beside me.

"Is that an invitation?" Sadie said huskily before she winked and bit her lip. Lane laughed before she groaned in pain, wrapping her arms around her body. I'm just gonna sit here and pretend to know what the hell is happening right now. *Oh, are they mates?*

"Zia, meet Sadie." Suddenly it clicked why she looked familiar.

"Oh, you were singing last night at the club." I remembered seeing those same glasses on the singer. "Why do you look so familiar though?" I ask more to myself because I still have that nagging feeling like I've seen her before last night.

"Lan," She says blanky, "She just said I looked familiar. Me, familiar." Sadie said pointing to her face. Lane again burst out laughing, finding something funny. Sadie faced me, removing her glasses as she raised a brow at me.

"Do I look familiar now, lune?" She asked. Then it clicked.

"You're Sadie K!" When Alek and I stayed with Maya, she was obsessed with this up-and-coming American wolf singer. She was blowing up and selling out arenas. I had no idea she came from this pack. I've never seen her around before last night.

"You're the biggest popstar in the world right now. Maya is going to die when she finds out you're from here."

"You flatter me, lune." Sadie said smirking now that I recognise her.

"Why do you keep calling me that?" Did she think my name was something else?

"What lune?" I nod. "You're going to be Luna one day, silly." *Oh, lune short for Luna. Got it.*

"So, Laney has told me a lot about you. Mostly good things." *Don't know if I believe that.*

"Sorry, I just have to ask, are you guys' mates?" I ask innocently as they both break out in laughter.

"Hell no!" Sadie said repulsed. "Gross being mated to *that.*" She said as Lane let out a playful warning growl. "Her mate is-"

"WHERE IS SHE?!" A voice boomed down the hospital corridor.

"-coming, apparently." Sadie said. Suddenly the door flew open, slamming into the wall making a doorknob sized hole. Her mate stormed straight to her, looking royally pissed as he reached down, picking her up from the bed and slamming his mouth against hers. Lane was a few years older than the rest of us which is why I never saw her at school.

"Oh my," I said starting to feel like I was intruding.

After a couple of seconds kissing, her mate reached down and grabbed the backs of her legs, hoisting her up into the air, wrapping her legs around his waist. He was shirtless, looking like he had just shifted before he came barging in. They were getting incredibly heated to the point where I started to think they weren't going to stop anytime soon. His hands slid from the backs of her thighs down to her ass. He grabbed her roughly, making her moan. I felt my face heat up. The need to mark Cairo was strangely growing. *I have to get out of here.*

I ran to the door, Sadie following as she closed it behind her.

"You would not believe how often that happens." She said exasperated. "Well, they're gonna be busy for a while so I'm gonna go and get something to eat. Bye!" She said before she briskly walked off.

I stepped forward, peering into the window. Lane's mate lowered her to the bed as he stood back up, unbuttoning his pants before he stripped them off. *They're not really going to fuck in the hospital are they?* I was so preoccupied watching them that I didn't hear Cairo come up behind me until he spoke.

"There you are." I jumped, face burning bright red as I spun around to face him.

"I wasn't" I rushed out guiltily. He looked confused, bare chested with blood sprayed across his chest.

"What were you looking at?" He asked curious.

"Nothing!" No way was I going to tell him I was about to watch Lane and her mate, well, *mate.* But then she moaned. Making me scream inwardly from embarrassment. Cairo smirked, now knowing exactly what was happening in that room. My face couldn't have been more red. I had no words. Nothing. All I could do was smile and pretend nothing R rated was happening right now.

"Were you watching them?" He teased.

"Would you believe me if I said no?" I ask wishfully thinking. He laughed; a deep belly laugh that made my insides tingle.

"Let's go back home, shower and change. Then we can come right back. They should be done by then." I nod, wanting to get out of these dirty clothes.

It took half an hour before we were walking back into the hospital heading for Lanes room. Cairo was right, they were done as we walked through the door. Seeing Lane and her mate now dressed.

"You done?" Cairo asked the second they looked at us.

"Hey, you know how it is. Can't keep your hands off em'." Lane's mate said as he pulled her into his side making her roll her eyes as she giggled.

"They haven't marked each other yet." She said elbowing him in the ribs making him grunt. "And they don't smell like each other." She whispered but obviously we heard. Cairo shifted uncomfortably beside me, audibly swallowing as I smiled awkwardly. We both breathed a sigh of relief when there was a knock at the door. A pink haired nurse appeared, wearing a stethoscope, navy scrubs and white tennis shoes.

"Oh good, you're still here." She said to Lane and her mate. "This saves me the trouble of having to repeat myself. Cairo, please make sure to relay this information to the Alpha. He has asked for updates." He nodded, crossing his arms across his chest ready to listen.

"Why wasn't Lane healing last night?" He asked getting straight to the point.

"Well, that's a complicated question. The rogue that attacked Lane had enhanced claws." All three of them looked confused. But I knew what she meant.

"I have heard of rogues willingly pulling out their claw nails and replacing them with silver claws." The nurse said. All three of them reacted the way I knew they would. They were confused, repulsed, angry. Not comprehending why any wolf would willing do something so barbaric. "It's not well known or practiced, but it seems in recent years it has become a thing some of the more savage rogues are doing. I take it from your face, Miss Zia, that you know what I'm talking about."

"Yes.." It's a big practice with the rogues in Russia. The winters are colder, packs are harsher from their more traditional ways, food becomes scarcer as the animals hibernate. Competition gets fierce so rogues need to be fiercer. Doesn't mean they don't enjoy using them.

"What happened to the rogue? Did he get away?" Lane asked, breaking the silence.

"Oh, he ran. But not far enough. You got him good, baby. He had to stop and rest to heal from his wounds." Lane's mate said, praising her.

"We got there just before he finished healing. So, we brought him in for questioning." Was all Cairo said. That's why he was covered in blood this morning. He was in that room. That room Alek and I could have easily ended up in if he had only crossed their pack instead of skirting town. I don't know if I would have had the strength to last if my mate had to torture me. Would that old Cairo continue hurting me knowing I was his mate? Or would the rogue factor be too great for him to stop?

"What did you find out?" Lane asked, distracting me from toeing the rabbit hole. A deep rattle sounded from Cairo's chest making me jump. I looked up at him, orange eyes staring at the wall at the back of the room. I didn't have to be mated to feel the anger rolling off him in waves. He was practically vibrating. Then he growled, unable to speak words. I was starting to feel uneasy.

"The rogue was hired to track and kill Zia." *Me?! What?!*

"Do we know who hired him?" Lane asked, making the scar across the bridge of her nose and up between her brows redden.

"No, he didn't see their face." Her mate said making a shiver run down my spine. Someone's put a hit out on me. *Someone wants me dead.*

"Do you believe me now, Zia." Lane said giving me a pointed look. I know exactly what she's talking about. She was right all along. My past is somehow connected to this rogue attack. It has to be. I don't think I've made any enemies here besides Jordan, but she wouldn't go this far would she? She wouldn't do this to Cairo. Damn her dreams to be this packs Luna. I don't believe for a second she could hurt Cairo like that. But this attack, if babushka's warning was anything to go by then my time is running out. I need to come clean to Cairo and soon before more of my..my pack members get hurt.

I need to tell him today.

"If that's all, I'd like to go home." Lane said looking back at the nurse.

"Actually, before you go. Lane, Nile, there's one more thing I need to speak to you about." She spoke with a note of concern.

"What is it?" Lane asked as her mate, Nile, began to look worried.

"Well, as you know we took some bloods this morning to

make sure all the silver was out of your system." The nurse said as Lane nodded. "Well, we found elevated hCG levels in your blood. A higher count than last night's tests."

"What does that mean?" Nile asked making the nurse giggle.

"You're pregnant, Lane. Very early which the hCG levels indicate, but it is confirmed. You two should start to smell the change in Lane's scent soon as well and after that, you'll be able to pick up the little heartbeat." Cairo, Lane, and Nile all gasped as my blood ran cold.

I breathed in and out.

In and out.

In and out.

"Sorry, I'm being paged. Congratulations you two." The nurse said before she was off, racing to the door and out in a split second.

"That's what you get for mating like rabbits." Cairo joked, making Lane look proud. Nile looked pale, then his eyes rolled in the back of his head sending his body crashing down to the floor.

"GET OFF THE FLOOR, NILE!" Lane snapped as Cairo laughed.

In and out.

In and out.

I couldn't do this...*I can't do this.*

"I'm so sorry, Lane. I put you and your pup in danger. This is all my fault."

CAIRO

"Zia!" I called out to her before I even realized she ran. "Sorry, I have to go after her. But congrats, this is great news." I wish I could have been happier saying that but I couldn't stop the worry from taking over.

Zia sounded...different. Like she truly believed this was her fault. How could any of this be her fault? One thing I know about Zia is that she is innocent. I don't know what happened in the twins past but the more days that go by, the more I realise it wasn't their fault. It couldn't be.

It took me a while to find her. She ran quick and the wind was strong today. It blew her scent around me everywhere I went, tricking my nose. Eventually as the winds shifted, I caught her scent. The trail grew strong as it led me to the back of the pack where our lands meet neutral land. There's a massive lake there, pebbled sand and planted palm fronds. It was the closest thing we had to a beach. During the colder seasons a mist rolls out across the water, hiding the land across, giving it the appearance of the sea. She was looking out across the water, sun setting, colouring the sky an array of orange and yellows. But as I looked closer, that red hue was back. I knew it the moment that Priestess *Glinda*, spoke about the curse. That cursed red hue followed Zia wherever she went. The signs were there. I would have seen it sooner but I wouldn't know what a curse would look like if it wasn't for the Priestess.

"Baby?" I said softly approaching her. She was watching the sun go down. It wasn't until I stopped behind her that I could smell the salt from her falling tears. I could hear her faint sniffles that she tried to hide. Nothing hurts more than hearing your mate cry. We're not even mated and my heart already feels like it has a fist clenched around it, squeezing tightly. I don't know what made her cry but what I do know is that I will do everything in my power to make her happy.

"Baby?" I try again. "Look at me...Please." She turns, her eyes red from crying, making the aqua blue stand out against the red. They were like glowing sad puppy dog eyes. *Shit.* Her eyes were ten times brighter. The whites of her eyes were bloodshot, more tears threatening to fall as they brimmed the edges just waiting for me to say something wrong. Her lip trembled slightly as her emotions clouded the air. Her emotions were almost screaming at me and if we were mated I would probably be on my knees from them. I *want* to feel her emotions, hear her thoughts. I want to know how I can help her.

I sigh. All I can do right now is try and distract her from her thoughts.

"For someone so little, you sure do run fast. Them little legs..phew, got some speed to them." I said feel fucking stupid but it worked. She laughed; the escaping tears that threatened to fall, fell from the big belly laugh.

"That," she sniffed, "was the lamest," she hiccupped, "joke I've ever heard." I laughed feeling accomplished. Her furrowed brow smoothened and her breathing slowly became even again. She gave me a small smile.

"There she is. Come on, you can give me a bigger smile than that." She breathed in and smiled as she exhaled, shaking her head.

"I'm sorry for running. It's just, Lane was so close to losing her pup because of me. Everything is always my fault." She finished as she whispered.

"Hey, don't say that. This wasn't you fault. He..he came after you. You didn't tell him to do that did you?"

"You sound like Alek." She said rolling her eyes making me laugh.

"Then I must be right." I joked making her roll her eyes again before laughing. "Will you come with me? I want to take you somewhere."

"Wait. I..I want to tell you about my past." She says but I stop her.

"No."

"What? B..but you want to know.." She says confused, head tilting like a puppy.

"I do want to know. But not today. Not when you feel forced and feel like you have to because of what happened to Lane. I want you to tell me when you *feel* ready, when you don't feel like your heart is going to burst and your full of cold sweats. Now come on, someone is expecting us." I say grabbing her hand pulling her along with me.

"Where are we going?" She asks, skipping her steps to keep up with my quick strides.

"Why, to the pack tattoo studio. Can't have you being the only one with tattoos. I gotta up my sexy game." I laugh as her eyes go black and a blush creeps up her neck. "Cute."

Chapter Twenty-Nine

Troubles

Jordan

"What are you doing?"

"What does it look like I'm doing, Bethany!? I'm dying my hair back!" I say to my dim-witted friend who apparently can't see the stupid hair dye in my hair. "I want my beautiful honey blonde hair back. Not that disgusting silver grandma toned hair."

"Why did you dye it in the first place? I...if you didn't like it." Did she miss the fucking memo?

"Why do you think? So, Cairo could notice me again instead of that flea ridden bitch." I clenched my fists, hating that bimbo bitch for ruining my life.

"What are you going to do now?" She asked timidly. She always annoyed me having no backbone, but it helped when I needed her to do things for me.

"I don't know. Maybe get sexier clothes?" I ask more than tell. I'm running out of options here. I already tried coming into his room in the morning but she had already moved in, digging her claws into him. I only have a short time left before he marks her and my chance is gone. I sigh, feeling that tension headache coming back. "Anyways, I have to pick up my ball dresses tomorrow so, I'll get new clothes then. Now come and wash this dye out of my hair." I snap. I need to get back to my normal self so I can lure him back to me. And if he won't reject her, then I'll just have to make her reject him. Then he'll come back to me.

Chapter Thirty

History

ZIA

That familiar buzzing sound that reminded me of another time filled the room. I couldn't deny Cairo looked hot as hell sitting in the black leather chair, shirt off, muscles and abs on display as he got his arm tattooed. His shoulder to elbow sleeve was coming along nicely. It was a complex pattern that he said was his grandfather's Egyptian tribal tattoo. It was like the intricate pattern crisscrossed and wrapped around his arm until ending just below the elbow. A large scarab beetle on the outside of his shoulder, as if the tribal designs came from and flowed around it. It was beautiful. I spent hours watching him get tattooed and listened as he spoke. He told me the origins of this pack and how his family became the Alpha Family. His Grandfather, Alpha Zosar's father was born in Cairo. There weren't many werewolves who lived in Egypt, so their pack was small. As the years went on, his grandfather noticed they were getting sick and their powers were weakening. So, he made the decision to move to America. Most of the pack followed. They settled down here in this neutral territory, turning it into the pack I see today. Once they settled down, they began to get stronger, healthier again. More women were getting pregnant, more babies were being born and more people were joining the pack. Their wolves needed Earth beneath their feet. They needed soil, water, land to run through. They needed a terrain that a wolf could survive and thrive in. That beach as Cairo called it, that he found me at this afternoon, the sand that I stood on wasn't always there. His grandfather and wolves from Egypt missed the sand beneath their paws. So, he bought tons and tons of sand, dumping it all along the massive lake. Which explains why it felt like a beach but wasn't. Then when Alpha Zosar turned twenty-one, he took over. He expanded the pack lands, accepted more people into the pack and grew it into the hundreds. He became a strong, loyal alpha. He signed treaties with our neighbouring packs, gave support and warriors when they needed.

Now this pack is one of the strongest and largest today. There were over four hundred pack members. He said I will see most of them at the ball. Then I asked just where the ball was being held and he said there was another building on the pack that I haven't seen yet. His grandfather when he and his pack first arrived here, they built a big stone like palace building where everyone lived together. It wasn't until Alpha Zosar became alpha that he started building separate housing for the mated couples, a building for everyone to eat in, to train in, a pack house for the Alpha Family and their betas, delta's and so on. As the years went on, an orphanage was built. In the beginning the rogues were relentless. They were attacking the pack like they were a flock of sheep. But with the treaties made and Alpha Zosar training his warriors to his standards, this pack became strong. It was fascinating learning all about the history of this pack.

"Alright, you're all done." The artist said, wiping the excess ink off Cairo's arm. He stood up, walking to the large mirror on the wall to inspect his new tattoo. He smiled, nodded his head to the artist and walked out. I followed seeing him wait for me.

"What do you think?" He said proudly. *I think I want to rip the rest of your clothes off,* I don't say. I think my pitch-black aroused eyes were enough for him to read my mind. I find myself biting my lips as my eyes trail down his chest, hands burning from the need to reach out and touch.

"That's how you feel, huh..." Cairo said, black eyes mimicking mine. He stepped forward, my breath hitching in my throat as he reached out, finger tucking under my chin as he lifted my head up to look at him. "Why don't we take this back home?" He said, breath fanning against my face.

"Mmm," Was all I could say. The electric feeling from his small touch was making my body go haywire. Then I purred, my wolf also wanting to show her happiness. He laughed, licking his lips as his eyes drop down, focussing on my lips.

"The pull towards you is getting harder and harder to resist. But I must." He said, sighing as he stepped back. I breathed in his scent, exhaling as I held in a whine. I didn't want him to stop touching me.

"I don't think you've ever told me how you got your tattoo?" He asked changing the subject.

"Oh, uh, this man he protected us from his pack. He found us on his morning run. Owned a tattoo shop and gave us free tattoos." I said shortening the story.

"Just like that?!" He said incredulously.

"Well kinda. When we met him, Alek and I could feel his soul was hurting. It almost felt like it was screaming at us to help. When we got to his shop we saw a photo of him and his mate. He saw us looking at it and told us she had died the year before. That was when we really understood what the Goddess meant for us. Why she gave us these powers and what our job in this world was. He was the first official person we ever sent to the moon. When he came back, he had this bright glow around him. A light was back in his eyes and his soul wasn't hurting anymore. It was healed." I said smiling as I remember the feeling when he woke up. The whole atmosphere changed.

"Wow, that sounds amazing." Cairo said smiling.

"After that he couldn't thank us enough. He wanted to repay us but we really had no need for money or anything like that. And being teenagers with access to tattoos well, we didn't give up that opportunity." I said, laughing to myself remembering the way the guy burst out laughing saying he knew we were going to say that.

"D..don't take this the wrong way, but I didn't think pack wolves tolerated rogues." Cairo said quietly, afraid to even mention the R word.

"They don't. He was just different. He could tell we weren't like other rogues. That and we were just kids. What harm could we really do?" He gave a tight smile, looking away before he cleared his throat.

"We should get going. It's late and we missed dinner. I'll make us something to eat." I nod, taking his hand in mine as we headed back to the pack.

Cairo tried to hide the gasp he made when I grabbed his hand, shocking him from my sudden movement. I looked up at him, he turned his head, trying to hide the blush painted across his face. Even in the dark I could see it. I laughed, finding his embarrassment cute. I looked ahead, smiling as I enjoy this moment. Though his hand was way larger than mine, it felt weirdly perfect. Like they were made for each other, moulded to fit into each other's hands. I really couldn't be happier right now. The smile on my face was so wide my cheeks were burning. But this is one pain I will always savour.

Chapter Thirty-One

The Plan

Unknown

I had to wait until everyone was asleep before I could go to this secret meeting. Choosing somewhere in the neutral zone so no one could overhear us. This was treason in its finest. We would be killed if anyone were to find out. I was meeting my partner, the man who was helping me with this insidious plan. He was already there, waiting in the spot we've met once before.

"What the fuck!" I said as I stopped in front of him. "She was supposed to die! Not get saved!" I said, feeling the anger I've managed to hide all day rise.

"Lane wasn't supposed to be there! It's not my fault." He growled out, just as annoyed that our problem wasn't solved already.

"It is your fault! That single rogue was supposed to be

multiple rogues. What the fuck happened there?" If he had just followed the plan we agreed on, everything would have gone smoothly. "You were supposed to give them the silver claws."

"First of all, fuck you. Do you know how hard it is to not only sneak away, but to find a fucking rogue? I had to wait during school hours so that I could run to the next city over looking for the fucking mongrels. Even then I only found one. And yes, I gave him the claws. He was more than happy to do the job and get paid extra for it."

"Well apparently you didn't pay him enough. He was supposed to kill her."

"That was out of my control, -"

"Don't say my fucking name you idiot. We had rules we agreed on. We don't say our names out here, we cover ourselves up and mask our scents."

"Stop being a bitch, it was his fault he wasn't feral enough."

"How fucking hard is it to kill one small rogue bitch!" I growled. This plan was supposed to be so easy. Now it's gotten complicated.

"You do it then! You're the one that wants her dead so badly." I scoff, glaring at him.

"I'm not the only one that wants her dead. Have you looked in the mirror lately? YOU came to me, remember? Not the other way around. You were too bitch to do this by yourself. You needed help." I finished saying as he growled, baring his teeth at me.

"Well, what are we going to do now?" He said annoyed.

"I don't know! I'll...think of something." I was at a loss. We looked at each other, eyes wide as we heard someone approached. Twigs snapped beneath their feet, leaves rustling as they stopped just before us, hidden in the shadows. Their scent was masked, face hidden by the darkness.

"I..I can help." The soft voice said. They were nervous. I

could hear the jitteriness in their voice, the fast beating of their heart.

"Come out of the shadows. We can't trust you if you don't trust us." I said crossing my arms against my chest and raising a brow in waiting, not that anyone could see it. My partner looked like he was trying to hide his panic at being caught but I wasn't worried. This person obviously heard our whole conversation. They didn't run and tell the Alpha or Cairo; they didn't get help. They stayed, listening. And now they finally approach us, wanting to help of all things. They hate the rogue twins just as much as we do. But I want to know who and why. He made a noise from beside me. I looked at him, seeing the shock and confusion on his face as the new hidden figure stepped out of the shadows into the moonlight. I looked, gasping as I saw their face.

"YOU?!" There was no way. No fucking way they would help me, us! "Why!?" My mind was blown. They were the last person I ever expected to help us get rid of Alek and Zia.

"I..I have my reasons." Was all they said. I would kill to hear them.

"Why are you here? What do you want?" I said, still reeling from the shocking reveal.

"I know how to get rid of Zia."

Chapter Thirty-Two

The Ball

Zia

In the days leading up to the ball, everything went back to normal after the rogue attack. But I could tell it was still eating away at Cairo. He was hovering over me, acting like a bodyguard as he walked behind me instead of beside me when we walked to and from school. He was getting distant and quiet. At home he never let me out of his sight. With the slight bags under his eyes, I think he hasn't been sleeping either. Something has been worrying him. When he wasn't acting weird, he'd have me in his room, hovering above me as he kissed me like his life depended on it. Not that I didn't love the hot make out sessions, but I was starting to miss Alek and miss hanging out with everyone else. I haven't seen Maya, or Lane or Sadie. But Cairo did say Sadie was going back on tour so she wouldn't be here very often. I didn't get the chance to see if Lane and her baby were okay. Cairo reassured me I would see everyone at the ball and that I could ask then.

And finally, it was time.

The ball was a few hours away. I was excited and nervous. I decided tonight would be the night I tell Cairo everything. After the ball, I'm going to take him somewhere quiet and let go. I'm going to show him the real, true me. Open my heart and soul up to him. I can only hope he takes it well. I don't know what I'll do if he doesn't.

The Luna shocked the hell out of me when she asked if I could look after Sarana for a little bit while she went and checked the last-minute preparations for the ball. I was flattered and speechless she trusted me to look after her. I promised I'd guard her with my life. We were in Maya's room, the last spare room in the pack that also had a spare bed, a shared room. There was a couch in middle by the windows and a big white fluffy rug where Sarana and I sat. She was playing with her wooden coloured blocks with the alphabet on them. I sat beside her, smiling every time she held up a block, while Maya sat crossed legged on the couch watching us.

"She is absolutely adorable." She said as Sarana stacked one block after another.

"I know, right. You should see her with Cairo." I said giggling as I think back to the day she put the bunny ears on him. Also, the first day I ever met her.

"Bubba?" She said perking up at his name.

"Yes, that's right! Bubba." I said smiling at her cuteness.

"So, are you ready for the ball tonight?" Maya asked excitedly.

"I am. I'm a little nervous about meeting everyone though. Cairo said not everyone were at the Trials when we fought. He said most chose not to come and others were out of the pack visiting other packs or tending to jobs they have in the human world like Sadie." She gasped.

"Omg, I can't believe she's from this pack! Like I am literally in the same pack as the world's hottest singer right now." I laugh.

"I knew you'd be excited. Can you believe I didn't notice her the night we went to the club OR when she was sitting right in front of me?"

"I wouldn't blame you for not noticing. They always look different up close. Plus, you've had a lot of stuff going on lately." She said trying to reassure me.

"Wook, bocks." Sarana said making me giggle before I looked down amazed.

"You are so good at that, Sarana! You'll have to teach me." I said as she nodded away, already dismantling the block building to make something else.

"What are you, three?" Maya joked.

"*Cala-te.*" I said telling her to shut up. I do know some Portuguese words to speak.

"I see you've been practicing your Portuguese. You said that almost perfectly. I heard the Luna yesterday speaking Portuguese. Does anyone know you can understand and speak it?" She asked.

"No," I said smiling sheepishly, "I don't want anyone to know just yet. Helps me listen in on conversations when they think I can't understand. I've already heard the Luna say to Cairo she wants grandbabies." Maya bursts out laughing, grabbing her stomach as she wheezes.

"No way! That's so embarrassing. But also, what a cheeky devil you are! Why didn't I think of that?" She said looking annoyed.

"Because you *estupido.*" I said teasingly. She squinted her eyes, mouth opening ready to speak when a knock at the door sounded.

"Saved by the knock." She muttered looking pointedly at me.

We looked towards the door, seeing the Luna appear as she entered. "Thank you so much for looking after her. I would have been here sooner but there was an incident with the ball room preparations that needed immediate attention." She said apologetically.

"That's okay, I really enjoyed looking after her." I said and it was the truth. I love kids and always pictured myself having them but after everything that happened I guess I forgot that.

"Well good because she never stops talking about you every time she sees you." She says whispering. "Okay, missy. Time to go." She says looking down at Sarana who started collecting her blocks up in her small arms. "These girls need to get ready for the ball and so do you!"

"Ball!" Sarana said excitedly dropping blocks as she jumped. We all laughed, then said our goodbyes to the Luna and Sarana as they left. Maya turned to face me, telling me the next time I saw her my jaw would be dropping. I rolled my eyes, getting a reaction out of her before I laughed.

"Okay, meet me at my room when you're finished?" I asked and she nodded. I said goodbye and left for my room. When I walked in, I was pleasantly surprised when I saw Cairo.

Goddess, I could get used to this sight, I thought as I watched Cairo dry himself off. His long hair on top was already styled in its usual bun, the sides of his head looked cleanly shaven with that fresh fade look. The solid black stretchers in his ears shined in the light. His new Egyptian tribal tattoo that spread across half his chest and down to his elbow made me almost moan. How could one man look so fine. It wasn't as if he wasn't hot before. But now he's mouth-watering. Watching him dry himself off makes me want to jump him right now just watching the way his muscles bunch and bulge as he moves. I have to hold myself back. He would probably regret it afterwards if we did something other than kiss. Feeling like I may have been rushed. I know he wants to do something romantic and I know I should wait for that but...Just look at him! At this point it feels psychically impossible to hold myself back anymore. His strong toned legs, powerful thighs hidden behind that evil white towel...*Goddess, I want to burn that towel so much right now.* Ever since he got that tattoo, it has been driving me wild. I always pictured my mate having tattoos and when I saw Cairo didn't have them I was okay with it. But now he does and I feel like I'm constantly aroused all the fucking time. We better mark each other soon because that thread of tension between us is just that, a thread. It's so damn thin that one more brush of his hand against my cheek or anywhere on my body and I will snap.

Suddenly he spins around, hands grabbing the ends of his towel holding it together around his waist as it tightens around his ass, moulding to his muscled buns. "Can you please take those socks off." He says as he clears his throat like there's a lump stuck in there. Confused, I look down.

"My socks?" The floors felt a little cold today so I put a pair of knee-high socks on. I didn't think there was anything wrong with the outfit I was wearing. A teal flowy tank and black shorts with these socks can't look too bad, can it?. "What's wrong with the socks?" I asked still confused after analysing myself.

"Zi, baby," He pleads, "Did I ever tell you one of my fantasies is of you in knee high socks?" He says, voice shaky.

"No?," I say because we definitely haven't had that type of talk yet. "What does that mean?" I ask, still confused.

"That means, pumpkin, that if you don't take those god damn sexy socks off your sexy little legs, I'm going to do it for you. But if that happens, then you won't be able to walk the next few days." He says making me gasp as it finally hits me. I'm turning him on just by wearing these socks. *Oh, that's why his towel tightened.* I blush. Many, many scenarios running through my head and none of them PG. "Do you understand now, baby?" He asks softly, almost like he's pleading. I purr softly, unable to dispel the R rated thoughts from my mind. I'm seriously tempted to keep them on. Tempted in seeing if he would keep his promise to keep me off my feet for a few days.

He growls, smelling my arousal as his head drops back, staring up at the ceiling before he starts shaking his head and muttering. "Please take them off, baby. I don't want to ruin the surprise for later." He said begging but I could also detect the note of worry.

"Okay." I bend down, rolling the socks down my legs before pulling them off my feet. I could hear the worried tone in his voice, worried that whatever this surprise is would be ruined. "What surprise?" I ask as I tuck the socks into my back pocket.

"I want to take you somewhere special tonight, after the ball." He says smiling as he turns around. He breathes in and out, a blush creeping up his neck as he does. "I want to mark you tonight, Zia. I feel like I'm going to go crazy if I don't do it soon. Everyday my wolf gets a little closer to taking full control." He says before he walks towards me. He stops, looking down at me with his dark, lust filled eyes. "I know you feel it too. I smelt your arousal the moment you walked in. I smell it more strongly every day. The longer we wait, the stronger your scent gets and the harder it is for me to hold back. And I need to hold back, because I want this moment to be perfect for you because you deserve it to be." My heart was pounding so hard at his confession that pain started streaking across my chest. But then I could hear my pulse in my ear, getting louder as the guilt became unbearable. He was wrong, I don't deserve it. He doesn't deserve to mark a **liar**.

"Cairo," I begin but he continues speaking.

"I'm sorry but I will have to meet you at the ball. I have to go set up our surprise before it so it's all ready for us after." I nod, feeling my throat go dry.

"Okay."

"I'll see you in a few hours." He leaned down, kissing me softly.

I watched him walk to the wardrobe, coming out holding a fancy black glossed bag that held his suit. He had quickly thrown on a pair of pants before he walked out, flashing me his gorgeous smile. I watched sadly as he left, disappearing behind the door, holding back my guilty tears. I ran to the bathroom, slamming the door before quickly walking over to the large tub. I turned the tap all the way, letting the steam fill the room as I striped down and stepped into rapidly filling tub. There was a bottle off to the side so I grabbed it, reading the label before squirting the contents into the bubbles. I swirled my hands through the water, forming bubbles as they grey and multiplied while my thoughts began to swirl just like the soapy water. *Goddess, I'm such a hypocrite.* For weeks Cairo has been nothing but amazing. He's been genuine, kind, loving, caring and loyal. He's been *trying*. He wants to mark me tonight to complete our mate bond and there's nothing I want more than to do that. But he still doesn't know everything about my past. Even if it is staring him right in the face. He just hasn't looked close enough to *see* it.

When we first met I punished him for hooking up with Jordan. I punished him for not staying loyal to our bond. I never should have done that. I should have been open with him from the start, but instead I kept everything inside. Instead of trying to protect myself, I have and will, hurt everyone else around me. I will have to be completely honest with Cairo tonight if he wants to mark me. I just hope he will still want to after he learns the truth.

ALEK: *[Zi?]*

ZIA: *[Yes, Alek?]*

ALEK: *[Ya chuvstvuyu tebya, Zia. Don't be sad today, stop thinking just for a few hours. For me?]* He says, telling me he can feel the storm brewing inside me. But he doesn't know why I'm feeling that way. He's just assuming it's the normal depression.

ZIA: *[He wants to mark me tonight, Alek. For real this time. What..what if he sees?]*

ALEK: *[Then you tell him the truth. I see the way he looks at you, Zia. You won't scare him away with your past. Remember, on byl sozdan dlya tebya.*

ZIA: *[Okay.]*

ALEK: *[Good, now get your little butt ready or else you'll be late again.]* I roll my eyes, annoyed at his parenting.

ALEK: *[I felt that.]* He says making me laugh.

I unplugged the bath, letting the soapy water drain as I stepped out, walking to the shower. Quickly rinsing the soap and bubbles off, I did the usual, washing my hair and shaving. After getting out, I dried my hair, putting some moisturiser on so that I could wear my hair down with its natural wave. Then comes mascara, making my eyes pop especially with the neutral, natural colour eyeshadow I went for. Finishing everything off with a light blush toned lipstick, I was ready to step into my dress. It really was beautiful, magical even. When I saw the racks of dresses Jordan had put on hold, I knew she would have grabbed a bunch of the new dresses not even bothering to look at them. The dress I chose was hidden within the rack. It was fate that this dress found me. I stepped into it, pulling the soft material up my legs, pulling it over my hips before it sat into place perfectly on my waist. I reached around, zipping up the back as it came together, tightly hugging my body. I gasped as I looked at my reflection in the mirror. The lilac-coloured lace dress looked like it was made for me by the Goddess herself. Strapless, the top part of the dress hugged my body in a corset. My breasts were held in place with a slight push up bra, my sternum, ribs and back were exposed, only covered by sheer lilac lace that had floral and diamonds embroided on it that went down the rest of the dress. The floral lace was thick around my waist with a split up the side. I felt like a fairy in this dress. It was beautiful and delicate. It complemented my skin and made my eyes pop. It was definitely a show stopping dress. I could see myself dancing in a meadow with Cairo as we dance to natures lullaby. I even pretended we were there, hands raised in the air as I closed my eyes, practicing what it would be like to dance with him. I was smiling hard and enjoying my daydream far longer than I should have. My phone alarm had been beeping for a few minutes before reality set back in. I exhaled, feeling like I really was in that meadow with Cairo. But as they say, all good this must come to an end. I just hope that one day we can be there again, for real.

I was running late again. I told Maya I'd meet her there as well as Alek. There were cars taking everyone to and from. No one would be wanting to walk so far in heels, let alone get their dresses dirty before the event. I hopped in one car and a quick drive through the pack, down a dirt road and I was there. From the outside it looked like a large stone building, just like Cairo described. The car came to a stop near five long steps that lead up to the large wooden doors with iron hinges and a black iron doorknocker with a large wolf head holding the ring bar to knock. I could hear soft music coming from beyond and my heart picked up in excitement. Walking in there was a large foyer beyond the doors, cream glossy tiles, cream-coloured pillars, and a gorgeous marble staircase in the middle that led up to another set of wooden doors that looked old but in better condition than the sturdy ones out front. There were gold fixtures accenting the room, ferns in the corners and a red rug that laid over the stairs. Sadie, Maya, and Lane stood by the bottom of the stairs, each looking beautiful in their short and long gowns and beautified with their hair and makeup done.

"You guys all look so pretty!" I said as I walked towards them, stopping beside Sadie in her short, tight, blood red leather dress. "*Absolyutno krasivaya.*"

"I have no idea what you just said." Sadie said turning and Lane agreed as Maya laughed.

"I know a small amount of Russian. She said we look absolutely beautiful." I nod, smiling as Sadie and Lane primp their hair agreeing with my statement.

"She got that right." Sadie said, putting her hand on her hip.

"Are you performing tonight, Sadie?" I ask. Her attire doesn't seem entirely fitting for a ball.

"Yes I am my dear, Lune." Maya squealed, looking excitedly at Sadie as Lane sighed.

"Great, a fan."

"Hey, don't be jelly that I have fans and you don't." Sadie said as she finished with a *hmph.*

"Please," Lane said rolling her eyes, "I am not." She looked at Sadie annoyed, who then laughed and said *'tell that to your face'* which caused Lane to growl and then Sadie laughed again as they both started bickering back and forth like an old married couple. But then all laughter and chatter stopped as we heard snickering come from behind the doors. They opened, in walked Jordan with her heals clacking against the tiles obnoxiously as she began walking up the steps but stopped when Sadie spoke.

"Oh, look. The pack slut walked in." Sadie muttered making my jaw drop while Maya laughed and Lane shrugged her shoulders as if to say she wasn't wrong. Jordan slammed her heels into the ground, growling out.

"Sadie." She said through clenched teeth. "Is that my dress?!" Jordan screeched out as she looked down at me from the first step she was standing on. Her fists clenched by her side; she couldn't keep her eyes off me. They kept shooting up and down, examining the dress and her nostrils flared as she deemed me beautiful and hated that she thought it.

"Aw, you noticed!" I said not helping myself. She screamed, making all our ear's ring from the echoing scream like a microphone was held to a chalk board as nails dragged down it.

"Y..you..you're the one that stole all my dresses!" She stuttered and stammered out, full of anger as she accused me. *Rightly so.*

"First of all, I didn't *steal* anything. They were offered to me and I only chose one. Secondly, they looked better on me anyways." I said loving the pure look of fury crossing her face. Her long red dress matched the colour of her face making the two almost blend together. "Now *otvali.*" I say, telling her to get lost.

"Oow!" Sadie said exclaiming, "This I have heard before. She said get lost, bitch." Jordan screamed again as we all laughed.

"I'm so sick of you!!" She screamed at me. She turned, red faced glaring at Maya before shooting a look at Lane and Sadie. She quickly disappeared up the staircase, opening the door and slamming it behind her.

"Hey...That bad smell is gone." Sadie said referencing Jordan. We all laughed, trying hard not to tear up and ruin our makeup.

"You know, I don't think I said exactly that." I said to Sadie as she smirked.

"Oh, I know!" She said happily before winking at me.

"Are we waiting for the guys?" I asked, looking back at the door.

"They're all inside." Maya said. "We were waiting on you." I felt my face heat, feeling embarrassed for making them wait. I feel like I'm always late around here.

"Yeah, let's go girls! I've got a stage to own!" Sadie said turning as she waltzed up the stairs with a sassy sway in her hips. Lane rolled her eyes watching Sadie retreat.

"You better not be rolling your eyes at me, Laney Pooh." Sadie said as she reached the top step and turned, looking down at Lane with her hand on the iron doorknob. Lane laughed and kissed her hand before blowing the imaginary kiss to Sadie.

Sadie pushed the doors, holding them open as the rest of us quickly walked up the steps and entered the ball room. Marble tiled floors, two massive crystal chandeliers hung from the ceiling lighting the room. There were large curtains covering the windows on the walls between large pillars. There were warriors lined up all around the room, guarding as they kept a watchful eye. Waiters weaving in and out of the crowd holding chrome trays of champagne and finger foods. The music was light and soft, perfect for a ball atmosphere. Some people stood and conversed; others were dancing. Jordan stood beside Jaxon, who seemed to be one of the warriors on guard duty tonight. The ugly scar on his face did nothing to stop the annoyed expression on his face as Jordan tried to speak with him. He looked like he wanted to be anywhere else. The Alpha and Luna stood near the back of the room, watching over their pack proudly as they wore matching coloured suit and dress. I spotted Zack in the middle of the dance floor dancing like a goof as Sarana stood in front of him in a cute pink tutu dress, laughing hysterically at his dancing. I smiled, seeing Alek and Keiran holding each other close as they danced to the music. And just when I thought I couldn't find Cairo, my eyes landed on him. He looked so handsome in his crisp white button up shirt, the buttons were black, matching the bowtie and suit jacket. His pointed leather shoes tied in the outfit and my heart seemed to skip a beat when he looked at me. He was dressed just how I envisioned him in the meadow. His mouth popped open, looking at me in shock., eyes trailing up and down my body repeatedly. He finally gave a shy smile as he looked back to my eyes with a blush on his cheeks. I smiled back, feeling like I am, a shy schoolgirl in front of her crush.

"Damn, the Luna went all out." Sadie said as she reached over and took a glass of champagne off a waiter that walked by.

"Definitely. I'm gonna go find Nile." Lane said before she was off, worming her way through the crowd. I looked at Maya, seeing her on the verge of a panic attack.

"Maya? Are you okay?" She looked off into the sea of people. Every few seconds she would breathe in like she was smelling something.

"Yeah..I just..." She stopped as she continued looking, even standing on her tippy toes. "Do you smell that?" She asked as Sadie and me both inhaled, not smelling anything out of the ordinary until it clicked.

"Maya! You're smelling your mate!" She gasped, confusing me with her reaction. I could see her eyes shimmer as she connected with her mate, but she looked worried.

"I..I am." Maybe she was just nervous about meeting him so suddenly, just how Alek and I were when we found Keiran and Cairo.

"Well! What are you waiting for? Girl, go get him!" Sadie exclaimed. Maya smiled brightly as she nodded before she took off.

Jordan stood in her way, on her phone texting as she blocked Maya's path. But that didn't stop her. She pushed past, knocking Jordan over as she said and I *quote 'move, bitch'*. We laughed, watching her on all fours as she snapped her head up and growled. Jordan wasn't off to a great start. Stolen dress, insults, accidental tripping's...

Sadie saw her own mate, excusing herself as she met him halfway on the dance floor. I was alone by myself but that was okay. I said hello to the pack members that came up and greeted themselves. Not a single person treated me like a rogue. They were all accepting of me. I couldn't have been more happier knowing the pack I will one day help Cairo lead, accepts me. And soon enough I had greeted nearly everyone in here. I looked over to Cairo, seeing him standing there watching me with a proud smile on his face. I walked to him, trying to calm the nerves in my body. I don't even know why I'm nervous. It's not like I'm meeting him for the first time.

"Wow...you look...beautiful." Cairo said, sounding like he almost couldn't get the words out.

"So do you, Cairo." I say looking up at him through my lashes.

"May I have this dance, Zia?" He said holding out his hand. I could feel my face heat up as he stared down at me lovingly.

"Of course." I said curtseying. He laughed at my antics before I gently placed my hand in his.

It felt like time slowed down and everyone around us faded away. He guided my hand up as his other one rested against the small of my back. I laid my free hand against his arm, holding it gently as he led the dance. I could feel Cairo's beating pulse through our joined hands and I could hear his heart pounding rapidly against his chest, mimicking my own hearts rhythm like they were in sync. He really has no idea what this moment means to me. What it truly means.

At fifteen I thought my chances of finding my mate were slim to none. Because of what *Vladik* did, I thought my mate would never want me or that I would never find him. But I did, I found Cairo in a place I never expected. In a place that was supposed to be a temporary stop so we could abide by the laws but then it became a permanent one. It became a home. He's everything I wanted him to be and more. Yeah, the start of our relationship was rocky but the place we're in now is one I only dreamed of. I just hope we can stay in this bubble of bliss. I don't know how he will react and can only hope he wants to stay with me once he learns about my past. Once he learns what I'm hiding.

I don't know how long we danced for, but it had to be hours. We were so entranced by each other, never looking away from each other's eyes. I heard faint speeches being held, a spotlight shined on us at one point and people trying to get our attention. People danced, people laughed and ate and drank. But nothing would break the spell we were under. It was just him and me. Before long there were only a few people left. The night had officially come to an end. The guards had left once most wolves were gone. The only reason our spell broke was because one of the waiters dropped a tray of empty champagne glasses, shattering across the tiles. We pulled back, arms aching from being in one position for hours. I rubbed my arm as Cairo spoke.

"I'm going to get our bags ready. I packed some of our clothes and some food and blankets." He said just as my stomach made a noise. He laughed, shaking his head as he continued. "I'll come back to get you once I retrieve them." I nod, turning as I watch him walk to the large wooden doors. As the doors closed behind him, my eyes focused on Maya who slowly approached me like a creepy little stalker.

"Somethings wrong with your face, Zi." She said making me frown before she started laughing, making fun at my blushing cheeks. I roll my eyes, sighing as I speak.

"What do you want." I state more than ask while pretending to be annoyed at her teasing but I could never be mad at her. So, the smile fighting to break free won.

"Well, I forgot my purse here and when I came back in I saw you staring after lover boy." She said and I shake my head, blushing furiously. "Haha, no but seriously, are you okay?"

"I..I think so. I'm just nervous. Cairo's taking me somewhere and he's going to mark me. I know we've come close before but that was in the heat of the moment. But this time my head is clear and my mind can't stop racing. I can't stop the worry that everything is about to go so wrong." I say taking a big deep breath in to calm my nerves.

"You haven't told Cairo you're already **marked**?" Maya said worried. I thought I heard a gasp but I wasn't focused on my surroundings, only the deepest, darkest secret that Maya just spilled.

"Be quiet!" I snapped. "No one can know about that!" I said afraid as she rolled her eyes.

"Zia, we are the only ones left in the ballroom. Calm down no one will know anything tomorrow anyways as your old mark will be gone when Cairo marks you. So, it will be our little secret."

Oh, how I wished that was true. One minute I was talking

to Maya about her mate and what he was like when we jumped, hearing a roar come from outside. “That was Cairo!” I said panicking. Sadie came running in, screaming my name as Maya and I ran to her. “W..what happened to Cairo? Sadie??” I spoke frantically.

“I just overheard Jordan talking to Cairo about you being marked and he’s completely wolfing out!” *No, no, no, no, no! He can’t find out like this! He can’t find out from anyone but me!* It wasn’t supposed to happen like this. He wasn’t supposed to hear it from Jordan of all people! I screamed, letting my anger pulse through my veins as my wolfs eyes shined through.

“Why can’t she leave us alone!” My voice was dark and sounded terrifying even to my own ears. My wolf was angry, furious. Sadie shook, scared for her life as she gingerly pointed to a door on the far side of the ball room. Assuming that’s where Cairo was, I headed straight for the door. Heels smacking down against the tiles as my claws extended, hands flexing as the rage pulsing through my body was beginning to boil over.

The last thing I heard before I pushed through the door was Maya’s small voice telling Sadie she was going to get Alek. I stepped out onto a big balcony. I could see across the pack land, the moon shining brightly down as a lake I hadn’t seen before shimmered the moonlight back. Cairo stood near the old stone railing, back to me as he listened to Jordan whose eyes flicked to mine. There was a glint in her eyes sparkling pure joy and excitement as she spoke lies to Cairo.

“YOU!” I said looking straight at Jordan.

It’s about time I deal with her once and for all.

Chapter Thirty-Three

The Mark

"I should have killed you when I had the chance." I said, my wolfs voice mixed with my own. "You've been nothing but a pain in my ass since the second I got here. I knew you were a desperate slut but I never-"

"THAT'S ENOUGH, ZIA!" Cairo snapped as he turned to me. He looked at me with pure hatred as his wolfs eyes shone brightly through. Jordan giggled as he spoke, only making my hackles raise more.

"You're defending her?! I'm your mate! ME, not her!" I yelled back as my hands shook from the white-hot rage coursing through me.

"Did you not whore yourself out and let another male mark you?" He said, ripping the air from my lungs. He looked at me in disgust. His lip curling as he spoke the words.

"Don't you dare say that!" I said, voicing cracking. I could feel my lip trembling from my heart beating so fast. He was breaking my heart with his words.

"Well, did you? Because right now the only whore I see

here is you." I couldn't hold it in anymore. My wolf was furious and would not let her mate disrespect us any longer.

"I was raped!" Her guttural voice broke through my own broke one. "The Alpha of my pack held me down and marked me as he raped me!" I screamed through the tears. "Do you know what that feels like to be marked by someone who's not your mate?! It's excruciating! I still feel the burning pain **every single day** since it happened. I still have the reminder of what Vladik did to me on my neck as he forced his mark on me! That *mark* burns me every day because my body is constantly fighting it. For three years I have been forced to bear the mark of my rapist!" My knuckles were white from the pressure, my chest was heaving up and down as I let everything out. Tears silently streaming down my face.

"No..." Cairo's voice was barely a whisper. His hazel eyes were back, his wolf had repelled back into his mind the second I spoke. I could hear him crying as my own growled back, hating her mate in this moment.

"I always knew you were weak. That's why Cairo will choose me as his Luna." Jordan spoke as if she had won.

Rage unlike anything I've ever felt before coursed through my veins like molten lava. I'd never felt such an urge to kill someone before. But I can't get Jordan's smug face out of my head. Then I felt it. A surge of power washed over my body, strengthening every bone and fibre in me. I could see a purple glow bounce off the walls beside me. I couldn't look to see where it was coming from because all I could see was Jordan. All I could feel was how much I wanted her dead. Then my vision blurred before it came back, clearer than it's ever been. Everything had a purple tinge to it and it was like I was seeing *through* Jordan. I could see into her soul and was as black as the night sky. There would be no redeeming for her.

She is rotten to the core and always will be.

Cairo

There are moments in my life that I wish I could take back. Moments I truly regret. But I regret nothing more than the things I just called Zia. I will regret it the rest of my life. The hurt in her eyes pierced my heart deeper than any knife could. The way her lip trembled, the way her wolf whined at my words. Even my own wolf repelled back into me, hating himself for letting his anger cloud our judgement. I hope with all my heart that I haven't fucked this up for good this time. I've fucked up too many times to count. Zia will only put up with me for so long before she realises she deserves a better mate. Better than what I've been.

The air around us whipped and whirled as it tunnelled, getting sucked straight into Zia. It was hard to breathe, hard to even move. The pressure in the air became so thick that it would take all my strength to take one step forward. Time slowed down, not just from the power rolling off Zia in waves but from my realisation. Everything clicked into place. Why she slapped me that day in the cafeteria when I threatened to tell my father about her and Alek. She was afraid her Alpha would come for her. I accused her of doing something to get kicked out of her pack when it wasn't. I flaunted myself and Jordan in front of her when we first met. Even though I didn't know we were mates, she was right. I did whore myself around. I never waited for her, never waited for my fated one. I slept with Jordan the first chance I got because she was easy and willing. I hadn't met my mate yet, and I didn't care about waiting and finding her. I attacked Zia for no reason. She did wait for me; she still has even after all the hurt I put her through. Her innocence was taken away from her because of an alpha and I'm no better. I just shattered her light and trust by calling her those cruel words and believing Jordan's lies. She told me she overheard Zia speak about already mating with another male. Already being marked by another. I never should have trusted her. She's a power-hungry snake that has always been after the luna position and I let her think that because she was an easy lay.

Zia will never forgive me now.

I growled out at myself, hating myself more than anyone else could. I turned, ready to slam Jordan up against the wall and punish her for her lies, but then I heard her gasp. I looked back, seeing her eyes wide as her hands went to her throat. She was struggling to breath under the pressure from the power Zia was expelling. She collapsed, unable to bear through it. A wave of power rushed over me, pulling the air from my lungs. I looked back at Zia. I've never felt this kind of power before. It felt like the power of ten alphas put together. I almost felt suffocated by the amount of power but managed to draw in a small breath. Jordan continued being crushed against the ground by the sheer force of it. I was barely standing, barely able to hold my composure as I looked upon my mate. The ground was shaking, dust falling from the stone roof as chandeliers jingled and smashed to the ground inside from the earthquake size power radiating from Zia. A purple hue glowed around her as the air cracked, lighting cracking from her. This is what Alek warned me about. She was beautiful and scary. Her bright aqua blue eyes were gone. They were now a violet shade of a starry night sky. Her eyes looked like they were a portal, no longer looking like eyes. There was an eerie depth to them that made them appear deeper. They looked like a gateway to another realm, thousands of tiny stars shone brightly through. I was terrified. They weren't the eyes of my mate anymore. They were the eyes of a God. A powerful, vengeful God.

I didn't see Alek until he was screaming in my face, pushing me back as his eyes looked crazed.

"What did you do?!" He yelled, losing his footing as the ground shook harder. We both fell to the side, grabbing onto the stone ledge, holding ourselves up. "I warned you not to push her!" He screamed, gritting his teeth as his claws came out, scraping through the stone.

"I...I.." I tried to say but couldn't. The power was getting too strong, my body was becoming weak.

"Do something before she kills us all!" Alek said slamming his claws into the stone, trying to hold himself up as an invisible force pushed him back down.

"She won't kill us! She's not a killer!" I said through my own gritted teeth. If there's one thing I know about Zia it's that she could never hurt anyone.

"She is going to slaughter us all to get to Jordan. I can hear her thoughts, Cairo! She wants her dead! You have ten seconds to do something before we all die!" Alek screamed just as blood started running from his nose. His face scrunched up in pain as he fell to the ground, claws scraping through the stone leaving jiggered marks.

I felt something wet on my neck. I gingerly brought my hand to my neck, wiping up to my ear as I brought my hand back down, seeing blood. I looked behind me, seeing a pool of blood already starting to form around Jordan's unconscious body. The stone walls started to crack, rubble falling down around us. I could hear the glass windows shattering, the screams of terrified pack members in the distance filled the air. I looked to my mate as I pushed through the pain and pressure. I couldn't lift my feet but I could slide them across the ground. I was counting down inside my head, counting down the seconds I have left to save Zia. I didn't want to do it this way but there was only one way I can stop her. The only thing I could think of.

I push through the pain, slowly making my way to her as my heart slams into my chest. I stop as a crack appears beneath my foot. My heart was pounding in my chest, sweat running down my forehead as I continued on. Her glowing purple eyes were still trained on Jordan unconscious bleeding body. With only a few seconds left before the cracks connected and the ground below us gave way, I reach for her. I grab her, hands burning from the pure electric energy coursing along her skin, and throw her head back with accidental force before I extended my canines and sank down into the junction of her neck.

Finally marking her as my mate.

"You're awake." A voice said above me.

I blinked, the darkness fading to light as my blurry vision became clear. Alek stood above me, staring down with no emotion on his face. I could see his jaw clench, nostrils flaring as he looked at me, lip curling up in a sneer.

"Wh..what happened?" I asked. My throat felt scratchy and my voice was barely above a whisper. He wiped the blood from his nose, trails of blood dripped down his ears, staining the collar of his white dress shirt. He exhaled roughly as he walked around me. I was laying on the ground, back aching from the little chipped stone rocks on the ground beneath me. I turned my head, looking at Zia as she lay peacefully on the ground beside me. Her neck bleeding as I didn't get a chance to close the wound. Her face looked peaceful, no longer clouded in hate. Her hair fanned out, looking like a halo around her. I reach over, ready to wipe the blood away as Alek speaks, with a darkness to his voice I haven't heard before.

"Touch her, and I break your fucking fingers." He said, looking ready to kill me. If my body wasn't exhausted as it was, I would have shivered. These twins were...terrifying when they want to be. I watched as he scooped her up, tucking her into his chest before he walked away, leaving me and Jordan on the ground. I looked over to her, studying her chest, waiting to see any signs of life. My ears still rung so I couldn't hear her heartbeat, but I saw the slow rise and fall of her chest. I sighed, glad no one died. I couldn't bring myself to stand up, my muscles burned and shook as I tried to move. I closed my eyes, willing sleep to come as I'm not going to be able to move right now.

"Son! Son!" My eyes struggled to open, refusing to as I heard heavy footsteps approach. A large hand touches my shoulder, squeezes before it lays on my cheek, frantically patting. "Son? Are you okay?" The hand goes to my chest. I try again. Forcing my eyes to open as I look up into my father's eyes.

"Dad..." He sighs in relief, large shoulders relaxing.

"What happened?" He looks around, taking in the damage as someone walks past us to Jordan.

"She's breathing, Alpha. Barely.." The warrior says grimly.

My father sighs, "Get her to the infirmary. Give me your hand, Cairo." I lift my hand but nothing moves, not even a finger. I breathe in and out, trying again but this time trying to move fingers and wiggle my toes. My body was so exhausted that I literally had no control over it.

"I...can't." He frowns, looking over my body.

"Don't think." Is all he says before I feel him probing into my mind, watching my memories.

The Alpha has the ability to look into pack members minds and see their memories. They can communicate with us privately or with the entire pack. They can feel our emotions when we're near and he can demand anything of us if he Alpha commands us. Right now, I can see him watching the events that just look place. His eyebrows look like the pair are entwined in a dance, moving up and down, frowning and lifting as he watches my memories. I feel when he leaves my mind, he sighs, shaking his head as he looks at me.

"You need to deal with Jordan. You made this mess; you clean it up." He says as he stands, dusting his suit pants as dirt disappears into the air. "Do you need help?" He questions. I shake my head, watching as he nods once before he walks away. I can't move and I have a feeling if he sent warriors to help pick me up and carry me to the infirmary then I will be in more pain than I'd like. I'll stay here, staring up at the cracks in the stone and thinking about how I'm going to deal with Jordan and Zia. She doesn't know I've marked her and considering how hurtful I was to her; I don't think she'll be able to forgive me for this.

Chapter Thirty-Four

The Aftermath

ZIA

Everything was dark, but for once in my life I didn't feel pain. I didn't feel the constant burning, searing, throbbing pain in my neck. I didn't feel dread or anxious. For once I felt...at peace. Like those plaguing thoughts had finally washed away as the storm inside my head receded.

I try to open my eyes but I had little success. They felt heavy, no amount of strength could pry them open until my body was ready. I don't know where I am, but I can feel soft material beneath my hands. I can't tell if it's my silk-lace dress or a thousand count thread bedsheet. My mind and body felt muddled, but I could sense someone was in the room with me. I don't know where, but I can hear the steady beating of their heart, the sighing of their breath. Their presence made me feel warm and weightless like I was floating on a cloud. Suddenly, their thoughts appeared in my mind like someone just turned on a speaker and started talking.

Please be alright...

I'm so sorry, baby. I didn't know what to do.

You...I..I panicked.

Please wake up. I'm so sorry for everything I did.

You must believe me. I wish I could take back everything I did.

Every single mistake I ever made since the moment I met you.

At first, I thought it was Alek, but the voice sounded different. It sounded deeper, broken. It was Cairo. But how can I hear his voice? What happened last night after the ball? I don't remember anything after I screamed at Jordan. I only know it's morning now because I can hear birds tweeting as they fly past the opened window that's somewhere in the room. How could I lose so much time?

Suddenly, I started feeling a wave of energy wash over me. My fingertips tingled as the sensation made its way down my fingers, through my hands and up my arms. When it met in my chest, it exploded out, sending the electric vibrations through my entire body. I could wiggle my fingers and toes again. I squinted as my eyes opened, being blinded by the morning light. I was in our room, laying on our bed. I was right before about the bedsheets but wrong about the dress. It didn't feel like I was wearing a gown.

Cairo?

I thought as I wait for my blurry vision to clear.

"Zia!" He exclaimed from the window to the right of the bed before the bathroom door. He raced over, feet slamming into the ground as he reached the bed quickly. I gingerly sat up, elbows wobbling as though they might give way at any second. I breathe out once I'm seated up right, legs hanging over the bed as I look at Cairo. "You're okay! Baby, you're okay!" He exclaimed happily and relieved.

“What happened?” I asked, slowly sliding off the bed to stand. He reaches out, ready to grab me if I become unsteady. I look down, seeing a pair of black shorts and a black and white hoodie zipped up on me. “Where’s my dress? What..” I was so confused.

“It’s okay, take a deep breath.” He says and I do. “A..Alek changed your dress after the ball. It had blood on it and I guess he grabbed the first thing he saw in my wardrobe.” I gasp as he said blood. *Please, tell me I didn’t kill Jordan.*

“W..why was there blood? Did-” I couldn’t finish, afraid to ask encase it was true.

“I,” He begins but stops as he looks at me with worry in his eyes. “I marked you, Zia.” I gasp.

Everything suddenly came back to me. I remembered everything from the moment I felt that rage flow through me. Everything came crashing back, assaulting my unprepared mind. The ball, dancing, eating, drinking, Cairo’s surprise, Sadie running in talking about Jordan. *Jordan.* That fucking snake. She told Cairo I was marked. Told him I had mated with another. I gasp again, looking up at him as I remember telling him what really happened with Vladik. What he did to me and why I was marked. And my powers...I’ve never experienced anything like that. The amount of power that coursed through my veins was indescribable. It felt amazing and terrifying. Then I remembered what he said. He believed her over his own mate. He called me the whore when she’s practically ridden the whole pack.

I couldn’t contain my tears any longer. They fell, hot and heavy in a constant flow. Cairo exclaimed, placing his hand on my arm.

“Baby, what’s wrong?! Please don’t cry, it’s okay. I will get your dress dry cleaned. There wasn’t that much blood.” He says cluelessly.

“It’s not about the dress you idiot! You marked me without my consent, and you believed the lies Jordan told over me! You never let me explain what happened to me. You never gave your own mate the benefit of the doubt. You trusted the pack *bliad'* who's only after the power you can give her! Can't you see she's been using you?! She's tried to pry us apart the moment I arrived. Or have you always known and not cared? And you called me a whore!" I screamed, letting everything out as Cairo looked defeated. "How...how could you?" I whispered out. There was a lump in my throat as I watched and waited for Cairo to reply. And after a minute, he did.

"Zi, baby, I'm so damn sorry. I should never have done that. I should never have done so many things. A part of me knew she could be lying but another part of me also believed she may have told the truth. I didn't know about your past, I thought maybe that's why you were so hesitant to tell me. And when I came to that conclusion my wolf snapped and took control. I am guilty of egging on his anger as well. I thought I had the right to be hurt."

"Save it!" I snapped. "I've heard your apologies already." He went to speak, asking how I knew but I stopped him. "I can hear your thoughts, Cairo. I've heard everything you've felt since the second I became conscious." I turned away, walking to the wardrobe, and grabbing a bag I had hidden at the back of cupboard. It was an emergency bag.

"Wait, wh..what are you doing? Where are you going?" He rushed out as I stopped by the bedroom door, hand paused on the handle ready to turn.

"I'm leaving, Cairo. I-"

"No!" His voice deep gravelly voice shocked me as I looked at him, his hazel eyes taken over by sunset orange. His wolf was in control again. His head flung back before he looked back down at me, Cairo back in control as his wolfs eyes melted away before they were replaced with Cairo's hazel. "Please, baby, don't leave me." He begged, tears brimming his eyes as he looked at me.

"I'm sorry, Cairo." I sighed out. I stared at him through my own tear-filled eyes, feeling that familiar ache in my chest. "I can't be around you right now, Cairo. How can I when my own mate doesn't even trust me." He sucked in a breath, heart beating as he repeated my words in his head. Then anger took over his face as he snapped.

"Oh, don't even start with the trust issues." He said, crossing his arms across his chest snarling at me. I copied him, ready for the fight. "You knew I was your mate the moment you smelt my scent and saw me. Why did you lie and conceal your scent? Then you slapped me and still didn't tell me after I felt the sparks. I should have known then but okay, yeah I was stupid not to realise. Even when I felt the tingles I thought it couldn't have been real because my mate would never conceal herself from me. Trust started with you, Zia! You hid your scent from me even when I asked you to release it. You hid yourself from me! Who does that!" He exclaimed angrily. My hand shot out on its own accord, connecting his cheek as I growled.

"Don't you get it! I was a rogue!" I screamed as I fisted my hands by my side. "We were attacked every time we encountered another pack, or pack members even if we didn't cross into their territory! They still attacked us just because of the fucking title. So how do you think we felt when we were told we had to go to school that was full of pack wolves? That we were forced out of hiding to attend high school. And let's not forget that you're the future Alpha of this pack. My whole life was ruined because of an alpha. Do you think I could forget all the shit he put me through? I know you remember." I finished as another lump appeared in my throat, threatening to release my built-up tears. I turned, needing to get out of here but his soft, sad voice whispered across the room in defeat.

"Please don't leave me."

I didn't turn, giving him my back as I looked down at the door handle. "I'm not leaving you, Cairo. You're my mate. We're destined to be together. But right now, I can't stand to look at you knowing you trusted her over me. I'll come back when you know the true meaning of the word mate. Because it seems like you never did." I turned the handle, ready to open the door before his hand landed on my arm, pulling me back and around to face him.

"I do!" He begged, tears brimming his hazel eyes that made the colour look brighter, more intense. "I do know the meaning! *I love you*, Zia!" My heart clenched at his words

"I'm gonna stay with Maya. There was a spare bed in her room." I turned back to the door.

"Zia, I'm-" He began but I stopped him.

"Save it, Cairo! I don't want to hear it. I just-" I stopped to calm myself down. "I need some time."

I went to step forward but his large, warm hand slid down into mine, entwining our fingers together.

"Stay." His broken voice was barely above a whisper.

I pulled my hand from his, tears falling as I opened the door and closed the door behind me. My body thudded against the closed door as I let the tears stream freely down my face, chest heaving from the pain of leaving him.

Before the door closed I could hear his own tears winning the battle.

I wiped my eyes, breathing in deep and exhaling before I stood up straight, hand tightening around the bag strap as I headed off to Maya's room. She wasn't there when I knocked and entered.

I know she wouldn't mind me sleeping on the spare bed and since she found her mate she probably won't be spending much time here. I dropped my bag by the foot of the bed before I sat down, laying back as I let my tears stain the pillow behind my head.

Alek

I laughed, watching Keiran bat a bug that tried mercifully to get into his mouth. It wasn't until his eyes changed and his wolf growled out that the bug got the message and fucked off. I leaned in now that the air space was clear and kissed him. His lips were soft, so kissable and addicting. Now that Cairo had marked Zia, albeit not how either of us planned him marking her would go, but now that it was done, I could finally mark Keiran. First, I just had to stop kissing him long enough to do it. I chuckled as I tried to pull back, his hands clinging to my shirt, keeping him close to him as he deepened the kiss making me groan.

"I love kissing you." He said as he eventually pulled back while I continued to peck at his lips and cheeks. "It's my favourite thing to do."

"The only thing you like doing?" I teased making his cheeks blush a cute shade of red.

"Well, n..no," he said clearing his throat, "I like the other thing we do too." He said looking anywhere but me.

"Good. Don't you forget it." I smile, staring lovingly at him. "Or else I might just have to show you how much you like it every day until you won't ever forget it." I smirk as his chest rattles from a purr. "That's more like it." I say winking. He leans in, mouthing parting as I join, ready to connect our lips but then I gasp, abruptly pulling back.

"What are you doing?" He says watching me as I stand up, wiping the grass clippings off my pants.

"Zia's awake, I gotta go." I rush out, turning but he stops me as he hurriedly stands up.

"Stop!" I jump from his change of tone. I've never heard or even seen him angry before. "Stop going to her all the time!"

He screams at my back making me jump in shock. I turn to face him, seeing the anger lines mar his beautiful face.

"She needs me, Keiran!" I snap back, angry that he's stopping me from going to her.

Last night after Cairo marked her, they both flew back, crashing into the ground when he marked her. Her power that began building expelled out in a small explosion. Even I was thrown back from the blast. Cairo would have been hurled the other way if he wasn't holding onto her. They were both knocked out cold. It scared the fuck out of me, but it worked. His mark stopped her from losing control. It was probably two, maybe three minutes later before Cairo started stirring awake. Zia was still passed out by the time I brought her back to their bedroom and changed her out of her dress. I wanted her to be comfortable when she woke up. I knew she would probably freak out finding out she was now marked and what happened last night. I only agreed to let Cairo stay with her when he finally arrived a few hours ago because I had to see Keiran. We snuck off to our special spot deep within the pack land. There was a break in the forest, almost like a secret meadow with a small view of the pack. The breeze was beautiful up here and the air was so fresh. It was also quiet. The perfect spot for us to spend some time together. And unfortunately, perfect for the fight we're about to have.

"I need you too!" Keiran said, grabbing his chest where his heart is. "I always needed you, Alek. I've just never said anything because I know you two have an unbreakable bond. But I'm your mate," he said softly, tears welling in his blue-grey eyes, "I deserve your love too." It hurt hearing his words.

"Keiran I...I had no idea you felt like this." I said looking down at the ground, feeling ashamed and guilty for neglecting his feelings.

"I didn't want to come between you two but enough is enough, Alek. She has her mate, now I want mine. Let Cairo be there for her. He's going to be there for her for the rest of her life. He's also made for her, he's the only one that can help her now. She doesn't need you anymore, Alek." His words sent a chill down my spine, heart restricting in my chest as I spoke.

"No!" I snapped. *She doesn't need me anymore.* That felt like a knife in my chest, piercing my heart as the blade twisted. "She will always need me, Keiran. What she went through, what we went through is something we will never forget. These scars you see all over my body are from rogue attacks. What happened to Lane, happened to me countless times. The rogues in Russia aren't like the rogues here. They are vicious and extremely savage. They savour the pain they feel every day from having silver claws. They enjoy it. I had to fight many rogues to get us to where we are now. That's something you couldn't ever understand."

"Why just you? I know Zia can fight. I saw it during the Trials." He questioned unsure.

"Zia nearly died. You know how I told you a little about what happened to Zia that made us leave our pack?" I ask and he nods. "Well, what I didn't tell you was that when he forced himself on her, he marked her. But he didn't just mark her, Keiran. He tore her throat open doing it." I stop, feeling my lip tremble as flashes of that dreaded day flash through my mind. "There was so much blood. The only way I could save her was by searing the wound with a silver blade. The wound never fully healed because of his mark and him not being her destined mate. She was in constant pain every day. I was there every night she woke from nightmares. I was there when she would cry from being in so much pain. I was there when she'd cry herself to sleep, clutching her neck at night and thinking that she would never get a mate now because he had ruined her. Do you know what that does to a person? No, you don't. But I do. I felt everything she felt and I heard every thought in her mind. Do you know how many times she thought of just ending it all? Do you know how hard it was to sit there, day after day, hearing my own twin sister, my *best friend*, contemplate killing herself? The thought of being alone in this world terrifies the fuck out of me, Keiran. To think I could lose her..." I stop as my voice breaks and wipe a stray tear off my cheek.

"Alek," He begins to say but I cut him off.

"We can't live without each other. We were born together and we'll die together. So, yes, Keiran. She will always need me. Just like I will *always* need her." I turn my back, walking away as the wind carries his sad whispered words.

"What about me?"

Chapter Thirty-Five

Mother Knows Best

Luna Ohana

Last night could have gone better, I admit. But we're dealing with teenagers. Two who have unnaturally strong gifts. Not to mention when they walk past I can feel the alpha power rolling off them like tidal waves. Zosar filled me in on what happened last night. I warned Cairo about Jordan but of course that boy doesn't listen. Which is why I am on my way to his room now. My son needs another lecture.

I knock once, opening the door as I look away, waiting to see if there are any objections. I don't hear any so I walk in, finding Cairo on his knees.

"Baby?" I ask and gasp, feeling my heart clench as he looks up at me with sad red rimmed eyes and tears streaming down his face. I run to him, getting down on my knees as I hug him to me. "Baby, what's wrong? What happened?"

"She..she.." He starts but can't manage the words through his heaving.

"Take a deep breath," I encourage, and he does.

"She left me, *a mãezinha*." I sigh, rubbing his back. It's been a long time since he's called me mum in my mother tongue. He used to do it as a child when his emotions got too much to bear. But as the years went on and he continued to grow, he no longer called me that. "She's gone." He whispered. I try to contain my smile as I pull back. Teenagers can be so dramatic. Even though both he and Zia are eighteen and not technically children anymore. But they will always be my babies in my eyes.

"What happened?" I ask again.

"Well.." He begins, explaining everything from the day he first saw her right up until this morning when she awoke. I was surprised at how much he had bottled up inside. My boy holds the world on his shoulders, always has. Always thinks he needs to be strong all the time.

"Don't worry, baby. I'll talk to her." I say smiling reassuringly.

"No don't. You'll just make things worse." He says looking exhausted.

"Excuse you, I will not. Believe it or not, I can help her." I stop, calming myself before I say something I don't want him to hear.

"Where are you going?" He says watching me stand.

"I'm going to fix this. Mumma knows best." I give him a reassuring smile, smoothing back his unkempt hair before I exit his room. I need to find Zia.

It's time we have a chat.

Chapter Thirty-Six

A Mirrored Past

Zia

KNOCK KNOCK.

I turned from my seat on Maya's couch. There was a quick rapping at the door before it opened. I hurriedly wiped my face, clearing away all evidence of tears encase it was Alek. He'd worry too much if he saw me crying and I don't want to worry him anymore. He needs to start living his life without my problems burdening him.

"Hello, dear." The Luna stood by the door, dressed in a black business style dress. She looked casual and ready business all at the same time, adorned with a beautiful jade bangle and matching earrings. I gave her a small smile, willing myself off the couch to go greet her.

"Morning, Luna." I said weakly.

"Good morning, dear. Would you like to take a walk with

me?" It sounded like a question but I had the feeling it was more of a command.

"O..okay." I tuck a strand of hair behind my ear and pat my clothes down, trying to make myself look more presentable.

"Good, follow me." She turned, confidently walking to the door, and held it open.

She led me through the hallway, down the stairs and out the packhouse. I followed silently behind her. We ended up on a cobblestone path, winding through gardens and forest until we came out to an opening right next to a river. I keep forgetting there's still so much land I haven't explored yet. There's so much hidden beauty ready to be discovered. This river winded and twisted around banks of trees, disappearing off into the distance. The Luna stopped along the edge of the path, looking out at the water. I stopped a few feet behind her, wondering why she brought me all the way out here. She didn't turn to face me as she breathed in and out. She spoke, voice softer, losing the confident authority tone it always held.

"Have you heard the story of how I met Zosar?" She asked. "Not many know it, but the elderly wolves do. I catch them talking about it from time to time. I always worry Cairo may accidentally hear one day. Goddess knows how he would react." I shook my head before realising she couldn't see me.

"No, I don't think so." I said quietly.

"I didn't meet him until I was nineteen. But by then the damage was already done." *Damage?* I thought as she turned around, a look of sorrow etched across her beautiful face. "My first boyfriend was the future alpha of my pack. I know it was wrong to love someone other than your mate, but we were young, and we did really love each other. At first, he was amazing. He was my best friend before we started dating when we were sixteen. As I got older, I watched all my friends meet their mates and I had started longing for that feeling. Longing to feel the sparks they all spoke of and the unconditional love they felt. So, when I broke up with him, he didn't take it well. We had never done anything except kiss but that night he went further. He didn't stop, even as I begged him too." I breathed in, hearing the words I've spoken before. "After that he went mad with jealousy. I didn't realise how much he loved me until I met Zosar. He was a young man at the time, travelling the world going from pack to pack." I smiled. I couldn't see the Alpha being a young carefree man. "I was out for a run that day and I didn't realise I had run across our neighbouring pack land. We were very close so it wasn't unusual for it to happen but we generally liked to ask permission first. I was just so caught up in my head trying to get away from Tomás." She stopped, clearly her throat before she continued.

"Zosar thought I was from the neighbouring pack. I hadn't seen him but I smelt him. I knew I found my mate; I just didn't know where. I followed his scent but the wind misplaced it, taking me back to my own pack. I didn't know he saw me that day. He later said he tried to follow me but the wind confused him too. He figured I went back to the pack, the one he was staying with. So, when he tried to find me again, he didn't until weeks later. By then my wariness turned to fear of Tomás. That day when I arrived back home, I told him I wanted to break up. That I smelt my mate. He flew into a fury. Telling me he chose me as his mate and nothing was going to change that. He chained me to his bed in silver cuffs, had his way with me whenever he wanted until Zosar came. Turns out, Tomás's mate was from the neighbouring pack. That alpha had found her crying one day, saying he rejected her. Her alpha and Zosar came to my pack to demand answers as rejecting a mate wasn't a practice wolves ever did. And when Zosar came, I had to greet him as my pack's future Luna. I had silver scars around my wrists and once he saw them, all hell broke loose." She smiled remembering the day.

I looked down at her wrists, a scratching thought at the back of my head compelling me. Everytime I've seen the Luna, she always wore bangles and bracelets on her wrists. And when she lifted her hand to brush a strand of hair out of her face, I saw it. Faded scars wrapped around her wrists from silver cuffs. I sighed; we have more in common than I thought. Her past almost mirrored my own. *Almost.*

"Then Zosar took me far away from that awful pack and brought me here, to America. I met his father, a lovely man, and his mother was undeniably beautiful."

"What.." I began, unsure if I wanted to continue my question but the Luna nodded, giving me a warm smile. "What did Tomás do when you left?" I feared her answer.

"Well one of the warriors that came with the alpha and Zosar was his mate. He never actually locked eyes with her that day he smelt her scent and rejected her. He closed them, unwilling to let me go. But that day he was caught off guard and once their eyes locked, he felt the bond snap into place. He never had eyes for me again after that. The mate bond is a funny thing." She mused as she looked away, remembering old memories.

"What happened to them?" Now I was just curious. Maybe...maybe if Vladik found his mate he could forget about me.

"Well, he eventually started a pack war because he thought he had the right to more land and power. He eventually died, the neighbouring pack alpha won and merged the two packs. Tomás's mate ended up being the new alphas second chance mate."

"Second chance mate? That's super rare." I said shocked, I've only heard stories of second chance mates.

"Just like twins?" She mused making me giggle and blush.

"Luna," I asked, frowning at the ground. "Why did you tell me this story?"

"Because I know what you're going through. I could see it in your eyes the moment I saw you. You've known pain like that. I went through it too, and I survived. But not without the help of Zosar. I know what Cairo did was wrong and stupid of him to believe that...*girl*." I snickered, loving that there really isn't anyone in this pack that likes Jordan. "Take a day or two to think about everything that's happened and move on. You're marked now, that won't let you forget about him. Not even for a second. But he's hurting just as much as you are. And remember, he's still young. You both are. He'll make mistakes just like you'll make mistakes. I would say we're all human but we're not really." She says making us both laugh.

She looked up at the sky, studying the shades of orange beginning to mix with the blue. With all the crying and drama of the day, I didn't realise how much time had passed since I left the bedroom this morning.

"We better get going. It's going to get dark in an hour or two. I'm sure dinner will be ready soon as well." I nod and follow her back down the path.

"Where is everyone? I thought we were going to dinner?" I asked when we arrived at a different place than the pack house. From what I could tell it must be a back entrance to the dining hall.

"Oh, we are. It's a pack night tonight." She said as I looked confused. "Every couple of months we have a big feast in the hall. It's our way of thanking the pack for always being there for us. It's basically a werewolf version of what humans here call thanksgiving. Except we do it every three months." She said proudly as her accent thickened. Some peoples accent like mine, will thicken when I get angry. You can hear Alek's accent the strongest when he's sad and I see Luna's accent gets stronger when she's happy.

"That's really beautiful." I say truthfully. "My..my old pack used to do a big bonfire with pig on the spits and everyone would also bring a dish of sweets or savoury during the colder months. There was always so much food. Our pack doesn't have electricity so fire was the only way we could get warm during the winters and I guess it was almost like this thanksgiving." The Luna smiled, enjoying listening to me speak. "At the end of the night," I said laughing as I remember, "all the little kids would be passed out in the snow from eating so much food they couldn't move." I laugh again, remembering how Alek and I used to laugh seeing their little pot bellies poke out of their jackets.

"That sounds wonderful." The Luna said smiling, mahogany eyes shining back her warmth. "I will make sure we do that soon."

"Really?" I couldn't contain the excitement. It's been a long time since we did anything that reminded us of home.

"Of course, honey. You're my daughter now. I want to make you feel at home here, anyway I can." I couldn't help the tears that burst out from her kindness. She reminded me of my mama. "Oh, darling, please don't cry. Come here." She said pulling me to her as she wrapped her arms around me. I cried into her chest; her hand brushed through my hair as her other one rubbed circles on my back comforting me. I cried and then sniffled, feeling her dress against my cheek become wet from my tears. I pulled back, wiping both eyes as I apologised for crying.

"Sorry, y..you just reminded me of my mama. I," I stopped, swallowing the lump in my throat, "I miss her."

"Oh, honey I understand. Do you want to invite her here? We can pay to fly your parents over here." She said smiling.

"No." I say sadly. "I can't risk it." That was all I said, all I *could* say.

"Okay, I won't push." She said nodding understanding. "Do you-" She stops as a loud crash came from the door behind her.

"ARGH, YOU STUPID-" The screaming voice stopped mid yell. My heart was racing from the sudden sound but the Luna looked unfazed.

"Come with me, there's someone you should meet." She

said amused as she opened the door behind her and held it open for me to follow. We walked into a storage room of sorts. Then we passed through a second room, shelving lined both sides of the walls holding containers of fresh fruit and veg, along with all the other pantry essentials. The Luna continued, sliding the door across, we stepped into a massive industrial, large restaurant sized kitchen.

"What have you done now?" The Luna said in a stern voice but when I looked up at her she looked amused. The fiery haired woman dressed in chef whites turned, dark eyes glaring our way.

"Someone threw out all my non-stick pans for these cheap pieces of shit!" She said angrily waving a whisk in the air. I tried to hide my smile; I know she was annoyed right now but the way she waved the whisk around was making me laugh. Then she turned, shocking me as she threw it across the room, jumping as it clattered on the ground and skidded across the tiles. Next, her hand reached for the fry pan on the stove.

"Now, Joanna. You better not be reaching for that pan to toss across the room." The Luna said, squinting her eyes in question as the chefs back rose and fell as she breathed in and out, hand paused by her side. *That's totally what she was going to do,* I thought. Suddenly, she turned and almost flew across the kitchen before she stopped in front of us panting like a dog on a hot summer's afternoon.

"Oh, my Goddess, you *are* pretty!" She exclaimed looking me up and down. "It's so nice to finally meet you! I've been waiting ages to meet Cairo's mate." She says bouncing up and down on the spot like she's had way too much coffee.

"Don't mind her. She's jacked up on caffeine." The Luna said making me laugh as she read my mind. "She said it's great to meet you."

"Oh, it's great to meet you too, Joanna." I said smiling. "Whatever you're cooking in here smells amazing. My mouth is watering." I said as I took a deep breath in. It really did smell amazing in here.

"Why thank you." She said as she stopped bouncing to primp her wild hair and pushed the now loose strands back under the hair net. "I'm cooking creamy garlic and lemon chicken with a side of greens topped with parmesan and bacon. And a few other dishes not worth mentioning." She finished just as my stomach grumbled.

"That sounds so good." I said rubbing my belly.

"Alright, you go on ahead dear, get ready for dinner. I'm gonna stay behind for a bit and help." The Luna said as she turned to me. "I'll help crazy pants here with dinner before she destroys the place." She whispered making me laugh. I nodded to Joanna, saying my goodbyes before I left through another door the Luna pointed out to me. It led into the empty hall with the tables free of people. Now that I know where I am, I can easily make my way back to the pack house.

I couldn't find Maya anywhere and I really needed to have a shower. I felt all grimy from all the tears I shed today but I didn't want to just randomly use her shower without permission. So, I dared going back to our...Cairo's room. I hope to Goddess he isn't there. I can't face him just yet; I still need time. I stop at the door, lightly knocking as I wait for a response. After a minute and no reply, I twisted the knob, gingerly opening the door half expecting to see him sitting on the bed. But the room was empty. His scent smelt faint, meaning he left some time ago. I shut the door behind me, leg it to the bathroom as fast as I could. I stripped in what felt like two seconds before I was squealing as I jumped under the cold-water spray. The coolness felt refreshing, giving me a kick of energy. I showered as quick as I could, getting out and drying myself off in record time. I put my used towel in the dirty laundry basket along with my clothes. Then I beelined for the wardrobe, grabbing a pair of black underwear and sliding them up my legs quickly before I turned, grabbing the first dress I saw hanging up. I caught my reflection in the mirror once as I smoothed the dress down. Thin straps, the short flowy white sundress with little yellow sunflowers embroided on it was cute. I looked pretty in it. But the wet ends of my hair made me look half-dressed and definitely rushed. I didn't have time to do more. I didn't want to get caught. I quick stepped to the door, quietly closing it just as a voice spoke from behind me.

"Fuck, Zia!" Alek exclaimed making me jump. I had pins and needles shoot down my body was the sudden jump scare. "I've been looking everywhere for you. First, you were already gone from the bedroom by the time I came back to see you. Then I checked Maya's room but I had just missed you. I followed your scent all the way out to that river but you weren't there either. I figured you went back to Maya's so I tried there and big surprise, you weren't there, *again*. Now I find you sneaking out of here acting all jumpy. What's going on?" He finally finishes his little rant.

"Nothing. Just...mate stuff. You?" I ask. Alek only ever rants when he's troubled. He either keeps it bottled up, constantly frowning or something will set it off and he'll rant for a good ten minutes.

"The same." He sighs, giving me a tight smile. I nod, tightly smiling back. What a pair of siblings we are.

"So...How's the weather today?" Maya asked from across the table. Alek sat on the end, Sarana sat across from him tapping away on someone's phone next to Maya who tried and failed to ease the tension in the air. There were two spaces between me and a dejected looking Cairo. Keiran sat across from him, and Zack sat between him and Maya who was looking at all four of us as we all shared the same look. I kept stealing glances at Cairo, but he never looked up from his hands crossed on the table.

"*Ty v poryadke?*" Alek asked checking on me.

"*Net. Ty?*" I said quietly, asking if he was okay back. He breathed in, looking over at Keiran a long while before he exhaled.

"*Net. Vsyo raspadayetsya na chasti.*" He said sadly as his lip trembled, saying everything is falling apart.

"*Ya znayu.*" I said sniffling. I couldn't agree more. Just when we were starting to feel overwhelmingly happy, it all comes crashing down. He pulls me towards him wrapping one arm around me as his own lip starts to quiver. He turns his head, hiding from prying eyes.

"I...should really start learning Russian. I didn't understand a word of that." Zack said making a joke but I didn't laugh. No one did.

"He asked if she was okay." Keiran said, speaking up softly.

"You know Russian?" Cairo said finally looking up surprised.

"A...a little. Alek's been teaching me." He said quietly like he didn't want Alek to hear. He pulled back, watching Keiran as he spoke. "I've also been studying in my free time and got a tutor at school to help." I could hear the tension in Alek's jaw from clenching his teeth. He looked like he wanted to run over there and kiss him but he stayed, looking troubled. I wonder what happened between them.

"She said-" Keiran began but Cairo cut him off hurriedly.

"Sarana! Get off the table!" He said panicked as he struggled to get out of his seat fast enough.

"Bubba, shush!" She snapped back at him making him stop, confused. "Eya, sad." She said pointing at me with her little fingers. "Sasa hug!" She said making me laugh breathily through a sniffle as I wiped my tears away.

"Okay." Cairo said sitting back down but still watched her closely. I lifted my hands up, letting her grab a hold as I helped her down off the table and into my lap. Her little arms were around my neck in seconds, hugging me with her small strength. I smiled, no longer feeling sad as this toddler hugged away my sadness. My eyes were dry by the time she pulled back, pig tails bouncing as her face stopped inches from mine.

"Betta?" I smile brightly, nodding as she clapped.

"All better now, thank you, Sasa." I say smiling as I brush her little overgrown fringe out of her eyes. "Sit down on my lap and we'll have some yummy dinner together.

Shortly after, Joanna appeared, following behind her were a line of waiters as they brought plate after plate out of that delicious creamy garlic lemon chicken she spoke of. I was one of the lucky ones who got said chicken. After that was all gone, she brought more mains out of different chicken recipes that almost smelt delicious. I grabbed Sarana's miniaturized plate, cutting the chicken into bite sized pieces for her before I sat back, staring down at my food as I salivated. I felt bad Joanna and her staff spent so much time cooking all of this, thinking they would miss out of the dinner but when they came back out all holding one plate each, they headed to the remaining empty spots around the hall. It was only after they sat down that everyone began eating. I smiled, looking across at the sea of faces, admiring how caring they were to wait for everyone to be included before the dinner commenced. I fall in love with this pack more and more as every day goes by as I see a new side to it or new places recently discovered. It's a pack worth dying for.

Chapter Thirty-Seven

A Pack Tradition

"Wakey, wakey eggs and bakey." Alek said in a sing song voice as he walked to the middle of the room, already dressed in his school uniform. "Are you girls ready for school?" I don't know why he bothered asking. Clearly we are still in bed, hair a tangled mess and sleep in our eyes as our ears ring from his sudden singing.

"Pshhh," I wave my hand blindly in the air, "not so loud.." I begin to drift off as his voice speaks again.

"Zia, we all leave for school in ten minutes. Think your ass can be ready by then?"

"Probably..." I mumbled under my breath. I stretched out like a cat, savouring the tightness in my muscles.

"Be quick. I feel like we've missed too much school. I don't want to fall behind. I want us to be able to graduate with the rest of the group."

"I know." I say as I stand up. I don't want to be left behind. "We missed out on a lot, huh." Three years of schooling missed, three years of *living*, missed.

"Everything will work out. It always does...eventually." He

said the last word quietly as to not jinx it. I'm sure I even saw him knocking on the wooden door.

I nod, before leaning down, grabbing my uniform I folded last night. Alek heads to the door, saying he'll wait for us outside. Maya had already hobbled off to the bathroom the second Alek woke us up.

"How do I look?" Maya asked, twirling in her uniform.

"Good? Are you going somewhere other than school?" She nods before a blush coats her cheeks.

"My mate is gonna walk me to school. I think he might mark me today!" She whispered excitedly.

"That's amazing! I know how much you've wanted to find your mate." She nods.

"I'm excited but nervous." She said shyly, rubbing the back of her neck.

"Which is understandable but don't be. It's gonna be amazing." I say as I lift my plait up, waving my hand to fan some air on my neck. My hair is like a curtain of heat sometimes.

"Okay," She breathes out, "I'll see you at school then." She gives me a quick hug, looking slightly awkward as she wrapped her arms around me. I smiled at her, reassuring her.

We walked down the stairs before we part ways. She headed for the exit in the mudroom while I went to the front door. Alek was waiting by the path that led to and from the pack house front door and if it was a normal human home I would say he'd be waiting by the letterbox at the end of the path. He was in conversation with Zack. Kitty stood next to him and watched me approach with a small smile on her face. She tried to hide it but I saw her eyes flicker, dropping down to my neck, trying to get a peak of Cairo's mark. I'm sure by now everyone has heard what happened or at least our friend group has. Zacks got a loudmouth. I stop beside Alek, brushing my hand against his arm letting him know I was there. I looked for Cairo, who stood by the large tree in front of the pack house already watching me with sad eyes. I could feel the half link between us, knowing he could now feel my emotions from his mark or hear my thoughts which I could only hear his because I wasn't like most wolves. He could feel my longing for him, feel my hurt. *I miss you, Cairo.* I think as I shield my mind, knowing he won't be able to hear my thoughts if I do that. I wish I could say that to him but things right now are awkwardly tense. Just like Alek and Keiran, who stood beside Cairo, staring at the ground like he's trying to hold back tears. Alek wouldn't look at him and I know it's because if he did, all his resolve would disappear and he would march right over there and take him into his arms and kiss away their problems. But sometimes things aren't that easy. No matter how much we wish it was.

"Are you guys excited for today!?" Kitty exclaimed happily.

"What's today?" I asked confused, looking between Kitty and Zack who were absolutely buzzing with joy.

"Our pack tradition for the seniors!" She said as Zack nodded.

"I've heard it's one of the best field trips our school does." He added.

"Where are we going?" Alek asked, just as confused as I was.

"And what are we doing?" I said, almost mirroring Alek's question.

"It's a senior field trip where we basically just chill out the whole day. A rite of passage for us wolves before we join the pack as adults." Zack said proudly.

"Yeah, we have one class this morning but it's really just like a roll call and explaining the events of today, then we go to this massive, special lake. The location is a secret until you get there. Like Zacky said, it's a rite of passage for the seniors."

Kitty explained, violet eyes looking brighter the more she spoke.

"Yeah, none of us actually know where this Lake is. Some even say it's been spelled so we can't find it until today." Zack said peaking Alek and my interests.

"If you were to ask any pack member for the location they won't tell you. But if you ask them tomorrow they would." Kitty said rolling her eyes at the same time as Zack did.

"So, it's like a coming-of-age type experience?" I ask and they nod. "Well, I guess I gotta get my swimsuit then." I say as I begin jogging back to the front door.

"Get mine too!" Alek called out.

"And a change of clothes for afterwards!" Zack interjects.

I run up the stairs, quickly not to take too much time so the group isn't held up waiting for me. I dart into my room, grabbing the first swimsuit and change of clothes I see before I head to Alex and Kieran's room. I don't waste time peaking around the room. I head straight for the chair in the corner that has a pile of Aleks clothes all stacked on top of each other. I pull out a shirt, pair of pants, one swim trunks and his flip flops. Which reminded me I also needed a change of shoes.

I hurry outside, one bag over each shoulder as I stopped next to Alek. He takes the bag with our shoes and clothes before he begins walking. Zack and Kitty held most of the conversation on the way to school. Alek and I joined in here and there but every time we caught a glimpse of our mates we quieted. Feeling the loneliness that we were used to seep in.

"Good morning, class! I expect you all know what today is." The teacher said expectedly with a huge grin on her face. The students in the class whooped and hollered in excitement. Some were clapping their hands together and others were making drum sounds on their desk. The teacher laughed, waving her hands in the air to silence the noise. "Okay, OKAY, calm down. As it is tradition, we will not be traveling by bus today. Since most of you are werewolves you will be shifting. Lina, you will be vamp running and Bailey," the teacher said addressing the only male human in the class besides Somner, "well, pick a wolf to ride. Everyone gets to embrace what they are and experience this day with each other. You will graduate together and most of you will be running the pack together some day. Since Somner has a mate, he will be taking her. Which just leaves Bailey. Would anyone be kind enough to let him ride on your wolf?" She asks as her eyes scan the class. I looked around the room, noticing no one was raising their hand to volunteer.

"He can come with me if he wants." I said, not wanting him to feel left out. I know how that feels. Suddenly, a vicious growl tore through the room. We all jumped, turning to see Cairo, bright eyes of his wolf shining through as he looked directly at Bailey like he was prey. We could hear the rattle in his chest, the deep heavy puffs of air exhaling like a bull staring at a red flag ready to charge. Bailey audibly gulped, feeling the target I had accidentally put on him. The teacher cleared her throat, trying to get everyone's attention but the air in the room became tense as we all watched Cairo. Fearing his wolfs reaction.

"Okay, well, I..is there anyone else?" She asked nervously.

"He's coming with me." Lina announced, looking at him with a twinkle in her eye.

"No! Last time you vamp ran with me I threw up." He exclaimed.

"Because you are weak." She teased.

"Am not." He replied.

"Prove it." Lina whispered leaning in as her fangs shone in the light. Bailey leaned forward, nose almost touching with Lina's as he spoke.

"I think I already have, remember..." He said and I think it all clicked for everyone. These two were mates. I don't know why she didn't volunteer in the first place but if vamp running makes him sick then I guess I get it. Or maybe she was just teasing him.

"Uhm...o..okay then. Let's head out everyone."

This was our first time running in a pack. We never got the chance to do this when we first shifted. We were supposed to run with the Alpha and the pack a few days after our fifteenth birthday but then...Vladik happened. It felt amazing and I could feel a deep connection forming with the people in my class. Cairo led the group, his large black wolf, fur glistening in the sun as he bounded over fallen trees, leaping through the air, and landing strongly on his paws. We ran for miles. Eventually, my wolf ran by his side, naturally falling into place. Our wolves loved running together and everyone could tell. Every couple of minutes Cairo's wolf would turn his head, making sure his mate was still running safely beside him. Her tongue would shoot out, licking his snout as he huffed out, puffing his chest up proudly. His wolf was such a show pony. I really do miss him. We've both made so many mistakes and after everything I've been through in my short life, in this moment I'm realising it's time to stop wasting precious moments. Why are we worrying about the petty little stuff when I could be telling him that I love him back?

We made it back to the pack, running across pack lines as we made our way deeper into the forest. I could feel the teacher linking Cairo, telling him where to go. After a couple of minutes, that familiar sound of running water floated through the air, getting louder the closer we got. Everything smelt so fresh and everything looked so green. I could hear the birds tweeting in the air. Even the fluttering of butterfly wings as they danced around all the colourful flowers that bloomed. I feel like I was made to live in this pack. Once we got to a clearing, the teacher shifted back, changing behind a large tree before she addressed the class one last time.

"Alright guys, you can shift and change into your swimwear. We'll be here all day so enjoy yourselves. We'll also be having pizza for lunch, so come when I call you or else you'll either be eating cold pizza or you'll miss out." She finished speaking as she pulled a branch back, the foliage revealing a crystal blue lake. The water shined like it was made of crystals, birds flew down, dangling their little feet in the water as they surfed by. There was a bank a few feet from where the teacher stood. Thick grassy patches surrounded the water, almost looking like moss beds. There was a large esky placed by a palm like tree with three piles of fresh towels. Everyone cheered, running ahead as they raced through the water, splashing each other as they got deeper. Alek and I stayed back, changing into our swimsuits. The teacher joined in, letting the tree branch go, shielding us from the stunning view. We looked at each other, nervously nodding as Alek pulled the branch back, letting me walk through first before he followed. I wiped my forehead, sweat droplets forming as I looked out at the water. Some were knee deep in the water, others waist deep or doggy paddling in the deeper parts.

"I love when you guys' match. It's literally adorable." Maya said as she popped up in front of us. We looked down, seeing the same shade of canary yellow on my one piece and Alek's swim trunks. He gave me a look, making me laugh as I put my hands up defensively.

"I swear I didn't plan this. It just happened." I said as he made a face and *mmm'ed* me as if he didn't believe me. Maya laughed, shaking her head at us before telling us to come swim with her before she turned, running through the water squealing.

"It's not that deep..." I whispered to Alek, wiping my forehead nervously as sweat built up again. "Right?"

"I..it looks shallow enough. We should be fine. Just take it easy, Zi." He said just as quietly.

"I will. You too, Ali. It's just like when we swam in our wolf forms, right?" Our wolves were excellent swimmers, their natural instincts letting them survive through any terrain.

"Exactly. They swam absolutely fine. So, we should too." I breathed in and out, feeling hot and sweaty from the rising heat building within me from stress. "You okay?" He asked. "It's just a little water and it looks pretty still. If we stay to the front we can stand."

"No, it's not that. I just feel a little hot and overwhelmed." I confess.

"I'm nervous too, but there's so many people here that we'll be fine. Okay?"

"Okay." I repeat. Alek walks ahead, gingerly walking into the water as he heads over to Zack and Keiran. Maya waves to me, calling me over to her and Somner. I breathe in and out, calming my nerves as I took a tentative step into the water. *I can do this.* If Alek can do it, I can too. *Just one foot in front of the other.*

Chapter Thirty-Eight

The Misstep

CAIRO

Running alongside Zia's stunning ash-white wolf felt incredible. Truly indescribable. I felt the strongest I've ever felt with my Queen running beside me. I could see our future; see the way we'd run our pack together. It was like all our problems suddenly went away as we ran. Now, as I stand chest deep in the water, I watch Zia as she apprehensively walks into the water. I'm gonna man up, speak to her and be the mate she always wanted. Just as soon as I stop feeling so damn anxious. I feel like a fuckin pup again. *Wait...I don't feel anxious*. So, why? *What the hell?! Why do I feel scared now?* I gasp, looking to Zia. These are her emotions I'm feeling, not mine. My mark on her ties her feelings and thoughts to me. She's fucking terrified right now. Then the realization hits me like a ton of bricks. She can't swim.

I growl, tearing through the water trying to get view of her again as people splashed and swam in front of me. *Where is she...where is she...* I thought, beginning to panic until she suddenly came back into view. I push my hearing out, focusing on her over the waves and splashing. Her heart is beating like a little hummingbird. My breath rips from my lungs just as I spot the drop in the lakebed. She's not looking down; she can't see she's about to step off into a deep part. It's like I was in a nightmare, I was running as hard as I could but the water slowed me down, making me feel like I wasn't running at all. She dropped, eyes flashing in fear as her head went under, arms wailing in the air as she thrashes about. People around mistake her panic for fun. I inhale and dive under the water, kicking my feet out as I glide through effortlessly. I could see her, screaming for help as she tried to claw her way back up to the surface with no success. She was drowning, heart hammering away. I reached her just as her eyes started to flutter.

Everything happened so fast.

I pushed off the ground, shooting us straight to the surface as she gasped, pulling in as much air as she could, clinging onto me so tightly that her clawed nails pierced into my shoulders, but I didn't care. She was safe, I got her in time. Both of our hearts felt like they beat as one as her chest pressed tightly against mine. She was shivering, shaking like a leaf and I tightened my arms around her, rubbing circles on her back as I whispered in her ear, telling her she's safe. That I won't ever let her go. I could feel the petrified, terrified feeling through our one-sided bond. I could also feel her relief, the more she breathed in and out. Then that relief turned to a staggering amount of love. I felt my heart restrict tightly as my eyes began to tear up. *She loves me.* I didn't think she did after all my fuck ups but she does. *She loves me.* She slowly pulled back, just enough so that she could look deep into my eyes.

"Cairo...You saved me.." She sounded surprised. I frowned, feeling anger bristle under my skin.

"I will always save you, Zia. Always." I promised as her eyes teared up and she began to sniffle. "You're my whole world. You're the reason I wake up in the morning happy like a kid on Christmas. Just seeing your gorgeous smile is enough to make my whole day. I'm going to marry you one day, Zia. You are my soul mate, my other half. If something were to happen to you, then everyone should mourn twice because I can't and won't live without you. You're my everything, Zia." I said as she suddenly wrapped her arms around my neck, breasts pushing into my chest as she held me tight.

"I love you, Cairo. I love you so much my heart hurts. I should have said it back to you. I should have-" She continues but I cut her off.

"I know, it's okay." She leaned back, looking at me with tear filled eyes as I leaned in, kissing her tears away.

ZIA

My slowly breaking heart was mended the instant I felt his strong hands grab my waist and hauled me up out of the water. Alek and I never learned to swim in our human forms because the lakes near our home were almost always frozen. Our wolves could swim because it's their natural instinct to be able to swim and survive, but with us we never did. I think we both tried to conceal our actual feelings and panic as we looked out at the river. I felt Alek the second he walked into the water and realized it wasn't as deep or scary as he thought. But me on the other hand, I was scared. Too anxious to feel anything else. I blocked off my bond to Alek, not wanting to ruin his day with my dread filled feelings. I'm glad I did because when I felt the ground beneath my feet disappear and I dropped down into the water, he would have drowned himself trying to save me. The pack would have lost two wolves today, not one. I remember trying to scream as water rushed in, filling my lungs. My heart seemed magnified under water, pounding fast as my life was threatened. I remember looking up at the surface as it got further and further away. My last thoughts were going to be thinking that I was going to die. But then I felt his hands. Cairo. He raced to save me without a second thought. I tried to call out to the others but they just smiled and turned their backs. I don't think they knew I was drowning.

I had my doubts when Cairo told me he loved me. I thought it may have been a manipulation tactic to get me to stay with him but the moment he pulled me out of the water I knew he really did love me. His actions and hurtful words in the past meant nothing to me anymore when I almost lost my life. Nothing compared.

The rest of the morning flowed by without incident. Cairo and I stayed in the shallow end, sitting on the sandy banks with the water swaying against our chests. He couldn't keep his hands off me and even growled when anyone tried to come close to me, even to the females. He was extremely apologetic, having no clue why his wolf kept growling at everyone. It seemed both him and his wolf didn't want to let me go. He was constantly kissing my neck, kissing his mark heating my body up as the water fought to cool me down. I'm sure if I didn't have supernatural healing I'd be covered in hickeys and my lip would be bleeding from how hard I've been biting it trying to conceal moans. I wish we could have made up sooner because I couldn't get enough of him. My hands felt like they were glued to his body. I'm glad we were in the water; it hid our arousal. Although I don't think it would take a genius to realise Cairo and I were horny making out in the water.

After lunch, having finished eating the homemade pizza's Joanna and her team brought, we all went back in the water and played this Marco polo game that Alek and I had never heard of, but it was a lot of fun. We were easy targets by staying in the shallow end but I think everyone kinda figured we weren't the best swimmers because the IT person didn't really go for us after a while. Which was fun because it was more enjoyable watching the person swimming blindly trying to catch the person nearest to them. When the sun started to set, the teacher called us out of the water, explaining there was one last senior event we had to attend. The pack BBQ. I had just finished changing when Cairo grabbed my hand, pulling me away from the group saying he wanted to show me something. It was only a couple of minutes' walk before we came to a small cave opening. He led me in through the dark, pushing the hanging vines out of the way as he held my hand tightly, pulling me up if I tripped. Suddenly there was light. What looked like thousands of blue fireflies lit up the cave ceiling, revealing another hidden lake inside. They shimmered in the water's reflection below, making the cave have a magical atmosphere.

"Cairo, this place is breathtaking." I exclaimed; mouth opened as I took in the wonders of the cave. I could hear running water, leaking down the rock walls, flowing into the magical hidden lake. There were tunnels to the back of the cave splintering off in different directions. It was an underground cave system connected to the lake we were at all day.

"I found this place when I was a kid." He spoke from behind me. "I know this is everyone's first time here but it's not mine. When I was younger I.." He stopped mid-sentence, breathing as he looked past me out at the tunnels. "I had a younger brother." He said so quietly I would have missed it.

"Had..." I whispered, feeling sorrow as I looked into his sad hazel eyes, tears forming as he nodded his head, brows furrowed.

"He was a year younger than me." He said breathing in. "When I was seven, we were playing near the pack borders when there was a rogue attack. My brother he...he didn't make it. The rogue turned on me next but before he could attack me my father appeared out of nowhere and tackled the wolf to the ground. His wolf fought the rogue, while I stood there frozen, holding my brothers bleeding body as he died in my arms. By the time the rogue was dead and dad turned back to grab Siron, he...he was already gone." I cried, holding my chest. His brother was only six when he died and Cairo was seven when he witnessed this. "That's why there's a big age difference between Sarana and me. My parents they took his death hard. Like most of us did and would if we had children. But he was their child. Then, one day a few years ago my mother found out she was pregnant. It was a blessing; *she* is a blessing. The older she gets, the more like Siron she is. It's almost like the Goddess gave him back to us." He said as he sadly smiled. I took a deep breath in, stopping the tears as he continued. "That's also why you didn't meet her straight away. My mother, she was worried. And so was I." Because I was a rogue. Now it all made sense. Why he hated me from the second he met me. Why the whole pack looked at us with disgust and hate before they even knew us. "I'm so sorry I treated you so badly when you came here. I was trying to protect myself and act like I was this big tough guy but I was anything but. I was scared. Scared that you would be just like those rogues and I was afraid I'd lose Sarana, just like I lost Siron."

"I would never hurt her, or anyone-" I began but he cut me off.

"I know that now, we all do. We knew it the moment we saw you two in the Trials. Anyone else would have taken the kill, but you and Alek went out of your way not to kill our warriors, not to kill your opponent's when everyone before you did." I slowly nod, killing was never an option for us. We didn't really believe in killing unless it really was life or death.

"This cave?" I ask quietly.

"It was a dark time for the pack after Siron's death. I ran away from home and found this cave. I stayed here for weeks, crying and being angry at myself for not protecting him better. My parents knew where I was but they let me be. They had someone drop off baskets of food everyday so I wouldn't starve. We all needed time to ourselves. After the haze of guilt and anger left, I realized how beautiful this place was. That was when I decided I would start focussing on my alpha training. I gave up my childhood to become strong. I trained mercilessly every day, only ever coming back here when things got too much to handle. I uh," he stops, rubbing his neck nervously as a blush begins to colour his cheeks, "I've never shown anyone this place before. I made a promise that I would take my mate here when I found her. This is where I wanted to take you the night of the ball."

"So, you...you never took Jordan here?" I asked feeling stupid and insecure.

"No." He said looking disgusted before he breathed out. "Look, Jordan was just...easy. I knew she only wanted me because of the chance to become Luna. I was young and stupid and she was always up for some...fun." He barely whispered the last part. "I didn't..didn't realize how sacred the mate bond was until I met you. You don't know how many nights I laid awake at night wishing I never touched her. Wishing that I had saved myself for you." My heart clenched as my lip trembled.

"I...I wish, I wish...I.." I tried to speak but my words failed me, heart too afraid to say the words that plagued my mind since Vladik happened. "I wish you were my first." I finally said, staring at the ground refusing to look up at Cairo.

"Hey, I will be." He said gently placing his finger under my chin, lifting my head up to look at him. "Don't even think about him or that. Okay?" His tone was so conflicting. He was angry but trying to be reassuring at the same time. It made me smile.

"I'll try." I say as a sudden wave of heat overcomes me. I inhale and exhale, breathing in and out as sweat begins to drip down my back. I feel like I'm going crazy because it's not that hot here in the cave. It actually feels cool. My shirt begins to feel like latex stuck to my skin. I need it off, need to breathe. I grab the hem of my shirt, crossing my arms over as I pull it over my head, exposing my bra to Cairo.

"Ahem..." He clears his throat as he turns, giving me his back. "Zi, baby? W..what are you doing?" He asked rubbing the back of his neck as he gulped.

"Oh, sorry, Cairo. It's just so hot," I say fanning myself again. "I've been hot all day. The water actually helped a lot. But since we've been out I've gotten hot again. Am I sunburnt?" I asked as he turned around. I watched as he looked at my face, over my shoulders and down my arms. It wasn't until he looked at my chest that his eyes widen, gasping as he quickly reached forward placing the back of his hand on my forehead checking my temperature.

"Shit!" He repelled back as if he got burnt. His eyes were as black as night, canines extending and chest rising and falling in a quick manner.

"W..what's wrong?" His hands clenched and unclenched; brows furrowed like he was fighting himself. His closed eyes snapped open as he began to stalk towards me. Making my heart skip a beat.

"It's your Heat, Zia." He said, growling under his breath as his eyes lowered, searing me with his look. "That's why you've smelt so fucking addicting today. Why I haven't been able to keep my hands off you, why my wolf has been so territorial." He licked his lips as I followed the movement, breathing out a silent gasp as my body shook. We waited too long in between marking. It didn't matter if one of us were marked or both of us marked each other. The second Cairo marked my neck, the heat began. Getting stronger every day that past. If wolves refuse to mate and complete the bond, the female goes through excruciating pain. We call it Heat because that's what it feels like. Our bodies heat up, getting aroused by the smallest things or even the simplest touch by our mate. If I refuse any longer the pain will begin, incapacitating me to the point that I will feel like I'm dying. It's a biological trait of our bodies do to make sure our bonds are completed and our souls are finally joined together as one.

"Cairo," I said as the blue in my eyes shifted, midnight taking over to show my mate I was feeling the same arousal.

"Yes..." He said so breathy my knees wobbled, threatening to give way. He saw, hands instantly grabbing me as I moaned from his touch.

"Take me, Cairo. I'm yours." And he did.

Chapter Thirty-Nine

Heat

Cairo crashed his lips against mine, kiss searing me as I opened my mouth, tongues dancing together as his hands snaked through my hair. My body felt like it was on fire, melting into his as he pushed our bodies together, free hand roaming down my back. That deep burning sensation blossomed within me and would only stop from Cairo's touch. My pants felt restricting, encasing the heat within my body, making it almost painful. I whined as I pulled back, purring as I unbuttoned my pants, letting them drop down my legs before I kicked them off to the side.

"Cairo...Mark me, take me..." I panted. The moment those words left my mouth he was on me again, taking me down to the ground as kissed down my jaw, across my neck and to his mark. He kissed it repeatedly, making me moan and thrash beneath him from the tingling sensation that shot through my body every time he touched his mark. He growled possessively as he lifted his head, glaring at my bra like it was the enemy. He looked up, smirking as a claw descended on his index finger. He hooked it under the front of my bra. He tugged, bra snapping open as my breasts spilled out, nipples hard from my heat. He looked down, purring. He lowered his head, taking a nipple in his mouth as his tongue swirled around. I moaned, pushing my chest into him as I reached down with my own clawed fingers, wanting to rip my panties off the same way he did my bra but he stopped me. Large hand circling my wrist as he held it against the grass beside my head. His mouth left my nipple with a pop. "Please..." I begged. I tried to move my other hand but he smirked, grabbing that one too. I bucked my hips, words failing me as I frowned up at him, the heat becoming unbearable.

"There's no rush, baby. I'll take the pain away, I promise. Just let me enjoy this, I'll make you feel good." He said, his deep husky voice making my body shiver.

He moved down further, hands hooking onto either side of my panties as I lift my hips up, helping him pull them down my legs. I was now fully naked, a bed of long soft grass at my back, the sound of our breathing and running water sounded throughout the cave, making me really feel one with nature in this moment. Just the way our ancestors would complete their bonds. He lowered his head again, breathing in my cores scent as my face heated. If my mind wasn't clouded by my heat and lust I would be screaming from embarrassment at how much I liked that carnal move. I was instantly wet the second he breathed me in and growled. I gasped as his head disappeared between my legs, tongue licking slowly up as my body began to vibrate. I shuddered as his tongued entered me, it was warm and wet, heating me to a breaking point. He moved ever so slightly, tracing circles with his tongue as his hands slid under my thighs and over my hips. He placed his hands on the inside of my legs, spreading me open as he brought me closer and closer to the edge. I was a panting mess, back arching off the ground as my hands went to my breasts, holding myself as he took his time. He was feasting on me, enjoying the taste of me on his tongue. He slowly moved one hand. The second his fingers slid down and circled my clit, I exploded. I screamed out, hearing it echo across the water, hips bucking against his head as he clamped his mouth down on me. My hands dug into the grass, holding on for dear life as my body shook and shuttered, before slowly coming down from my sudden high.

"C..Cairo..." I panted out, watching as he leaned back, mouth wet from my core as he looked down at me through lowered lids, chest rising and falling as he caught his breath. His tongue slowly slid out, tracing his lips, tasting me again.

"Mmm," He growled, eyes trailing down my body. I swallowed as my mouth dried when his hands moved to the zipper on his pants.

I watched with intent, eyes flicking back up to his face as he smirked, knowing exactly what I want to see. He pulled the zipper down ever so slowly, teasing me. I let out a warning growl annoyed he was taking too long making him laugh. Finally, he pushed the waist band down, raising each leg one at a time to pull his pants off, tossing them aside with my own. I licked my lips, taking in his God like body. Dark honey tanned skin, muscles rippling as he moved above me. I feel his length against me as he crawls up my body, the muscles in his arms bunching and stretching as his hands stops either side of my head. I reach out, feeling his peck muscles beneath my hands. I slowly trail down, feeling every inch of his chest and muscles until I stop, gasping as I grab him hardened self in my hand, feeling the sheer size of him. He was so hard, like I was holding a steel rod in my hand.

On instinct, I guided him into me, letting the tip stop at my opening. He leaned down just as I moved up, meeting him halfway in a searing kiss. His tongue dances with mine as my hands go to his head, pulling him into me more. I want my lips swollen and my breath taken away. And he does exactly that with one, slow, deep thrust. The moment he was fully seated inside me, our lips parted, heads thrown back in pure bliss as the extent of our full mate bond snapped into place. Our breaths were stolen, fingertips tingling as we stayed still. That whimsy thread of our bond we felt the moment we recognised each other as our mates was now a thick, braided rope, entwined around us. I could feel him but he felt dulled. Like the volume was turned down. Then I realised I hadn't marked him back. He was still frozen above me, feeling the full effects of the bond. I couldn't hold back anymore. The heat had begun to burn through me again, urging me to mark him now more than ever. While he was distracted, I let my canines extended, running my tongue along the sharp tip. Then I moved, suddenly flipping us over in one clean sweep as I straddled him. Before he could comprehend what happened, I strike, clamping down on his neck, instantly marking him. He yelled out, body shaking beneath me as he came. He bucked against me, my teeth pulling at his skin as his blood entered my mouth feeling like pure ecstasy. I let go, placing my hands on his chest and slowly pulled back. He looked at me, mouth open as I saw myself in the reflection of his dark midnight eyes. I could see his blood dripping down my lips like I was a vampire. Now it was my turn to smirk. His eyebrows were raised, shocked at what just happened. I laughed finding the look on his face absolutely priceless. He groaned when I slowly began to move my hips, large hands grabbing my hips but he didn't stop me. Our slow paced picked up speed as he used his hands on my hips pushing me back and forth fastening our rhythm.

Goddess, this feels amazing.

"Could agree more." Cairo said as he flipped us back over. With him back on top, he fisted the grass beside my head with one hand, the other slid under the small of my back, scooping me up as he pressed us together, letting him slide in deeper.

"Fuck!" I exclaimed. He was so much deeper in this new position.

I could do this forever.

Cairo's laughter filled the cavern once more, hearing my unshielded thoughts. The sound echoing back in a symphony of deep bellows before they were replaced by the sounds of our sex. Both being vocal as the feelings were incredible. This was unlike anything I had ever felt before.

We spent hours making love as we explored each other's bodies. The stamina of werewolves really was impressive. I thought we would have burned out hours ago but we were only just now slowing down. One final orgasm later and we were collapsing back on the grass, catching our breaths as we lay naked, hot, and sweaty. I would die if anyone were to accidentally stumble into this cave right now. I mean just two seconds ago my ass was in the air so that would have been a sight to see.

Cairo pulled me to him, wrapping his arm around me so I lay against him chest. I bring my knee up, laying it over his waist as I listen to the steady rhythm of his heart.

"Wow." He said, musing aloud.

"Yeah, wow.." I said with a smile on my face.

"What a sport." He said making me laugh. "How are you feeling?" He said raising his hand to my forehead, feeling my temperature.

"I'm good. The...heat, subsided a while ago." He chuckled, removing his hand as he laid it on his stomach.

"I didn't know you could be feisty like that." I pushed at his chest as I gingerly sat up.

"You thought that was feisty?" I laughed.

"Zi, baby, words cannot describe." He said making me laugh. "You can definitely ride me anytime. Shocked the hell out of me but fuck if I didn't like it."

"Stop.." My face felt like it was going through its own heat. He winked, making me swat his chest before I stood up, walking over to our pile of clothes.

"What are you doing?" He asked as he held himself up by

the elbows, muscles rippling in his chest and you guessed it, he was hard again.

"Cairo..." I said groaning as I turned away. "Can you...put your dick away?"

"Why? Your seats all ready for you."

"My sea-" I began but it clicked when he made his thing wave at me. "Oh, my, Goddess. I can't deal with you right now. Can you just get dressed? We have that barbeque to go too. Encase you missed it; my stomachs been rumbling like crazy. Plus, I need to get a dress from home first." I slip my underwear on, then my jean shorts. As I bend over to pick my shirt and tattered bra, I feel him come up behind me. Turning around, my nose brushes against his chest. I step back, shaking my head and smiling to myself as I pull my shirt over my head. The second the shirt is down; he takes my lips in his. One hand threads through my hair, holding the base of my neck while his other slides slowly down my stomach. My breath hitches as his fingers push past the band of my pants, before he slowly enters me. I moaned into his mouth, feeling two fingers slowly thrust in and out as he pushes his palm into me, rubbing friction against my clit. My head drops back as I moan, ecstasy taking over as I breathe in and out. His slightly hunched over form bends further down as he kisses down my jaw to my throat. His tongue darts out, teasing his mark as his fingers continue to bring me back to that blissful edge again.

"I g...I guess...we're going to be late..." I panted out, just before his teeth bit down, marking my red raw neck, making me explode.

"Goddess, Cairo!" I exclaimed. I couldn't believe my eyes. Fairy lights hung across the big, opened space, three large, long tables lined up at the back of the pack house, filled to galore with food. There was music, people dancing off to the sides and people chattering away with drinks or food in hand. There was even a small bond fire near the back, children sat around it with marshmallows on sticks, holding it in the fire and giggling as the puffy white goodness caught fire. I looked through the sea of people, seeing the Luna smiling at me from afar. She looked proud.

"We don't usually have a bon fire, that's new. But mum did say she was going to make a few tweaks because of something you said. A...about your pack?" Cairo said quietly behind me just as the Luna nodded before she looked away, speaking to a pack member who just walked up to her. My tears acted on their own, falling hard and fast as my heart strummed. "Baby, what's wrong?!" Cairo said spinning me around as he felt the sudden change of emotion within me.

"I. Nothing." I said as I sniffled and wiped my tears away. I didn't want to stain my off the shoulder dark teal dress. It twisted in the middle of my breasts pulling the neck down into a V neckline. There was a diamond shape cut out hole just under the twist and the dress was tight fitting, hugging my body perfectly as it stopped mid-thigh. I felt pretty in this dress and didn't want to ruin it with my tears.

"The changes, they remind you of your parents." He said reading my thoughts.

"I miss them. I don't know if my papa is even still alive." I said, feeling my lip tremble.

"What happened at your pack, baby?" He asked and I could feel the genuine concern through our bond.

"I..I want to tell you. But not here." I whispered, looking around to see if anyone was listening in.

"Okay. I know the perfect spot." He said making me laugh.

"Just how many *'perfect spots'* do you know?" I said quoting him with my fingers.

"Ah, that's for me to know and you to find out." He said as he winked. My stomach thought this was the perfect moment to make itself and its hunger known. "I think we should get some food in that belly." He said laughing as he walked past me.

"Hey! Wait for me!" I said as my little legs kicked into gear, trying to catch up with his long strides. He already had a plate ready and started shovelling food after food onto in. I watched as the pile got higher and higher before I had to tell him that was more than enough.

"Eat." He said handing me the plate.

"You're not going to make me sit on your lap are you." I said eyeing him as he laughed.

"That is absurd. How will I eat?" Well, he's got me there. I turned, hearing familiar laughter seeing Sadie, Lane, and Maya off to the side all chattering away happily.

"I'm gonna go say hey to the girls really quick." He nods, telling me he must see his parents and that he'll get me when he's ready to go. I pick at my food, eating as I make my way over and great the girls.

"Hey!" The second I spoke they all repelled back, holding their nose as if a foul smell had assaulted them. "What?" I looked down at my feet, making sure I didn't step in anything unfortunate.

"Did you not happen to shower before you came?" Sadie asked, face crumpled as she held her breath.

"Uhm, no? We were running late and we only had enough time to change. Why?" I looked at all three confused.

"Goddess, Zia." Lane started. "Did Cairo happen to lick or rub his face all over your body?" She asked as my cheeks heated.

"There was...a lot of rubbing and licking involved. Why?" I feel like a broken record, how many times am I going to have to say why. Sadie laughed as Lane rubbed her forehead as if a headache just appeared. "You probably left your pack before you were able to learn this but alpha males especially, have the ability to create special pheromones. They rub this scent all over and in...some cases...into, their mate as a possessive mark. Cairo's basically warning other males to stay away from you." Lane finished blankly. *That sneaky fucker.* That's why he fingered me before we left the cave, why he rubbed his hand all over me. I should have questioned him but I was dick whipped and too blinded by his magic fingers. The bastard.

"Well, that explains why no one looked at me when we arrived." I sighed. "Explains even more why all your mates ignored me when I tried saying hello earlier." I can't believe Cairo was marking his territory thinking he was fucking sneaky and shit I fell for it.

"Now that you're fully mated to him, he will be even more possessive than our mates. You're the future Luna of this pack. His protectiveness towards the packs Queen is essential. A pack will always be stronger with both alpha and luna. Plus, he won't be leaving you alone for long either if you catch my drift." Lane said giving me a pointed look while Maya laughed and Sadie winked.

"Speaking of, where did he go?" I say standing on my tiptoes as I look for him. I felt him before I heard him. His husky lust filled voice making my body shiver as he spoke behind me.

"Right here." He growled low and I didn't have to turn my head to know his eyes were pitch black. "Time to go." He said as his hand encased around my hip, pulling me back into him ever so slightly as I felt his hardness against my back.

"But I'm still talking to the girls." I tried to say but he growled, chest rattling against my back as the girls gasped and squeaked. *I can't believe he growled at me,* I thought as I remembered this time to shield my mind. I also couldn't believe how incredibly hot that made me. One growl from him and I was ready to go, Goddess knows what number this round would be. What has happened to me?

"Yes, Alpha.." I said low, succumbing to my lust. His lip lifted in a smirk as he pulled me with him, disappearing through the trees. I laughed as Lane's voice softly carried through the air.

"Never expected Cairo to be such a horn dog." She said as all three laughed.

We eventually joined the party once more. We had just experienced our first time against a tree which was... eventful. I don't know if I'm a big fan of the scratchy bark against my skin. Half the time I was worried my hiked-up dress was going to get torn to shreds. I also can't believe my insatiable lust for Cairo. I cannot keep my hands off him, one look from him and a waterfall happens inside my body, gushing out as my body prepares itself for him again. The mark on my neck is so raw it hurts. He's marked me over and over, teeth piercing the same spot. But then he'll kiss it, and my body is ready for him to mark me once more. I always heard about the uncontrollable lust you feel right after you complete the bond, but I guess I just thought it was bullshit. I now know it's not. One thing I didn't know was the scent thing alphas could do. It was safe to say that no male dared to look my way tonight. Cairo well and truly marked me as his in every sense of the word. The second any male caught whiff of my scent they immediately turned and headed in any other direction. It made him laugh but I was getting pretty damn annoyed. No one wanted to talk to me. I either repelled them or repulsed them.

I stood by the flower beds, red plastic disposable cup in hand as I slowly sipped my drink and watched the pack interact with each other. Cairo caught my eye again when he was talking to his father, but it wasn't from lust or anything sinister like that. He looked taller, muscles slightly more bulkier than what they were at the beginning of the day. He used to be a couple of centimetres shorter than the Alpha but now he was the same height. Even the Luna was looking at him up and down trying to figure out how he grew over the span of a few hours. He smiled to himself as he made his way back over to me. He told me it was a survival technique for male wolves. Obviously hearing my thoughts again, he explained that when they mate and mark their mates, they become stronger. Their protective instincts become borderline overbearing and they become more dominant. Not that I'm complaining, my body feels well and truly exhausted and satisfied by said new feelings.

But now it was finally time.

"I'm ready." I say feeling my nerves begin to buzz anxiously.

"Ready?" He said mind going straight to the gutter but then he stopped smirking. Listening to my thoughts, feeling my apprehension, and rising stress course through my body.

"I'm ready to tell you everything. My whole miserable life story."

Chapter Forty

Every Single Detail

We walked silently through the forest, hand sweating as Cairo's own entwined in mine squeezed every couple of minutes to reassure me, giving me strength. I was nervous, finally about to tell him everything. No more distractions, no more interruptions. I was nervous to tell him that I used to love my abuser. But that is a long story, which is why he led us to the beach.

We sat on a grassy knoll that ended right at the peak of the small hill, long strands of grass growing over the edge as our legs hung over, brushing against the sand that licked at our feet as they swayed.

"It's beautiful here." I speak quietly. The breeze was cool, carrying the freshwater smell across the tiny little waves bouncing and bobbing up like they were trying to get a peek at us. The moon was out, shining brightly in her half crescent phase. Stars lighting up the night sky, shimmering down as I stare back, swallowing my fears and willing the Goddess to give me strength.

"It is." Cairo said beside me as he looked out at the water.

"I've been many places, Cairo. But this...this place is truly beautiful." And it was. No pack compared.

"There is still more that I have to show you." He said making me chuckle.

"And you will." I promise him. "I know," I begin but pause, working past the lump in my throat, "I know I've said it before but I want to say I'm sorry. I never should have treated you the way I did. I should have been honest with you from the start. I should-"

"It's okay, Zia. It's hard to be honest with someone who hates you, hates what you are. I let my emotions affect how I treated you. My fear won. I never gave you the chance to show me who you really are. Alek was right with what he said. I never saw you as anything but rogues. I never saw the beauty and innocence within you. I judged you because of a label and for that I'M sorry." He said before he paused and inhaled, taking a big breath in before he expelled it as he shook his head. "I should have given you a chance from the start and gotten to know you before you let your scent out. I don't want to be one of those alphas that kill first and ask questions later. I want to be compassionate and caring. I want my pack members to come to me without fear and judgement." He said opening his heart to me.

"You will be. We've all seen a change in you lately and I know our pack is going to love you when you become alpha."

She said our pack!

I laughed, Cairo's inner thoughts sounded like a little bashful child, excited by something his first crush said. His cheeks heat, forgetting that I can hear his thoughts too. We really need to remember that little detail.

"The sky here reminds me of home." I said looking back up as Cairo followed. "The stars I mean. Our pack was traditional. We were miles away from the nearest human settlement. We didn't have electricity or technology really. We'd only go to the nearest town every month for supply runs or clothing. Our homes were these beautiful log cabin types that were made from the trees surrounding us. The more the pack expanded, the more we chopped down trees to build new cabins and houses. The scraps were used for our wood fires, or the big bonfires we did. Nothing ever went to waste. The trunks of the trees were turned into little stools and other furniture of the sorts. In the winters we would have bonfires every night and ate together as a pack. We were all one big family." I paused, looking over to see if Cairo was listening. He looked down, smiling as he nodded.

"I am. I'm ready." He said leaning in as he placed a kiss on my cheek.

"I suppose that's why no one stopped the obsession Vladik had with me." I continued as Cairo went silent. His breathing slowed, growing quiet so he wouldn't miss a word as he looked back out at the water. "We were best friends, Alek, Vladik and I. He was three years older than us and he was the Alpha's only son. His mother died during childbirth so he just had his father. My papa was the Beta and they were best friends. During summer the bonfires weren't as frequent since we didn't need the large fires to keep warm, so Vladik and *Pyotr*, the Alpha, were always over. But they were often at our house during all the seasons so it didn't matter about the bonfires-" I stopped, feeling like I was just babbling away. I cleared my throat, getting back on track.

"I think I was around five when I realized Vladik saw me as more than a friend. His infatuation with me had begun. I remember the moment he first changed around me. He hid it well from everyone."

"Ali? ALI!" I called out for him but the earmuffs were clouding my hearing. My feet crunched through the snow, sinking in from the extra layers that snowed overnight. I know Alek and Vladik were around here somewhere. I lifted one of the earmuffs as I held my breath, listening for them. They loved hiding from me. They'd always jump behind trees and crouch down into the snow so I'd

overlook them. But I heard it, the giggling. I smiled, running forward as they came into view.

"Ali, you forgot your earmuffs!" I said pulling out his pair from my winter jacket.

"ZyZy, I told mama I'm not wearing them. I'm too big now."

"But...I want to match." It was my favourite thing to do with him. We were already wearing the same jacket and pants; our scarfs were a shade off and the only thing missing was his earmuffs.

"I don't want to. We're always matching!" He said making my eyes water. I could feel my lip beginning to tremble.

"Alek," Vladik cut in, "Can you ask your mama if I can sleep over tonight." He asked but it didn't sound like a question. Alek nodded his head happily as he ran back to our house.

That was the day I noticed the change in him. When he sent Alek away, he just stood there and stared at me, and being the young naïve girl that I was, I started growing attached to him. My first crush happened. I didn't know what mates were so I didn't think twice and neither did the pack. They thought we were cute together and from the way Vladik grew possessive of me, everyone thought that was the early signs of us being mates. Because of that, no one thought to stop his growing obsession with me. I was too young to realize how dangerous it could, *would* become.

"I'll wear them, ZyZy." I smiled, happy that he wanted to wear them when Alek didn't. I jogged to him as he bent down on one knee, with his hand resting in the snow holding himself steady. I tried to put them on his head but they were a size too small.

"They don't fit.." Tears welled in my eyes again.

"That's okay. It looks better on you anyways. You don't want us silly boys wearing them." I laughed at his joke.

"Mama said they keep my ears warm." He nodded once and stood back up.

"She's right about that. Let's go back home, I don't want you getting sick from the cold." He said smiling down at me.

"But I'm a wolf, Vlady. I can't get sick!" I exclaimed.

"We haven't shifted yet, ZyZy. You know this." He said before his smile dropped, a cold hard look crossed his face. "I said, I don't want you getting sick." His voice sounded different; I couldn't understand why but something in me told me to listen to him.

He wouldn't leave me alone that night. Usually when we had sleepovers we would sleep on the floor of our room. Our bunk beds could only fit one person on each mattress. So, we'd lay down heaps of blankets on the floor and all three of us would sleep there, telling our best Baba Yaga stories. Alek always slept in the middle. Vladik was on one side of him and I was on the other. But that night, Vladik slept in the middle. Alek didn't think anything of it but I couldn't fall asleep. That was the first night I felt separated from Alek. Our mama and papa always said we would scream as babies and not fall asleep unless we were together. But that night we weren't. Vladik had watched me toss and turn for hours with a blank look on his face. His eyes looked all void of life, not one emotion crossed his ice blue eyes. Eventually he asked me what was wrong. I said I couldn't sleep without Alek next to me and I still remember what he said. '*You don't need him anymore. I'm here.*' I remember the panic that coursed through me, the fear of just the thought of losing Alek and he smiled. Vladik smiled at me because he saw the fear. Over the years I often thought if that was his first threat against me and I was just too young to realize it or detect the threat within his subtle tone.

"Then came the day when he turned fifteen and shifted for the first time. He came straight over to see me but when he stood in front of me, he was furious. I was standing on our deck, relieved that the wooden railing acted as a barrier between us. I didn't understand the anger, didn't understand why he was so angry with me." I said shivering as I remembered.

He grew fast. By the time he was fifteen he was tall and towered over me. Standing on the deck it brought me face to face with him. I'd never seen him this mad before and I didn't realize until years later that it was because I wasn't his mate. He smelt my scent and it hadn't changed. It stayed the same. I think what I said next was the moment that really tipped the scales for his obsession. It was so innocent, and I laid awake countless nights wishing I never said anything to him. But then, maybe this was always supposed to happen. His infatuation with me started a long time ago and nothing was going to stop him.

"Are you okay, Vlady?" He didn't speak. Just continued to look through me. "Oh! How was your first shift? Did it hurt? And what does he look like? Do you think I could meet him? Would he let me ride on his back?" I asked a million questions. I was three years shy of meeting my own wolf. I was excited about seeing his, feeling his soft platinum fur and watching him play in the snow. He looked at me differently when I stopped speaking. His eyes shifted to black, boring into mine as his body leaned forward ever so slightly like he was going to pounce. But he didn't, it looked like he stopped himself at the last second.

"You can." He said looking thoughtful as his eyes shifted back to their normal colour. "But there's something I have to tell you first." He said smiling. "You're my mate, ZyZy."

"I am!?" I didn't know any better. I wish I wasn't so excited. He jumped up, leaping over the ledge in one quick movement.

*"Yes. You're my mate, ZyZy." He said leaning in a he picked up one of my braids. "**My Luna**."*

That day he told everyone we were mates. I hadn't shifted yet so I didn't know he was lying. I always had a crush on him so I assumed it must have been true. From that day on we were together. He never left my side. He was constantly with me, never wanting to be away from me. He would always kiss me on the cheek and make me laugh, cuddling me and holding hands.

"I..I.." I stop as a rattle sounded from deep in Cairo's chest as he read my thoughts, hearing the way another guy kissed me. It made me laugh and weirdly feel safe.

"Go on." He spoke stoically.

"It wasn't until Alek and I shifted that I realized Vladik lied. That he wasn't my true mate. There was only one person who had their doubts about our bond. Our papa. The day we first shifted, Alek and I accidentally sent him to the moon. When he came back he began looking troubled. I think someone up there may have warned him or said something because he started asking questions." That was one of Alek's biggest regrets. That he didn't notice sooner like papa did.

"What happened when you saw him? After you shifted." Cairo spoke quietly.

"I was terrified."

We had just come back from our run with mama and papa's wolf. We went inside to change and Alek called out saying Vladik was here. I took a few minutes extra to do my hair up in a cute high ponytail, brushing my fingers through my bangs before I left my room. I could hear the Alpha outside talking with our parents as Alek joined in. I was confused as I closed the door behind me. I couldn't smell Vladik, but his scent was the same. And when I saw him it clicked. I stopped beside Alek, he and my parents were focused on the Alpha. Vladik knew in this moment that I knew we weren't mates. That he had lied for three years. My heart was pounding, my breathing began to pick up. The look on his face terrified me. His eyes were vacant as he watched me, daring me to say something. I didn't, wouldn't. Alarm bells were ringing in my head, telling me to turn and run as fast as I could.

"ZyZy?" Alek asked as he turned to me.

"P...pardon?" He chuckled as he playfully shoved me with his shoulder.

"Aren't you gonna run into your mates' arms? I know I would if I found mine." I swallowed, faking a smile as I spoke.

"W..we...we already knew we were m..mates.." I exhaled, feeling

my throat constrict as I looked at Vladik. His eyes hard darkened, no one saw or felt the sudden danger.

"Yeah, but now it's official." Alek said as our parents laughed this time.

"Y..you're right. W..we should celebrate.." They all agreed, immediately planning a last-minute feast. I watched Vladik as he mouthed for me to come to him. And I did. He smiled when I reached him, putting his arm around me as he tucked me into his side. I put my hand on his back, hiding my hands because I couldn't stop them from shaking. He chest rose and fell on a silent laugh, feeling them through his jacket.

"I never told anyone. Never spoke a word of his lie. I was worried he'd do something to my family or Alek. He'd whisper things in my ear like what would I do if Alek died. What would I do if I was no longer a twin, if I was all alone, an orphan? I tried my best not to be caught alone with him. I knew what he was planning to do, I knew I couldn't let him do that to me. But...two days later he got me alone. He orchestrated the whole thing, had my family and I over for dinner. Then he asked if I could stay the night announcing to my family that he wanted to mark me. I couldn't say no. Couldn't let them know he was going to hurt me. But I planned on telling the Alpha as soon as Vladik left the room." I leaned down, undoing the straps from my sandals, letting them roll down the sandy hill. I stood, sliding down as I walked over, stepping into the water, letting my feet submerge to distract my mind. I could hear Cairo behind me, preparing himself for the worst. He didn't move, just stayed seated as he waited for me to talk.

"The Alpha decided to walk my parents out. Alek said his goodbye and as soon as he was out of view, Vladik grabbed my wrists, hauling me up out of my seat and dragged me down the hallway to his room. He pushed me, shoving me through the door as he closed it behind me, locking me in. I started to panic, running to the window trying to pry it open but it was also locked. Then I ran back to the door, trying the knob to see if my new strength could break it but he switched the handle to silver. He planned everything. I was trapped. Then I heard his footfalls down the hall. The second he walked in and shut the door, he stalked toward me. Telling me his father was down the hall and that I needed to not make a sound. My knees hit the back of the bed causing me to fall back. And that's when he did it. He put his hand over my mouth and held me down as he marked me. By the time his father broke the door down and saw me in the foetal position on the floor, clutching my neck as I writhed and convulsed from the pain, he knew. He was screaming at Vladik, demanding an answer. But he didn't speak. He just smiled at him. Then," I closed my eyes, reliving the painful, horror filled memory, "Vladik killed him. He shifted so quickly the Alpha didn't have time to fight him off. He killed him so quick and didn't care he just ended his father's life."

"He...he killed him?" Cairo asked as he stood up, sliding down the sand as he made his way to me. "That's how he became Alpha?" His face was delirious, unable to believe Vladik could kill his own flesh and blood.

"The moment he took his last breath I saw the alpha power transfer to Vladik. He shifted back, naked, covered in blood as he pulled me up by my hair and threw me back on the bed. That was the first time he raped me."

"T...the first?" Cairo's voice broke as he spoke. I felt a single tear run down my cheek as he stopped breathing. Then he was at my back, spinning me around as he hugged me. I felt safe in his arms, safe enough to continue.

"He kept me there for a few weeks before Alek came to see me one day. Vladik alpha commanded everyone to leave me be. None of them knew he was the alpha yet and he did the command so subtle they had no idea. When Alek came, Vladik was fast asleep. He didn't hear Alek call out or knock on the door. I saw him look through the bedroom window. I cried seeing the look of horror on his face as he took in my naked, bruised body. Alek ran, getting my papa but Vladik was awake by the time they both came back. Every time he marked me, he would call me his Luna, every time he...when he..." I couldn't say the words again.

"He would call you that." Cairo finished for me. Remembering he day he said those words to me. Now understanding why I reacted the way I did.

"Vladik was crazed when my Alek and papa came charging in. Papa screamed at Vladik, challenging him but Vladik just laughed. Papa tried to charge at him but he didn't know Vladik was the Alpha now. He just commanded him to stop and bow before him. I've never seen such fear in papa's face when he realized how dangerous the situation really was. Alek grabbed my arm, pulling me towards him but Vladik was stronger. He pulled me back to him, spinning me around so I faced them with my back against his chest. He laughed and taunted them, saying how easy it was to fool everyone for years. How they let their little girl get r..." It was too much, I hated these memories, hated my past but I had to finish the story. Cairo needed to know everything.

"I remember their screams when he told them."

Vladik had commanded my father to stop, but he knew the loopholes to alpha commands. If you're not clear, then there are ways to break them. So, Vladik hadn't expected him to lunge at him, let alone move. But he threw me towards my father at the last second, throwing him off balance. Alek tried to attack but it was no use. Vladik was too strong. He kept screaming how dare they try take me from him. He focussed his wrath on my papa. The last thing I remember from that night was Vladik grabbing him by the throat as he dug his claws in and slashed down his chest.

"I...I could see the bones through his torn skin. He wouldn't stop bleeding."

That's when I first attacked Vladik. My wolf acted on instinct, clawing at his face savagely. Then I blacked out. It was a week later when I woke up, wrapped in a blanket still naked and covered in dried blood. Alek said Vladik pinned me to the ground and tried to mark me into submission, but he was too feral. He didn't control his own strength causing him to rip my throat open.

"I only survived because what happened to me at the ball happened that night. Alek said Vladik was thrown across the room and hit his head on the fireplace. He said he used his power on me to calm me down and it worked. He said he didn't have time to think because Vladik started stirring awake. He ran, hand holding my throat together as he tried to stop the bleeding. But he didn't take me home. He knew we had to leave or else much worse would have happened to me and him."

When I awoke, it was a week later. He looked exhausted, black bags under his eyes from little sleep, his body was stiff from running for as long as he could, stopping only when necessary. He apologised profusely to me. I hated hearing the heartbreak in his voice as it broke, his sobs ringing though my ears and I'll never be able to forget the sound.

"His tracking wolves early caught us a few times. Then he sent rogues after us, which is how we ended up at the port, jumping on a cargo ship that was headed for Portugal. We hid below, not knowing when the ship would stop sailing. We got caught stealing food though but because they couldn't find us the crew started saying there were child ghosts on board. That kept us entertained." I said remembering all the sounds we made, hands clamped over our mouths trying not to laugh as grown men screamed. "Eventually we came to America. Then those new laws came out and then I met you." I couldn't believe the weight that lifted off my chest. I've been holding all of that in for so long. It was hard telling him everything. Every word I spoke felt like I was being pulled back to that day, then suddenly I was back here, in Cairo's arms speaking through my pain and everything stopped. The ticking of my heart, breaking of my voice. The feeling made me laugh. I felt crazy for laughing but I felt free. For the first time in my life, I was free. Free of my demons, my nightmares, that cold hand of anxiety that felt like it was always around my throat or punching into my chest. I felt like I could breathe. I was happy. I no longer had the burning pain in my neck from Vladik's mark. It disappeared the night Cairo marked me. The night my true, fated mate marked me. It erased my pain, my unwanted mark.

"That's what the scar on your neck was? Why you always wore your hair over that shoulder. You were hiding your scar?" I pulled back, nodding sadly as my hand went to my neck. The mark was gone but a thin scar remained.

"I thought I always covered it well." I said quietly.

"I first saw it after the Trials. Then again when my wolf first tackled you to the ground. I could see it when the braid moved. It looked like a painful scar so I never said anything. My dad has scars that he never talks about."

"Thank you. For never asking about it. I hated it, hated the memories that clung to it. I hate that you weren't my first, hate that you weren't the first to mark me." I began but stopped when I felt the surge of anger course through me from him.

"Don't say that, Zia." He said crossing his arms over his chest as his knuckles went white from the pressure. "Did I mark you on your scar side?" He asked, voice softening but his face was still stern.

"No..."

"Was I the first to mark you on that other side of your neck?"

"Yes..."

"Then you see, I was the first to mark you. I was the first to mark there wasn't I?" He said smiling, nodding his head. Tears fell silently as his words rung true. He was right, he was the first in a different way. The guilt inside me began to lessen from his words.

"Thank you for telling me, baby. I love you, and I will never stop loving you. This doesn't change what I think of you, I want you to know that. Don't let those dark thoughts cloud your mind. I can't stop thinking about how fucking strong you are and I'm not just talking about your powers. To go through what you did and to feel that *and* be reminded about it every day, that... no one could survive that. But *you* did." His hand was on my cheek, thumb wiping away a fallen tear. "My strong beautiful mate survived that. That's why you will make the best Luna and mother." I choked at his words.

"M..mother?" Why did that make my heart flutter?

"Of course. I want little Zia's running around." He said as his voice deepened, eyes twinkling in mischief.

"How about we practice right now?" I tease but also with a note of truthfulness. He laughed, looking down at me as hazel eyes began melting away as black replaced it.

"Now you're speaking my lang-" Cairo began but he stopped mid-sentence. His eyes flicked above me to the sky, brows furrowing as I followed. The clear night sky was no more, thunder clouds had rolled in. My head tilted as I studied the clouds, they were strange. They looked almost unnatural.

"Do they look-" I said as Cairo answered for me.

"Red." I gasped, feeling like a wall suddenly erected between us. Cairo blocked me. I couldn't hear his thoughts; I couldn't sense his emotions. He was hiding something from me. I went to speak, wanting to know why he cut me off but suddenly the Alpha appeared, bursting through the trees as he screamed.

"Cairo!" His deep voice commanded hastily. "With me, now!" His eyes were sunset orange, almost yellow as his wolf front in his mind.

"Dad? What's wrong?" Cairo quickly spoke as his heart started beating faster.

"NOW, CAIRO!" He spoke no more. He turned, sprinting off into the tree line as we followed.

I tried to mindlink Cairo, but he was still shut off. I couldn't link Alek either because he had done the same thing. I hadn't seen him at the party either, him and Keiran were missing. Thin low hanging branches cut at my arms and cheeks. Something was going on and we didn't have time to waste. The Alpha was running so fast we lost him for a few seconds before he appeared again, meters ahead of us as his arms swung out, pushing foliage out of his way. We were nearing the party but no music played. I couldn't hear any conversation and when I stretched my hearing, I couldn't detect any of the hundreds of people that were there at the start of the night. As we drew near we could hear someone crying, their sobs filling the air.

"Mother!" Cairo yelled out as we came into view. She was on her knees, clutching Sarana to her chest as she cried. The Alpha pulled her up and she clung to him, hands shaking as she held onto Sarana. "Where is everyone? What's happening?" Cairo asked confused and worried.

"There's a rogue." The Alpha said, eyes still golden yellow.

"Where?!" Cairo growled, his own eyes shifting.

"The northern border. A rogue had trespassed the border and evaded the warriors. I sent the trackers out. They found a camp of rogues in the neutral zone, gearing up."

"Gearing up?" Cairo repeated. "How many?"

"Cade and Jaxon counted eighty."

"Eighty!" The Luna stammered as she stopped breathing. She began to hyperventilate, hand going to her chest as her eyes widened in fear.

"Oha, calm down. Everything will be okay. Take Sarana back to the house, go to the safe room. I'll come join you once I know what's going on." The Alpha said as he turned to his wife. He leaned down, kissing Sarana on the cheek as he tightened her loose pig tail.

"Go with mummy, Sarana. Daddy loves you. I will see you soon, okay? Go to sleep and when you wake up I'll be there." She softly nodded, not understanding what's happening. Once they were out of earshot, the Alpha continued. "Alpha Wesley, our neighbouring pack Alpha has had trouble with rogues lately. He's been pushing the boundaries of the neutral zone trying to expand his pack. I've been thinking the rogue that attacked Lane was from that group." He finished but I looked up at Cairo. He knows that rogue was after me. He looked to the sky again, gears shifting in his mind as things began clicking. He still blocked me out. "Do you think they're gearing up for war with them?" Cairo said but something in his voice didn't sit right with me. It felt like he wasn't saying something.

"Possibly." Alpha Zosar said. "I fucking warned Wesley not to take the neutral land." He snapped out.

"Alpha!" A warrior appeared, rushing out his words as he ran towards Zosar. "The rogues want to speak with you. They sent a messenger." Cairo growled lowly as he stepped in front of me, shielding me.

"Where's the rogue?" The Alpha spoke.

"Jaxon! Cade!" The warrior called out as he turned to the direction he came from. Seconds later the rogue appeared. Skin dirty, his feral red eyes scanned each of our faces. He had a large scar across his face, a skull tattooed on his chest and black hair grazing against his shoulders.

"Speak, rogue. What do you want?" Zosar said as his body leaned in ever so slightly.

"Do not command me." Sneered the rogue. "You are not my Alpha." He said as he spat at the ground.

"If you don't want your tongue ripped out of your head then I suggest you speak," the Alpha said almost flirty like as he smiled at the rogue, "RIGHT FUCKING NOW!" He roared, making Cairo and I jump from the sudden shift in his tone. The rogue scoffed, rolling his eyes unafraid.

"My army will not attack your pack on one condition." Cairo exhaled, not looking shocked as the Alpha did who tried to hide it.

"And that is?" Zosar said.

"You will give us, *Zinoviya*." I gasped, breath ripping from me as I start to panic, bile rising up my throat.

"We don't even have a Zinoviya in our pack. You're mistaken, rogue." Cairo said.

"Oh, I don't believe I am." Red eyes flashed to me, winking as spoke. The rogue spoke my real name. I hoped and pleaded that he didn't mean me but his eyes said differently. He did mean me. They're here for me. Babushka's warning was true. This is what she was telling me about.

He's finally found me.

Chapter Forty-One

Lost and Found

My fist pounded on the door, heart racing in my chest as I screamed Alek's name. Everything was happening too fast, I should have had more time, I *need* more time!

"ALEK!" I pounded the door again. I grabbed the doorknob, twisting and shaking as the metal wouldn't budge. "ALEK!" I raised my hand, ready to thrust it forward but the door swung open, Alek's fear filled eyes found mine as he spoke.

"What is it?! What's wrong?" He looked me up and down, seeing the tears fall from my panicked face.

"*On nashyol menya, Alek! On zdes!*" I rushed out as I told him Vladik finally found me.

"*Chto?!*" Alek said repelling back like he got slapped.

"Zia!" Cairo called as his heavy feet slammed against the steps, skipping two at a time before he reached the top, quickly turning the corner as he spotted me at Alek's bedroom door.

Once the rogue left, the Alpha called his men. Telling them to hunt down *Zinoviya*, giving them permission to kill her as a warning to the rogues not to enter this territory. I ran without saying a word. I needed Alek. He still wasn't answering my link, still hadn't been heard from since the lake. I prayed he was in his room and my prayers were answered when the door swung open and there he was. Shirtless and marked and mated. But I didn't have time to congratulate him, he needed to know we were in danger.

"What's going on?" Cairo said worried as he looked between the both of us, still clueless to our native language.

"*Ya ne mogu sdelat' eto snova, Alek. Mne nuzhno uyti. On ub'yot vsekh. Mne strashno, brat.*" I had too much to say too little time. I could hear Cairo's wolf whine, wanting to understand what I'm saying but I can't let him know. Can't let him know I'm planning to run away.

"*Chto sluchilos'?*"

"*U nego Celaya armiya rogues. Oni vse ishchut menya. Oni sprosili Zinoviya.*" I said to Alek, filling him in on what happened.

"Alek? What's going on?" Cairo begged, hoping he would answer him.

"*On znayet, chto eto ty?*" Alek said, looking back at Cairo. I shake my head. He doesn't know I'm the one the rogue was asking for. I looked down at my feet. "*Skazhi emu, Zia. On poymyot.*" He's right. Cairo will understand. He listened to me when I told him about my past, he didn't run, he didn't scream or yell. He understood and listened. He did it once, he'll do it again. He loves me...

"I need to tell you something, Cairo. But not here." I turn without looking, walking straight to our bedroom door.

"Baby, what's wrong?" He asked the second the door was closed. "I can feel your fear through our bond. What's going on?" I hadn't realised he unblocked me. I focussed inwards, feeling his angst and confusion.

"It's me, Cairo. I'm Zinoviya." I expected him to look shocked but all he did was sigh sadly as if he wished I didn't say those words.

"Why did you not tell me Zia isn't your real name?" He asked sadly. I could feel the hurt through our bond.

"I trust you with my whole heart, Cairo. But it's hard to feel safe when my demon is still out there looking for me. I guess, it was my last safety net. If I didn't speak my name, then no one would hear it, *he* wouldn't hear it."

"Is your last name even James?" He asked curiously making me laugh.

"No," I smiled lightly shaking my head, "its *Alekseeva*." It's been so long since I've spoken my own name. I've been just Zia for three years and Zia James for a few weeks since we started school.

"Wait, so, Alek's name is Alek Alekseeva?" Cairo said confused making me laugh.

"Alek Alekseev." I laughed again. "I..it's complicated. But Cairo, if your dad finds out the rogues are here for me, he'll kill me. You heard what he said." That fear began to take over again, that hand of anxiety restricting around my throat.

"He won't do that. Believe it or not, he has experience with this. My mother doesn't think I know but-"

"She told me, Cairo. About what happened to her." I said, knowing where he was going.

"She did?" I nodded. I went to him, wrapping my hands around his waist as I placed my ear against his chest, listening to the beating of his heart, soothing my own erratic one.

"I'm scared, Cairo. This pack has been so good to Alek and me. I don't want to be the reason they all die. They don't deserve that. I'm so sorry, Cairo." I sniffed, tears watering my eyes as my guilt overwhelmed him.

"Why are you sorry?" He asked softly, hands rubbing up and down my back soothingly.

"Because everything is always my fault. I'm a screw up! I made us leave our pack, I forced Alek to become a rogue when he didn't want too. I'm the reason we never had the chance to say goodbye to our family. Everywhere I go, chaos and death follow. Every single time we came across rogues, Alek had to fight them because of me. They smelt me! An unmated female. And he fought them all, every single time! I.. I made him a killer." I said pulling back from his embrace.

"Zia..." He reached for me but I stepped back.

"I can't let anyone else die because of me, Cairo. I need to hand myself over."

"No!" He snapped storming towards me. He grabbed me by the arms and shook me. "You listen to me right now. We wouldn't be a pack if we didn't protect our future Luna. We're a strong pack because we're protective of each other. If you, so help me Goddess, even think about handing yourself over, I will lock your ass in this room until the war is over." My mouth dropped at his possessives and my stupid body reacted to it. But now was *not* the time. "We'll address the pack in the morning, after we speak to my father. Then you'll see how much the pack cares for you. They may have only known you for a short while, but I can already see the love in their eyes. I hear the way they talk about you. They've already accepted you as their Luna to be, Zia. And so have I." I cried at his words; his reassurance was enough to help strengthen my weakened resolve.

"I love you, Cairo. I love you so much."

"I love you too, baby. Now, let me draw you a bath."

"A bath? Cairo, the rogues-" I began but he lifted his hand in the air to stop me.

"Have given us twenty-four hours to hand you over. That's twenty-four hours to rest, recuperate and come up with a plan to tell them that they can fuck off if they think they're gonna take you. Now as I said, let me draw you a bath, I will join, keep you some...*company*," he said lowly making me laugh when his eyes shifted to black, "then after our bath, we'll get into bed, *cuddle*," he said again in the same sultry tone, "and get a good night's sleep. It seems tomorrow is going to be a long, complicated day." I laugh, I sigh, I nod. Already feeling the tidal wave effects off tomorrow.

"Alright, draw the bath." I conceded.

After our *sensual* bath, Cairo patted me down with my towel, dried my hair, massaged some argon oil in, then led me into the bedroom and picked out a fresh pair of pyjamas. I felt so spoilt and the permanent blush on my face kept Cairo amused. He was so sweet, so caring. I've never seen this side of him before. Sure, little glimpses here and there but this? Was something I could definitely get used too. Then we laid down and he brought me close to him, lifting the sheets up to our waist as I laid my head down on his chest, loving the familiarity of his heartbeat. It lulled me to sleep in no time.

In the morning I awoke before Cairo. I was busting for the toilet and decided I may as well brush my teeth and get ready for the day. I felt the second he woke up, it felt like my heart beat doubled, feeling like there was a whisper of a second heart inside my chest. Then his thoughts started to slowly enter my mind, heating my cheeks as he replayed our bath scene last night. I laughed, of course that's the first thing he would think about. But then his link went blurry. He was mindlinking, and soon enough he called out.

"Hey, baby?" I could hear clothes rustling as he got dressed.

"Yeah?" I called through the door.

"Are you ready? Dad linked; he wants to speak with me." Cairo said last night that we were going to go see his father together and talk about the situation, work out a plan.

"Almost!" I said, quickly pulling on my jean shorts. "I can meet you at your dad's office."

"Alright, I love you." I smiled.

"I love you too!" I called back. Once I heard the door shut I let out a breath. I was ready the second my pants were on but I wasn't mentally ready. I couldn't stop the what if's flying around in my head. What if the Alpha got angry? What if he decided that I wasn't worth risking the safety of his family and the pack? *What if, what if, what if.*

I brushed off my worries, steeled my back and exited the bathroom. I slipped on my shoes and made my way out the door, down the hallway and to the stairs. I was felt dread as I approached the Alpha's office.

Inhale, exhale.

"What did I tell you about wearing those shorts?" I heard the Alpha say as I opened the door. Sarana sat on his desk, legs dangling over the side as she gave him a sassy little sigh.

"Daddy, it fiiiine." She emphasised. "Mumma said." I laughed; Cairo snickered as the Alpha shot us a look. I tried to hide my smile as I walked to Cairo's side. Sarana turned her head, noticing me as her eyes lit up.

"Bubba! Eya! I pretty?" Oh, she was good. Had both of them wrapped around her little finger. Cairo laughed as Zosar grunted.

"Of course. You're the prettiest little angel there is." Cairo said as she stood up on the desk and clapped her hands.

"Devil more like it." Zosar mumbled under his breath, making us laugh. Then Cairo sighed, exhaling as he looked up, pointedly looking at his father before he spoke.

"We need to talk to you." Alpha Zosar watched Cairo thoughtfully as Sarana mimicked him. He nodded his head, then she nodded her head. He crossed his arms, still looking at Cairo as she crossed hers, turning to also look at Cairo. Zosar leaned down, whispering in her ear as he smirked.

"I see you copying me you cheeky little pup." She giggled, pigtails swishing as she turned and jumped in his arms. Cairo looked down at me, smiling before his eyes widened. He gulped, looking away quickly and blocked his scent and bond. *What in the world was that about?* I thought.

"Eya!" Sarana called out.

"Hello, Sarana." I said waving at her. Cairo gulped again, eyeing my socks. I hid my smirk, knowing these knee-high socks were Cairo's kryptonite, his one weakness. I thought wearing these could take his mind off the coming doom and it seemed to work because it distracted him enough to let his block waver. I could hear him chanting in his head.

Calm down, calm down, calm down...They're just socks.

This is no time to get excited.

I cannot get hard in front of my father.

My hand flew to my mouth, trying desperately to hold in a laugh. Thankfully the Alpha was blissfully unaware.

"Hello, Zia. What can I do for you? *You,* need to speak with me?" He asked knowing that's the reason I was with Cairo here in the first place. I breathe in, counted to three before I exhaled, releasing my built-up tension.

"My name is *Zinoviya Alekseeva.* I am the one they're after. Those rogues are here for me." I crossed my arms against my chest, hiding the tremors in my hands. My nerves were fried, so afraid of how the Alpha would react. And he did. He repelled back, gasping as his brows furrowed.

"Ah. Well, I didn't see that one coming." Was all he said. I sighed in relief, feeling the weight leave my shoulders. I was worried for nothing. Cairo's hand touched my back, rubbing circles to comfort me. "Why are they after you?" We didn't have time for me to tell my story again, but I had a shorter, quicker way to speed up the story for Zosar.

"My old Alpha, he has an obsession with me. He is like *Tomás.*" Cairo looked confused at the name but the Alpha's eyes darkened. He growled lowly, making my hackles rise. He didn't speak for a long time, then he suddenly snapped.

"These fucking alphas! They think they can force people to become their mates. Let them come, let *him* come! I'll kill them all." He vowed strongly.

"Daddy, bad word!" Sarana said spinning around to face

him. He exhaled, rubbing his head before he looked down at her, kissing her forehead and spoke.

"Shit." His head snapped back, realising his mistake as we laughed. "Uh, I.. I mean sugar?" He asked Sarana hoping she'd buy it. "Sorry, pup." He said when he realised she wouldn't. "Cairo, take Sarana back to your mother. I need to call a meeting with my warriors. We've already lost some hours from our twenty-four-hour deadline the rogue gave us and I don't trust that they'll keep their word for long." He nodded, and looked at Sarana, picking her up as she leaned in, kissing Zosar on the cheek. "Zia, do no worry. You are my daughter in law. I won't let anything happen to you." He spoke firmly.

"Thank you, Alpha. Thank you for everything." I clutched my chest, tears welling in my eyes. He accepted me into his pack, his family.

"There's nothing to thank. The mate bond is sacred, and my son deserves all the happiness a mate brings." Cairo looked at Zosar, eyes wet as his lip began to tremble. His father spoke words Cairo had longed to hear for such a long time. "Zia, stay for a moment. I want you to tell me about your Tomás." I nod.

Cairo left, taking Sarana back to their mum as I stayed, telling the Alpha what Vladik is like. I could only speak on what he used to be like, what I remembered of him. But three years have passed. I don't know him anymore. He'd be twenty-one right now, Alpha for three years. I don't know how he runs the pack, what type of alpha he is and how his obsession has evolved over the years. Zosar understood, saying his years of experience can help, especially with rogues. He's fought his fair share; he knows how they think. He's trained his warriors and the pack in rogue fighting. Then he dismissed me. I went down to our level of the pack house, ready to splash some water on my face or seduce Cairo to take my mind off the pending doom. *Eighty rogues.* That's eighty feral wolves, eyes blood red from the savagery of their wolves. Packless, blood-thirsty, they hold no loyalty to anyone. Which leaves me plagued with one question. Why are they fighting for Vladik? *Why?!*

"Oh! Sorry..." I said as I rubbed my forehead from walking straight into Cairo as we collided turning the corner at the same time.

"You okay? Your mind is all over the place. I can't tell if you're horny or worried. Or maybe you're horny AND worried..." I laughed at his absurdity. But he wasn't wrong, I was both worried and horny. Being mated has shot my sex drive way up. This incessant biological need to procreate that is wired into wolves DNA will literally be the death of me.

"I'm okay. I do need to find Alek though." He nodded in agreement.

"I'll link Keiran to meet us here. I need to talk to him and I know they'd be together."

"Okay, I need to pee so I'll be right back." I said but his eyes had already glazed over.

I did my business quickly before coming back out. My hand paused on the doorknob as a familiar scent assaulted my nose. Jordan. I didn't stop and listen this time. I stormed down the hallway, turning the corner ready to deal with her but my heart stopped at what I saw. Jordan and Cairo were *kissing*. His hands were on her stomach, she was on her tippy toes, leaning up as they kissed, hands flat on his chest holding herself steady. I could hear the blood rushing through my ears, heart pounding as I watched on in silence.

Suddenly, Cairo threw her back. She gasped, hands reaching out, clamping on her door frame as she steadied herself.

"Get off me!" He growled, his wolfs voice was present, mixed within his as they looked on at her in disgust. Her dull green eyes flicked behind him, looking straight at me as she spoke.

"Oh," she giggled, "Zia! I didn't see you there." She said brushing a curled strand of hair out of her face before she touched her lips. Cairo spun, a million thoughts rushing through his head and our bond. He didn't need to speak for me to know the truth but he did anyways.

"Baby! It's not what it looks like! I swear!" He pleaded; eyes wide as he panicked.

"It's exactly what it looks like. Cairo was shoving his tongue down my throat and telling me how much he still loves me. How much he misses fucking me." Jordan said, delivering her speech with such happiness.

"HE WHAT?!" Alek appeared behind Jordan as he reached the top of the stairs, wolfs eyes presence as his chest heaved up and down. I could hear the cracks in his knuckles as he focussed on Cairo. Keiran stood behind him, looking concerned as he tried to figure out what the hell was happening.

"It's true, he couldn't keep his hands off me." Jordan said as she turned to Alek, fuelling his rage. He screamed and the ground shook slightly.

"No, it's not! Stop fucking lying!" Cairo said as he grabbed Jordan, roughly turning her to face him.

I would never do that.

I love Zia.

I wouldn't...I wouldn't....

"Baby, I swear. I would never touch her. I love you. Pleas," Cairo begged turning back to me and pleaded in both words and his mind. But I couldn't focus on him or anyone. Jordan winked, smirking as if she had won. And I snapped, but this time, I was in control.

"Get back." I said to Cairo as I looked at Jordan.

"What?" Cairo began but I bristled, hackles rising. I didn't have time for this. There's a damn rogue war coming and we can't be dealing with Jordan's jealous antics anymore. We were wasting time.

"I SAID GET BACK." Power rippled through the air, walls shaking from the violence of my command. Cairo's feet moved on their own, compelled by the command.

"Zia! Don't!" Alek screamed, looking across at me as he shook his head, pleading not to do what I'm about to do.

"What's happening?" Keiran asked, eyes wide as he looked between us and back to Cairo submitting to my will.

"She's drawing power from the moon..." Alek began before he grabbed at his chest, groaning in pain. "And me." Jordan left me with no choice. I was sick of dealing with her. I pulled on my bond with Alek, drawing his strength into me as I commanded Cairo to get out of the way.

"Zia, stop!" Cairo tried to grab my arm but he yelled suddenly pulling his hand back, getting zapped by the power surrounding me. It was buzzing along my skin, strengthening everything inside of me.

"Why do your eyes look almost white? What are you?" Jordan demanded.

"I'm the moons warrior, bitch! And I've had a fucking enough of you!" I said raising my fists.

"Oh, bring it! I've been waiting a long time to hit that skanky face!" She screamed as she copied my stance.

"The only skank here is you." My fist flew forward, connecting with Jordan's face. I felt a crack as she screamed, blood instantly flowing from her nose. She grabbed her face, pulling her hands back as she screamed again at the blood staining them. I smiled, baring my teeth as I reared my fist back.

"Cairo! Do something!" Keiran demanded. He was holding Alek up as he begged.

"He...can't!" Alek said through groans as his face scrunched in pain. "She gave him a command to get back. With her drawing from the moon and me, she now has the power all alphas. An alpha's Alpha!" Jordan barely dodged my hit, but her hand connected with my ribs and I grunted, savouring the burn to push me on.

"You have to do something, Alek!" She hit me again, connecting with my chin. Cairo tried to pull me back, distracting me from her but I growled, launching myself forward, taking her to the ground. I straddled her waist, hands raining down on her as she attempted to block me. Tunnel vision began as I focussed on her face. Blood started coating my hands but I couldn't stop. It felt amazing.

"I..I've got something. Cairo, when I say, extend your claws and scratch across your ribs as quick as you can. With both of our bonds to her, that should be enough to shock her out of her rage. I don't know what else to do."

"Okay!"

"Now!" Alek yelled.

I screamed out, searing pain burned and blossomed on both sides of my ribs. I stopped my onslaught, having trouble breathing as the pain incapacitated me. I was so distracted by the pain I never saw Jordan's fist fly out until it was too late. Everything went black.

Chapter Forty-Two

The War

Cairo

I dived, catching Zia mere seconds before she hit the ground. She was out cold, a bruise forming on her temple from Jordan's fist whose head thumped against the floor, exhausted from the beating she received from Zia. *This is great, just fucking great. Just what we need.*

"CAIRO!" Zack screamed as he reached the top of the stairs, chest heaving up and down as he caught his breath.

"What now!?" *What could possibly be happening now?*

"The rogues! They're attacking!"

"FUUUUUCK!"

"What are we going to do?" Keiran asked panicked.

"Zack, Keiran, Alek, go help my father. I'll take Zia and Jordan to the infirmary, then I'll be there." Zack and Keiran nodded, immediately springing into action as they left quickly descending the stairs. Alek hesitated. "Alek, man. The rogues, they're here for her. We need to stop them." I said as he breathed, looking at her one last time before he nodded and turned, running after Zack and Keiran.

I picked Jordan up, slinging her body over my shoulder as I leaned down, gently scooping Zia up. Cradling her against my chest, I quickly began my descent down the steps, out the front door and picked up my pace as I headed in the direction of the infirmary. My wolf and I just needed to make sure Zia was okay before we joined the fight. I needed that reassurance or else I wouldn't be able to fight as well as I can, mind too distracted.

The nurses rushed out as I linked them, taking each of the girls as they placed them onto beds and wheeled them into a room. They checked their vitals, hooked them up to drips and injected a booster shot to quicken their healing. I watched the clock hanging up on the wall. Five minutes quickly passed before ten soon approached.

Come on, baby. Please wake up.

I need to know you're okay before I go fight.

I don't know what it's like out there, but I know they'll need my help.

"C...Cairo?" Zia spoke softly under her breath. The bruise on her temple already begun to fade. I sighed in relief, bending down as I touched my forehead against hers.

"You're okay." I breathed a sigh of relief before dread soon seeped in.

"What happened?" She asked as she looked around confused.

"Baby, I don't have time to explain. The rogues attacked; I need to go fight. I just needed to know you were okay. You're safe here. I changed your top. It was bloodied and I know you don't like waking up seeing blood on you." I said but paused as someone's link was coming through.

"Cairo?" She asked worried.

"Alek's on his way," I said, my mind clearing from the

mindlink, "he'll stay here with you and protect you encase the rogues decide to attack the hospital. Some warriors are coming with him as well. I love you, Zia." I kissed her on the lips, savouring it as she kissed back.

"I love you too, Cairo."

ZIA

I grabbed the control for the bed, pressing the button as the back started lifting. Watching the door close behind Cairo. I couldn't stop the apprehension and unease that slowly sunk in. A mixture of our joined feelings were muddling together. I never want to doubt Cairo, but he's never fought a group of rogues before. I should be out there helping him but if I did that, I'd only distract him.

Looking to my right at the sound of groaning, I turn, legs hanging from the bed as I sat up, eyes instantly rolling as my lip curled, Jordan stirred awake from the bed across from mine. *You gotta be kidding me. They put me in the same room as that meddling bitch.* Her eyes slowly fluttered open, hand rising to her face as she felt around, noticing all the cuts and lumps have quickly faded and began to heal. She jumped, head snapping to me as she glared.

"What the hell are you doing in my room?!" She snapped as she ripped the bed controller off the hook, manicured nails tapping away at the settings trying to get the help button to work.

"First of all," I begin, "I'm not in *your* room, we're in the hospital. Secondly, we are sharing a room. If you couldn't tell what the two beds meant." I look at her with distain as she continues to glare, now sitting up right. She copies me, legs dangling over the side as she crossed her arms against her chest, pushing her tits up as she does so.

"I can't believe they put me in a room with you. I want my own room. Nurse!" She yelled, making me jump from the sudden volume change, instantly pissing me off.

"Goddess, you're so fucking selfish!" I snapped standing up, clenching my fists down by my side. The last thing the hospital needs is to be taking care of us after another fight. Now is not the time. "There's a fucking war going on right now and all you care about is getting your own room! I don't know how you ever thought that you could make a good Luna. You're selfish as all fuck, you single minded bitch. Your pack members are fighting for their lives out there!"

"A what?" She got off the bed, frowning at my words. I sigh. I was about to re-tell her that a rogue war has started but she gasped, looking down at my chest.

"Wait, why are you wearing Cairo's shirt?!" She snapped with her painted nailed finger pointing at me. I yell out, having enough of this shit.

"BECAUSE HE'S MY MATE! Why wouldn't I wear his shirt?! I'm wearing his fucking mark; his scent is all over me! All *in* me!" She screamed, hands shaking as her tantrum hurt my ears. I turned away from her as I linked Alek, wondering where the hell he was. He should have been here by now.

ZIA: *[Alek? Where are you? Cairo said you were on your way. Alek?]*

I asked but it was like white noise was coming through our bond. The link felt fuzzy like something was in the way blocking it. I try again.

ZIA: *[Alek? Are you oka-]*

ALEK: *[ZIA, RUN!]*

Fear, pain, confusion, hurt blasted through our mind. I paled, hearing the pure terror in Alek's voice as he screamed. I tried to link him again but something severed our tie. I couldn't feel him anymore. *No, no, no, no, no.*

ZIA: *[ALEK! ALEK!!]*

He didn't respond.

The door creaked opened; Jaxon suddenly appeared. His hand moved behind his back, slowing revealing a gun. Jordan gasped beside me, shaking her head erratically as her eyes widened in fear. "W...what are you doing?" I asked as he raised the gun, aiming straight at us as he mouthed something.

Then, he fired twice.

I looked down, not seeing a bullet hole or blood before my mind went fuzzy, everything started blurring. I heard a thump beside me, Jordan fell, clutching something in her hand. I felt a sharp pain in my chest, looking down again, I found the source. A tranquilizer dart. No, no!

C...Cairo....

I tried to link him, tried to call his name in my mind but it was too late. Jaxon slowly approached as everything started fading fast. The last thing I saw before the tranquilizer effects took its full effect, was Jaxon smiling as he leaned down, grabbing me by the hair before he kissed me roughly.

"Rogue bitch." He spat just as everything went black.

Chapter Forty-Three

Goodbyes

Cairo

I growl as my fist breaks through the wall, cracks splintering up the plaster. I rip my hand out, pulling back as I swing again. I will burn this whole fucking world down starting with Vladik. He will pay for what he's done. He's now taken everything from me. Everything! Alek is...Zia is...

"FUUUUUUCK!" I scream.

My wolf rips forward, fur sprouting from my skin as my bones snap out of place. The transition from man to wolf happens quickly. I can't do anything right now. My heart has been shattered.

He's in control now.

SIX HOURS LATER

As soon as I left Zia, I ran as fast as I could, heels digging into the ground as my feet took me to the battlefield. Jumping over fallen trees, ducking under low hanging branches, hands scraping against tree bark as I pushed myself off, trying to gain extra speed. I could hear the snarls and growls of my fellow pack members engaging in battle. I could hear the rogue's jaws snapping, claws dragging through the ground. Their growls were feral, dangerous sounds that could be heard for miles. I heard yelps and howling, and the closer I got, the more fur I could hear ripping, more bones crunching, and the smell of iron tainting the air. When I finally broke free of the tree line, the sight had stopped me in my tracks. The smell of blood was even worse as the stench of death lingered. I scanned the battlefield, shifted and non-shifted rogues fought. Warriors and their wolf partners fought valiantly, keeping the rogues back. We were winning, some rogues laid dead left and right. A few warriors retreated, hands holding their wounds as blood poured out. I felt a sense of pride, seeing how strong my pack is. They moved in union with each other, stepping left, ducking right as each fought like a team taking on the rogues. A foul-smelling stench assaulted my nose, getting stronger when I felt a presence come up behind me. I remembered something my father told me when I began my alpha training. He told me rogues are dirty fighters. They'll use any and every way they can to win a fight. They don't have goals; they don't have purposes. They fight for the fun of it. They love the thrill of it. They're not afraid of death. They welcome it. Just like the rogue behind me, sneaking up on me to surprise attack me. But these rogues forget one thing. They *stink*. There's a particular horrid stench that clings to them. I wasn't worried, my father specifically trained me for this. I remember the way the rogue that killed Siron moved. He was twitchy and aggressive, never studying his opponents moves.

I stretched my hearing, listening to the miniscule sounds behind me. His elbow cracked, knuckles quietly popping as the rogue fisted his hand. I ducked and spun, kicking my leg out taking the rogue to the ground. I reacted on instinct. I extended my claws before I swiped out, mauling his thighs where I know a main artery is. He'll bleed out quick. Suddenly I was tackled to the ground as four rogues surrounded me. I steeled my nerves, focussing on the smaller female rogue in front of me. Her movements were quick but sloppy. I ducked and weaved, hitting out as her nose broke beneath my fist. I strengthened my arm, pulling back just before I stepped forward, but I staggered, faltering as I dropped to the ground. A sharp stinging pierced my chest. I looked down expecting to see the injury but nothing was there. No blood, no red mark, no gunshot wound or silver burns or claw marks. Nothing. My chest was bare.

"No..." My eyes widen as the rogues laughed. *Zia!* Something was happening to her, and the rogues knew it. They all shared a look, an amused glint in their eyes. I turned, ready to run back to the infirmary but they boxed me in, taunting me.

"No, no, you stay." One said.

"Play with us," Another sang.

"She's not yours anymore." My head snapped to the brown-haired rogue. He winked at me, red eyes glimmering as he and the other three rogues all attacked at once.

I screamed as their claws pierced my skin, silver burning the wound. My eyes changed; my wolf slammed forward in my mind. My hand shot out, clamping down on the neck of the rogue in front of me. He wasn't laughing anymore. We used our strength to crush his throat. We dug our claws in before we ripped out pieces of the rogue's windpipe as he watched in horror. All blood drained from his face before his lifeless body dropped to the ground. The other rogues faulted, grips weakening as they took a feared step back. It was now my time to smile. Blood sprayed my face as I launched into the air, taking another rogue down as we mauled at his face and chest. The last rogue turned and ran. I stood, ready to go after him but a fierce growl and yelp tore through the air.

"DAD!" Time slowed down as I ran to him. The same rogue that spoke to us the night before was here. The silver dagger he held in his hand was embedded in my father's chest, aimed straight in his heart. I froze, father's eyes locked onto mine as the light slowly started to fade. The rogue let go, stepping back as he smiled one last time at me before he raised his hand in the air and turned, leaving the battlefield. Everything went silent. The fighting ceased as the other rogues followed. We were now alone; the war was over. But not without its casualties.

ZOSAR: [*Cairo..*] His weakened voice entered my mind.

ZOSAR: [*Tell..y...your mother...I..I love her...*] His breathing became gargled as blood rose up his throat, spilling out of his mouth as he dropped to his knees.

ZOSAR: [*T..tell Sarana...I love her..an...and that...she will always be...my...little girl..*] I shook my head, refusing to hear his last words. Even in his mind he was too weak to speak. Running to him, I caught him as he fell back. I didn't know what to do, my hand shook over the blade. If it was in his heart he would die in seconds, maybe instantly if I removed it. But if I leave it in, he can live long enough to have a chance to survive.

"Dad!" I shook him lightly as his eyes fluttered open. "No, please! Hold on! We...we can get help! Somebody help!" I looked up, tears in my eyes as I screamed at the pack for help. Some were on the knees, head bowing to the alpha in sorrow, some stood still, looking on in horror. Others cried and wept, knowing what was coming.

ZOSAR: [*Cairo...I...won't...make it. I'm...sorry I was never..a good...father...to you.* I never...] He coughed as more blood filled his lungs.

ZOSAR: [*Never...blamed you...for Siron. Blamed...myself. You* *look...just like...him*] He coughed again, heart weakening as his pulse slowed down dangerously slow.

"Dad, please! I can't lose you!" I cried, tears falling on his face.

ZOSAR: [*I'm...sorry, my...boy. Y..you will be...a..great...alpha...*]

"DAD!" He looked up, smiling at the sky as his eyes faded. His head fell back, body going limp in my arms.

Storm clouds rolled in and blanketed us in darkness. The rain started to fall as everyone's eyes were on us. I sat there holding my father in my arms, pulling him against my chest as I hugged him, wishing this was all just a nightmare. But it wasn't, it was real. I listened to the last beat in his heart, seconds after I gasped, feeling the Alpha power transfer to me. I threw my head back, screaming to the sky. I didn't want this! I didn't want to become alpha this way!

"*Take it back!*" I screamed to the Goddess, wishing she could hear my cries, but she ignored me. Forcing me to go through this transition alone. It was overwhelming. I felt strong, more powerful, more dominant. But that could do nothing to stop my falling tears. My father was dead, and I was now the Alpha. Not only had I lost my brother, but I had also lost my father. I couldn't save them. How am I meant to be Alpha now? It's all my fault. I should have fought harder, should have fought quicker. Should have...should have...

A warrior approached, looking distressed as he called out.

"Alp-Ca...Cairo..." He stammered, knees giving away as he dropped down, head bowing in sorrow. He rushes his bow, paying respect to my father before he looked back up, brows pinching together as he spoke. "Alpha Cairo." My eyes close, hating the new title. He should be saying my father's name, not mine. I'm only eighteen, I wasn't ready to take over the pack yet. But fate had other ideas. She's caste her hand down upon me, cursing my life.

"Speak." I address my warrior.

"It's Alek, sir." *Please, Goddess, don't do this to me.* "We found him unconscious not far from the infirmary. He's been stabbed, and..." He pauses, looking concerned as he continues, "he's not waking up. The doctors believe it's wolfsbane."

"W...wolfsbane?" I stammered. Someone attacked Alek and poisoned him? What the fuck is going on? "Send men to the interrogation room. Check the wolfsbane supply. See if any is missing."

"I..I will. But," *No. No, I can't hear anymore. I can't take anymore.* "The hospital was attacked. Two nurses are down and-"

"Zia, where is Zia?" I ask calmly, eyes closed.

"She's gone."

"Cairo! Can you stop putting holes in the walls and act like a damn alpha!" Zack snapped. "What do you want us to do?"

"What do I want you to do?" I laughed. "I WANT YOU TO FIND THAT FUCKING ROGUE!" I roared as I turned, facing Zack and the seven warriors behind him.

"Yes, Alpha." They all said in union, turning as they marched out of the hospital room. I caught my reflection in the door window, eyes yellow and rabid.

"Cairo," Zack began. He seemed to be the only one level-headed. Caleb was in one room down getting his head stitched up, Keiran was, well, as good as could be expected. Then there was Zack. I chose right for my beta. "Have you seen your mum?" Just the memory of my father's death had my wolf growling, teeth baring as he whined in pain.

SLAP

My wolf repelled back from the shock, throwing me back in control of my body. We didn't see Zack's hand swing out, slapping us as he snapped. "Pull yourself together! You're the Alpha now. You need to control yourself!"

"I lost my fucking dad and my mate, Zack! I can't even smell her fucking scent anywhere other than the room I left her in. It's as if she disappeared into thin-fucking-air! I have failed everyone! My mother lost her mate, I don't even know if mine is even alive. I can't even feel her, Zack! And do you want to know what the worst part is? I can't even begin to find her because the one person who would know where she was taken too is laying in that hospital bed behind you on the verge of fucking death!" Alek is the only one that knows where their old pack is. The only one who knows where Vladik would have taken her. They were so secretive, worried he would find them if they ever spoke their names or their home. But he came anyways.

"The doctors don't know if he will ever wake up." Keiran spoke quietly as tears fell. He clung to Alek's hand, waiting for any sign of life. Anything to let him know his mate was okay. Because of the wolfsbane coursing through Alek's system, Keiran can't enter his mind. Can't pull answers from him or even feel him.

"I have every right to lose control of myself when my whole world has been taken from me. Six hours ago, she was safe, hearing me promise her that I'd be back in no time. My only salvation is Alek and..." I don't finish but I don't need too. "If it's orders you want, I can give orders. I can be a fucking Alpha. Find that fucking rogue, he knows where she was taken. You'll know him when you see him. They all listen to him. And when Caleb is finished getting stitched, send him to me. I have a job for him."

"No, need. I'm here." He spoke from the doorway. "What can I do?" He asked as he straightened up, ready to obey as an array of stitches covered his face.

"I need you to find a witch. Find *Glinda*."

Chapter Forty-Four

Home

ZIA

I awoke in a dark room on a thin mattress. My hand felt around, feeling cold concrete inches below the mattress. I could hear a steady drop of water dripping away in the distance. *Where am I?* My eyes slowly adjusted to the dark. It was night. The small window with thick silver coated bars on the cobblestoned wall to my right, had a single streak of moonlight streaming in, but this place was so void of all light inside this stony place that the small beam of moonlight didn't do much except slice right through the darkness. I could hear someone breathing, slow and steady.

I groaned, placing my hands on the mattress in front of my knees as I pushed myself up to stand. I caught myself on the cobblestone wall. I squinted, looking ahead seeing a tall figure standing in the dark. They moved forward, leisurely stepping into the moonlight as the streak lit up their body slowly before it stopped, lighting across their face. Ice blue eyes gleamed in the light.

"Hello, *my Luna*." Vladik said. I couldn't breathe, fear licked up my throat, chills going down my spine as blood rushed to my head. *No, no, no. I can't be back here...I can't be back here!*

"You're even more beautiful than I remember, ZyZy." He stepped forward, stopping as he looked down at me. He was so close I could feel the heat from his body, warming my paled, clammy skin.

I couldn't move, frozen in fear as I stared up into those dead pale blue eyes of my tormentor. My abuser, the demon and man who lived in my nightmares for as long as I could remember. The man who scarred my past and shaped my future. My future, which is now in his hands. He's changed so much from the eighteen-year-old I remembered. His jaw had sharpened, no longer rounded from his youthful age, he was taller, more muscled. His eyes, the ice blue, dead pale looking eyes I remembered but it was the scar down his left eye I didn't recognise, until I did. *I* did that to him. The night my papa and Alek tried to save me. *Papa...*

"It took a long time to find you, baby." His dark voice spoke, making my heart plummet. "You-" He began but stopped, suddenly sniffing the air. My eyes widen, my scent, it was different now. Cairo...My heart began beating rapidly as his eyes shifted, I could feel his fury. His body started to shake in anger as his hand shot out. He fisted my hair, ripping my head back as he pulled me forward into the light. His eyes were trained on my neck, staring at Cairo's mark. I cried out from the pain, his claws extended, pressing into my scalp as he shook me roughly.

"YOU'RE MARKED!!" He roared, voice ringing in my ears. I whimpered, afraid of what he's going to do to me. "YOU'RE MINE!" He shook me again as my feet scraped against the ground as he dangled me in the air. "YOU'RE MY LUNA!" He declared but something in me snapped.

I wasn't his Luna, I was Cairo's.

I kicked my legs out with my sudden burst of energy, connecting with his stomach as his hand in my hair let go. I fell to the ground, catching myself at the last second before I shot up, wolfs eyes shining brightly through the dark as I spoke, letting the sudden flash of rage lead me. "YOU, are not my mate. I let my TRUE mate mark me! You are not and will never be my mate, Vladik. You are not him!"

He stilled, dark eyes shifting back to his piercing blue eyes as he stalked closer. Once he moved out of the light, he moved too quick for me to see. Hit after hit, he wouldn't stop his attack. My face throbbed as he continued his assault over and over again until my vision clouded. Soon everything went black. But the sound of his voice still lingered echoing through the room.

"You will learn, *Zia*."

I don't know how long it was before I awoke again. My face throbbed, skin burned to touch, and it was hard to breathe because of my swollen cheeks. They will go down soon enough and the bruises sometime after that, but I know this won't be the last time. The look on Vladik's face was pure, controlled rage. He hit me with precision. He wanted to hurt me, punish me for being marked. He was stronger, taller now and could easily overpower me as he has done many times before. But I'm all alone now, Alek's miles away in a different country. I have no way to draw extra strength without him by my side. If I'm going to survive this time at all, I'm going to have to survive on my own. For the first time ever, I won't have someone to save me.

I was laying on my stomach, still in the short jean shorts and

Cairo's white button up shirt. I breathed in, smelling the faded scent of blood, sweat and dirt mixed deep within the mattress. I laid quiet for some minutes, keeping my breathing slow and steady encase Vladik was lurking somewhere in the dark waiting for me to awaken. As the minutes trickled by, the swelling in my cheeks slowly went down, my vision became clearer from the swelling and my eyes had adjusted to the dark. *Is that?* I push up on my elbows, squinting as I get a better look at the body laid on the ground. My mouth dropped open on a silent gasp. *It's Jordan!* I watched as she finally stirred, wondering why she was taken too. But I wasn't alone when Jaxon came into the room. He probably panicked and when he apologised, he wasn't looking at me. He was looking at her. I sit up, knees against my chest as her head lifts, blinking eyes looking around before they landed on me.

"W...what?" She gasps, eyes widen even further as she shoots up with a sudden burst of energy. Her eyes dart around the cell, heart beating a million miles a minute before her confused and terrified eyes found mine. "Where the hell am I?" She screams. I stand up, wobbling as my head still feels dizzy.

"You are in Russia." I blanch, dumbing it down, not wanting to repeat myself with her right now.

"What?! No! I can't be here!" My eyes roll on their own. *No fucking shit.* "This wasn't part of the plan!" My blood ran cold.

"...What plan?" A bad feeling overcame me as she screamed again, feet slamming against the ground as she pointed at me wildly.

"Only you were supposed to be taken!"

"What did you do?" A lump formed in my throat, there's no way she could have done this.

"We had a plan, Jaxon and me. Those stupid rogues were supposed to distract the pack while another group grabbed you. I was never supposed to be in that hospital room. I was supposed to be out getting my nails done, having an alibi! But you just had to snap. Had to ruin the fucking plan. Jaxon should have fucking left me there! Not given me over to the rogues with you." There was no air in my lungs. All I could hear was the sound of my own heartbeat as her words replayed in my head.

"Y..." I tried but that lump in my throat stopped me. I breathed in and out before I tried again. "There's no way you could have found him. I was careful! I never...I never..." She laughed; an evil glint twinkling in her eyes.

"Even if I didn't hear that pathetic little sob story you told Cairo after the ball, it wouldn't have mattered. I knew about Vladik long before." My body trembled, so many questions flipped through my mind like papers blowing around from a gust of wind. There was no way she would do this to the pack she longed to rule over for all these years. And she knew about Vladik? How? "Someone you love, betrayed you. After that it wasn't all that hard. I got in touch with him, then he sent me some rogues who were well paid and willing to get the job done. Your Alpha here likes to use rogues. Quite smart if you ask me. Rogues are disposable." I growled lowly, feeling my wolfs hackles raising at her words.

"Once the rogues knew of the plan and distraction, I just had to get Alek out of the way. But of course, he wouldn't trust me, so-"

"What did you do to Alek?!" My eyes changed; claws extended as I waited for her to speak.

"Well, if I got my measurements right then he's dead. If not, then he won't ever wake up from the wolfsbane poison I created. It's not like I cared about the measurements. Just as long as he was out of the way. Cairo would naturally gravitate to the battlefield and I didn't need another knight in shining armour coming to the rescue since you're always a helpless little dove." She scoffed, lip curling in disgust. My tears fell on their own accord. That's why I couldn't feel Alek anymore. I can't even feel the slightest bit of our bond and without him, I can't go to the moon and see him if he was there. She took my brother from me...She truly was evil.

"That's what was in the tranq I gave Jaxon. Just enough to knock you out and get you to your Alpha. Your *mate*." She laughed, enjoying seeing my tears.

"It was quite the plan." Vladik's deep voice resonated around the room as keys jingled. The steel barred door opened, then he stepped forward. Jordan gasped, heart beating rapidly as I looked over at her, seeing her wolfs orange eyes shine through. "I wanted Alek too. I was going to kill him for taking you from me. But her plan was better. It had little to no flaws at all. She-" He turned, facing Jordan as he stopped mid-sentence. His eyes changed too, ice blue shifting to his wolfs orange. Both recognising each other as their mates now that the dulling tranquilizer had run its course through her body. For a split second that light at the end of the tunnel, the small light of hope was so bright, I could almost taste my freedom. They were mates! He wouldn't want me anymore. But then I saw his eyes. They turned so black the rims of his eyes started staining red. He was furious, beyond furious. *No...*

"Oh Goddess! You're my mate!" Jordan exclaimed so happily, hands waving in the air as she spoke. *No, no, no, Jordan stop...* "Wait, you're the Alpha! That means I'm your Luna!" She was so in her own world she never saw the danger coming. The moment she said she was his Luna, his hand shot out, wrapping around her neck as he squeezed her throat tightly. Her eyes widened in shock, hands slapping and clawing at his as his grip tightened.

"What makes you think I would ever want a mate like you?" He asked, voice void of any feeling and dripping with acid. "You reek of male. You will never be my mate."

He spoke with so much hatred as he lifted her up, legs dangling in the air as her eyes went bloodshot. Then I heard it. The crackling of her joints and the snapping sound of her neck echoing through the silent room as her body went limp. I froze, unable to move. Fear gripped me tighter than it ever has. Through everything I've ever gone through, this moment will forever stay with me. He killed her, his mate. That was the moment I knew he would never let me go. He killed his own mate because of me. *How could he? His own mate...*

"Shame," He finally spoke, pulling her to him as he held her body, inspecting her face closer. "She was beautiful." His words sent a chill down my spine. He brushed her hair out of her face, feeling the skin on her check. Then, he let go, letting her body drop to the ground making an audible thud like she was a piece of trash. "Now," He turned, smiling as he stalked towards me. "I've missed you, baby."

"S...st..stay away!" I stammered out, choking as sobs wracked through my body.

"Aw, now, you know I can't do that." He said smiling before his face dropped, eyes darkening. "I need to fix that mark of mine."

"No!" I screamed.

I tried to run, but he was quicker. One arm wrapped around my back, holding me tightly against him as he grabbed my hair, straining my head back as I thrashed against him. His canines extended before he marked me. I screamed; pain seared through me. His mark fought Cairo's. But his mark would never win the battle. He finally pulled back; my blood smeared across his lips as he spoke.

"I missed that taste."

Then he kissed me, tongue pushing passed my lips as he grabbed my cheeks, forcing my mouth open. Once he had enough, he dropped me the same way he did Jordan and left just as quick as he entered. I laid down on my side, cradling my legs as I cried myself to sleep the best I could with my bleeding neck. *Cairo...* I whimpered before exhaustion finally took me.

Chapter Forty-Five

Sarana

Cairo

I'd never been to a real beach before. I'd only ever seen it in movies and on TV shows. I've never smelt the salt in the air as the wind carried it across the waves. But tonight, I could.

The wind carried my tears as I looked out across the water of our makeshift beach. The moon was high in the sky, cloudless, and full of stars. The pack has been quiet ever since the rogue war happened. They lost an alpha, gained a new one and lost their new Luna all in one day.

We lost a few good men and women, but the rogues lost more. Funerals are being planned, ceremonies put off and classes have temporarily stopped.

The pack mourns.

"Cairo?"

I should be there, acting like an alpha, being the Alpha, they need right now. But I just can't. I need time. Time alone.

"Cairo?" Caleb said again.

"Let me guess, Zack sent you."

He's been on me ever since our argument in Alek's hospital room. He wants me to step up, be strong for the pack but he doesn't understand, nobody does.

"Does he want you to calm me down?" I've felt him in my head all day, trying to link me but I've blocked him.

Doesn't mean I can't still feel the little woodpecker in my head, attacking the wall I erected between us.

"Everyone's worried about you, C. You're the Alpha now. We-" His words fell on deaf ears. He's just like Zack.

"Where's Kitty?" I asked.

"W..what?" He was confused, as he should be.

"Where, is, she?" My chest rattled low, my wolfs anger quickly rising to the surface.

"She's at home..." He said quietly, still unsure.

"Exactly, Caleb. Your mate is at home, safe and sound probably sleeping on her soft bedsheets and thick comforter. Do you want to know what's happening to my mate?" I ask, voice dropping as my skin bristles.

I could feel the moment Zia woke. Our bond came back and I could feel her again. She was alive. But that's where my happiness ended.

That's why I've been standing here, looking out at the water for hours.

"Wh..." Caleb began but he stopped. He breathed in, holding his breath before he exhaled. "What's happening to Zia?" I could hear the hesitation in his voice.

"She's being marked." He sucked in a breath, heart picking up its pace as he listened. "I felt it an hour ago. Since then, the pain hasn't stopped and I'm not talking about my own pain from someone trying to break our bond. I'm feeling *her* pain. He's marking her over and over again. He hasn't stopped. And you know how I know? Because my neck hasn't stopped feeling like it's being skinned. Occasionally I'll feel a throbbing in my face but that's okay. Do you know why that's okay? Because she's alive. So, I guess now that I know that I can calm down and control myself. Be the Alpha I'm supposed to be. Right?" I ask but he doesn't reply. He stays silent.

"RIGHT?!" I turn, my wolfs eyes shining through, fists clench as my voice deepens from rage.

"Cairo, I'm-"

"You're what? You're sorry?? Or are you sorry that your mate is home safe while mine is out there getting fucking tortured!?" My chest heaves, nostrils flaring as I watch him cower his head, showing me his neck.

"You're right..."

"NOW LEAVE!" My voice boomed out as my alpha command rippled through the air.

He instantly dropped down to his knees, bowing his head as he submitted and show me respect.

I looked away, back to the water as he waited a few seconds before he rose. He breathed out and turned, sand crunching beneath his feet as he walked away. No one will ever understand my pain.

Zack hasn't found his mate yet and Caleb's mate is safe. He knows where she is.

The only one who can feel even a whisper of what I feel is Keiran. But that's where our similarities end. He can hold his mate, touch his mate.

I can only feel the whispers of our bond, feel the pain her body is in. Feel the sadness and fear washing over her.

"Zia..." I speak to the stars, hoping wherever she is that she could hear me. I need her to know. "Hold on, baby. I'll find you. I promise."

FOUR WEEKS LATER

KNOCK KNOCK.

The door opened slowly, hinges screaming as they're pulled apart. I growled, the pillow in my hands ripping as I screamed at the intruder. "GET OUT!" A small squeak sounded as Sarana appeared, hands clutching her chest as my head shot up. "I'm so sorry, Sasa." She looked scared, big eyes tearing as she looked at me. "Come here." I give her a small smiled and nod, pushing away my sorrow. She looks wary as she approaches in her frilly pink skirt, grey and white stripey sweater, red polka dot flats, a boho style scarf around her neck and a pink tiara on her head.

"Bubba, okay?" She rubbed her arm as she spoke, a slight tremble in her lips and her chin wobbled. I was sat on the floor, clutching Zia's pillow, and breathing in her scent when Sarana came in. She was still a head shorter as I sat down. Facing her as I tried to smile away the pain.

"I'll be fine. Don't worry about bubba, he's a big boy." I saw referring to myself. She nods, rainbow bangles on her wrist jingling every time she moved. "Sasa, what are you wearing?" I chuckle as I look at the violet feather clip on earrings clipped to her ears. She looked like a colourful peacock.

"Mama always crying," she said, tiny tears slowly dripping down her cheeks, "so I dress myself." My eyes close, refusing to see the truth in front of me. We neglected her. *I* forgot about her. I didn't even think about what she would be going through. I'm here losing my shit and mums too sad to take care of her daughter. I'm a horrible alpha and big brother. History was repeating itself. I couldn't protect my younger brother and I wasn't protecting my younger sister. That needed to change. I need to focus, need to be the backbone this pack needs. I need to be stronger for everyone, I need to get my ass into gear, need to find a way to save Zia.

"Bubba?"

"Yes?"

"Where's daddy?" Like a knife to my chest, a ball formed in my throat, threatening to make my voice crack as I spoke.

"He..." *Inhale, exhale*. "He died, Sarana. There was a big fight and a mean rogue hurt daddy. He couldn't heal fast enough." *Inhale, exhale.*

"Will I see daddy again?" She said with a note of hope in her small voice. I reach forward, bringing her to me as she wrapped her arms around my neck.

"No, bubby, you won't. We won't." I think she got it then. She started crying, repeating she wanted daddy over and over again. "I know...I want him back too."

I cry with her, knowing I'm the only one right now who can understand her, who can understand and share her pain. If she had her wolf already, I would silently command her, to ease her pain away. She's too young to know this kind of pain. Too young to be crying these sad tears. Too young to lose her father. I felt guilty for having spent more years with him than her. I hope she doesn't grow to resent me.

Soon her little heaves slowed down, her sniffles soon stopped, and her breathing deepened as her body went lax in my arms. She cried herself to sleep. Exhausted from toll our father's death has had on her. I tucked her into my chest, picking her small body up and lay her down gently on my bed. I tuck her in, taking the tiara off her head and placing on the bedside table. Then, I sit and watch her. Watch the peaceful look that washes over her face. I wish I knew peace like that. But I won't know it until I get Zia back.

Chapter Forty-Six

The Surprise

ZIA

It's been four weeks. I've counted every day the sun rose and set. Four weeks since I've eaten a proper meal. I get a cup of water a day and a piece of bread thrown on the ground like I'm a dog. Four weeks since I last saw Cairo, last touched, last felt those mate sparks. My heart aches for him every day and my mind is trying so hard to stay strong and sane for him. But I'm not strong. I've seen the movies where the girl gets kidnapped and when she wakes she fights like hell to get out and escape. But that's not real, Vladik is my nightmare and to be back here again with him is killing me slowly. I'm not strong enough to escape. I'm just barely strong enough for me to survive. Survive the torture he puts me through every day. When Vladik visits me, he marks me. Opening the wound on my neck as he forces his mark upon me. Then he watches as it heals and fades, Cairo's mark expelling his from my neck. Then he gets mad, beating me before he holds me down and has his way with me. Then he marks me again before he leaves, always holding hope that Cairo's mark will be the one to disappear but it never does and that...that is what I draw my strength from. That Cairo's mark and love is so strong that no matter what Vladik does to me, no matter how many times he marks me, it will never go away. And for that, he's punishing me.

He left Jordan's body in here. He's not even affected by the smell of his dead mate. He won't even spare her body a glance when he comes in here. I can't stand the smell anymore. Werewolves can pick up the smallest scent from miles away. So, in this tiny cell, it feels like I've got my nose pressed up against her body. Even shutting my senses off, I still throw up every day. It started the second her body started decomposing. I slept standing under the little barred window. Breathing in the fresh air as it slowly blew in, granting me a millisecond of relief before the stench of a decaying corpse assaulted me once more.

"How is my mate today?" Vladik asked from beyond the bars, hidden in the dark as he watched me from the shadows like he usually did. He often stood there, watching me as I slept. I'd wake for a few seconds before my skin crawled, feeling his eyes on me.

"Please...Vladik, please take her body out. I can't...I can't take the smell anymore. I feel sick.." I beg him, staring in the direction I know he's in. I plead with my eyes, hoping, and praying he will grant me this one wish. "She doesn't deserve this." I whispered. "Please, Vladik." He stepped forward, keys clanging as they hit the lock. The steel and silver doors creaked as he pushed them open with his steel capped boot.

"*I like the way you beg, ZyZy.*" He placed his finger under my chin, lifting my head up so that I look into his cold ice blue eyes as he spoke our mother tongue. "*Okay, my Luna. I'll remove the trash.*" He spoke without an ounce of remorse. *Trash*...I'm so sorry, Jordan. What you did was despicable, but the dead don't deserve to be treated like this.

A warrior I recognised appeared at the gate. He bowed, eyes slightly widening as he looked at me. Not believing who he was seeing. Vladik growled lowly, the warriors head instantly snapping down in submission. "*Get rid of the body.*" He nodded before he gagged, picking up what he could of Jordan's body. He would need to come back a few more times until my cell would be clean of her. Vladik sniffed the air, turning as he looked down at me. "*I think you need a bath.*"

"*No...*" I shook my head, fearing what he had in mind.

"*Yes, I have a surprise for you. You don't want to smell like filth do you?*" His hooded eyes pierced me with a look that dared me to defy him. I shook my head making him smile.

He grabbed my hand, leading me out through the cell, down the pitch-black cobblestoned path before we reached a metal door. We walked up some stairs, pushing through another door before light stung my eyes, making me clasp my hands over my eyes. I was so disorientated by the sudden light I lost time. I don't know how long we walked or where he took me, but soon his hands were on my shirt, unbuttoning it before he tossed it aside. I felt the breeze on my naked body. I shuddered, eyes focusing as we stood before a lake. Vladik striped beside me. Walking into the water, he dipped under the surface, little waves rippling as he resurfaced. Platinum blonde hair slicking back as he ran his hand over his head. His alabaster skin glistening as the water dripped down his body. I shivered, hating that I once saw him attractive. He was a pale ghost in comparison to Cairo. He was kissed by the sun, green Earth coloured eyes and hair as dark as the night sky. He was a warm summers day where Vladik was a winter storm. He was cold, icy, frosting everything he touched.

"*Zia,*" Vladik spoke the name I had for three years, amused, loving the way it made me flinch every time he said it, "*come here.*" He left no room for argument. No room for me to disobeyed him.

I clasped my hands together, hiding their trembling as I stepped into the water. I held my hands up, covering my chest as his eyes roamed down my body looking appreciatively through the crystal-clear water. I closed my eyes when his hands touched my body. He washed me, letting the water clean my stained, dirty skin. He turned me to face him, hands grabbing my jaw roughly. Then he pushed my head down, holding me under the water as I thrashed around. His face was distorted from the waves, but I could see his smile. My arms flailed about, lungs burning as I screamed. Suddenly, he pulled me back up. I gasped for air, breathing in as much as I could. After that he pulled me out of the water, tossing Cairo's bloody and torn shirt to me. I quickly swirled it around in the water, wanting to get the smell of Jordan's body out. I prayed and prayed to the Goddess that Cairo's scent still clung to it when I pulled it out. I quickly followed Vladik, wringing the water out of the shirt before I put it back on. He stopped when I reached him, grabbing my hand again making my fingers go white as he squeezed my hand. I dared not to make a sound. I didn't know this Vladik. I didn't know how to talk to him, how to do anything. He's got a hair trigger, and anything could set him off. I looked through the woods, missing my home more than I thought. I could see my child self, running and laughing through the trees with Alek behind me. Like distant memories, the ghosts played happily, blissfully unaware of the nightmare coming.

We came up on the old stone building. I've only seen it once before and it scared me as a child. And now I knew why. I knew the horrors that lay deep within. The stench of death that fills the air. I breathed in one last time, not knowing when I will smell the fresh crisp air again. I was pulled back down the ways to my cell. Water droplets still echoing in the air, a musty smell mixed with dirt from the Earth. I almost retched but I held it in. Thankful that the cobblestones no longer smelt of death. They were wiped down; small puddles of soapy water lay in the stones crevasse as they dried. The ground was swept, all evidence that Jordan was here was gone. I walked to my mattress in the corner, bending down to sit but I wasn't alone. Vladik came down with me. He rose above me, smiling down as his eyes went black and canines shimmered in the dark. My hands went to his chest, pushing him back as he placed his knee inside my thigh, prying my legs open.

"*Vladik...please. Stop...it hurts.*" I cried but it was of no use. He took what he wanted and marked me, my pleas falling on deaf ears. As everytime this happens, I was floating in the air, watching my bruised body trying to fight him but he easily overpowered me. My face still held defiance to it but as every day passed, little by little, I lost a piece of myself. When he rose up, he kissed me roughly. I hated tasting my blood on his lips, hated seeing the satisfied look on his face like he's won.

"*You are such a good girl, my Luna. I think you deserve your surprise now.*" My body wouldn't move, tears all dried once he removed himself from me and left without another word. He could leave the door open but I would have no energy to escape.

I turned my back to the bars, tucking my legs into my chest as I lay in a ball. I held the collar of my shirt close to my nose, smelling the faintest scent of Cairo. Then I cried. I missed him dearly, missed him more than the air I breathed. I don't know what happened to him that day. Everything is still cloudy. I know Jordan and Jaxon teamed up. Those two I'm not surprised. Jordan thinks I stole Cairo from her and Jaxon never liked me. He despised me for being a rogue. Then Cairo attacked him during the trials and it only makes sense that's the reason he did this, his hate deepening because of it. Cairo permanently scared his face from that attack. And that too is my fault. I hid my scent from him, making his wolf snap and panic when it was released into the air with my blood. If I had of just told Cairo, let my scent out when he asked then that wouldn't have happened. He wouldn't have attacked Jaxon. But there's still that third person that helped them. Someone Jordan delighted in keeping their identity a secret.

Someone I love, betrayed me.

Footsteps echoed as they grew closer before they stopped, keys clanging in the lock again. The door slowly creaked open and my body began to shake. Not healed enough from Vladik's last recent visit. But he was bringing me a surprise.

"Please...Vladik. Stop this..." I barely whispered. I expected to hear his deep cold voice, but instead I heard two sets of gasps. Two hearts beating rapidly, breathing becoming irregular as they looked at me. Something about them familiar...

"...Pup?" I gasped, quickly looking over my shoulder. *Papa!*

My arms shook as I tried to push myself up but I fell, too weak to move. He stepped forward, quickly catching me. He pulled me up, hugging me tightly against his chest as he breathed me in. Mama stood behind him, tears in her eyes and hands clasped over her mouth as she looked my body up and down. I could see everything in her deep-sea blue eyes. The same emotions Alek felt for years, she now showed. But there was more, there was fear, panic, and pure terror swirling around. She closed them, unable to see me anymore. But she ran forward the last few steps, encasing me in her warmth. All three of us cried and held each other in silence. I could hear the wind blowing outside the window, whistling as it blew in and swirled around us. I missed the way they smelt. My papa's pine and maple wood scent, mama's sweet strawberry honey swirl that always had a hint of blackberry nestled away in it. They pulled back, each one holding a hand as they squeezed taking me all in. Seeing their baby girl after years of knowing nothing.

They looked the same but not at the same time. Papa had new healed scars around his throat and jaw. His black hair began to grey on the sides. He was as tall as Alek and standing just as strong as I remember. Mama was short, my height. Her light blonde hair was curled, styled, and tucked behind her ears. She was just as beautiful as I remembered. Alek and I looked so similar to our mama. The only difference were our eyebrows were dark like papa's and we had his straight nose.

"*Mama, Papa...*" Relief filled me, I longed to see them for years but feared the consequences of contacting them. But none of that mattered anymore, I was back, and they were right in front of me, in the flesh.

"*My baby!*" Mama's voice softly echoed through the room as her dainty hand delicately touched my healing cheek, finger tracing my healed scar. She never saw what I looked like the day we left the pack. Vladik had already cut my face. Her chin wobble, a single tear separating from the pool of tears in her eyes. I smiled at her through my own tears. I looked to Papa, focusing on the scars on his neck and replaying the day those appeared the events that led to both of our markings. He exhaled, nodding his head as he smiled reassuringly down at me. Babushka said she never saw him up there but I saw what he looked like that day. I saw the complete savagery Vladik was and had done to papa. I feared he could not survive a new, young savage alpha who had just rose to power. But papa is strong.

"*My pup, look at me.*" Papa spoke, squeezing my hand ever so lightly as I opened my eyes after closing them from shame of not believing he could survive. "*Alek, is he here?*" Mama gasped as my chest heaved, pain souring through me at the thought of Alek. It wasn't a question I could answer easily or truthfully because I didn't know. I don't know if he's alive or dead. I have only been able to feel my bond with Cairo. The bond I had with Alek was now a gaping hole in my heart. A void. I didn't know if he was here on Earth still or if he was somehow still alive after Jordan's malicious plan. "*Is he?*" My Papa asked again, this time with more steel to his voice. He needed to know, needed to know if he had to mourn a child. They both looked at each other then, breathing in at the same time before my papa's voice was barely above a whisper. "*Is he dead?*"

"*I don't know, Papa. I can't feel him anymore.*"

"*What happened, pup? How are you back here?*" He said sadly.

"*We...we found our mates.*" Mama gasped, tears halting their trail down her cheeks as she spoke.

"*You did?*" I nodded. "*What are they like?*"

"*Alek's mate is sweet. You would like him.*" She gave a small smile, brows frowning as tears began to fall again.

"*And yours?*" Papa asked.

"*He's alpha blood. But we...we had a rough start. I wasn't so trusting and he..he wasn't either. But I love him. He's protective of me and loves me too.*"

"*How did he find you?*" Papa asked, quietly emphasising *he*. I know who he meant; Vladik.

"*There was a girl in the pack. She wanted to be Luna. She was vindictive, always trying to tear us apart. She found out about Vladik and somehow tracked him down. She brought rogues to the pack and she...*" It was getting harder to breathe the more I thought about her betrayal. "*She did something to Alek. Wolfsbane.*" Papa growled as my mama cried out. "*She said she wasn't sure if she got the measurements right. He..he could still be alive, but I don't feel him anymore. I have only been able to feel my mate since I woke.*"

"*What pack? W...we can find him! Your mate, he can help!*" Mama said as I nodded, knowing I finally had a way to contact Cairo. I went to speak but my father stopped me, shaking his head as he looked at the both of us.

"*No. Do not speak a word. He will just command us. He has done it before. I will find a way. I promise you.*" Then, he shared a look with mama. She nodded, both agreeing on something.

"*Okay, papa.*" I pulled my hands out of theirs, gingerly wrapping my arms around the both of them as I hung my head.

They joined in, heads leaning against mine as I let the

beating of their hearts give me strength. They left soon after that, both of their eyes glazing over as a shimmer followed. Vladik had commanded them out. They each kissed me goodbye before they disappeared into the darkness.

Vladik didn't come back. I haven't seen him in a week. I was left alone with the rats that steal or now *stole*, my food. Not even they have been back but I did warn them off. Everyday I've been talking to myself, writing imaginary diary entries in my head to keep me sane. It won't be long before he comes back, before he hurts me again. I need to keep my wits about me if I'm going to survive. Because when he comes back, and he will, he may just kill me.

Chapter Forty-Seven

Friend or Foe?

TWO MONTHS LATER

GHOST

"Yes?" I said into my phone after I couldn't ignore the silent buzzing any longer.

"You need to come back. Somethings happened." It was Aleksei.

"What's happened?" He never rings me, we had a code, a rule we never break.

"He's *happy*." I shivered. Bumps raising along my arms at the thought. Vladik was never happy and when he was, he was sadistic. A happy Vladik meant danger. "I heard the soldiers speaking, he has two female captives. I need you to come back, Ghost. He's watching me closely; eyes are following me wherever I go. Updating him. Only you can find out what he's up to."

"It will take me a while to get back. I can't...escape so easily this time." The less he knows the better, it's how Aleksei prefers it.

"Please, hurry. I do not have a good feeling about this." I agree.

"I'll see you as soon as I can. You won't know when I arrive, but I'll link you once I'm there." I hang up, not another word was exchanged.

I wasn't going to stop until those twins were found. I needed to find them before Vladik did. I couldn't let him get his hands on them...on her. I needed to protect them.

It took me a week of planning, escaping, running, and finding a black-market flight, but I eventually made it back. I was *home*. I know every secrete passageway, every route the warriors take that patrol the pack. I knew how to sneak in undetected, how to blend into my surroundings. There was a reason why I was called Ghost. You never know I'm there until it's too late. I masked my scent, scaling a tree careful not to break any branches not even a single twig. I'm not the way I am without being meticulous about the details. If I need cover, I take it. I blend, like a chameleon. On this branch I perch, waiting for the sun to set before I make my descent. The patrols are slower, less routine and slopy than they used to be. I head straight for the building, hidden deep in the pack land, the cobblestoned building quickly came into view. I cross the short space, rubble flicking but no one notices. There's no sound other than silence of the night and my shallow breathing. I circle the building looking for something before I find it. The window. I crouch down, looking through the bars as I find the figure bundled just below. A wave of relief washes over me, there she was. Safe, *for now*. It's takes mere minutes for me to pick the multiple locks, navigate my way through the dark before I'm at her cell. Her hear rate spikes, breathing becomes irregular and rapid. My chest tightens, my head knows her fear is not directed at me, but she shouldn't be feeling this way. She's too young to know this type of fear. Her sniffles reach my ears, she's trying to hide them.

"Th...that was quick..." Her small shaky voice spoke.

"Not quick enough, cousin." She gasps, head snapping my way as her eyes widen. I contain a growl; her bruises were as clear as day. Both on her upper body and lower. She stands up, knees wobbling and hand grabbing the wall to hold herself up.

"Grace?" I nod, smiling as I slowly approach.

"Don't speak so loud, keep it hush. No one knows I'm hear except Aunty and Uncle." She looks confused, muttering something to herself.

"Wha...what's going on?" She asks quietly.

"I left that day when all hell broke loose. It was a few hours after you and Alek left. Once Aunty linked me I knew I had to run. I was the best tracker our pack had and I know if I stayed, I would have been forced to track you down. Forced to bring you back to him. But Alek was always so smart. Even I couldn't track you. But I never gave up. I searched and searched for you. I kept Aunty and Uncle updated. I searched every Russian pack, even the neighbouring countries."

"America. That's where we've been hiding. Grace, I...if you left then, why are you back now?"

"I didn't know until now. Until I saw you. But they brought me back to save you. They told me you are mated. I'm going to find your mate, Zi. I'm going to find him, and I'm going to kill Vladik. For everything he's done to you, to our family, to our pack. To all the innocent people he has killed over the years. He will pay." I vowed.

"I missed you so much, Grace." Her tears made her bright aqua blue eyes shimmer in the dark. They were haunting.

"I missed you too. Now tell me, what pack is your mate from? What is his name? His father's name? If I ask for the Alpha it will be less likely that I'll be thrown in a pack prison like this." She nods quickly, listening intently so she can rattle off all the information I need to know. But I frown, ears straining as I hear quick footsteps approaching.

"Someone's coming. Fuck! I thought I had more time."

"No, it's Alina. She...she brings my food now. She's coming back with a blanket."

"Zy," I touch her cheek, "I love you. You are strong, you are resilient. You have more heart and strength than you know. Please, keep hope. Hope will get you through this. I'm going to find him. I will be back." Her hot tears fall over my hand. She placed her small one over mine, eyes closing as her brows furrowed. I need to pull away, not having enough time before Vladik comes back. Uncle linked, it's not Alina coming, it's Vladik. He cannot find me here.

"Grace," her eyes are open, a seriousness has taken over her features, "be...be careful when you find him. Cairo...He's hurting."

"Don't worry," I pull her to me, hugging her as I reassure her worries, "I'm tougher than I look." I kiss the side of her head, breathing in her scent before I turn and run. I shut the door and slink back into the darkness. I take an old secret passageway out. I won't cross paths with Vladik and he won't know I was ever here. He doesn't even know this passage exists.

But I do.

TWO WEEKS LATER

It was harder finding Zy's mates pack just with his name alone. I needed the pack name, the town it's near or the closest one to them. But I'm determined, I'm going to find this damn pack, I'm going to get her mate and I'm going to save my family and my pack. I spoke to my Aunty and Uncle again, they told me what happened, how she was captured and what happened to Alek. But if what that snake said was true, then I need to find some vervain to counteract the wolfsbane coursing through Alek's blood. I've learned many tricks through the years *travelling*. When I stayed with a coven of vampires, they were the ones who taught me the benefits of vervain and wolfsbane and how they counteract and cancel each the other out. That traitor was stupid. Stupid to think that Vladik would ever want her, too stupid to see how obsessed he was with Zy. I'm glad she's dead. You never, ever betray your pack. But what she did was worse. She was malicious and evil, only worried about self-gain. She wanted to hurt my baby cousins but she never realised she was hurting her pack.

I got the first flight out of Russia. Then I searched high and low for this pack but to no avail. I needed to find some vervain. I had a feeling no wolf pack was going to have it. I needed to find some vampires. They can sniff this plant out like their life depended on it. I know a bit about the covens in America from the last one I spent time with. I know there's one close by. I just have to run around and listen for the distinctive sound of speeding footfalls. Dead giveaway if you know what vamp speed sounds like. But their scent smells of iron and when you're amongst nature, it's an odd placement. It took a few hours jogging around the area before I finally heard it. I jogged towards the sound, they stopped a distance away, shielding themself in the cover of the trees. I could smell the faint iron scent lingering in the air but it was mixed. I couldn't place it, couldn't figure out what was different about this scent. I breathed in, blocking out the sounds around me as I do, listening to the heartbeat strumming quickly. It wasn't an adult vamp. It was a child.

"Hey, little vamp!" I called out, hearing a small gasp sound behind the tree ahead. I moved forward when I realized the child wasn't going to come out. I approached slowly, hands in the air knowing they had the speed and fangs to fuck me up.

I've fought full grown vampires before but child vampires are different. They're faster, they move rapidly and don't follow any rules. They fight savage and there's no way to track their movements.

I look around the tree, seeing a little copper haired boy standing in a little opening. He looked cautious but curious. His hair was slightly curled and shaggy. I waved and went to speak but suddenly another child appeared.

"Hey! Don't you talk to my brother! If you hurt him I will have to hurt you back." He spoke with such determination but his voice was shaky as if he was afraid of me. He looked identical to the other little boy; the only difference was his hair was a little shorter.

"Oh, there's two of you. Don't worry, Little Vamps. I have no intentions of hurting you." I say as I nod reassuringly. I still keep my hands out in front of me so they can see. The second boy's eyes kept flicking all over my body, waiting for danger. "I actually need your help." This next part I was slightly worried about. I don't know how they are going to take the request.

"With what?" The second asked, the same curious look crossing his face that the first had.

"I need to find some vervain." They reacted just like I thought. Their heads reared back, fangs extending as they hissed at me. Fingers becoming jittery as the blood lust rushed through their bodies. When vampires hiss their adrenaline glands go into overdrive, helping them to hunt and kill. "No, no!" I raise my hands higher, slowly crouching down to show I mean no threat. "I need it to help my cousin. I promise you; I don't want to harm you or any vampires." They retract their fangs, breathing in as they calm down. The first boy looks angry, little arms crossed against his chest as his twin spoke.

"What do you need it for?" He looked curious, able to take the situation in better than his twin.

"My cousin was poisoned with wolfsbane. Vervain is the only thing that can counteract the effects of wolfsbane. I need to save my cousin. He's dying and his twin isn't doing much better. She won't last much longer without her brother and her mate." They looked at each other, a silent conversation happening before the first twin nodded his head. The second twin that spoke for the both of them turned and left the way he came, speeding off. Minutes passed but the second twin still hadn't returned. The first one had stood there the whole time staring at me, hardly even blinking. It was unnerving. "I'm feeling judged, little vamp." I say trying to break the silence between us.

"Do you promise you won't hurt us?" He suddenly asked. "Our daddy is not a nice man. He'll hurt you if he finds out we helped you." My heart clenched, hating the look that passed through his eyes. His father doesn't just hurt other people.

"I promise, Little Vamp. I won't hurt you or any other vampire. My cousin was kidnapped by a very bad alpha. He wanted her to be his mate so much that he killed his own mate to be with her. But my cousin already has a mate that she loves very much and he's not doing so well without her either. He can't find her and I can't find him. I don't know what pack he's from." Some people would frown and disagree with me telling a child these things. But I need him to know the truth, need him to know I really do mean no harm. If he knew the details then he wouldn't have to be scared.

The second twin was back, speeding across the distance as he placed the vervain in my hands. I gasped, head snapping back as I look down at his own. Vervain was poison to vampires but he wasn't burning! There were no blisters forming, no look of pain spreading across his face as he passed it off to me. "How? How are you holding vervain? You're a vampire?!" They giggle looking at each other.

"Your nose isn't that good." The first twin said smirking.

"We're hybrids." The second twin said proudly. "Our mum was a wolf."

"Was?" I shouldn't have said that. I hit a nerve, both boys

immediately looking down at the ground as tears emerged in their gold eyes.

"What pack are you looking for?" The first one said as they both looked up with stoic looks on their faces.

"I don't know, I didn't get the chance to ask. Do you know any packs with a Cairo in it?" They shake their heads, dread setting in as I fear this is going to take longer. They look at each other again, nodding as their brows rise and fall as they speak silently in their minds. "Alright, this little twin bond is getting creepy." It was like I was looking at the male version of the twins from the shining.

"We heard our dad talking about a big war with rogues that happened with the Dawn pack a few weeks ago." There it was, hope.

"That's gotta be it! Do you know where it is?" Their little heads shook from side to side.

"No." That's okay, it's more than enough. I just have to go to the closest pack and they will know where this Dawn pack is.

"Thank you so much, Little Vamps. I'll find a way to repay you one day."

Chapter Forty-Eight

The Prisoner

THREE MONTHS LATER

GRACE / GHOST

"Let me out of here!!" I rattle the bars, not caring the searing heat from the steel burns and scars my hands. Every day I grab these bars, every day I shout to be released. Every day I scream that I need to save my cousins. And every day, I get ignored, I get laughed at. "I need to get to the Dawn pack! I need to see Cairo! It's about his mate! And give me my jacket back!" The first pack I came across after the twin hybrids gave me the vervain, immediately threw me into their cells. They try and beat me, *try,* and assault me but no matter how hard they try, they never succeed. They love having a rogue to torture. Love having someone to spit at through the bars, to taunt and watch as I burn myself on the silver. This Alpha and his guards just want something to play with. They don't care what I have to say.

"You will never be getting out of here, rogue. You'll die here. The only reason you're still living and breathing is because the Alpha has taken a liking to you. He likes to play with his rogues but you're his favourite." The long-haired guard said and he unlocked the door and walked in carrying another plate of food. I hide the smirk as I snatch the paper plate off him, pretending to mad as I shove the food quickly in my mouth. This is the third day in a row they've fed me well. *Big mistake*. "He likes to b-" He begins again but I cut him off.

"Break them before he kills them. Yeah, yeah, I've heard it all before." I toss the plate to the side, watching as he growls in annoyance.

"You think that scar across your face is the only thing he'll do to you?" He says reminding me of the day I first met this packs Alpha. I didn't see him pull the silver blade out before it was too late. It sliced me, down my forehead and across my nose to my cheek. He laughed and laughed as I screamed. My blood still staining the concrete beneath my feet. I had to hold my face together the whole night so my quick healing could close the wound without the help of bandages.

"Will you shut up? Shit you're like a fucking parrot that's learnt how to talk. You squawk so much." He growls, eyes shifting at my disrespect. But that's good, I need him mad. He's an idiot, he won't fight smart. He'll fight stupid. "You know, all of you have been smart up until now."

"What are you talking about?" He growls.

"You idiots have barely fed me, barely given me water. You've tried to beat me every day and left me unconscious most of the nights. But then your Alpha wanted me to heal so he could torture me all over again. And then *you* came in here." I laugh.

"So? You're still a weak pathetic rogue."

"Man, you are thick." I roll my eyes; it still hasn't clicked for him. "Your Alpha," I say slowly, "wanted me to heal. Which means I've been fed breakfast, lunch, and dinner for the past three days. I've had uninterrupted sleep, and I am now healed. Which means I'm no longer weak." I laugh again, watching as his face morphs from confused to shock then fear, blood draining from his face. It's finally clicked. "You just walked straight in here with a trained, *healed* killer." I swing out quickly, using the weight of my body as I push forward, hand connecting with his face in one clean hit. His body drops, out cold as a cracking sound is made when his head hits the concrete.

It's time to save my family.

I quickly and quietly opened the cell door after I patted the guard down. The halls were dark, filled with a musty smell, paint started peeling and claw marks were scattered all along the walls. There wasn't much blood on the ground but each cell I walked past had more blood stains on the ground than the next. I turned the corner, spotting a female guard as she stood wearing my expensive leather jacket I was gifted from the coven of vampires. My lip curled up, I was hoping and praying they didn't search through the interior pockets. I had stuffed the vervain in them. They'd probably be dried out by now but that would make it easier to ground up into a powder. Her ears prick to a sound, just as she turns I attack. She was easy to take down, just as quick as the last guard. Both unaware, unprepared. I roll her body over, slipping her arms out with caution as to not break them. It was a bit of a fiddle but I finally pulled the second arm out. Rolling her body back over, I cringe at the sound of her teeth clinking on the concrete. I'd probably care if this pack weren't scum. Plus, I remember her. Two days after I was captured she came bye. She wanted to see the new rogue. The usual insecure girl comments happened. She made fun of my silver hair, my light ashy tone skin, the violet shade of my eyes. I was a seer. And not once did I have a vision here. I get incapacitated me when a vision comes through. I have a feeling the Goddess never sent me any because she knew I'd need my wits about me, knew I was in constant danger.

I make it out of the maze of a building, following the rubble path before I branched off, remembering the way I ran when I found this pack. Since I'm a seer I don't have the ability to shift. But that doesn't matter, I don't need one. It was easy enough to escape the pack borders undetected. Sometimes it helps that I don't have a wolf. I don't set off the same alarms as wolves do.

I run for miles, eventually slowing down a few hours later once I reach a little opening in the forest. I catch my breath, breathing in as I speak to the Goddess in my mind. *Give me a sign, a vision, anything. I need to find that pack. I need to help your warriors.* There it was the rush of energy filling my body as my breath was pulled from my lungs. My neck arches, head raising to the sky as her vision takes over.

I see it! The pack! I see the Alpha, but he's blurry. Dark hair, tall, commanding. I see the town, the school, the city streets, then, a sign. The town name printed boldly for all to see.

Just as quick as the vision takes me, it leaves. My heart slows, adrenaline lessons as my vision becomes clear. I can see the world again, but now I have a mission. I know where I need to go, I can find Zy's mate, find her pack and save my family.

Chapter Forty-Nine

The Truth

CAIRO

Every night it was the same thing. I'd see flashes of chains, whispers of pain all over my body. Burning sensations in my hands, my fingers throbbing. My heart would pound, I'd see Zia. Alone, in the dark, crying my name, her sweet voice shaky as she asks why I didn't save her, why I never came for her. She was haunting my dreams, plaguing my mind when I'm awake. I barely managed to control my wolf. It took months to calm him down and gain control back, and once that happened, I was able to focus. Form plans, send out scouts and trackers looking for the rogues, Caleb was still out hunting for the witch. I know she can help or maybe I hope she can. She was the one who warned me about Zia being cursed. I know she's around here somewhere. Sometimes when I go for midnight runs, I'll catch her in the shadows. Only for a split second but I always see her smile, her eerie, yellow reflective eyes. Then as a small breeze blows past, she's gone, disappearing as quick as she appeared. I feel like she's watching me, waiting for something to happen. I never try go after her because her scent is never there. Not even a whisper of it lingers after she leaves. I end up running to clear by head but come back with more questions and clouds.

As usual, I wake up body covered in sweat, sheets soaked and my wolf on edge. The top sheet is scrunched up and balled by my feet. I get up, sighing as I walk to the door, ready to run again just like every night. It seems to help so I don't stop this new routine. And as I open the door, there stood Caleb, hand fisted in the air as he prepared to knock on my door. He looked tired, the last time I saw him he had just gotten new cornrows in. Now they were gone, hair frizzed up and unkempt. He gave me a small smile, lowering his hand as he spoke.

"I found her." I stopped breathing, mind hopelessly thinking he was talking about Zia. "The witch."

"Where?" Finally, a little ray of hope slithered through the dark tunnel I was lost in. This is it, I'm one step closer to finding Zia.

I followed him down and out of the pack house. He didn't need to tell me where he was going, I already knew. It was the same spot I saw her every time. Except this time, I smelt her scent. It was herby, like sage, lavender, myrtle, and frankincense. There was no doubt she was a witch just by her scent alone. It was so overpowering I dulled my senses. A headache was forming the closer we got, my wolfs nose picking up her scent from a mile away. It got easier once my senses were dulled.

We stopped in front of her, she was dressed in her dark cloak, but when the breeze blew the front open I saw pointed boots, a beautiful blood red silk and lace dress. Around her neck were chains, crystals, stones, and all sorts of pendants. That's why it always sounded like there was chimes surrounding her. Her long dark hair fluttering in the wind. Her yellow eyes landed on Caleb, making him squirm and tighten up beside me.

"Thank you, Caleb. You can leave." She said lightly, smiling as she watched his facial expressions change.

"I don't feel safe knowing you know my name." He said, eyes flicking to me as he linked, telling me he didn't like this.

"Don't be afraid, I'm a good witch. Isn't that right, Cairo." She smiled at me, teething morphing into sharp razor blades before just as quickly, they were normal again. I won't lie, she does give me the creeps. She was like one of those 3D pictures where she looks normal on one side but then she turns and she looks completely different, terrifying.

"It's fine." I nod to Caleb, watching as he sighs and looks at *Glinda*, one last time before he leaves. The second he's out of earshot I speak.

"Have you been watching me?" She laughs, a delightful sound but there's a frequency to it that hurts my ears.

"Yes."

"Why couldn't I smell you?"

"I was projecting." She looked amused.

"Why? Why are you watching me?" I thought about this question for weeks. Why me? What is she gaining from this? What does she want?

"I'm curious what will happen. I was intrigued by the girl, that was a powerful, rare curse that was placed on her. Then you, Young Wolf, appeared watching the sky and you were open. You weren't afraid of me. Many are."

"What does this curse do?" I didn't think to ask this the first time I saw her.

"Hmm, it links you. The one who took her, who has her," She already knows what's been happening around here. She must have been watching for a while. "He had her cursed, linking her to him. He could do what he wanted. He could feel her, influence her dreams. If he is as malevolent as he appears to be, she would have a darkness that would be clinging to her like black sticky ink." My blood boiled, hackles rising as I looked up at the sky. He was fucking with her all this time. The dark thoughts she has when she's asleep, the nightmares, the sudden panic attacks that take hold of her so suddenly. Part of that is her post traumatic stress disorder, but the other part was him. He's been amplifying it all this time.

"Where is she." I say more than ask. I'm sick of waiting, I need answers now. "Where does he have her? At her pack? In Russia? Where?!?" She raises an eyebrow, looking at me as though she's staring through me. Similar to the way Zia looked at me the night of the ball when she lost control. When her eyes turned to stars.

"I do not have those answers. But I do know someone is coming, and soon." I went to ask who, ask more questions but she disappeared as a gust of wind suddenly circled us. Her voice lingered longer than her body did. "Prepare yourself for what's to come." Then she was gone.

My head was a mess, I had no idea what to think after this visit. I needed some clarity, some piece of comfort and the only place I've felt comfort lately is visiting Alek. He's my last link to Zia. I head off in a different direction than the pack house. To the infirmary where my mates twin and Keiran were. He's not once left Alek's side, barely showering every couple of days only because the nurses have forced him to. A twig snapping to my right drew my attention.

"Maya?" She gasped, turning as the strings of her hoodie swayed.

"Oh, Cai-Alpha! Sorry. I guess I'm still getting used to it." She said sadly as she approached. I hadn't seen her in months, Zia's kidnapping hit everyone hard. I know if I wasn't Alpha I would have hidden myself away. Shut out the world.

"Can't sleep?" I ask as she nods, she had dark circles under her eyes, her hair had grown a little but looked messy. She was wearing a baggy grey oversized hoodie, probably her mates since it had a male scent to it, and black track pants. She looked different, didn't dress the same but then neither did I. I too stopped taking care of myself. The absence of Zia just took the light and energy out of me. Out of everyone.

"Yeah," she said sighing, "can't seem to sleep. I miss her." Her eyes welled with tears, chin wobbling as she looked at the ground. I knew that feeling all too well.

"You-" I began to speak but stopped when I felt Maya's emotions. It was strange being an alpha. I could link any pack member, even if they try to block me. I could command anyone, even feel their emotions when they're nearby. And right now, I could feel Maya. I could feel her pain, her sadness, but what made me pause was how much guilt and regret was riddled through her. But there was also anger and so much hate for Zia.

"Are you okay?" She asked, looking up at me.

"Why..." I began but had to stop so I could breathe, calming the rising tension climbing up my throat. "Why do you feel guilty?" Her eyes widened, she immediately masked herself, a wall suddenly erecting in her mind.

"Maya! There you are." Her mate Evan appeared, smiling before he stopped, watching the sudden fear take hold of her as we stood, staring at each other. "What's going on?" He looked between us, steeping closer to Maya as he touched her back.

"Answer me, Maya. Why, do you, feel guilty?" Tears started falling, she shook her head and took a timid step back from me.

"Babe? What's going on?" Evan asked again, firmer this time.

"**ANSWER ME**." I roared, commanding her as Evans head snapped to me, his wolf rising to the surface before he realized the command wasn't said to him.

"I...I....no..." She was trying to fight it. Her hands began shaking, forehead sweating as my eyes shifted to my wolfs. My hackles were up, anger rising as the missing pieces of the puzzle started to fall into place. "He...he made me. Vladik....he... he killed everyone but me. He...cut my hand..." She was still trying to fight it but the more my wolf stared back at her, the painful it became for her to resist my command. "He made me join his pack! He commanded me! He was now my alpha; I couldn't disobey him!" She screamed out as she cried, hands grabbing at her throat.

"What did you do?" Evan asked as he dropped his hand, stepping away from her.

"He commanded me to find Zia. He said if I found her I had to contact him. B...but I didn't...I...I..." I growled lowly. She started fighting the command again. Whatever words were fighting to come out, she didn't want me to hear. "I had help! Jaxon and" Suddenly Evan grabbed her, shaking her as he screamed, realizing his mate had betrayed the pack.

"WHY!? Why would you do this!" He shook her roughly before he let her go, looking hurt as his heart was breaking.

"When?," I asked as a thought popped into my head, "when did you contact him?" She snapped her mouth shut, lips going white as she refused to speak. "**WHEN?!**" I commanded her again.

"A...a..aaa...after the ball!" The worlds flew out of her mouth. Evan came to the same realisation as I did. He shook his head, stepping back further as put distance between him and Maya. She looked at him, a hurt look crossing her face.

"You..." He began but stopped when he wiped a stray tear off his cheek. "You are the reason the Alpha is dead. The reason his Luna is in the hospital and the reason Cairo's mate, our new Luna is gone. It was you!"

"Evan..." She reached for him but he pulled away.

"My father welcomed you into this pack before the ball. You had no allegiance to Vladik anymore. You betrayed this pack and your friend of your own accord." My wolf was frothing at the mouth, so angry at her betrayal. He wanted her dead.

"Friend?!" She said deliriously, facing me as she laughed. "She is the reason my whole pack was eradicated! If she wasn't so weak she could have been happy with him. Then he wouldn't have killed my family! Everyone would still be alive!"

My wolf ripped control from me so suddenly I could do nothing to stop him as he clenched our fist and swung, connecting straight into Maya's chest with full strength, right above her heart. She flew back, a cry escaping as she hit the ground roughly. She panted and struggled to breathe, eyes wide as her body began shutting down. Evan and I both heard the crack in her chest the second my fist made contact. She laid still, unable to move as blood began spilling out of her mouth. Evan walked towards her slowly, looking down at her as she stared up at him. She tried to reach for him but he stepped out of reach.

"I reject you as my mate." Was all he said before he turned around and left without another word. If her lungs weren't filling with blood she would have cried out. Her hand slowly went to her chest, clawing at it as the pain of their bond snapped. We can never reject our mates but I have heard the Goddess can grant it. I've never known anyone who has successfully rejected their mate until now. I walked over to her, looking down as I see my wolfs eyes reflect in her wide teary ones.

"I," she coughed, clearing her throat before she smiled, teeth stained with blood, "I poisoned Alek." Everything stopped in that moment, my ears were ringing. I now knew everything. But I couldn't believe Maya could do such things. Never believed she could kill. She laughed, the sound coming out as a gargle from the blood pooling in her mouth. Then her heart gave out. I should have seen this sooner. Why would anyone seek out the person who was responsible for getting your pack killed? She came all this way, showed up so suddenly, so out of the blue. I should have seen this sooner. I won't make that mistake again.

I stood in front of the hospital room window, watching Keiran sleeping peacefully as his head lay gently on Aleks chest. He was breathing on his own but he needed help with an oxygen mask. He had these purple veins across his body and his lips were blue. The doctors said that was the result of the wolfsbane poisoning. Keiran kept Alek's hair trimmed, the same length it was the last time he was awake. He lost a little muscle mass but the fluids and feeding tube helped keep his weight even.

"Bubba?" I look to my left, seeing nothing before I looked down, shocked to see Sarana here instead of at home sleeping.

"Sasa, what are you doing here?"

"Zacky bring me to see Mumma." Right, it was Zacks turn tonight to look after her. Ever since my father died my mother couldn't handle the loss. Her wolf went rabid and none of us could control her. We had to sedate her and put her in an induced coma. It's what we must do if our wolves go rabid and we're unable to pull them back in. I wish Sarana never had to see our mother like that. Just losing Zia had brought me to the edge of losing control forever but my mother lost her mate. My father died. The pain of losing a mate is too much to bear. I guess that's why my mother tried to *be* with my father. I couldn't thank the Goddess enough for Sarana not being there that day.

"Bubba, why doesn't mummy wake up?" She asked, her big brown eyes boring into me with such sadness and confusion. She lost both parents six months ago.

"Because mummy's safe. She missed daddy too much so the doctors gave mummy some medicine that helped her fall asleep. She will feel better when she wakes up. Which will be soon." I smile but the hope inside me was paper thin. I have no idea when she'll wake up and no idea if she'll be changed or not.

"Where's Eya? Everywon was happy when she was here." It hurt knowing even the children of the pack could tell something happened. We try to protect them but they're smart, they see things, sense things. It's harder for Sarana because she's lost her whole family. Our mother, our father, me as I can't spend enough time with her lately and Zia was also gone.

"I know, bunny. I know." I smile sadly, trying to be strong for her. "Why don't you go find Zacky and make sure he takes you back home. You can come back in the morning and see mummy when everyone else is awake." I could feel Zack's panic from my alpha link as he ran through the hospital trying to find Sarana after she walked off. I send him a quick link, telling him Sarana's on her way back to him. I watch as she turns the corner, happily skipping out of view before the smell of rogue assaults my nose. My hackles go up, spinning as I look down the opposite corridor. There was a rogue in the hospital! I turned, making sure Sarana really was gone. I need to keep her safe.

The smell got stronger, hints of Alek and Zia mixing with the rogue. My ears pricked at the sound of footsteps falling quickly behind me. My knuckles cracked as I steeled myself, getting ready to spin and take the rogue down when suddenly a weight pushed past me, knocking me as I lost balance.

"Sorry!" The female rogue called. I stand up quickly, hearing Alek's hospital door open before she slammed it shut, hearing a click lock into place. I watched as the seer rogue ran right to Alek's side, startling Keiran awake. He growled, running around the bed to her but she was quick, she muttered another apology before she swung out quickly, fist connecting with Keiran and he was quickly knocked unconscious, body crashing to the ground. Her hand went inside her jacket, pulling out a powdered substance that had a lilac tint to it. I raced to the door, yanking on the doorknob but it was locked.

"Fuck!" I had reinforced steal doors installed in all the hospital rooms ever since Zia was taken. But now that meant I couldn't break it down. I ran back to the window, banging on the newly installed bulletproof glass. "Open the fucking door!" The rogue rummaged through the draws, finding a small bottle of saline. She mixed the powder into the bottle, closing the lid before she shook it, mixing the two substances together. Then she grabbed a syringe, opening the packet before she grabbed the needle, pulling the cap off with her teeth and jammed it into the bottle before she extracted the powdered liquid. "Don't fucking do it!" I growled out as I tried my best to break the window down. I know what she was planning to do but I couldn't let her kill Alek. I had to do something. I threw my body against the glass but it only repelled me back. She grabbed the IV bag, injecting the needle right into it. I could do nothing as I watched the lilac substance stain the bag. My heart was in my throat, watching Alek's heart monitor as his rate stayed the steady rhythm it has been for months. Wait...*He wasn't dying...What the hell did she do?* "Open the fucking door right now!" I said again, watching as she finally turned around, looking at me blankly through the window with only the glass separating us

"I don't think so." She said casually crossing her arms against her chest. "I'm feeling threatened." She looked amused. I growled, eyes flashing orange as I banged on the glass once again.

"What did you do to him!?" I had to know. I wouldn't be able to face Zia ever again if I saved her only for her to find out I couldn't save her brother.

"I didn't hurt them." She said, hands going up in the air. "Well, maybe the one on the floor I did. But how was I supposed to save Alek if his mate wouldn't calm down and let me near him. There's no way he would have listened to reason."

"You," I pause, replaying her words. She came here to save Alek? Who she already knew the name of and that Keiran was his mate. "You saved him? How? And how did you get past the border undetected?" I need to update the border patrolling plan. If she could get passed my warriors undetected then so could anyone else.

"I've been doing this a long time."

"Why-" My breath hitched in my throat. She smelt so familiar my heart hurt. "Why do you smell like Zia?" She laughed before she smiled proudly.

"I'm her cousin, Grace. You radiate alpha energy but Zy never said you were the Alpha. Are you Cairo?" She asked shocking the hell out of me. How did she know my name?

"I. That's me..." I was so confused. I didn't know what the hell was going on.

"Nice to meet you, Cairo." She breathed in, holding her breath before she exhaled looking at me sadly. "We have a lot to talk about." Then she walked to the door, unlocking it as she opened it for me. She stepped back, walking to the back of the room as she waited. Closing the door, I slowly approached her, still unsure of her. She was a head shorter than me, still taller than Zia but her features were similar. They had the same eyes. Though hers were violet, it felt like I was looking at Zia wearing violet contacts and ashy skin tone. "Man, you are big. I consider myself tall but you make me feel short." I chuckled. The now foreign sound sounding strange to my ears. "No wonder ZyZy loves you. You must make her feel crazy safe." She said amused but just like that, all the humour washed from my body at the thought of her and how I couldn't keep her safe.

"Can...can you tell me if she's safe? I.. Is she okay?"

"I wish I could give you a proper answer, Cairo. But I last saw her three months ago and Vladik..." She stopped, a single tear falling as she slowly blinked, brows furrowing. "I don't know if she's hurt anymore or not."

"She is." I said as she looked at me confused. "Hurt, I mean. I feel when he beats her. But a few months ago, our connection stopped. I only feel it sometimes now, like faint flutters of pain that last seconds before it's gone again. She's still alive. That's all I know."

"I'm so sorry." She looked at me, sadness clouding her violet eyes as she clutched her chest. "I tried to get here as fast as I could but I got captured by the Northern Rise pack."

"We're allies...Did you not give them my name?" She growled, eyes darkening as I spoke.

"I didn't but that fucking Alpha cun-" She stopped, closing her eyes as she breathed in and out. "I did." She said as she looked at me again. "Every single day for three months I said I needed to find you. But he didn't listen. Said I was his *plaything*." Her lip curled in disgust as she spoke the word. "He did this to my beautiful face!" She touched the scar across her face, before her fingers went white as she clenched her hand in a fist.

"Three months..." That Alpha knows exactly who I am. I met with him two months after I became Alpha. We signed a new treaty and everything. I'll be paying him a visit once this is all over. I don't bother asking how she got out. She got into my pack unnoticed, I have no doubts she escaped that pack undetected either.

"Are you the Alpha?" She questions and I nod. "ZyZy didn't say you were the Alpha." She looked me up and down, eyes boring into me as she sensed the power within.

"She doesn't know. The day she was taken was the day I became Alpha."

"I'm sorry for your loss." She was genuine. She went to speak again but stopped when the door opened. Zack walked in, dressed in his usual ripped jeans and a fitted black tee. His hair was longer now, tied up in a small bun.

"Hey, C. Sarana's back h-" He paused, looking past me towards Grace. His mouth dropped open, eyes widening as they flashed orange. I turned upon hearing a gasp. Grace mimicked his stance, her mouth opened as her eyes shined so bright.

"MATE!" They both spoke at the same time. Then they bit their lips and looked each other up and down, purring as they liked what they saw. I groaned, knowing there's now two of them. Zack is the pack shit stirrer and from the short time I've known her, I just know she's the same. Not unlocking the door because she felt threatened. What bullshit. She didn't even look scared. She looked amused. That was such a Zack move.

Suddenly she grunted, hands fisted by her side as she frowned. "Sorry, *malysh.*" There was the Russian again. I have no clue what she called Zack and neither did he. "I'm gonna have to mark you later. First, I need to save my cousin. Cairo," she spoke addressing me as Zack continued to purr behind me as he checked her out, "there's something you should know about the attack."

"Cousin?" Zack finally spoke, her words now penetrating his mind after the cloud of lust cleared. "You mean Zia?" He said shocked. She smiled and nodded.

"Come to my office. This way." I headed to the door, stopping as she walked to Zack, her long nailed finger going under his chin as he smirked.

"Goddamn, you are sexy." She gave him a heated stare, licking her lips as she looked down at his lips.

"Could say the same about you, babe." His head inched forward ever so lightly, ready to take her lips in his.

"Oh, I know I am." She spoke confidently and he laughed. "I have to go talk with your Alpha, but once I'm done." She leaned in, tilting her head up slightly as she whispered in his ear. "I hope you're ready for me. You ain't never met a wolf like me, baby." She kissed his cheek, lingering a few seconds longer before she pulled away, walking towards me as I held the door open.

"Don't I know it." He muttered, watching her leave. She had a sway in her step and didn't need to turn around to know Zack was staring right at her ass. She smirked at me, knowing exactly what I was thinking before she left, walking down the hall towards the exit. The last thing I heard before the door closed was Zack's voice.

"Keiran? What are you doing on the floor?

Chapter Fifty

The Mission

"You said something about the attack? And what of this plan to save Zia and Jordan." I asked Grace as I sat down in my father's chair, now mine. It still felt so foreign. Like he was about to open that door any second and demand me out of his chair. His mahogany desk was filled with piles of paperwork that I hadn't had the time to get through. It just slowly built up as the weeks and months passed.

"Don't you dare say that traitors name!" She snapped, shocking the hell out of me from her sudden outburst.

"What? Jordan? She's many things but a traitor isn't one of them." My words seemed to piss her off more. Her violet eyes darkened drastically.

"Who do you think was the one to poison Alek? Or hire the rogues that attacked Zia the first time or helped contact Vladik and formed a plan with him and the rogues to take Zia? I saw it all. All those months ago, before I was captured the Goddess showed me everything. How she met with Jaxon and Maya. How she came up with the idea to poison Alek so he couldn't interfere with the rogues taking Zia. Or how Maya helped them, gave Jordan Vladik's number and watched as she called him then and there. She was the fucking mastermind behind the whole attack!" I refused to believe it.

"I dealt with Maya. I know she was the one who poisoned Alek. She wanted to get revenge on them for Vladik destroying her pack. Jordan wouldn't do that...she wouldn't."

"Wake the fuck up, Cairo!" She yelled, hands flying out in rage. "She was a power-hungry cunt that did everything in her power to get Zia out of the way. She did more than you know. I've seen it all. She called him, Cairo! CALLED HIM! You may feel what Zia felt, but you didn't see where she's being kept or what he's doing to her. You only feel *whispers* of it. He's using her parents against her to keep her in line. He left Jordan's dead body in her cell for weeks and let's not forget about him marking her or beating her or r-" She stopped, not speaking another word as her mouth slammed shut and she closed her eyes. I couldn't believe it. This was too much...*Jordan's dead?* He..he killed her? I feared the worst about Zia and was ignorant to what he was doing to her beside the beatings and the markings. I didn't want the other to be true, but Grace just confirmed it. "So, don't you dare say Jordan wouldn't do that because she did, and now we have to go save my cousin before it's too late."

"I..." I began but she cuts me off, not afraid of talking back or disrespecting an alpha.

"I had a vision. The Goddess showed me where Alek was, showed me this town and the pack. But that wasn't all. She showed me something else the moment I crossed your border." She breathed in and out, eyes watering as she looked up at me. "She...she dies, Cairo. The Moon Goddess showed me Zia dying in that cell and *soon*. She was extremely weak and her body couldn't hold on anymore. They..she died." My heart pounded, chest tightening as her words replayed on a loop. There was no more time. We were now out of time. We must save her now. "It's going to take us a week to get there. Getting into Russia is the easy part. Getting to the pack is not so easy. The other packs don't dare go against him because of how crazed he is. They all know his agenda. The person of his obsession and how deadly he is when it comes to her. If they even get wind of an American coming for her, he'll know it instantly. He'll be alerted the second we're spotted."

"I'll ask again. What the fuck is your plan?" I was over it. Over the power trip this fuck was on. He's taken enough from me and I won't let him take her life too. He's taken enough from her.

Grace voiced her plan. The two of us, Caleb and Zack will head to Russia. She will lead us, getting us to the pack undetected. Vladik doesn't have guards because everyone is afraid of him, but his beta will help us. He'll lure Vladik away. Most of the pack resent him, hating him for killing their Alpha, his father. But she said there are some who are loyal to him. Who will do anything he says, kill anyone for him. I was shocked when I asked why his beta would betray him. Zia's father was still the beta, he was never replaced when Vladik took control of the pack when he came into power. Grace explained that Vladik knew Zia's mother helped her escape. He still thinks Grace left with Alek and Zia. He kept their father as beta so he could keep an eye on him. Knowing that if they ever contacted him, Vladik would know instantly. Their father has been watched closely over the years. He was commanded to inform Vladik if he ever heard or spoke to Alek or Zia.

"You kept them informed." I guessed as she nodded. "How did they not tell him?"

"There are many loopholes to the alpha command. Not many people know that. They think once you are commanded, that's it. You cannot oppose it. But you can work around it if you listen to the actual command. We used a code name for me. They call me Ghost. The day I left they no longer called me Grace. I was known only as Ghost. So, when Vladik asked where *Grace* was or anything about me, my uncle could answer truthfully. He never knew where Grace was. But he knew where *Ghost* was."

"Wait...Ghost?" She nodded, seeing the gears turn in my head. "I've heard that name before. My father, he once spoke of a Ghost rogue. A highly trained assassin, they find you. Offer their skills in return for a favour. But that's just a myth, my father never believed it. Are you...Are you saying the Ghost rogue is not only real, but *you?*" She nodded once more.

"I've done many jobs, all over the world. Even a few here in America but I made the mistake of thinking my little cousins wouldn't be here. That they were still hiding out in Russian or the surrounding countries. I worked while I searched for them, growing my favours for the dreaded day that Vladik would find them. I would have an army ready to protect them. But I never planned on them being betrayed. No one saw that attack coming. And now with the new vision, I don't have time to gather and call in my favours. We don't have the time. We have to save Zia ourselves...and now." My mind was such a mess. A headache formed from all this new information and revelations. First Maya, then Grace showed up and all the information she brought with her.

"Alright, Grace. I'm trusting you. Trusting that your plan will work. If you didn't save Alek then I never would have listened to you. Family or not."

"I understand. We've got one day to gather our things, a handful of weapons and leave. I have an aircraft carrier that can get us there. That's when the hard part starts." She finished, turning as she walked to the door, but she stopped. "This will work, Cairo." She said looking at me over her shoulder before she left, leaving me alone in silence.

Everything happened quickly after that. I dropped Sarana off with her nanny, promised her that I would be home soon with Zia. She was excited, gave me a big hug and said her little goodbyes. Then I spoke to Keiran, leaving him in charge of the pack. He was pissed about Grace but shocked at finding out she was mated to Zack. Alek also woke up. Pulled a memory loss prank on Keiran which nearly gave him a heart attack. But then we had to break the news to him that Zia was gone. He feared the worst of course, he couldn't feel Zia either. He refused to stay behind, hating that his body was failing him when he tried to get out of the bed. He wouldn't listen to anyone until Grace walked into the room. His jaw dropped, then he was happy. So, happy that he cried. She talked some sense into him, then scolded Keiran for giving her the stink eye the whole time. My mother was the last person I spoke too. I know she can't hear me but I hoped she could. I told her I loved that, that it was okay to wake up. That Zia was gone and that I was going to save her. I reminded her of Sarana. How she visited her every day, told her what she was wearing, if she dressed herself or who did her hair. She told her about her day and who let her do piggyback rides on their wolves. I told her she needs to wake up for her daughter. She is missing too much. Sarana has gotten bigger, looking more like a little girl as the days go by. Making new friends, learning new things from sitters and day care and anyone who has her for the day. Then I said goodbye, kissed her cheek before I left.

Caleb was already at the meeting spot. We just had to wait for Zack and Grace, then we were leaving. They were running late but Keiran came, looking nervous as he spoke.

"What do I tell the pack? I...I've never run a pack before."

"Tell them the truth. That I've gone to save Zia. And you'll be fine. You've had your training; you've seen what your dad did for mine when he had to leave the pack. I'll have my phone if you need me. Not sure if I will always have service but you will have Alek by your side and your father as well." He nodded, still unsure but he masked his face, reassuring me that he could do this.

"Good luck. All of you, be safe. When do you leave?" He asked.

"As soon as Zack finishes marking Grace. I heard them going at it a while ago." I shuddered.

"Ready?" Grace said as her and Zack came out from the tree line.

"More than you can know." I said, Caleb nodded beside me and Keiran came in for a hug. His eyes glazed over, Alek linking him back to the hospital.

"Did you pack winter clothes?" Grace asked as Keiran left.

"Why? We're werewolves." She of all people should know this. "We can handle the cold." She laughed, shaking her head as she looked at our incredulous faces.

"Oh, trust me. You're gonna need it." And she was right. We did need it.

Four days later we were in Russia, on the outskirts of the town closest to the pack, freezing our fucking asses off. It was a whole winter wonderland over here. It snowed every day, making our legs scream from using more strength just to walk than what we were used too. Our wolves refused to shift. They weren't used to these artic temperatures. Though it did snow back home during the winter, this was a whole new level. Caleb, Zack, and I stood shoulder to shoulder as we used each other for warmth. The snow jackets, double layered pants and scarfs did nothing to stop the shivering and tremors that griped our bodies. We could barely hear Grace speak over our teeth chattering.

"Right," She spoke, standing a few feet in front of us, hands on her hips as we looked at her back. "I've mapped out the best route to take that will get us there undetected. If we leave now we can get to the pack in three days. We'll have to take a longer route but if we want the element of surprise then this is our best bet. The snow will be picking up, making it a hard trek but we can do it." She finally turned, facing us before she rolled her eyes. "You can't be serious." She blanched.

"No offence babe, but it's fucking freezing. I can't feel my crown jewels." Zack said making her laugh. She looked so unaffected by the cold, still dressed in her leather jacket and jeans. She did change her boots though, so I guess that's gotta count for something.

"You guys are a bunch of pussies."

"Shud up." Zack said as he breathed into his shivering hands trying to warm them up.

"The sooner we save Zia, the sooner we can get back to your little warm country. Now let's go." She moved without another word. The three of us followed, eager to do just that.

The trek was extremely long and hard. The snow was up to our knees but as it continued snowing every day, the inches slowly crept up our bodies. We were going through untouched territory. If we had gone the way the pack does then we'd be easily able to get there in half the time. Nights were the worst. You couldn't see your feet, couldn't even see the person in front of you. Grace refused to light fires or even a torch. She was strict and meticulous, but I liked that. It gave me the hope to push on, knowing if she can do it, then we can too. When it felt like our bodies were too frozen to continue, she dug into her bag and pulled out these little heat packs that you had to activate. I put one in each glove; Caleb did the same as well as Zack. But he went one further and put one down his pants. Needed to warm his ass up he said.

Finally, we made it. We were stationed just outside of pack lines. The sun had just come up, casting a warm orange glow that made the snow sparkle like a sea of crystals. The air was unbelievably fresh and crisp here. My lungs almost burned from the quality and coolness of the air. I could see why Zia still held love for this place. Vladik could never take that away from her.

"Where is she?" I asked, looking ahead as the adrenaline

slowly started building up. I was so close to her, so close to holding her again and bringing her home. I had no more tears left to shed, only determination filled me.

"We have to wait here," I swallowed the growl that threatened to spill. My wolf was on the edge, stalking back and forth in my mind. He wanted his mate just as much as I did. "We're waiting for someone. And keep quiet." Grace said shooting us all a look. She had changed the second we arrived. She was no longer playful; a ruthlessness took over her. Now she meant business. "Not everyone knows about this place, but Vladik still does. But I doubt he'd ever come here now that he has ZyZy."

"Not for long." I growled lowly, eyes flashing before they settled back into my hazel ones. Grace hushed me, spinning around as she looked ahead pointedly. She was hearing something, something we couldn't. This terrain was her home, she grew up here, she knows how to work around the complete sounds of nature. No buzzing of electricity, no traffic, or industrial sounds. It was pure nature.

"Someone's coming." Zack whispered low as he stood next to me, eyes flicking from Grace to the person coming as we all braced for oncoming danger.

"*Gracie! Is that you?*" She gasped as a man appeared. He had blood stained on his hands and shirt, raising my hackles as he took Grace into his arms.

"Is it just me or does he look like-" Zack began and I answered for him.

"Alek."

"Could be twins. Except the hair colour." I couldn't agree more. Alek was the spitting image of this man who could only be their father. The only difference was the black hair, beard, and scars.

"Thank the Goddess." He spoke as he looked down at Grace. "We were so worried about you. Milana isn't doing too well. She's taken over the job of delivering food and water to

Zinoviya. She's..." He stopped looking, a haunted look crossed his eyes. They watered, threatening to spill as he looked away. My heart skipped a beat. I don't know what I should expect but if it can almost bring Zia's father down to his knees, then it can't be good. "Is this them?" He looked beyond Grace, studying Zack before his eyes flicked to Caleb then me. They lingered, looking me up and down before Grace spoke.

"Quick introductions. That one there is Zack, my mate." She nodded towards him.

"Mate?!" He frowned, nostrils flaring as he stared at Zack who I could hear gulping beside me before he spoke.

"He..." He cleared his throat. "Hello, Sir. I'm Zack." Grace winked as her uncle behind her laughed.

"*You're going to break him.*" He said crossing his arms across his chest as Grace laughed. We didn't understand what he said but I have a feeling it may have been a little jab at Zack.

"That's Caleb and the one in the middle is C-"

"Cairo." He said shocking me.

"You know who I am?"

"Boy, I can feel the power rolling off you. You save my baby girl, and you have my blessing." *Okay, my father-in-law is fucking terrifying*, I thought as I smiled back at him. *But blessing I will get.*

"Now, Gracie, Alek. Is he okay?" He sighed in relief as Grace nodded again, reassuring him that he was recovering back at the pack with his mate. He nodded once, then got straight to business. "Here's the plan. Gracie, you take ZyZy's mate to her, get her out and as far away from here as possible. As soon as Vladik knows of the attack he will send his warriors to her. You two are with me," He looked at Zack and Caleb as they listened intently, nodding as he spoke. "I will pretend to have captured you and I will link Vladik here. Once he is, you two attack while I alert the pack and the attack will begin."

"The pack?!" Grace cut in. "But-" She began but he stopped her.

"I know what you are thinking but no. Most of the pack oppose his rule. They know he has Zinoviya. They're waiting for my word so they can help overthrow him. His warriors are the only loyal followers he has."

"No...The last time I was here the pack were following him too." His eyes flicked to me for a split second, but I saw something flash across his eyes. I couldn't tell what it was but I didn't have a good feeling about it.

"Something happened four months ago that made him change. He's killed close to a hundred pack members since. I just had to bury the last one this morning. He's out of control now. Which is why the pack will attack his warriors and his supporters if there are any left. We are all ready for change, for a new reign to begin. But that starts with Vladik's coming to an end." I couldn't agree more.

"Okay, Uncle. We're ready. Is Aunty Milana safe?"

"Yes, I've taken her to a cabin outside of the pack lines. Take ZyZy there. I'll link you where to go." She nods before she turns to me.

"It's time, Cairo."

Chapter Fifty-One

Zia

My heart was pounding so loudly in my chest I was afraid it would give away our position. Grace just led me down a dark tunnel as we entered the dungeons from a secret entrance/exit. She stopped near one of the doors, head flicking in all different directions before her soft voice spoke, eyes trained on the main door.

"I'll stay here, keep a look out. We should have at least five minutes before all hell breaks loose."

"Got it." I turned but she stopped me, hand on my arm as I looked back at her. "What is it?" I didn't like the look in her eyes, it made me uneasy.

"Whatever happens, whatever you see in there, you need to keep your cool. You cannot, under any circumstances alert anyone to our presence. Understand?" I nodded, telling her I won't be a problem. She hesitated before her hand unlatched and let me go, head training back on the door.

I continued down the dark cobblestone path, trying quietly not to make noise as my boots touched the ground. The cells I passed were empty but the smell coming from them was strong. My feet picked up the pace when Zia's scent slowly lingered into my nose. My heart strummed; breath came out in pants as I stopped at her cell. I grabbed the dagger that was strapped to my leg and jammed it into the lock, twisting as the bolts inside crunched, snapped and the door sprung open. The air was ripped from my lungs as I ran forward but suddenly my feet halted on their own at the sight in front of me. It took seconds for my eyes to adjust to the darkness in her cell but once they did, my heart shattered. *My mate...My beautiful mate...* Her hands were in cuffs, a long chain connected to a mount on the wall. *He chained her like a dog...*Her skin had paled, her once beautiful hair was now long waist length, tangled and knotted. Messy strands hung down over her face like a curtain, hiding her hollowed cheeks. The bones in her body were defined from starvation. Her lips were dry and cracked, wrists burned red and blistered from the silver cuffs burning into her skin. She still wore my shirt, the same shirt I put on her the day she was taken from me. It was ripped and frayed all along the edges, dirty and bloodied and the only pants she was wearing were underwear. She had faded bruises all over her body, scars all over her hands and fingers as if she used them to protect herself. The sight of her alone almost killed me, but what drove the knife straight through my heart was what she didn't do. She didn't react. She sat on the dirty mattress beneath her looking broken and lost. I couldn't lie and say I wasn't expecting her to run straight into my arms and then we'd both cry at our reunion. But she didn't more, didn't even sniff the air as my scent filled the room.

"Baby?" I said quietly as I slowly approached her before I squatted down. "It's me, Cairo." Nothing. "Baby?...Zia?" My hands shook, afraid of touching her in fear of how she would react. She so broken she didn't even know I was right in front of her.

"C..." Suddenly her eyes slowly cracked open. "Cairo?" Her voice was so small, barely above a whisper.

"Baby!" I couldn't contain the excitement.

"Is...it really...you?" She spoke slowly, eyes still open but not focussing on me.

"Yes! Baby, yes, it's me! I found you! I'm here!" I was smiling so hard my cheeks hurt.

"You...always...say that. You're...not hhere..." No, no, no. She closed her eyes again, believing that her mind was playing tricks on her.

"No, baby, I am here!" I promised and reassured her as her eyes slowly opened again.

"You...never..are." She closed her eyes as her body slowly slumped down, chain jingling as her hands went slack.

"No, no, no. Baby, please don't shut down on me. I'm here! Look at me! Touch me! Smell me! See," I reached out, slowly touching her hands as the mate sparks shot up my arm. I haven't felt those sparks in a long time. "I'm real!"

"My...Alpha?" The beating of her heart slowly picked up. Her eyes opened again, now focussing on me as tears welled in her glowing aqua blue eyes. "Y..you're...here.." I cried, nodding my head as I took her hand in mine, softly squeezing it.

"Yes! Feel my warmth, Zia. It's real, it's real. I've come to take you home."

"Home...Where is...home..." She sounded out of breath as she spoke, mind confused, unable to discern reality from whatever world she created in her mind to survive this Goddess forsaken place.

"With me. With our pack." I remind her, gently rubbing circles on her hand with my thumb.

"Ali..." She whispered Alek's nickname she often called him.

"He's alive. He's safe, he's healthy. He's waiting for you. Grace saved him." Holding her hand, I could feel the relief wash over her as her rigid hand relaxed. "Let's get out of here." She gingerly nodded, looking across to the chain mounted to the wall. I grabbed the silver cuffs on her wrists, pushing through the burning pain as I pried them open. She hugged her wrists to her chest, face scrunching from the pain and relief. Slowly and gently, I put my hands under her arms, pulling her up with me as I stood us up. She was wobbly but it didn't take long for her to stand on her own. I grabbed the hem of my woollen shirt, swiftly pulling it over my head as I handed it to her. "Here, take that shirt off baby and put this one on."

"I...I can't.." She whimpered softly.

"Please, baby. Your health isn't strong enough right now to handle the cold out there. My shirt will keep you warm and my scent will help with healing as well. Please..." She hesitated, looking at me with unsure eyes. A storm was brewing behind her eyes. I wish I could take that storm away, I hated seeing her like this. So timid, so afraid.

"O..okay, okay....okay..." She repeated unsure as she nodded her head slowly as if she had to convince herself to do it. She breathed in and out, looking at me one more time before she unbuttoned the last remaining four buttons on the shirt, watching as it fell to the ground.

My knees buckled from under me, sending me crashing to the ground. Everything stopped in that moment. The ringing in my ears got louder, the pounding in my heart got stronger as my breath was ripped from my lungs. It was worse than anything I could have imagined. I thought she was hesitating because of what her body looked like. But I was wrong. So, so, wrong.

She was sickly thin, ribs sticking out as she hiccupped, tears wracking her body as she watched me. Grace was right when she said I had no idea what she was going through. But we were both wrong, so fucking wrong. Everything suddenly made sense. Why her wolf disappeared, why I couldn't feel our bond anymore. Her wolf was using all her power to protect Zia's body and...her **baby**.

"You're...you..." The words wouldn't come. I tried again;

mouth dried as I looked at the sickly small baby bump. "You're **pregnant**."

"Yes." Her chin wobbled, tears falling as I stepped forward. Gently grabbing the shirt from her hand, I put it over her head, letting her slip her thin arms through before I pulled it down over her little belly. Then I hugged her, dipping my head into the crook of her neck as she cried. Out of all the many scenarios I thought of, her being pregnant wasn't one of them. I can't even tell if the baby is mine or not. Her wolf is still protecting the baby which means her scent is still masked. I can hear the little heartbeat strumming strong.

"CAIRO!" Grace screamed as she suddenly appeared at the door. "We need to leave now!" Her eyes flashed from me to Zia, giving her a small smile before she turned and left.

"I'm gonna carry you. We'll be able to get you to safety quicker if I run with you." She sniffled, eyes wide in fear as she looked back at the door, afraid Vladik was going to appear any second and stop us.

I swallowed a cry when I scooped her up. She hardly weighed anything as I tucked her into my chest. I didn't need supernatural strength to hold her. She was so cold to touch, skin almost frozen. She rested her head against my chest, listening to my heart as I ran. I don't know how long I raced through the snowy white woods following behind Grace, but all I knew was that I needed to get Zia out of there desperately. Both the life of her, and her baby depended on it. The vision Grace had; this is what it meant. If we didn't save Zia when we did, she would have died. There was nothing left to her anymore. Every little bit of strength she and her wolf had went to the baby. My wolf whined as I ran with her in my arms. The only thing that spurred me on and gave me strength were the mate bond sparks.

Soon we were at the cabin. Racing up the three small steps. The warmth hit us, shocking our bodies from the drastic change in temperature. There was a fire lit in the fireplace, blankets and pillows laid on the ground in front of it with a first aid kit, bandages, bottles of water and a fresh bowl of steaming soup. I quickly stepped forward, laying Zia down gently on the blankets. I grabbed the bottle of water, snapping the lid off as I brought it to her lips. She took small sips, breathing out as the cracks on her lips lessened as they became moistened. I grabbed one of the spare blankets, wrapping it over her shoulders before my hands went to the soup bowl. I didn't care what was going on back at the pack. I needed to take care of Zia. She needed food and water, warmth, and medicine. She slowly opened her mouth, letting me slide the spoon in. When the bowl of soup reached halfway she stopped me, shaking her head as she was able to eat anymore. I nodded, grabbing one of the bandages to dry her mouth. Grace's hand appeared, holding a small tube of pawpaw ointment. She pointed to her lips, making me nod understanding the task. I squeezed some on my finger, gently rubbing it across Zia's lips as relief look over her. Then her eyes fluttered closed as she turned on her side. Sleep quickly took over her exhausted body. I brushed a strand of hair out of her face, tucking it behind her ear as I watched her chest rise and fall.

"Where's her mum?" I said looking to Grace who now stood by the window looking out.

"She's nearly here. She ran back to get some medicine."

"I can't believe I held her in my arms again." I said looking down at Zia sadly. Suddenly Grace gasped, spinning around as a furious look crossed her face. "What? What is it?" I asked standing up. "Is it Zack?" They were mated now; she would be able to tell if he was hurt or not.

"Noo!" She punched out, cracking the glass as her fist made contact. "That fuck's escaping! Uncle Aleksei just linked saying Vladik ran when his warriors were overthrown. He can't get away with this!"

"Which way did he go." I didn't ask. I was going to end this, today. He won't escape me.

“What? East...No!” She said as she realised. “Cairo! No, you can’t leave her!” Grace panicked, eyes flicking from Zia to me.

“I don’t want to leave her!” I snapped. “But I have too. She won’t ever feel safe again as long as he’s alive. He needs to die. If he manages to escape he’ll come back for her and the baby!” Her eyes went wide as I slipped up.

“B...baby?!” I sighed, turning to the door getting ready to leave.

“She’s pregnant.” I said before I looked over my shoulder looking to Zia’s small sleeping form. “Take care of her. Tell her I love her.” My hand went to the doorknob.

“Cairo, don’t do this!” Grace pleaded. “What if you don’t come back?” Her voice broke.

“Then you tell her I will always love her.”

Chapter Fifty-Two

Vladik

When Grace said he ran my blood boiled to a breaking point. I couldn't let him escape. Every fibre of my being longed for his death the day he took her from me. He wants to run away from the fight? Then I'll bring the fight to him. It's time Vladik and I came face to face. Today is the day it all ends.

It took a while to find his scent but once I caught it, I locked on and ran straight towards it like my life depended on it. His scent lingered on Zia's skin like a disease. It was repulsive, clinging to her like another life form. The snow crunched beneath my feet, wind whipped around my body, snowflakes slicing into my chest like little razor blades. I was running too fast for them to melt as they touched my chest. I wasn't going to shift for this fight. I won't give him the pleasure of meeting my wolf. He's going to look into my eyes and watch as I rip his black heart right out of his chest. I want his death to be painful. I want to see him look at me with fear in his eyes as he realizes this is it, the end of his pathetic life. I want my face to be the last thing he sees. I slowed to jog, then I stopped. He was standing on the edge of a cliff, staring out at the vast white land.

“I knew you’d come.” His voice rose every hair on my body. “That’s why I ran. I couldn’t very well fight you where anyone could jump in and save you.” He said turning to face me. Eyes as blue as crystal, a scar down one of them and a smile creeping across his face. “I had to get you alone so that I could bring your head back to your little group and show them their Alpha is no longer.”

“You can sense me.” I state.

“Yes, but that’s not how I knew. I sent my favourite rogue to your little pack. Told him to say a special hello to your father.” My blood ran cold. My father was always going to die in that attack no matter what happened. He had planned everything. “When I found out my ZyZy had a mate, I knew when I took her you’d come one day. I told my rogue to kill your dear *daddy*, so that when the day came that you would stand before me as you are, it would be a fair fight.” *A fair fight*...No. “Alpha against Alpha.” I masked my face, hiding the hurt and pain that stabbed into my chest. He killed my father just so I’d be strong enough to make it a fair fight. “And how’s my little birdy Maya doing? She was perfect. I bet you never suspected a thing.”

“She’s dead.” His amused face dropped for a second before that malicious smile was back. He could see it in my eyes that I was the one who did it. He was overjoyed at the revelation. “She’s not yours. She never was.” His smile dropped, jaw clenching knowing I wasn’t talking about Maya anymore. “She’s mine and always will be. Don’t you ever wonder why your mark never stuck?” His jaw clicked, eyes bore into me as I smiled, knowing I hit a nerve. “Because you are not her true mate. You *killed* yours.” I smirked, watching the fury flash across his face.

“Such a shame I’ll have to kill you before you meet your

child." My smile faulted, heart pounding in my chest. *My child...Zia's baby is...is my baby? Not his...*

"It's mine..." I muttered, guilt overcoming me as I regretted leaving them both. He laughed, sound echoing before he spoke.

"Not for much longer. I will admit, once I smelt her new scent and saw the little bump growing, I was going to kill it." I growled at his words, my wolf was clawing at the ground in my head, just waiting for my control to weaken just the tiniest bit so he could lash out and kill him. "I was going to make her suffer for giving herself to another. But when I saw her pull her wolf from herself, how she made herself human so that all her strength would go to protecting the pup from the inside, I changed my mind. I decided I'd raise the child as my own. Raise it with hatred for you, so that one day when it was old enough, it would come find you and kill you. And you would never know you were killed by your own child."

I couldn't tell if the baby was mine. Her scent was masked and her belly was the smallest one I've ever seen. I've seen many pregnant pack members and my mother when she was pregnant with Sarana. But none of them had been the size of Zia's. Her body was anorexic. I understand why she pulled her wolf inside her. She needed that extra strength to protect the baby from the harsh conditions she was in. The starvation, the beatings, the rape. I don't know how our baby survived. But Zia is strong. She was always stronger than all of us. This time I need to be strong for her. I need to end her nightmare, starting with her demon.

"Hmm," He mused as he watched me curiously, "I expected tears to come from you hearing that news. I thought you would wolf out hearing that she's pregnant. Do you not care? I have her and your baby and you don't react other than saying it's yours!" He screamed making me smile. I loved how unhinged he was becoming from not getting the reaction he wanted. He truly was a psychotic wolf. But I know something he doesn't, and *that,* is eating away at me.

I have her.

"Oh, dear. I thought you were smart, *Vladik.* Guess I was wrong." I shrug, revelling in his anger.

"What are you talking about?" He snapped.

"Did you really think I came to you first?" I laughed. "Of course not. I came for my mate and I wasn't leaving without her. You, however, were a bonus. I didn't want to leave here without hearing you take your last breath."

"**YOU TOOK MY LUNA**?!" He roared, eye's flashing to his wolfs as he growled viciously at me.

"**SHE IS MY LUNA**! And you're about to feel the wrath of her mate!"

I lunged forward at the same time he did. We went down, both throwing hits as we struggled to untangle ourselves. We stood up; my fist flew out connecting with his jaw with a satisfied crack. He roared again, fists raining down on me too fast for me to dodge. He was quick. My face throbbed, arms burning as I used them to block his hits. I growled, stepping back as my own wolfs eyes shone through. He laughed like a maniac. I had enough. He had been toying with me this whole time, trying to get a rise out of me and he was still doing it. He played dirty, not challenging, or fighting the traditional Alpha ways. He wants to fight dirty? Then I am happy to oblige. It's time he finds out just how ruthless I can be.

Everyone has thought about killing someone they hate. They imagine scenarios, certain ways the person dies, how much pain they would be in or how their screams might sound. And I dreamed of killing Vladik. As he continued to laugh, distracted at the danger I lunged forward, clawed fingers digging into his shoulders as I held him in place. And finally, I did the one thing I've been wanting to do to him since the day he took Zia.

I marked him.

A sick joy coursed through me the moment my teeth pierced his skin. His blood curdling scream bellowed through the air, music to my ears as I felt his pain through our instant bond. I felt the second my mark began rejecting in his skin. He thrashed against me, skin ripping as he clawed at my chest, desperate to get away. But I didn't let up. I marked him again and again, more forcefully each time, letting him feel exactly what Zia felt when he forced his mark upon her countless times. He tried to punch me but I barely felt them. He became weaker, hands trembling as his blood spilled down his chest. His blood coated my tongue, staining my mouth but I revelled in it. I wanted him to hurt, wanted to feel everything Zia felt. And soon he stopped hitting, arms sliding down to his sides as his body went slack. He was there, on the edge of life and death. I finally pulled back, sucking in a breath as I grabbed onto the collar of his torn, shredded jacket. I walked forward, hearing his feet dragging in the snow before I stopped, dangling him over the edge of the cliff. His eyes were rolling in the back of his head, limbs hanging lifelessly by his side.

"I wish we had more time together." I smiled, enjoying the look that crossed his weak face. His mouth moved but no words came out.

Then, I let go.

I watched his body drop until he was no longer visible. The fog swelled and spiralled as his body whooshed through it. Then I heard the moment his body hit the snow. No sound followed, just the soft thud.

Vladik was dead.

I breathed a sigh of relief. It was finally over.

It took us a little over a week to get back home. Zia's health hindered us from going faster, but with Vladik gone there was no threat anymore. She was asleep most of the time. We had to sedate her. She was still scared of him, not believing us when we told her he was dead. I thought all her worries and fear would go away the second we told her but it didn't. She was still so afraid of him and I couldn't blame her. She spent seven months down in that cell. I don't know everything he did to her, only the things I felt from our bond or saw the bruises on her body.

After a few days she was able to stay calm. See reason and know that she was safe, that she had her family around her to also keep her safe. Soon she decided to shift. Her wolf was stronger than her, able to keep her going as we travelled to the airstrip where our plane awaited. It was excruciating to watch her shift. She hadn't shifted since the day before she was taken. She screamed and cried the whole time and I could do nothing to ease her pain. She wanted to do this for her baby...*our* baby. When she completed the shift, a wave of emotions hit me, sending me to my knees. Pain, sorrow, fear, hopelessness, hunger. Everything she felt for the duration of her captivity. I cried; her emotions were so strong they crippled me. It had been so long since I felt the full connection of our bond. With her now shifted our bond snapped back into place. With everything back, I still couldn't hear her thoughts. She still shielded them from me. When I stood back up, I nearly went back down again at the sight of her wolf. Her once beautiful white fur lost its sparkle. Her healthy glowing wolf with the strange blue-orange eyes was now faded, thin and skeletal looking. I vowed right there I would never let anything happen to her or our baby ever again.

My baby.

I could also smell our pup once she shifted. I never doubted Vladik. I knew he spoke the truth when I remembered the scars on her hands. They were defensive scars. I concluded she had tried to protect our baby once he smelt the change in her scent and saw her belly grow.

Finally, we made it back home. Keiran had done a great job

of looking after the pack while we were gone. As we arrived, it looked like the whole pack was waiting for us by the border. They cheered, hollered, and whooped as we got out of the car. I thanked them for coming but regrettably sent them home. We would have a celebration for Zia's return at a later date once she was feeling better. The excitement was too much for her. Her wolf was still in the car, head whipping from side to side with her ears pulled back and eyes wide with fear. They couldn't handle that many people yet.

Caleb left with Kitty, but Zack and Grace stayed behind. I hoped I would see my mother's face within the crowd, smiling brightly like she once did. But she wasn't there. Which could only mean one thing. She hasn't woken up.

"Baby, look." I turned to Zia's wolf watching me from the back seat. "It's Alek!" Her head whipped up, mouth dropping open as her tongue sprung out and tailed wagged excitedly. She lunged from the car as I dived for her. She was still too weak and pregnant. She could break a bone if she landed wrong or came down too hard. I slid across the ground, one knee scrapping as my other held me up. I caught her in the proposal position, wolf wiggling in my arms trying to get out of my hold. It felt like I just had a mini heart attack. We skirted the car just as Alek came into view. His footing faulted when he saw Zia's wolf. Keiran gasped, handing grabbing onto Alek holding him up when his knees threatened to buckle.

"*Sestra...*" He whispered. Then he collapsed, suddenly crashing to the ground as he screamed and cried, fist pounding on the ground. Zia's wolf stopped, whining as she slowly approached her brother. "What did he do to you..." He said through sobs, aqua blue eyes glowing as the whites in his eyes turned red from his tears. "I'm sorry! I'm so sorry!" Zia's wolf tilted her head up and let out a painful howl into the air.

My heart clenched at the sound, tears coming to my own eyes as we all watched her try and shift back. She had tried before but didn't have the energy. But now she was trying again and she was fighting hard. I could feel the excruciating pain she was going through but I could also feel her resolve. She wasn't going to stop. Not until she could hold her brother. They both needed each other.

As the cracking and snapping of her bones stopped, she abruptly stood up and ran as fast as she could to Alek. His head was still hung, shoulders moving up and down as he sobbed.

"Alek..." His head whipped up as she ran to him crying his name. He stood, pushing off the ground as he ran towards her.

Their reunion was powerful. I've never felt such strong emotions coming from Zia before. Never seen Alek cry or break down. He had always been the strong one, always been the rock Zia needed. It was breathtaking the love I could feel through our bond. The closer they got to each other, the closer the air started to feel charged. Like every atom was buzzing with anticipation. I looked at Zack and Grace. They could feel it too. Zack looked down at his arms, seeing goosebumps appear as Grace raised her hand, feeling strands of her hair start to float up from the static electricity charging in the air. Keiran looked up at me as all four of us realized what was about the happen the moment Alek and Zia embraced. But we were too late. The second they touched each other a loud crack sounded in the sky like lighting and a flash of violet blinded us.

The next thing I knew, I wasn't on Earth anymore.

"Cairo." A voice I hadn't heard in months spoke from behind me. I was standing on and surrounded by clouds with every colour of dusk as a sweet fragrant, almost spiced smell filled the air. I felt weightless. My mind was confused but my body didn't feel it. It felt happy, calm, at peace. A warm wind circled me, I felt crazy like the wind was actually hugging me but I couldn't see anything. Then the voice spoke again. "Cairo." I turned, everything stopping as my father stood before me. Dressed in his favourite suit. He looked exactly the same as he did the morning of the rogue war but the wound on his chest was healed, suit pristine. He didn't have his tie on and the buttons on his dress shirt were buttoned only half the way. He looked so carefree, the lines that always marred his face weren't there. And without them he looked younger. I couldn't speak. I was too stunned, too confused at where the hell I was and why I could see my father again.

"Whe..." I tried by my words still failed me.

"This is the Moon." He answered for me. I gasped, suddenly realising Alek and Zia sent all of us here by accident. I looked around but I couldn't see Keiran, Zack or Grace anywhere.

"This is unbelievable." I said as I looked around. "Are you... real?" He smiled warmly.

"Yes and no. Think of this as heaven."

"This is what Alek and Zia can do? What the Moons Warriors are gifted with?" He nodded.

"You can see me anytime you want. You need only ask them. Ah, yes." He said laughing. "There is someone who wants to see you." I frowned, watching him as he looked down. A little black-haired boy tugged on the leg of his pants.

My heart stopped.

Eyes instantly watering as I watched Siron step out from behind our father's leg. He smiled shyly, looking up at our father as he nodded. I was seeing a ghost. My baby brother, the same age he was when he died. He walked shyly towards me before he stopped, looking up at me as he waited. I gingerly crouched down, mouth open as he stepped forward and hugged me.

"Siron..." I hugged him. Squeezing him to me as I cried. There were too many emotions that coursed through me as I held his little body to me. His small arms were around my neck felt surreal. Seeing him now I realized just how much Sarana looked like him. The only difference was she had our mother's hair. But they had the same eyes. I forgot that.

"Mama?" He asked when he pulled back smiling brightly.

"I...I don..." I stumbled over my words. I was hearing his voice again, just like I remembered.

"She will come visit soon. Cairo has to get back to his mate now." My father said, walking forward as he bent down and scooped Siron up making him giggle. "She needs you, Cairo." His smile slowly disappeared as a look crossed his eyes. He didn't say more but something rang alarm bells in my head. I looked around, panic setting in just before a rough wind blew around me. Suddenly, I was back in the field. I was on my back, staring up at the sky as moans and groans sounded beside me. Zack sat up rubbing his head, Grace was breathing in and out rapidly and Keiran was looking around with a worried look on his face.

"Zia?" I said but she didn't reply.

"They're gone." Keiran said as his eyes clouded over, probably linking Alek. I went to link Zia but Keiran was suddenly back, fumbling to get up as he panicked. "Zia collapsed! She's in the hospital!"

No...

Chapter Fifty-Three

Mistakes That Define Us

ALEK

It doesn't matter how many times she or anyone else says it, this will always be my fault. I could have prevented all of this from happening. There were so many clues, so many times she said something when we were kids or she acted differently, strangely. Like the times she suddenly stopped asking for Vladik to sleep over or when she became scared of the dark. When she wanted me to start closing the curtain to our bedroom window because *he* was always standing there watching her. If I didn't brush her fears or sudden mood changes aside, I would have seen the danger coming years before he was too strong, before it was too late and before her life changed forever. I should have questioned why she suddenly felt scared the day she shifted and saw Vladik for the first time or even just how he clung to her after he shifted. I was ignorant, we all were. We believed him when he said they were mates. He conditioned us for years and by the time we turned fifteen and she realized the truth, it was too late. She must have felt all alone. Everyone celebrated their mating and no one knew the truth but her. Looking back now, I would have picked up on her flinching every time he moved his hands too quick. Would have picked up on how shy and quiet she became. It was my fault. Now she's lying in a hospital bed all skin and bones and I can't do anything to help her except sit here and hold her hand waiting for her real mate to come. I didn't have enough time to wake the others when we accidentally sent them to the Moon. She just collapsed right in front of me. She was so weak. Using our powers like that drained her immensely.

"Baby!" Keiran said swinging the door open as Cairo, Zack and Grace all ran in after him. "What the hell happened out there?"

"You went to the Moon." I replied looking at each of them. Keiran was the only one that didn't have red rimmed eyes from crying.

"I saw my parents." Grace said looking at me, smiling sadly. It was devastating when her parents died. She cried for days. This was back when we didn't have our wolf or powers. When we couldn't let her see them.

"I saw my grandfather." Zack said quietly.

"My dad and Siron." Cairo spoke next. Keiran looked at each of them, confused what they were talking about. Before he could ask, I answered for him.

"You've never lost anyone." I said as Keiran looked to me. "If you did, you would have seen them."

"But...It felt like someone hugged me. Gave me a kiss on the forehead." I smiled, knowing exactly who that was.

"That was the Moon Goddess." They all look bewildered but somehow not shocked. Like they all came to that conclusion on their own.

"How is she?" Cairo asked walking to the other side of Zia's bed. They had changed her into a gown, started an IV drip and one for antibiotics.

"She's stable. When we touched and our power exploded out from us, it completely drained her. I caught her just before she hit the ground. I brought her straight here and that's when they dressed her and hooked her up." I said looking up at the bags. "That's also when...when I...when I found out she's pregnant." In my haste to get to her I didn't see the little bump she had. It wasn't until the doctors examined her and confirmed the pregnancy.

"What?!" Keiran exclaimed before he ran to my side looking down at Zia. The others didn't look surprised at all. They just looked sad.

"I failed her. I don't deserve her or you." I said to Keiran letting my heart speak.

"Don't say that!" He scolded me. "You're not a failure." He said hearing my thoughts.

"I am though." I whispered quietly turning back to look at her. "She went through months of hell surviving him *while* being pregnant. I couldn't save her again because I was in a coma!" I never saw that attack coming. If I did I could have prevented this.

"You were supposed to be dead." Zia spoke softly.

"What?" I felt a wave of relief wash over me. She was awake and okay. But her words sent a chill down my spine.

"Jordan. She was the one who poisoned you." I growled, seeing the whole plan coming together. A rattle in Cairo's chest vibrated out. I looked at him, knowing he knew the truth.

"She couldn't have!" Keiran exclaimed. "She was in the hospital with you." He looked down at Zia confused.

"She had help. Jaxon and someone else. I don't know who." Zia frowned, looking down at the bed trying to think who it could have been.

"Maya." Cairo and I said at the same time.

"What? Oh, that's right, she's here. But..." Zia said stopping as she looked around the room before looking towards the door. "Where is she? I thought she'd be waiting here?" Cairo looked away, wolfs eyes shining as his jaw clenched. Eyes looking out the window above the bed.

"She's dead." He finally spoke.

"What?!" Zia and I exclaimed at the same time as we looked at Cairo.

I knew Maya was the one to poison me. She ran right up to my face, worrying about Zia. I was trying to calm her down when she reached into her jacket pocket and pulled out a syringe. I trusted her. That's why I never thought twice when she pulled it out and thrusted forward. I thought she was handing it to me, so, I reached out to grab it but she bypassed my hand and jabbed me right in the chest. The pain was instant. I asked her why as I dropped to the ground, feeling the poison burn through my veins but she never spoke. She just stood there watching me. I watched my veins form on my skin and spread down my arms fast until they reached my fingertips. The last thing I saw was Maya smiling before she took a breath in, exhaled, then ran, screaming for help.

She fooled us all.

"No! Maya wouldn't do that! She would never help Jordan! She hated her!" She looked between Cairo and me, seeing the grim and angry looks on our faces. She shook her head, unwilling to believe it. "Give me your hands." She wanted to see.

I looked at Cairo, not knowing if that was a good idea but he already had his hand out. She entwined her fingers in his before she looked at me with a pointed look. I closed my eyes, frowning as I went against my better judgement and put my hand in hers. Once she did, all three of us were joined. She searched my mind first, watching the moment Maya approached me like a wolf in sheep's clothing. Then we were watching Zia's memory of Jordan. The words she spoke when she revealed she was the mastermind behind everything. Then Cairo, feeling what he did when he spoke to Maya that night. How she blocked her link the second Cairo started asking questions. We watched in horror when he commanded her, hearing her spill all her dark thoughts. Her betrayal, her *willingness* to help Vladik. She continued to help him long after she joined this pack. His alpha commands wouldn't have worked on her anymore, but she didn't care. She wanted revenge. And she almost got it if it wasn't for Cairo being the alpha. I won't lie, I felt immense satisfaction when her mate rejected her and the Goddess granted it. Then as she laid there dying, I couldn't be more prouder of Cairo. He didn't hesitate in ending her betrayal. She let our hands go, not saying a word as we all processed what we saw. Memories of three combining.

There was a small knock on the door before one of the pack doctors walked in. She bowed her head towards Cairo, acknowledged Zack, Grace, Keiran and I before bowing again to Zia, giving her a tight smile but I could see the grim look in her eyes. From that look alone I know the worst was yet to come.

CAIRO

"Sorry to interrupt, everyone. May I please have some privacy so I can speak with Alpha and Luna." Zack and Grace nodded, already heading to the door as Keiran did the same but stopped when he noticed Alek wasn't moving.

"Alek? We need to leave the room for a second." He said softly.

"I'm not leaving her." Alek snapped.

"I never demand anything from you but I am now." My softly spoken friend said shocking me at this new stern side of him. "We *are* leaving this room and we *are* going to give them privacy. We will stand outside next to the window if you like so you can still keep an eye on her from the hallway. Now move it." I had to look away or else I was going to laugh. Keiran was never the type of person to stand up for himself or voice his opinions. If he were ever the Alpha he would be a gentle one. He has not one mean or angry bone in his body.

"Zi," Alek said after he sighed at Keiran, "I'll be right outside. Okay?" She didn't move or speak for a few seconds before she finally nodded. A single tear falling. As the door closed behind them, I prayed we weren't about to hear bad news but the doctor stayed quiet, looking at Zia with an uncertain look in her eyes.

"Alpha, please have a seat." She gestured grimly to the chair behind me. The hairs stood up on the back of my neck but I did it. I sat down, taking Zia's hand in mine.

"What is it?" I spoke.

"Firstly, I'd just like to say, Luna, you are the strongest wolf I have ever met. To go through what you did would have destroyed anyone. But here you are." She was right, if that were me I wouldn't have made it to this moment right here. I nearly didn't when Zia was taken. *If I knew she was pregnant then...* "And secondly. We have your test results back, Zia."

"Tests? What tests?" I asked worried.

"Because of Zia's health, we decided to do a full check-up. We tested her blood, did pregnancy safe scans, listened to both their hearts and so on. Now, werewolf pregnancies are usually a lot stronger and healthier than the average human pregnancy. The babies are born stronger, healthier with little to no help once they're born besides cutting the cord and clearing the airways. But your pup," There it was. The words I dreaded from the moment she said her tests were back. "Because of what you went through and the conditions you were accustomed to," she said looking at Zia sadly, "while being pregnant, your baby is a lot smaller than she should be."

"It's a girl?" I smiled, looking to Zia as her eyes watered, hand rubbing her belly softly.

"Yes, a little girl. We were able to see her gender on the scans. But...because of your weight and malnourishment, she is measuring smaller than what she should be at 34 weeks. This means her lungs haven't developed at the normal rate and if she survives birth, she will need to stay in hospital for a few months so we can monitor her health. She will need help breathing for the first few months until her lungs can continue to work on their own without assistance. That would also mean as she grows, she will have to take care of herself, including her lungs. She will have to carry asthma puffers, reduce her psychical activities and take care not to damage her lungs anymore or else she will damage them beyond prepare." I went to speak but she continued, reading the questions on our face. "Because of the damage already done to her lungs from the condition she's in, her lungs will never fully develop properly. She will need to be cautious of them. Since they will never be as healthy as ours, they will be fragile. Like I said, asthma puffers, reduced physical activity and such. I'm very sorry."

"You..." I began, swallow the lump in my throat as Zia started to cry, "you said, *if* she survives birth. What do you mean by that?"

"Because of how weak Zia and the baby both are, there's a chance one or both won't make it. But...Cairo, there might come a time when you will have to choose."

"Choose?! What do you mean by choose?" Zia's sobs quieted. I could feel her acceptance through our bond, she knew what the doctor meant. I think some part of me also knew but I didn't want to believe it.

"If complications happen, and both the life of your pup and mate are on the line, you will have to choose which one to save."

"I..I can't do that! I..I..."

"Cairo," Zia's hand softly touched my shoulder, "you will have too." She looked up at me with her big sad doe eyes, glowing brighter from the red rims.

"You...you can't ask that of me...Please, Zia. Don't..." I shook my head, tears falling as my heart pounded in my chest. "I...I want you both!"

"You will choose her!" She snapped at me, eyes flashing to her wolf as images flashed in my mind.

I saw the day she realised she was pregnant, the day her scent changed, when she woke up and saw her belly growing. When Vladik found out, attacking her bloody and blue as he tried to rip the baby from her belly. The moment she felt the first flutters, the first kick, the little hiccups she felt every day or the little foot that kicked out in the same spot. She went through everything with our baby. I get why she wants me to choose her. She fought like hell so that our baby could survive.

"Always her, Cairo. *Always her*." She said as she held her hand over my heart. She swung her legs over the bed, threw the blankets off her and stood up. I reached for her but she stepped back out of reach. She grabbed the cords and needles attached to her arms and ripped them out, letting them fall to the ground as small droplets of blood slowly trailed down her arms.

Then, she left.

Chapter Fifty-Four

Home Sweet Home

Zia

I was back but I didn't feel it.

Alek called after me as I walked down the hall, both he and Keiran having heard everything the doctor said. Shaking my head, I kept walking, ignoring him. I didn't have the energy to talk anymore. I barely had enough to keep one foot going in front of the other. I just wanted to be home, in my bed that felt like clouds and doused in Cairo's scent.

"Zia, stop!" I do, spinning on my heels as he comes to a stop in front of me.

"No, Alek." His hand grabbed my arm gently as I went to turn but I flinch, feeling the strum of hurt streak through our bond.

"Zia..." I could hear the distress and hurt in his broken voice which only made me feel worse.

"Leave me alone." I take a step forward, halting when he speaks again.

"Zi-" I snap. The ground shook when I clenched my fists, feeling a rush of power flow through me. The doors rattled on their hinges, glass windows and panels cracking.

"I SAID LEAVE ME ALONE!" I roared, watching as Alek's head snapped back, fear flashing through our bond. I cried, hating seeing that look in his eyes, hated knowing I was the one who put it there. I turned, now running, and pushed through the pain. I needed air, needing out of the confines of this hospital. Needed away from people.

I shut everyone out. Cairo, Alek, the pack. I wanted silence, I don't want to hear or feel anyone else's feelings. Don't want to feel their guilt, their regret at not doing something, their sadness, their pity! I want none of it. I just want to be alone, just me and my baby.

I ran until water was the only sound I could hear was the water. I thought about what the sand felt like between my toes for months, thought about what the breeze would feel like when the water carried it across right to me, blowing through my hair. I sat down on the grassy bank, running my fingers through the grass as I closed my eyes, letting the breeze lull me into a sense of calm.

"Thought that was your scent." Grace spoke as she sat down beside me. "What are you thinking about?"

"Nothing. I'm just taking everything in." My hand was on my belly, feeling the baby kick and turn before she settled in. "Just in case."

"In case what?" She asked, head tilted as she looked at me.

"In case this is a dream."

"This is real, Zy. Everything that happened the last two weeks are real. You're home, you're safe. It's real." She reassured me but she doesn't understand, no one does, no one could.

"That's the thing, Grace. It's always real. Until it's not.

Every dream, every vision, every delusion was always real. It always felt so real like I could taste, touch or smell. But they eventually disappeared, and I was alone again. Locked in a prison I could never escape from."

"Okay. Do you want me to leave?"

"Yes." I said as I laid back, feeling the grass brush against my arms as I looked up at the sky, watching the clouds slowly move and morph into different shapes.

She slowly stood up, waited a few seconds to see if I changed my mind. When I didn't, she nodded, turning, and walked back towards the pack house. I smiled, feeling her hiding amongst the trees watching me. If I wasn't so attuned to everything around me, I would have mistaken her for a tree or just a figment of my imagination. But I could hear her shallow breaths, the slow beating of her heart. She was amazing at blending in, camouflaging to her surroundings.

A few hours went by and I found myself asleep, dreaming of a life that never happened. When I awoke, there was an apple, two oranges and a bottle of water sitting beside me. I could smell Grace and Cairo's scent on the fruit. He must have come by when I was asleep. I'm glad he didn't wake me. I felt better, being back at my pack, amongst my mate, my family. Feeling all those bonds heal me. I watched as the blue in the sky faded, an array of yellow and orange painting across the sky. When the sun set and twilight was now upon us, I decided it was time to get up. My centre of gravity was way off, being eight months pregnant made doing simple, everyday mundane tasks slightly more difficult. But I did it, just like I did day after day when I needed to stretch my legs in that cell. *The cell...*I needed a bath, my skin crawled from the memories and the smell never stopped lingering. I could still smell Jordan's decaying body, the mud on the ground, my blood from months of abuse staining the cobblestone. The bucket I used as a toilet or when I had morning sickness as needed to throw up. Everything was still as vivid as if I hadn't left at all.

I saw no one on the way back to the pack house or when I walked inside and made my way up to our bedroom. I immediately stripped out of the hospital gown and turned the tap on in the shower. I watched the room fill up with steam, fogging the glass. I grabbed a hand towel, wiping down the mirror as my reflection came into view. My chin wobbled, tears falling as I looked at the defined cheekbones, sunken eyes and ribs sticking out. I looked like a skeleton, hands scarred and malnourished. I pulled a leaf out of my hair. My once beautiful platinum silver locks were matted, dirty and reached my hips. Now I know why everyone looked at me with shock and pity. Why most couldn't keep eye contact with me.

I shook my head, walking backwards away from the horrifying reflection until my back hit the wall. I slid down until I was on the floor, knees tucked up against my chest as I cried. Everything becoming too much, too much. I cry out, a sudden pain shooting across my belly. My breath escapes me, heart pounding as I'm frozen in place. Then, the pain eases, then disappears as my breath comes back.

My baby...

It's back, I squeeze my eyes shut, grabbing my legs as the pain takes over. My back cramps, sending white hot pain down my spine. A few seconds go by then it disappears again. It doesn't come back, letting me catch my breath. My chest rises and falls, ease washing over my body. *I'm okay. We're okay.* I stretch my hand over my belly, feeling our baby girl move. She turns, stretching as her foot pushes out against my stomach. I run my fingers across it, feeling how small it is. Without her, I wouldn't have survived Vladik. He tried to break me, but no matter how much he took from me, she was my strength. The little piece of Cairo I kept safe within me all those months ago.

I knew from the moment Vladik left Jordan's body that I was pregnant. Before her body even smelt, the morning sickness started. Then my wolf shifted in my mind and became aggressive. I thank the Goddess Vladik didn't know or the guards he left down the hall. I pulled her back, barely managing to get the reigns back on our control. If he saw how savage she became he would have pushed, asked questions, figured out I was pregnant earlier. If he did I would have lost her. I knew I had only a short amount of time before my smell would change permanently. I blocked my scent as much as I could but that could only hold him off for so long. Soon he would be able to taste the change in my blood. He stopped marking me that day but it was also the day he went savage on me. I threw my hands over my belly the second I saw his own descend. He snapped at my face, hands clawing at my belly. I pulled my wolf from my mind, shoving her straight down to protect our baby. She willingly went, pushing her power out to protect my uterus.

"I'm sorry…" I whispered to her. I already failed her. I couldn't protect her. She won't have the strongest health; she won't have a worry-free childhood. I damaged her. I'm the one that might kill her when I give birth. All because I'm not strong enough. *I'm such a failure.* How will she ever live knowing how traumatic my pregnancy with her was? And how much I suffered just to keep her alive. I don't deserve to raise her. *I don't deserve to live.*

KNOCK KNOCK.

"Zia? It's me, Gracie." She opened the door, closing it behind her before she strode forward, turning the shower off. Then she grabbed a towel, bending down she wrapped it around me. "What are you doing?" She asked softly.

"What do you mean?" I looked up at her.

"Why are you pushing Alek away? He didn't almost die for you to come back and push him away. I gave you space, gave you time."

"I almost died too!" I snapped. I grabbed the side of the bathtub, using it to pull myself up, ignoring her outstretched hand.

"I know you both almost died but you both also need each

other. I'm gonna tell you what Keiran told Alek after you left. The Goddess isn't finished with you two yet. You still have much work to do, work that both of you will need to do together. Have you asked Cairo about his mother?" She said, giving me whiplash from the sudden change of topic.

"N..no...Why? What's wrong with her?"

"She's in a coma, Zy. Her mate, husband and the packs Alpha was killed in the rogue war."

"What?" I repelled back, almost slipping on the slick tiles. "C...Cairo didn't say anything about it."

"He loves you, Zia. He's seen what you went through, he felt what you went through the first few weeks you were taken. Add that to losing his dad, taking over the pack and running it the best he could. His mother tried to kill herself, so overcome with grief that she wanted to be with her mate. He had to place her into a coma. I hear he also has a little sister he had to take care of. I know that is nothing compared to what you went through, and I know you have a lot of shit you're going through, but so is he. Yet he's being strong for you. I know you spent months being strong for your pup, but you aren't alone anymore. You have your pack who would do anything for you, your mate who's tough as shit and so caring. You have Cairo and Alek back. And me. Use us, let us help you through this recovery, let us be your support system. The rocks you fall back on when you feel like you can't stand. But Cairo and Alek, they need you too. And I'm sorry for the tough love. You know I've never been sappy." I laughed through tears, bending my head down to wipe my snotty nose and tears.

"How could I be so blind." If it wasn't for Grace I wouldn't have known any of this. "I can't do anything right."

"Don't say that!" She snapped. "You're here, aren't you? You have survived more than any of us ever have. Don't stop now. Push through it, take it one day at a time. One step at a time."

"O...okay." I gasp, folding over as the pain was back and

now twice as painful. My legs gave way, knees smacking against the tiles as I cried out.

"Zia!" Grace shouted, squatting down as she grabbed my shoulders. She brushed my hair back, tucking a strand behind my ear as her violet eyes were wide, worry flashing through them before she looked down, horror widening her eyes.

"It's...okay. It will pass...soon." I spoke through panted breaths.

"No...Zia, you're bleeding." She scooped me up just as everything went black.

I woke up minutes later seeing the yellow hospital lights flash by above me as they rushed me into surgery. The pain was back, blinding me as the doctors injected me with something. I tried to call for Cairo but nothing came out. My mind went fuzzy, eyes blurring before slowly, everything faded away.

CAIRO

I will never forget the moment Grace ran down the hallway carrying an unconscious Zia, screaming for help. All I saw was red. Zia's legs were coated in blood. My heart stopped, fearing the worst and it hasn't started back up ever since we pushed through those hospital doors. They had a gurney waiting for her. They ran faster than we did, rushing her straight into surgery. I was screaming, demanding to be told what was happening. All they could say was that they were going to do an emergency caesarean. The doctor warned us this could happen, but I never expected it would happen so soon. Never thought Zia would be bleeding out like this. They shut the doors on me, Grace and Zack holding me back as my wolf went almost feral. He didn't want to leave her or our pup. I prayed, hoping the Goddess could hear me. Prayed she could hear me begging her to save them, to save both of them.

"Cairo, don't make me hurt you. Step back from the door." Grace said as she put me in a head lock as she clung to my back. My wolf thrashed around, eyes brimming red. "If you want them to save her stop being a distraction! Zia needs their undivided attention. They can't give her that if their Alpha is trying to break the fucking door down!" My wolf suddenly stopped, pulling back as he let me in control. I pulled my hands from the door, unlatching my nails that begun digging into the wood. I pushed back, facing away as I frowned, closing my eyes as I tried to find Zia. I could feel her, she was there. But her heart was failing, beating slower as our bond got weaker. I spoke to her, praying she could hear my thoughts.

I love you, baby. You got this. You're strong, you can do this.

I love you.

I always will.

Chapter Fifty-Five

The Choice

An hour had passed, we stood in the waiting room, waiting for the doctor to walk through and say our baby was born and Zia was alive. That they were both alive, both healthy and stable. Anyone in this position would lose track of time but not me. I tracked every second that went by as the clock hands went round and around. Keiran was holding Alek as he cried into his chest, saying he couldn't lose her again. Keiran repeated that she was strong, that she'd make it. I wanted to believe that I really did. But the more minutes passed, the more my resolve began weakening. My heart was beating so hard in my chest I feared it would explode. I need her to be okay. I can't lose her. I can't lose my pup. I just got them back. I didn't even know I had a baby on the way but I already love her so much. I can't be the alpha I'm supposed to be if I don't have them by my side.

"Cairo!" Grace exclaimed. "The doctor is coming!" We all stood up, facing the swinging doors with hope in our hearts. But all of our smiles dropped when the doctor came running through, blood all over her scrubs as she looked at me.

"Tell me she's okay! Tell me they're both okay!" I rushed out before she could speak.

"I'm sorry, Cairo..." Those two words shattered my heart. I wasn't prepared for this.

"No..." I shook my head.

"Cairo, it's time." She said solemnly.

"T...time for what?" I asked, tears brimming my eyes as I blinked through them.

"It's time to choose. Both pup and Luna are in distress. We've tried everything we can but it wasn't enough. We can only save one."

No...

"I can't."

Time passed slowly in a blur. I wondered the halls like a ghost, refusing to move on. That was the hardest choice I've ever had to make. I wish I never had to make the choice in the first place. My whole world crashed and burned once those words left the doctor's mouth. *It's time to choose.* How is anyone supposed to choose! I...I'm still a kid! I'm nineteen next month, I just graduated from school not too long ago though I shouldn't have graduated. I never went back to school after Zia was kidnapped. I'm one of the youngest alpha's to ever be Alpha. I've had to run a whole pack while trying to find my mate. I couldn't even look after my sister once I lost my father and Zia. How am I supposed to make a decision like that? I couldn't do it, I couldn't choose. But I had too. How do you choose? Your mate? The person you are mated to spend the rest of your life loving more deeply than anyone else? Or your child? The one you didn't know you were having but have already formed a bond with. The little heart beat I hear every time the thought of my baby, my daughter, enters my mind. How do I choose? My heart was torn. All I could hear was Zia's broken voice in my head from this morning.

Always her.

In the end, I had to make a decision. One I hope I will never regret.

I stood in front of the glass window of the nursery, looking in as my heart beat wildly in my chest. My eyes welled with tears as I looked into the *empty* room. I wish more than anything that my daughter could be laying there in that little clear bassinette, swaddled in a cute pink blanket. I wish I could walk into that room, pick her up and cuddle her against my chest and protect her with my whole heart.

But I can't.

"I'm sorry, Zia. I'm so sorry." I whispered as a stray tear fell. I looked away, feeling like I'm leaving my heart in that room as I leave. I see the doctor coming out of Zia's room as I approach. She puts her clip board down, looking up at me apologetically. I could feel her guilt. She hates what she had to put me through.

"How is she?"

"She's doing good...considering." She says quietly. "Look, Cairo. What you had to do, the choice you had to make, you did what you thought was right. Don't punish yourself for that."

"It's hard not to punish myself when I feel like I betrayed Zia." I breathe in and out, feeling like a tsunami of tears was building inside me. "When I chose..." *Breathe in, breathe out.*

"Go in and see her, Cairo. She was just awake." She gives me a small smile.

"Yeah..." *Time to see her.*

When I walked in, Zia's eyes were closed. Her breathing was shallow, chest slowly rising and falling. I bent down, gently kissing her before pulling back. Then I turned, looking into the incubator at my baby girl. *Always her.* I wish more than anything she could be laying in that nursery. I wish she could be as healthy as any other pup, but instead I failed her as a father and as a result, she's here. She has a tube down her nose to help her breathe and cords attached to her little chest monitoring her heart rate. If I had just found Zia sooner, both of my girls would be safe and healthy. I wouldn't have nearly lost them both. It was only by a miracle that Zia was still here.

She doesn't even have a name yet. Zia never told me if she had any names picked out and I haven't had enough time to think of any. I should have asked Zia sooner. I was just worried talking about the baby would have been a hair trigger and set her off. The doctors were right. I need to stop punishing myself and be the father and mate Zia always thought I could be. My little girl needs her daddy to be strong for her. So, that's what I'll do. I'll be strong for her, for both of them.

I open the little circular window, reaching my hand inside so I could feel my little baby. She's so beautiful, so tiny. She's the perfect mix of both Zia and me. I chuckle, blinking away the fat tears. She's definitely got Zia's blonde hair. I can see little tuffs of the platinum blonde hair sticking out from underneath her little pink knitted beanie. I have to lean down closer to even see her little blonde eyebrows. They're almost nonexistent. She doesn't have the silver streaks like Alek and Zia have but I'm assuming that's their whole Moon's Warriors trait. Like how Kitty and Grace have a full head of silver hair and ash toned skin. I touch her arm, feeling the tiny limb and how soft her skin is. Her little arms were the size of my finger. I'm almost afraid to touch her in fear of breaking her. *I can't believe I have a baby.* I can't stop crying every time I look at her. The Goddess gave me a slice of the heavens when my daughter was born.

"Goddess, she's so small." I say as I hear movement behind me.

"I know." Zia said, sliding her hand in as she gently touches our daughter's cheek with the back of her finger. "But she's strong. She's our little warrior."

"She really is. I can't believe she's here. She's mine, ours..." There I go, crying again like a big baby.

"*We* made her. She's so beautiful, Cairo." Zia said as she placed her hand on top of mine.

"It's like she took the best parts of both of us. Our sweet, strong little girl."

"Hazel."

"Hmm?" I ask as Zia smiles up at me.

"Her name. Hazel."

"It's beautiful." I smile wide and teary eyed. "But why Hazel?" I ask curiously.

"When the doctors pulled her out of me, they placed her on my chest for a few seconds. And when they did, she had her eyes open. She stared straight up at me, Cairo. Like she knew who I was even before I spoke. She has your eyes. Your beautiful Hazel eyes." My heart pounded proudly in my chest.

"Hazel...It's perfect. I love it." We pulled our hands back, promising to hold Hazel soon. I faced Zia, her now washed and brushed hair was pulled up into a messy bun, lips no longer cracked but they still looked pale. But so did her body, she had lost a lot of blood during the surgery, during the birth. "I'm sorry, Zia. I chose her." I grabbed my chest, feeling the strained beat as she grabbed my arm.

"It's okay. You did what I wanted you to do. I felt what you went through when you had to decide. I'm the one that should be sorry. I wish you never had to go through that. But I'm alive, she's alive and that's all that matters. We survived. I know you feel like you betrayed me by choosing her but you didn't. You respected my wish." She said hugging me.

"I can't believe what happened. I thought I lost you."

"I know. The Goddess surprised us all." Zia said shyly.

Zia had a placental abruption. Her placenta detached from the inner wall of the womb and she was bleeding out fast. I had to decide whether they saved Zia or Hazel, who was in danger of losing oxygen and dying. Both their heart rates were dropping, sending the doctors into a frenzy as they worked to save them. But when it got critical and seemed like there was no other option, they needed my answer. So, I chose Hazel.

"The second you chose her was when I felt it. I felt the impossible choice you made and so did the Goddess. I remember feeling more empowered than I've ever felt before. That surge of power that washed over me, healed me. I remember hearing the nurses and doctor gasping in shock as my heart suddenly steadied. I felt my own body stitching itself back together. She saved me, Cairo. She saved me."

"Keiran was right. She's not done with you. You both have a job to do that you haven't really been able to do because of Vladik."

"I know. We're finally able to do what she intended for us to do and I know just who to start with." She spoke with determination as she pulled back, smiling up at me as her eyes glowed brightly.

"Who?"

"Your mum."

"You know?" I said unsure.

"I do." She smiled at me reassuringly. "Grace basically slapped me in the face with the truth."

"I'm sorry. I should have told you what was going on. I was just...worried you wouldn't be able to handle it."

"It's okay. It would have thrown me over the edge. But Grace has a way of snapping you out of things. Her tough love does work." She laughed, rolling eyes before watching me chuckle. Her tough love definitely works I'd say. This hospital would have a few doors less if it wasn't for her. "When the Goddess healed me, it wasn't just my body she healed, but my mind also. It was like she took all the darkness and pain and trauma inside of me and erased it. Replacing it with light and love. Of course, I'll still have nightmares and fears from the memories, but my mind is at peace. I'm not worried about the what ifs anymore. I'm not unstable anymore. Now I'm focussed on my family, my pack, and helping other wolves who are hurting." My cheeks hurt from how hard I was smiling. I am so proud of her. I'll say it every day until the day I die, she is the strongest person I have ever met.

"Knock, knock!" Alek said standing by the door. "How's she doing?" He asked beelining straight for Hazel.

"She's doing really good!" Zia said excitedly. "The doctors said her lungs have slowly started to work on their own. She will have to stay here for a little while until she puts on a bit more weight and can breathe without the tube's assistance. But the progress she's made already is amazing the doctors said."

"That's great. And does the little peanut have a name?" He said tapping on the incubator like a kid in a pet store. I slapped his hand away, lifting a brow as he shot me a look, mouth agape. I smirked, watching him cross his arms across his chest and squinting his eyes.

"It's Hazel!" Zia said excitedly.

"Ah, like your eyes." He said to me, now the one smirking.

"And how did you know that?" I ask.

"When you have a twin bond with someone who you can hear the thoughts of, then you'll know all about your *dreamy eyes*." He teased, eyes dropping down to my cheeks as they heat.

"Sorry not sorry." Zia said flicking imaginary hair over her shoulder.

"Here, take your clothes, trouble." Alek said holding his arm out with a bag of clothes as he continued to look down at Hazel.

"What are you doing?" I asked watching Zia walk around the other side of her hospital bed and start to change.

"We're going to see your mum, Cairo. It's time she woke up." She said tossing the white hospital gown on the bed with little baby blue flowers on it.

"We're going to take her pain away." Alek said smiling as

he walked to the door and turned, waiting for Zia to join him.

"Thank you." I breathed in and out, feeling a sigh of relief. Sarana misses her so much, I miss her. I know the pack does too.

"You look after Hazel, Cairo. We'll look after your mum." Zia said as she tightened a leather braided belt around her waist.

"Wait, I want to give you something." She tilted her head, confused as Alek said he'd wait outside. She walked towards me in a white top and a tan-brown boho style skirt with the leather twisted belt around her waist. She looked beautiful.

"What is it?" She asked as she stopped in front of me. I reached into my pocket, feeling for the delicate chain as I pulled it out. My hands slid around her neck, clasping the two ends of the chain together as I stepped back, watching her eyes widen as she looked down, holding the diamond ring attached to the chain.

"I had this made for you when you were taken. I had it with me every day as a reminder of you. Something to keep my fight going." Tears fell as she clutched the platinum diamond ring in her hands.

"I love it so much, Cairo. I really do." Her chin wobbled as she spoke.

"I want to marry you, Zia. The ring around your neck is my proposal. And no, I'm not asking, I'm telling." I say as she laughs.

"There would only ever be one answer anyways." She said eyes sparkling as she looked up at me. I kissed her, hands holding her head in place as I poured my heart and soul into our kiss. She returned it just as strong, sparks flying all over my body as we deepened the kiss. "I love you so much, Cairo." She said as she pulled back, resting her forehead against mine. "Now let me go so I can save my mother-in-law." I chuckled, nodding against her head before she pulled back.

"Thank you." I said one last time just before she left,

closing the door behind her.

ZIA

Once I left the room, I headed to Ohana's with Alek to heal her broken heart. Each step I took felt like I was getting stronger. We were finally able to do our life's mission the Goddess gave us. We've only ever healed one person on purpose before, everyone else was purely by accident. But here we were, standing next to Ohana's bed, entwining our hands together as our powers melded together. With her being in a coma it made it easier for her soul to transition to the moon. When people are awake there is always a bit of hesitation or resistance on their part.

Tears welled in my eyes as we watched Ohana's expression change. Her brows furrowed, seeing us with her at the moon. We had the ability to be in two places at once. Here on Earth with our psychical bodies and on the moon, with our astral bodies. We smiled at her before we looked behind her, watching as she followed our gaze. Then she gasped, seeing Zosar. He stood there smiling happily with a young boy who no doubt was Siron. He looked exactly like Cairo I thought although she was the perfect mix of him and Sarana. She cried as she embraced them both. Alek and I pulled ourselves back, not wanting to intrude on their time together. I know once she wakes she will be the mother Cairo and Sarana remember. Which reminds me, I need to see Sarana. I think she would like to see her daddy too. I haven't seen that little cutie in months and I can imagine it hasn't been easy for her.

"Wow, that felt so..." Alek said as he unclasped our hands.

"Right..." I say agreeing, already knowing what he was trying to say.

"Yeah." He chuckled. "That was crazy. It just...my heart feels full. You know? And I feel like I could walk on water." I laughed, shaking my head at him.

"You forget we can feel each other." He smiled shyly, rubbing the back of his neck as he spoke.

"I wasn't sure since you...since you blocked me." I felt horrible, I forgot I did that.

"I'm truly sorry for that, Alek. My mind, heart and soul were torn and broken, surrounding in a cloud of darkness with no light in sight. I didn't know what to do, what to think. So many things were going on in my head, I just needed time to think for myself. I went through months of not hearing or feeling anyone else's thoughts, only to be thrown right back into the middle of it. I could hear and feel you, Cairo, even the pack. Now that I'm Luna, I can feel everyone. It was too much. I needed to ease myself back into being a werewolf again." I breathed out, placing my hand over my chest as I felt my heart pounding.

"Your hands are severely scarred." He said looking down at them. "He used silver?"

"No." I say, able to see the memories in my mind but not be gripped by fear as I watch them. "When his eyes dropped down to my belly the day he smelt I was pregnant, I knew what he was going to do. I covered my stomach with my hands. He didn't stop his attack until a while later. By then I could see the bones in my hands. When he left my cell, I used some of my wolfs healing to stop the bleeding. I used just enough so my bones weren't exposed. It took weeks for my hands to heal from my human strength and healing abilities. I never used my wolfs strength again after that. But mama, she helped as much as she could."

"She did?" I could see the longing in his eyes. He missed our parents dearly.

"Vladik made her bring me food and water as a sick game. She knew she couldn't help me escape but she could help me in other ways. She snuck in medicine for my hands, bandages, and some vitamins for my pregnancy. She snuck back in once to bring me a blanket when the snow came in. About a month before I was saved, he ordered mama away. Paranoid that something was going to happen. One of papa's warriors snuck me food every chance he could get but once Vladik tightened the security, he couldn't come anymore. I had no food, little water from the puddles of snow that melted from the window. The winter was bad this year. It was so cold I could barely move some days."

"I'm sorry I wasn't there to protect you. I should have tried harder."

"Don't, Alek. No more beating yourself up. We couldn't have known how far gone Vladik was. Even as a child we couldn't have done anything to stop him. Remember what I showed you?"

"No?" I asked confused what she was referring too.

"That he and Joran were mates. He killed her and left her body there for weeks. I thought since she was his mate, he'd let me go and when he realised he didn't need to be obsessed with me anymore but I was so wrong. If he could kill his own mate for me, then there was never a chance to prevent any of this from happening. He was going to get me one way or another. If you had found out and tried to stop him when we were younger, he would have just killed you and his father sooner. So don't blame yourself anymore. I don't." Wrapping my arms around him, I hug him as tight as I could. "You warned me of the danger, but Jaxon was too quick. We couldn't have foreseen the three of them teaming up together. It was a coordinated attack that went perfectly. There was no way we could have known what they were planning." I pull back, smiling up at him as tears fell. "Now let's go. There's a few more people we need to help." He breathed in, wiping the tears from his eyes before he smiled back, nodding as he took my hand, leading us out of the room and down the hall towards the exit.

Chapter Fifty-Six

Ghosts of Our Past

The next few weeks were hard. We had a quick pack meeting in the hall to celebrate my return, we also discussed the new pack laws we made and then we introduced Hazel to the pack, showing photos and allowing visitors to see her through the hospital window, everyone walking past like a sushi train. To say there were a few surprised looks would be the understatement of the year when we announced the birth of Hazel. But instead of getting distrustful or doubtful looks like I feared I would get; they had the complete opposite reactions. I thought they would think Hazel was illegitimate, my captor's baby. But they knew without a doubt she was Cairo's. I had many men and women approach us, saying how much they admired my strength for going through what I did. Most of them said they knew I was someone special when I competed and survived the Trials. *The Trials...*

That was the first thing we changed. No more trials of any kind. No more hate for rogues. No one ever knows what a rogue is going through. Rogues are always judged too quickly and too harshly. Many forget that you can tell the difference between the type of rogues just by their eyes. The ones with red rimmed or blood shot eyes are the crazed and dangerous ones. The ones that give rogues a bad name. The ones that make everyone fear rogues. Alek and I were never like that. But no one cared enough to look into our eyes and see that we weren't feral. Being Luna of this pack, I'm going to change the way people see rogues and how they're treated.

Hazel has been growing stronger every day. She had grown in height and the doctors were happy with her weight. We were finally able to bring her home. She started breathing on her own, but she will still need regular check-ups and constant care. Which is okay because I can't seem to let her out of my arms, let alone sight. Unless she's napping of course. Cairo and I often argue over who's turn it is for cuddles. But I do have the advantage of having boobies so I always win. When Hazel starts having trouble breathing and her little lips start turning blue it's the scariest moments of our lives. But we listened to what the doctors told us to do. We place her in the position they showed us and rub her back gently to help. My heart thumps against my chest so loudly when that happens. I'm sure she hears it too because her little hand always lays against my chest, lulling it back into its normal rhythm.

Grace has certainly been fitting into the pack well. She's started training some of our male and female pack members who aren't just warriors. They were amazed at her stealth techniques and had all heard the stories of the Ghost Rogue. Cairo agreed with no resistance at all. Even he was impressed and gladly let her teach. I think he hopes that if there were any risk of another war in the future, that our pack members could defend themselves and their families without a second thought. So, now Grace has formed her own group of ghost warriors. And she's such a troublemaker, especially when it comes to her mate. I guess it runs in the family.

"Just can't keep your hands off each other can you." There

they were, right in the living room shoving their tongues down each other's throat.

"Have you seen him?" Grace said as she turned, flicking her long silver ponytail over her shoulder. "He's a babe." She said as Zack blushed as red as a tomato behind her, his own long hair hanging down past his shoulders.

"I have noticed. Zack, you're wearing your hair out longer now?" I asked. The last time I saw him before I was taken, he had shaved sides and the top half of his hair was longish, hanging down past his ears. Now it was all grown out past his shoulders. "It looks good." I compliment him as he continues to blush.

"Y...yeah, Grace-" She cuts him off.

"Tell her, puppy." She faces him, eyes darkening with lust. He rubs the back of his neck, kindly refusing to answer. *Oh, Goddess. It's something sexual, isn't it?* Poor Zack. She's traumatizing him.

"She..." He coughs, clearing his throat as she smirks at him, raising an eyebrow while she waits. "She likes it long so she has something to hold on to." His face could not have gone any redder.

"Damn straight." She winked at him. I couldn't help laughing.

"You look sexy in my shirts but if you don't go change right now I'll have to do something about it." He said making me feel like I'm intruding on a private moment.

"I better, I'm wearing nothing else." And I believed it. She wore one of his school jerseys as a short dress and I know Grace never lies so I know there's nothing else underneath.

"Grace. We are right in the living room." I say looking around to make sure no unsuspecting children heard anything. She laughs, still staring at Zack waiting for what she said to set in.

"What?! N...nothing else?" He says with a sheepish grin.

"Mhm, nothing else." She says as her phone vibrates. She

pulls it out, reading the text before she speaks again. "As much as I'd love to continue this and have some playtime, I need to deal with this."

"I..I'll go have a cold shower." Zack rushes out seconds before he turns, running from the room.

"You are so bad." I say watching her wink and look so proud of herself.

"How is little Hazel doing?" Grace says as she walks to me.

"She's doing great. She's loving her new cot but I'm pretty sure that's because Cairo put a teddy bear in there that he smothered his scent in and the sheets as well."

"Is she napping right now?" I couldn't help but think she was acting strange. Her questions were...I don't know. Just weird.

"Yeah, she was tuckered out from getting visits all morning." She concentrates on her phone, reading a new message rapidly before she starts hyperventilating, eyes widening in shock or was that fear? "Grace? What's wrong?" She turns away, breathing rapidly before her fingers fly over the screen. She lifts the phone to her ear, waiting for someone to pick up. Alarm bells started going off in my head. "Grace? What's wrong? Who texted you?" I asked now worried but she still didn't reply.

"Are you sure?" She spoke immediately as the person on the other end picked up. I couldn't hear what the person said but she hung up soon after, going white as a ghost as she looked at me.

"Grace, answer me! What happened?" She does just as I heard Hazel's wake up cry from her nursery.

"That was Uncle. It...it didn't transfer over." She said cryptically.

"What didn't?" I didn't have time for guessing games. My boobs had already started leaking from Hazel's cry. *Mummy instincts on point.*

"The Alpha power." My heart stops. *No, no, no.*

"What?!" My papa was Vladik's beta. The alpha power should have passed to him. "B..but Cairo said he killed him!" I rushed out, going over exactly what Cairo had said.

"But did he see the body, Zy?" Grace asked grimly.

"It doesn't matter." I said after I breathed in and out, calming myself down to think clearly. "I'm not afraid anymore, Grace. Everything will be okay. Go find Cairo and tell him what's happened. Maybe he remembers something." She nods once, waiting for me to finish. "I heard Hazel cry so I'm going to check on her and give her a feed. Go, Grace." I nod, smiling reassuringly as she finally turns and runs to the door.

As I approached the nursery, I could hear Hazel begin to cry louder. "I know, baby, I know. You're hungry." I say as I open the door.

"Shh, shh, shhh..." My blood ran cold, heart stopping as Vladik stood before me.

"V...Vladik....how.." I stared in horror as he held Hazel close to his chest. Gently rocking back and forth as he touched her cheek. Seconds past before he finally looked up at me smiling a chilling smile.

"Your mate doesn't know how thick the snow is, ZyZy. It was like landing on a soft bed. I will admit, more than a few bones were broken but the snow broke my fall, saving my life. It took a few weeks to heal from the damage but once I was healed, I made my way here. Undetected. You let your guard down, ZyZy. I met that wolf *Jaxon*." He spoke so calmy as Hazel refused to calm in his arms, unable to settle. "I wouldn't bother looking for him. He's long gone once he showed me how to get into your pack. Shh, shh, shh...Don't cry little one." I was frozen in fear. I screamed at myself to move but I couldn't. He was here, standing just a few feet in front of me holding my baby. *My baby!* His eyes were now red and rabid. "She's a pretty little thing, ZyZy. Almost as pretty as you." He said looking up at me as he smirked before he leaned down, kissing her cheek.

"Don't touch her!" I screamed taking a step forward but he

stepped back, giving me a warning look as he turned her away from me. Her screams were getting louder, I was afraid she was going to stress her lungs.

"Now, now, *Zia*." He spoke my name like it was acid on his tongue. He had a nasty looking scar on his neck, just like the one he left me with years ago but worse. "You wouldn't want anything to happen to her, now would you?"

"Put her down!" I growled, no longer fearing him. I will do anything to save my daughter, even if that meant giving my life for hers.

"She reminds me so much of you. I wonder if she'd look like you when she's older." He smiled, chilling me to my core as I saw his intentions written all over his face. I could see what he was thinking and it petrified me. But I knew one thing, I have the power to stop him. To stop him once and for all.

"You will NEVER have my daughter. Just like you never had me!" I growled, watching as he gently laid Hazel back down in her cot, her little body wriggle as she cried, tears now falling down her face making my heart clench in pain. He will regret hurting her.

"You-" I didn't let him finish.

I was done letting him rule my life. I was done letting him hurt me and the ones I love. I pulled every last bit of strength I had inside of me. I pulled and pulled and pulled until my feet left the ground. I was in the air, my hair floating up around me as time stilled. I threw my hands out as I screamed, but no words or sounds came out. Instead, violet strikes of lightening cracked around the room, thunder rolled outside in the sky as an unnatural wind whipped around us. I felt my eyes change as every atom and molecule in the room became visible. I let the power of the Goddess flow through me as I focussed the immense energy inside of me at Vladik. I could see the pure fear in his eyes, watching his life flash before him. Then every flash of violet lightning shot straight at him, going through him. Strike after strike he screamed as if he was being skinned alive. Then suddenly, the room disappeared. We were in the Forsaken place. Ice crystals formed against my skin as my breath froze in the air. Vladik screamed, feeling the pain of a thousand souls as his punishment began. I had brought Vladik's soul to Hell myself. Hazel's cry pierced my ears, pulling me back down to Earth just as quick as I appeared in the Forsaken place, leaving Vladik's soul behind. I ran to her, feeling drained more than anything but nothing matters in this moment, only her.

"It's okay, baby. It's okay. He'll never hurt as again." I say as I pick her up, hugging her to my chest as I begin to sway. Her beautiful Hazel eye's look up at me, tears and cries fading. I felt like she was studying me. "He's really gone." I whisper. She blinks once, then she smiles. Her eyes twinkle before they begin to get heavy. Then sleep finally washes over her.

I couldn't believe he's finally gone. I trust Cairo one hundred percent but I felt like I would never truly believe Vladik was gone until I saw his body myself. I couldn't believe he was alive but I knew it was a possibility. Evil like him always finds a way to cling to life. But now I finally felt at peace. There was no more monster lurking in the shadows. I had vanquished him once and for all. His subtle threat of taking Hazel and forcing her to go through and experience what I did cracked everything inside of me. Before when I've lost control of my powers there was always a degree of fear inside me. I always felt like I could never control my powers fully but I was so wrong. In that moment as Vladik looked down at my beautiful baby, I let that fear go and harnessed the raw power and energy I felt coursing through my veins. I tapped into something I've never tapped before. In that moment when the air around us cracked and splintered, I felt everything and nothing. I could still feel Vladik's soul even now, trapped in a vortex of his own making. I'm sure everyone could feel the moment I unleashed my power. It felt like I tapped into my own soul. A part of humans and supernatural creatures that can never be touched. A source of ultimate power. My heart was still beating hard like a hummingbird working overtime and the panic...no, not my panic. Cairo's.

I jumped and gasped as the door was ripped from the hinges. Cairo appeared, canines extended, claws out and wolfs eyes shining through as he scanned the room, chest heaving up and down. When his eyes landed on Vladik's dead body, he sighed heavily in relief. Then he stormed to us, pulling us into him as he wrapped his arm tightly around us. His heart was a loud symphony of drums. Hazel's tiny hand landed on his chest like she could feel his distress in her sleep. He calmed instantly but that didn't stop the tears from falling.

"We're safe." I reassured him.

"I was so scared, Zia. I...I was afraid I'd failed again at protecting you, the both of you.

"No, Cairo, don-" I began but he stopped me. There was a strange new look in his eyes. *Was that proud?*

"But then I felt you, Zia." He laughed. "You tripped me. I felt your power flow through our bond and I completely face planted." I laughed just imagining it.

"I should be sorry but I kind of really wish I could have seen that." He shook his head chuckling.

"I wasn't the only one that tripped though. Grace and Alek were with me and they fell too. We were just outside the house when you did something. It was like the pressure outside was so strong none of us could push up from the ground. All we could do was watch the house get circled by this strange violent-purple storm cloud. You should have seen the sky!" He said so excited like a kid on Christmas. "I've never seen anything like it! And Alek..." He said nervously, "We looked over at him to see if he could feel something I couldn't and his eyes were purple, Zia. Purple!! Like Grace and Kitty's eyes but he's not a Seer!" I laughed, watching the range of emotions cross his face.

"Something like this?" I blinked, feeling the molecules in the air become visible once more.

"YES!" I laughed before shushing him as I looked down at Hazel, feeling her stir in my arms. "How are you even doing that?"

"I was always afraid of my own power. But in this room, facing Vladik, I wasn't afraid anymore. Because it's not just me. We have a baby now. Once I let that fear go, I found this new part inside of me that I can access just like how I access my wolf.

"You've never been more beautiful and stronger that you are right now. I can't wait to spend the rest of my life with you."

"Me too, Cairo. Me too."

Chapter Fifty-Seven

Onto the Next

The next few weeks were pretty eventful. First thing we had to do was get Hazel settled and the pack reassured that no we didn't have an earthquake. It was just your Luna. Alek and I decided to open up our own healer's clinic. Our pack builders were quick to build our new clinic and as soon as the doors opened, we started healing our members. I don't think I've ever seen so many happy tears before. After every session I would tell our members to spread the word, tell their family and friends in other packs. We want to help as many wolves as we can, our pack and others, rogues and humans who were mated to werewolves. We also have discussed plans in the future to hold annual balls with all the packs we have treaties with and those we are trying to sign. This gives us the chance to make new alliances, help build our pack and let our members meet their mates and to also help us reach more wolves to heal that we normally couldn't see on a daily basis.

Then, it was time for my parents to visit. Papa had successfully calmed down the pack and exiled those who were still loyal to Vladik. But once the pack was stable, they decided to visit. They'll finally be able to meet Hazel and see Alek again after all this time.

"You're here!" I said as I ran into the living room where the front door just closed. There stood my parents, happy and safe.

"*Oh, my baby, you look so healthy!*" Mama said as she looked me up and down, tears coming to her eyes.

"*Where is Alek and the little one?*" Papa asked.

"I just linked Alek." I say speaking English as I know Cairo and everyone else can't understand Russian just yet. "He's on his way. And Hazel is-"

"Right here." Cairo said walking up behind me. "She's been waiting to meet you guys." He smiled at my parents.

"Mama! Papa!!" Alek shouted as he ran to them, almost taking them down to the ground as he came from the mudroom.

"Goddess, I missed you two so fucking much!"

"*Language, Alek.*" I laughed as mama scolded him.

"You haven't changed, mama." He mused.

"You have!" She exclaimed as they all separated. "*Look at our baby, Aleksei! He's all grown!*"

"*Yes. So big and strong, my son.*" Papa said proudly. "*And where is your mate?* I v'ant to meet him." Papa said, his English thick with his accent.

"I...I'm right here." Keiran said shyly still standing by the door. "Hello." Papa studied him as our Mama gasped.

"Oh, he is so handsome, Alek." She whispered making Keiran blush. "*And shy too.*" Alek laughed, turning to mama as he informed her that he could understand her too. Now she was the one blushing in embarrassment.

"Papa?" Alek said as he suddenly started walking towards Keiran, stopping only when he was standing so close that he could feel his breathe on his skin.

"Don hurt my son, Keiran. Or I will have to hurt you." He said with his thick accent hindering his threat. I rolled my eyes holding in a laugh as poor Keiran gulped and rubbed his arm so fast he could start a fire.

After all the introductions and subtle threats were out of the way, Keiran got the seal of approval from our parents. Then they met their granddaughter, and I could see papa had already become smitten with her. Hazel had quickly wrapped them around her little finger. I wish they could have stayed longer but they were only staying for a week. They spent their whole lives living in Russia, so change doesn't come easy for them. We asked them to move here but they were happy there. Before Vladik's darkness, the pack was beautiful. They love the cold winters and now that my papa was Alpha, they can return the pack to its former glory. We promised them we would visit every year or we would try too. Of course, I'll miss them, but I have my own life now. I'm an adult. I'm also a mother, a Luna, and the Moons Warrior. My future has never looked brighter.

A few days had passed and since my parents were only here for a few more, we decided to get married. I wanted them here for my wedding. It was a big day, Grace and Cairo planned everything. So, when I arrive at the place where I am to walk down the aisle, I will have no idea what to expect.

"Alright, Zi. Everyone's waiting, just gotta get you dres-" *Sighs* "ZIA!" Grace yelled, waking me with a fright as she stood by the door, hands on her hips and that damn eyebrow raised again. I thought I heard her come in but I was just so sleepy. I already had my wedding lingerie on and my white robe wrapped around me when she walked in seeing me asleep on the bed. It was the cucumber slices on my eyes that convinced me to have a nap.

"What was that for?! I was having the best nap." I snap as I bent down, picking the cucumber's that flew off my eyes from the floor.

"No time to naps, cousin. You're getting married today." She looked stunning in her long black dress, big platinum hooped earrings, a Victorian style choker around her neck and her silver hair pulled back. The scar across her face only accentuated her beauty as she wore a garnet-coloured lipstick that helped make her violet eyes pop.

"Do you have a baby?" I asked making her frown.

"No, not yet." She crossed her arms.

"Then let me give you a piece of advice. When you find the time to nap you take it!" I snapped. "That sweet little angel out there keeps me up at all hours of the night. So, if I want to nap on my damn wedding day, THEN I WILL NAP ON MY DAMN WEDDING DAY!"

"Fine." She said sighing. "I won't interrupt the sleeping mother again. Now, come on, put your dress on and I'll help you with your hair and makeup."

I nodded before I grabbed the dress hanging up in my closet. It was an ivory-coloured sweetheart style dress with lace sleeves that had stunning floral detailing. The dress sparkled and shimmered every time I turned. I felt so beautiful. Grace brushed, sprayed, and styled my hair into a princess braid. She curled the loose hanging hair before she clipped in a gorgeous blue sapphire hair clip. I started to cry but she said she'd hurt me if I ruined the makeup, so I stopped. She chose a blush-coloured lipstick and subtle eye makeup. She said she chose subtle colours and slightly bold lashes so my eyes would be the main feature. I loved everything about it. I looked so, so beautiful.

I know we were already seen as married in the werewolf world, but I know how Cairo feels. He wants everyone to know I'm taken and that I'm his. So, when he decided to plan the wedding and have the ceremony soon so my parents could attend, I couldn't have been happier. To spend the rest of my life mated and married to the man I love is more than I ever dreamed. He's done more for me than he will ever know.

"Thank you everyone for joining us today in celebration." The wedding officiant spoke as she looked out at our close family and friends sitting off to both sides of the aisle. The pack won't be joining us until the reception after the wedding. "Many wolves don't participate in the human tradition of marriage. But I am honoured today to be able to wed you two. Your love and bond is what makes the world a little brighter. Now, Cairo, if you would like to read your vows."

"Thank you." He said, nervous but I could feel how happy and excited he was. He looked so handsome in his black suit and bow tie. "Zia...I have only ever known you as Zia. Not Zinoviya, not ZyZy, just Zia, because I met you in one of the hardest times of your life. Little did anyone know; it was only going to get harder. Once I knew you were my mate, I vowed to never hurt you again. The start of our relationship was rocky as hell and you didn't deserve me as a mate then. But I promise you today, that I will be the mate and husband you deserve. I will be there for you in sickness and in health. I will love you until the day I draw my last breath." I never took my eyes off him, not even to blink. I said a sorry to Grace in my mind before I finally blinked, letting the fat tears roll down my cheeks. But then I had to hold my tongue to not laugh as she linked me and said she used waterproof makeup.

"Zia, would you like to read your vows?" The officiant said and I planned too, I really did but he took the words right out of my mouth and made me speechless. I only had a few words left to spare and I made them count.

"Fuck the vows. Kiss me, Cairo!" Everyone gasped, Grace and Zack laughed and clapped, the officiant too was shocked but not Cairo. He smirked and stepped forward, grabbing the back of my head, placing his other hand in the small of my back as he leaned down, kissing me just like they do in the movies.

After our kiss and the cheers from our family and friends,

we all made our way to the pack's beach. The large grassy patch was covered in fairy lights and they chopped a few trees down which they then turned into a large dance floor. There was live music and tables upon tables of food. Everyone was there, dressed to the nines and dancing away. I knew Cairo had chosen this place for a reason. It was where I told him the truth about me and my past, where we both learned to accept each other. This place held a special spot in our hearts. As our life together had finally begun, the lives of our friends and family were also about to begin.

Kitty and Caleb had approached us shortly after we arrived at the reception. They wanted our blessing to leave the pack and travel. Kitty had received a vision of a little pack, south of the country that was in need of help. They were excited for their new adventure and couldn't wait to leave. We would miss them; *I* would miss them. I felt like I never had enough time to really get to know them. Cairo told them to go and not to look back. That life was precious and to never take it for granted. He's really matured. I'm so lucky to have him as my husband and mate. But Kitty and Caleb leaving wasn't the only change coming our way.

"Well, welcome to the family, Cairo. Guess this means I can't knock you down a peg or two anymore." Alek joked but I had no idea what he meant by that as they both laughed.

"Oh, you can." Cairo said smirking. "I'll just be putting up a fight now."

"Good." Alek smirked back.

"What are you two talking about?" I squinted at the both of them. They were acting weird, laughing, and smirking at some sort of inside joke.

"Nothing, baby. Anyways, thank you, Alek. I'm-" Cairo went to continue but mama and papa had approached calling for Alek. Cairo and I watched and listened in as they spoke quietly.

"Papa?" Alek asked.

"Son, as you know I have been meaning to ask you something."

"What's he saying?" Cairo whispered into my ear like a buzzing fly.

"Shh, I'll tell you soon." I said hushing him.

"What is it?" Alek asked watching papa.

"Well, I am getting old." Papa said sadly which made Alek laugh and reply saying he knows which then made papa growl. He sighed, looking down at mama as she nodded at him. *"Since I was beta, I became Alpha once Vladik died. And since I am getting older, I wanted to ask if you'd like to be Alpha. It's within your right and I don't want to work anymore. I want to spend the rest of my days with your mama."*

"What?!" Alek said shocked.

Papa just asked Alek to be Alpha.

I said in my mind so Cairo could know what was going on.

"I am tired. I was beta for a long time. I want to spend time with your mama, telling her how she looks just as beautiful as the day I met her and how much I love her. I haven't been able to do that lately."

I repeated all their words in my mind, letting Cairo understand the conversation better.

"I love you, Aleksei. But look at him." Mama said as papa did just that. *"He's torn between wanting to make you proud and leaving Zia. He left the pack for her, Aleksei. He chose to become a rogue and put her first. We can't tear them apart."*

I didn't need to look at Alek to know he was tearing up just like me.

"Then who will be Alpha?" My father said in English.

"I think you know who, Aleksei." Mama said, smiling as a light bulb went off in his head.

He knew the perfect person for the job.

ZACK

A FEW WEEKS LATER

"I can't believe I'm an alpha." I said as I stood Infront of the large fireplace. I had said my goodbyes and left my pack in America, moving with Grace and her uncle and aunty back to their pack in Russia.

"Ahem." I smirked, turning as Grace approached. Dressed in a sexy red one-piece body or pants suit, whatever they're called that had a big V dipped neckline that showed off her big melons, a platinum choker and matching large, hooped earnings, and she finished it off with a large black fur coat that reminded me of a young widow who grieved her rich old husband that had just mysteriously died. "Let's get something straight, baby." Goddess her thick Russian accent was so sexy when she spoke English. "*I'm* the Alpha, *you're* the Luna."

"Yes, ma'am." That's right, Grace is the Alpha. My Alpha.

At the wedding her uncle had approached her, asking if she wanted to be the next Alpha. He had asked Alek who turned it down but there really was only one person who was suited for the job. Grace. I was more than happy to sit back and be her bitch while she runs the pack. She wants a hot meal cooked and house cleaned at the end of the day when she arrives home? I gotcha. I'm as whipped as they come but I couldn't be happier. I would kiss the ground she walked on but you know, germs...and poop. Couldn't think of anything worse than poopy paw prints.

Yuck.

Epilogue

Zia

We didn't get much time to celebrate after our wedding since everyone had started leaving. We threw a little going away party for Kitty, Caleb, Zack, Grace, and my parents. Kitty and Caleb had their new adventure awaiting and so did Grace and Zack as Alpha and a male Luna. But now that the celebrations and parties had died down, it was time I finally seduced Cairo. Goddess, I had missed him. We had yet to consummate our marriage and I had everything prepared so we could. Alek had taken Hazel for the night. I pumped as much as I could so there'd be no disruptions. Keiran was on alpha duties and the pack were advised, by me, not to contact Cairo or I for the night. Every question could be directed to Keiran.

Grace had left me a wedding present before she left. Her gift was the whole reason I decided to get Cairo alone tonight. She bought me a red lingerie set complete with the suspender thing that went around my waist and attached to the matching thigh high stockings. I felt so sexy but nothing made my eyes bug out more when I saw the red collar at the bottom of the bag with a big gold ring on the middle dangling down. I gulped and debated whether I should use it, but in the end I decided yes. I fastened it around my neck and stood back, looking at myself in the mirror. My long hair was washed and dried, hanging down my back in its natural wave that Cairo loved so much. I put some blood red gloss and mascara on. Then I was ready. I posed against the bathroom door, hands resting on the door frame behind my back just as Cairo walked in. His hand paused at his tie, mouth dropping open as he looked at my body up and down hungrily. His last thread of sanity snapped when I purred, eyes darkening. He slammed the door shut with his foot, kicked his boots off and ripped the tie from his neck. He tossed his suit jacket to the side as he stalked towards me. My chest rose and fell in anticipation. Once he reached me, he leaned down immediately grabbing the backs of my thighs and hoisted me up. He smashed his mouth against mine, eliciting a moan as he ground himself against me. He was so hard and ready. Always hard and ready.

"Fuck.." He said as he pulled back, spinning as he walked us to the bed. He tossed me down, watching me bounce as I giggled.

I was so excited I was on the verge of hyperventilating. His eyes darkened, staring at me heatedly as he slowly unbuttoned his white dress shirt. I bit my lip, watching as he popped the buttons one by one. Slowly his chiselled chest was revealed. Then his large hands grabbed his belt, sliding it through the buckle before he pulled it from his waist. He smirked, raising a brow as he watched me hide a moan.

He undid the button on his trousers, slowly pulling the zip down before he stopped. I opened my mouth, ready to protest but he lunged for me. His mouth was on me, kissing down my jaw as he made his way to my neck. He kissed and sucked on my skin, teasing his mark as my body shivered. I was so wet and ready for him I burned.

I looked deep into his eyes, letting him see just what he does to me. His hand went down, ripping the red lace panties straight off my body with one clean tug. Then he was pulling out himself out, stroking before he lined himself up and slowly began pushing it in. I threw my head back, moaning as he slid all the way.

I stretched around him painfully but if his finger were to brush against my clit right now I think I would probably explode right then and there. He pulled back, stopping as the tip was almost out. With my head thrown back I never saw him move. I screamed in pleasure, he slammed into me so deep just as his teeth pierced my skin, marking me. My body shook and thrashed against him as wave after wave washed over me. He groaned, feeling me clamp around him as he held still, waiting for me to finish my orgasm as his face contorted, eyes rolling back as he groaned.

Soon, he was thrusting again, hands either side of my head. I watched as his muscles rippled in his chest, my hands feeling the muscles in his back moving in symphony with his hips.

My breasts moved up and down, hypnotising his eyes as watched them bounce.

He soon slowed down, I could fill him get harder, larger and knew he was close.

"What is it?" I asked as he smirked, eyes darkening further as the wheels in his head spun.

Cairo

I was nearly at the edge of no return but I slowed, not wanting this moment to end just yet. The last time I was in her I got her pregnant.

I wanted to take her all in, burning this moment and her body into my memory. So many things had changed.

Since becoming Alpha, I noticed I gained more muscles and even a few inches in height...and *length*, as Zia was just now noticing. And while she hadn't grown in height, her body had changed.

Not from the power of Luna, but motherhood.

After weeks of taking medication, eating, and healing, her health was back to what it once was. And as I looked down at her body, I could see the subtle changes. Her light golden skin was glistening with sweat, milk-filled tits almost spilling out of the too-small bra she was wearing which was making it impossible not to rip the thing to shreds. I wanted to see those tits bounce freely.

My eyes roamed down to her slim stomach. Her hips were wider than they were before. I groaned; my child had inadvertently made her sexy.

I stopped moving and placed my hand on her belly, imagining what it would look like if she were healthy during her pregnancy. Her belly was so small with Hazel.

I smirk as a dirty thought crossed my mind.

I want to get her pregnant again.

And again, and again.

I bellowed out in laughter, seeing the look of pure shock cross Zia's face. That and the bright red blush. She heard every word I thought.

I laughed again and started slowly moving in and out of

her as her pussy quivered around my cock and her scent got thicker. The thought of me getting her pregnant again shocked the hell of her but surprised her at how aroused she became at the thought.

Soon her hips were slamming against mine as I thrusted in deep, quickly nearing an explosive orgasm for the both of us.

We both knew by the end of the night; she'd be pregnant again.

THE END...

You've heard her parent's story, now, it's her turn.
Hazel's story will be told...

Acknowledgments

Firstly, I would like to thank my partner for being my number one supporter. I couldn't have gotten this book finished without his help in looking after our daughter while I sat at my desk tapping away on the keyboard writing chapter after chapter. Secondly, I'd like to thank my little Blossom for being the best baby for me and allowing me to write while she napped longer than thirty minutes each day. To our new pup safely tucked away inside my belly, thank you for not giving me too much morning sickness!

I would also like to give thanks to the lovely Mary Begletsova (@marybegletsova) for the amazing art she did of Cairo, Zia, Alek and Keiran. She captured them perfectly and brought my characters to life in a way I could never have imagined.

And thank you to Lizzie James from Phoenix Book Promo for the amazing detailing and work you did in formatting this book!

Printed in Poland
by Amazon Fulfillment
Poland Sp. z o.o., Wrocław
23 July 2022

e918823b-c7f3-4961-bea5-0bc00cb0fe6aR01